NASTRAGULL

―――― BOOK ONE ――――

PIRATES

ERIK MARTIN WILLÉN

ASC PUBLISHING

Cover design, interior book design, and eBook design
by Blue Harvest Creative
www.blueharvestcreative.com

PIRATES: NASTRAGULL BOOK ONE
Copyright © 2012, 2015 Erik Martin Willén

All rights reserved. Except as permitted under the U.S. Copyright Act of 1976, no part of this publication may be reproduced, distributed, or transmitted in any form or by any means, or stored in a database or retrieval system, without prior written permission of the publisher.

This book is a work of fiction. The characters, incidents, and dialogue are drawn from the author's imagination and are not to be construed as real. Any resemblance to actual events or persons, living or dead, is entirely coincidental.

Published by
ASC Publishing

ISBN-13: 978-1508717676
ISBN-10: 1508717672

Visit the author at:
Twitter: www.twitter.com/ErikMartinWilln
Google+: https://plus.google.com/113109764948220499797/posts
Blog: www.sciencefiction-nastragull.blogspot.se

Visit the author on Google+
by scanning the QR code.

*For my sister, Anna-Sofia-Charlotta Willén,
who died from Lupus, SLE
at the age of twenty-four in Edinburgh, Scotland,
December 20, 2001.*

Life is too short to be taken too seriously, and too long for you to be concerned about other people's opinions.

ERIK MARTIN WILLÉN

PROLOGUE

HE watched his son and daughter, ages five and seven, with love in his eyes as they argued about what bedtime story he should read. He was in his late forties, his short hair and beard perfectly trimmed. His squared-off face and deep blue eyes gave him a cold and intelligent expression; and he hardly ever smiled, except when he was with his children. At the moment he wore a thick robe, giving the impression that he also would soon go to bed.

He closed his eyes, and then he took a deep breath. Aromas from hundreds of flowers mixing with the fresh air from the open window made him think of his wife. She had placed them there, she said, to make it easier. He had to be strong, to show no fear. Tonight was the last time he would put his children to bed.

After watching them fondly for a few moments longer, he said softly, "Tonight, children, I will tell you a different story. It is a story that you have never heard before."

Instantly the two children stopped bickering and sat straight up in the large bed. Their father smiled sadly, and tucked them in. His daughter said, "I want to hear about a princess who is rescued by a beautiful knight."

"And I want to hear about a knight," the young boy countered. "He doesn't have to rescue any princess, though."

His sister stuck out her tongue at him, and he stuck out his back at her.

The man swallowed hard, holding back his tears, and then said gently, "Actually, I am going to tell you the story about creation, the Tree, and the dragons."

"If there are dragons, it must have a princess," the daughter pointed out.

"Stories with dragons always have a knight," the boy added.

He wagged his fingers at the young ones. "No more interruptions." He regretted the words as soon as they left his mouth, because they sounded harsher than he had intended. Reddening a bit, he cleared his throat and then smiled down at his two loved ones.

"All right, then. In the beginning, there was a place called Fantaka. It was a beautiful place, perhaps the most beautiful, wonderful place of all time. The sun shone brightly over a landscape of grassy hills covered with colorful flowers. In the far distance were the highest mountains in creation; the sky was blue, and there were no clouds. Atop a small hill in the center of a wide plain stood a solitary tree with large green leaves. It was the Tree of Life. As time grew older, so did the Tree."

"Booooring," announced the little boy, yawning.

"Quiet. I like it, Father, please continue."

Again, the man gave his two children a friendly and patient smile. He lifted his eyebrows, ignoring his young son's mutterings about girlish crap.

"There were two colorful birds playing, flying, and singing over the hills. As they chased each other through the landscape, they crossed long, clean rivers and beautiful valleys filled with flowers, heading always towards the lonely Tree. When they arrived, they landed on a branch, playing with each other, and singing in joy. Their song was interrupted by a roar, far in the distance. It echoed throughout the landscape and they knew, as the roar increased in volume and became more frightening, that something was very, very wrong. All the animals in the valley begun to run for cover. The birds were just about to take off from the lonely Tree on the hill themselves when two black shadows passed over them—and two ravens attacked without warning, killing them almost instantly. They fell like stones onto the grassy sward, while the ravens took up the same position on the branch as the original two birds had."

The father paused and looked at his children, who looked back at him, stunned. He ignored their shocked expressions and continued in a rougher, more rumbling voice, "Soon the ground broke open, and from within it came a scream, followed by a huge, monstrous arm reaching up and beginning to pull itself out of the newly-formed fracture. A huge lizard-like leg took a step out of the crack, followed by another; and with each step, the ground trembled. It was an enormous black dragon with two heads. Everywhere it went; it devoured the landscape, and any animal in its way.

"Another roar echoed from the direction opposite the first one. This one came from a cave on the largest mountain. A second dragon emerged; and unlike the first one, it had only one head and it was white."

"Is it good, Daddy? Is it a good dragon?" the young girl cried out.

"Who cares? I want to be the black dragon," the son said, crossing his arms across his thin chest.

The father only laughed quietly before continuing, "The two dragons met below the hill bearing the single lonely Tree, the Tree of Life. The creatures snorted at each, and then they attacked. It was a fight to the death. You see, children, there could only be one dragon, not two."

"Why?" they asked in unison.

"Because only one dragon can guard creation; if there are two, then a conflict will erupt, just like this one did." He smiled at them solicitously. "Do you want to hear more, my lovelies, or are you tired?"

From their eyes, it was clear that he should continue.

"Very well. As the two dragons fought their mortal battle, all the other living beings in creation ran for cover. They fled, but there was no place for them to go. Still they fled, and more of the beautiful landscape was ravaged. The two ravens flapped their wings while screaming, taunting and encouraging the battling beasts. Then something happened that wasn't supposed to happen. From behind the ravens rose a large shadow, covering them and the entire landscape—yet there were no clouds. A snorting sound was heard, and soon it turned into a loud, clear tone, similar to that of a horn. The two ravens fell silent as they looked towards the strange shadow, and then they bowed their heads—and all the fleeing animals fled no more. They were no longer afraid. United, they followed the strange shadow. From its center shone a light that was brighter than any other light in creation. Then there was the third dragon…"

His tale was interrupted by a woman's cold voice. "It is done. It is over. They are gone." He looked down to see that his children were lying where they had fallen, eyes closed, and faces pale. Their little chests did not move.

He looked up as their mother entered the bedroom. Her eyes were cold, yet there was an exquisite sadness in them. She was younger that he, in her early forties, beautiful and haughty, a dominant expression frozen on her features. Her black hair was braided behind her head, and her dark brown eyes seemed almost black in the dim light. She wore a robe similar to that of her husband, but in her left hand she held some type of helmet. She half tried to conceal it behind her back.

Her husband looked down at the two lifeless bodies of his children, and he allowed a single tear to trickle down his face before his expression turned as cold as his wife's. He stood up, and reached for his own battle helmet, which lay on the floor under the bed.

"The poison worked fast," he observed tonelessly, as he toyed with his helmet's visor.

His wife walked over to the bed and kissed her children one last time. She faced her husband. Now she, too, had a tear trickling down her face; but it was a monument to her strength, and her coldness, that she allowed herself no more than that. "It is time," she said firmly.

"Yes, my Queen, it is."

They embraced quickly, then pulled back and looked at each other; simultaneously, each reached out to brush away the other's tear. Then they clasped hands, turned, and left their children's room forever, walking away through long hallways and corridors decorated with lavish art, ornaments and large gold statues, twice lifesize. There were military standards draping before every column, and hanging down from the ceiling were thousands of flags taken from hundreds of battlefields. Everything might have seemed normal if it hadn't been for the hundreds of dead bodies decorating the floor. Some of them faced each other, daggers sticking out of their chest. All the servants had committed suicide at their order. You couldn't buy loyalty like that.

When they reached the main hall, they dropped the robes. Both of them wore high-tech black battle armor underneath, similar but with different engravings and decorations telling their respective life stories. The engravings emitted a dim, bluish light, enhancing the contours of their armor. Releasing each other's hands, they put on their helmets. Each took the form of a monstrous creature out of a madman's nightmare. When they were properly caparisoned, they turned to face their troops: thousands of soldiers standing there quietly, all wearing burnished silver armor.

"Husband, where is our carpet?" she asked while donning her battle gloves. He gestured with his arm to a waiting officer.

The officer shouted, "Prepare the red carpet for our Queen!"

There were one hundred steps on the giant staircase. On each step, two prisoners faced each other, kneeling with their hands tied behind them. Each wore worn battle fatigues. Standing behind the prisoners were guards, waiting patiently. When the call went out, the eerie sound of two hundred sharp blades leaving their respective sheaths echoed through the hall. The queen walked down the one hundred steps, followed by her husband. For each step she took, guards cut the throats of the two prisoners on that step. A red carpet of blood spewed onto the white marble and onto the uncaring Queen as she descended.

When she reached the bottom of the staircase, the soldiers in the great room bowed their heads. In front of her lay an enormous beast with a saddle, waiting patiently. Its body was covered with scales and a thin fur, like silky grass. The eyes were blue, and they emitted a faint glow. The mouth was filled with long fangs; as it grunted, dark saliva dripped onto the floor, where it melted into the marble like acid. The beast used its long tongue to lick blood from the floor as it flowed into its range.

She mounted the beast. It stood up, and her husband handed up a battle standard made of white metal with a large down-pointed triangle on top. The Queen turned to her bodyguard and said, "Now, let there be thunder."

From outside, there came the din of horns and drums.

The Queen smiled coldly, then rode out, followed by her bodyguards. Her husband accompanied her on a smaller beast. They moved fast through a raging battle, ignoring friend and foe alike, headed towards a monument in the distance that had a thirty-mile radius and was as high as a mountain. Atop the monument was another beast bearing another rider, heading towards them; when the Queen dialed up the magnification of her helmet optics, she could see that the rider held a standard bearing a large eye. She nodded.

"Husband," she said after a while, "did you ever finish the story for our children?"

"No, my Queen, I did not. The end was too quick."

The Queen reined in her mount and looked at her husband. "Then let us finish the tale here and now, for all time."

ONE

BLOODY sweat poured down Alexa's face as she ducked the mercenary's blade. She kicked out toward his groin, but it wasn't there; instead she slipped on the blood-slick floor, a bright, sharp pain in her right ankle telling her she'd twisted it as she fell. She tried to crawl away, realizing that he was coming after her to press the advantage, bent on killing her or worse. His body-stink and heavy breathing warned her that he was much too close, so she reached quickly for her ace in the hole—or in the left leg holster, to be precise. She spun, kneeled, aimed, and pulled the blaster's trigger, grinning confidently.

Nothing happened.

In that instant, she realized that she was about to die. "Oh, shit," she hissed, still grinning stiffly, and saw the bastard grinning back at her; he understood her predicament, and was more than happy to exploit it. He kicked her hard in the face with one heavy black boot, sending her crashing into the bulkhead. Alexa spat out one of her front teeth, and blood oozed out between the fingers she instinctively put to her mouth; then her eyes rolled back, and she slumped to the deck. A harsh intake of breath resulted only in eye-watering pain as the cold air impacted the nerve in the broken tooth, but she betrayed nothing; she lay where she'd fallen, apparently helpless.

Alexa stubbornly refused to feel the pain; she was better than this. Instead of fear, her mind filled with anger: an anger that had been building, futilely, for the past ten years—from the very moment she'd been forced into piracy until now, when she might just finally die.

The mercenary grabbed her hair hard, and with surgical precision he made a small, deep cut on the side of her head. "Time to die, pirate," he grunted, "but not until I get me a souvenir or two." He yanked, and there was a ripping sound as he tore off part of her scalp, complete with several dreadlocks. Alexa screamed at top of her lungs as this new pain overwhelmed her.

The man was laughing now and shouting out loud, telling her in no uncertain terms what he would do to her. He swung her around, emitting a short victory cry, then forced her neck back and raised his knife for the final cut. For a just a second, he hesitated. The attractive little brunette was young, with a fine athletic body, a picture-perfect face, and dark golden skin. That gave him other ideas.

She knew it, too, and started struggling frantically. He ignored her as best he could and looked around for a more secluded area, where he could ravish her undisturbed. He started to pull her away from the bulkhead, and every time he looked at the little vixen he was all but blinded with lust. He moved his knife closer to her neck, hoping she would stop struggling.

Alexa spat out blood and fragments of her tooth, swearing and screaming, as if fighting desperately to survive—but she was craftier than that. She had more surprises hidden away, and a man who had to handle a hysterical woman didn't have time to pat her down for weapons. She saw from the corner of her eye a sudden reflection from his knife as it approached, and in one smooth motion she dove down, pulled out her own boot knife, and thrust the blade up and behind her, sticking the bastard in the gut. She pulled herself away from him even as his knife sliced into the side of her neck. She ignored the pain and the warm stream of blood dribbling down her neck; with all her strength, she shoved the knife deeper into his belly, twisting and turning it and jerking it around to inflict as much damage as possible.

His guts slipped out in a ropy red-gray tangle, his scream rising to a terrible pitch and then trailing off as his eyes went dull with shock and he crumpled, trying to hold his viscera in.

Coup de grâce time. She jumped on top of the man, holding him down with her legs, and revealed a new surprise. She jerked her right elbow up and a foot-long blade, hidden in the seam and attached to a scabbard sewn into her battle fatigues, shot out from her sleeve like a giant switchblade. She cut the man's throat with the elbow blade even as she pulled the boot-knife from his belly.

She could feel the blood trickling down her neck as she got up, but decided she might as well continue the fight.

Alexa pushed aside a lock of hair and took a deep breath. One of the ship's passengers staggered around the corner, took one look at her, and instantly turned tail with a shriek. No surprise there. She knew she probably looked a fright, bloodied and bedraggled as she was. She knew from facing herself in the mirror that her eyes were those of a battle-worn veteran, far older than her 19 years, and her combat suit was ripped and singed. Add to that the bloody bald spot on the side of her head where the merc had ripped away his short-lived "trophy," and it was no surprise her looks scared people. Hard to believe she'd once been considered attractive. She leaned back against the cold bulkhead, catching her breath, and then slid down into a sitting position, her vision graying out for a second. When she came back to herself, she was looking at the dead man next to her. In one of his hands he still held part of her scalp. Snarling, she kicked the body sharply, then collected her scalp and tucked it under her waist belt. Her scalp would be no one's trophy but hers, dammit.

There was a crystal viewport a few feet away for the benefit of any passengers who happened to want to see what was going on in the void. Alexa levered herself to her feet, and hobbled up to it. She peered out through the foot-thick quartz and watched as the destroyer class vessel pressed the attack against the much larger transport cruiser, its missiles raising blooms of fire and destruction from the transport's hull, its X-ray lasers ablating away the ship's armor in massive clouds of metallic vapor as they poured fire into it.

Once the target had been softened up sufficiently, one of the destroyer's cargo bay doors irised opened and vomited forth hundreds of pressure-suited troops equipped with jetpacks, opening fire with handheld weapons as they closed the gap between the ships. The transport proved it wasn't quite helpless by picking off several of the troopers with its return fire, but most soon clanged down onto the hull of the transport and attached themselves to hatches, handholds, and other helpful protuberances. They soon broke through by means of tools and explosives, opening a half-dozen minor breaches in the ship's primary hull. Alexa gasped as she felt the pressure differential shift before the emergency bulkheads thudded shut, keeping the transport from depressurizing all at once. She hardly had time to catch her breath before the destroyer rammed the larger ship and attached itself with a massive cylindrical arm. That slammed her hard against the bulkhead opposite the viewport, and she went out like a light.

On the transport, yellow warning lamps were flashing, Klaxons were sounding, and the overhead lights flickered as smoke began to filter through the passageways, causing the passengers and crew to panic. They scrambled *en masse* for safety in the escape pods on the lower decks, as a small security detachment ran in the opposite direction, pushing their way through the crowd.

An explosion peeled back the transport's main hatch—which currently lay at the terminus of the destroyer's cylindrical connector—and hundreds of armed soldiers swarmed through, shooting and hacking their way through security personnel, passengers, and crew with equal ease. The attackers were led by an enormous figure dressed in a powered battle suit that gleamed gray in the flickering lights. In his hands were two massive particle-beam blasters, and attached to his forearms were several large blades—all of which he used to deadly effect as he sliced a bloody path through the crowd. His troops followed his example, and began to spread through the ship.

The leader pulled off his helmet and bellowed, "Don't bunch up," in a voice like thunder. Then he emitted a deep roar as he charged the room. He was over two meters tall and enormously broad; his bulging stomach was proof of his one weakness, food. His long black beard was matched in length by his hair, both reaching below his waist. His face was covered with hair and old scars. Foam and salvia poured from his mouth as he roared; and from his under jaw two pale fangs, one broken half-off, thrust out. Pure evil seeped from his eyes.

Pale yellow light pulsed through the wisps of smoke and vapor, making it difficult for Alexa to focus. She'd barely climbed back onto her feet (how many times was that so far today?) when a familiar voice cried out "Behind you!" A figure emerged from the gloom and discharged an energy weapon in her direction; Alexa ducked and glanced back in time to see a security goon topple, most of his head gone. "Thanks, Nina," she croaked.

Nina stopped long enough to help Alexa to her feet. She gave her a puzzled look that made it clear she'd noticed the bald spot on Alexa's head.

"You all right?"

"Had a little trouble." Alexa brushed dust and gray matter from her battle uniform, then quickly checked all the gizmos attached to her waist belt and combat vest. Once she realized her equipment and weapons were intact, she put her right hand on the bald spot and winced at the throbbing pain. "Little woozy, but I think I can handle it."

Nina laughed in relief, and Alexa snarled back. Best friend or not, she didn't think this was a laughing matter, and she knew she looked like hell. Well, Nina didn't look much better. If anything, her battle fatigues were in worse shape than Alexa's—most of the right half was torn clean away, exposing the huge tattoo of two monstrous fighting beasts that covered most of the petite brunette's body. "Told you, you should cut your hair short like mine," Nina said. "Gives 'em less to grab onto."

"Yeah, yeah."

Nina jerked her head toward the fray. "C'mon, baldy, let's go!"

Alexa glanced from Nina to the dead man, and shouted back, "Where's the rest of the crew?"

Nina jerked her weapon up and fired past Alexa again; it was hard to tell if she'd gotten anything this time, because the smoke was turning the corridor into a yellow-tinged hell. "I dunno, but they better get here soon or we'll lose this prize! Who knew the bastards would put up this kind of resistance?"

There it was! Alexa snatched up her blaster from the interface of corridor and floor, checked the readouts for energy, and switched out the old magazine for a new one just in case. "Crap, if they keep it up there won't be much left to plunder," she muttered.

An explosion erupted far down the corridor, followed by shudder that all but knocked the two female pirates off their feet. That would be the second cylindrical arm breaching the transport. A howling maelstrom rushed past them as air, smoke, and loose debris rushed out of the ship; then the foam sealant that had deployed when the ships collided hardened enough to seal the air in. Now that the smoke was more or less gone, Alexa noticed, from the corner of her eye, a hint of distant movement through the viewport as several people—passengers, probably—gasped out their last few seconds, twisting in the void.

Collateral damage.

"There's your bloody reinforcement," Alexa shouted over the fighting. For a second, she forgot about the ongoing melee as she caught her reflection on a large wall mirror, placed on a pillar as décor. She snarled; she looked worse that she thought. She kicked the dead man's head hard with her boot, but it didn't make her feel much better.

They set off carefully toward the sounds of battle, their eyes trying to take in everything at once, blasters held at the ready. As they got closer to their comrades' position, Nina cursed long and hard, as only a pirate can. "The hairy idiot Captain is late as usual," she spat, gesturing towards the end of a hallway leading into one of the ballrooms. A voice from her wrist com confirmed Nina's comment.

Alexa gave Nina a tired smile and replied, "Don't let Zuzack hear you! You can only call him Captain because you're a pending crew member."

"I know. I know, my dear owner." Sounding very sarcastic, Nina gave Alexa a short bow.

"Don't call me that," Alexa warned. "I hate it, and you know it."

They ducked into a niche that, until recently, had apparently been an inset display case for some kind of ceramic art; it was just so much crushed powder now. As they caught their breath, the sounds of minor explosions and blaster fire ripped through the cramped space, accompanied by ragged shouts and screams from the injured or dying. The smoke was becoming dense again, hurting the eyes and making it almost impossible to tell friend from foe. Alexa knew from experience that some of the dead and injured on both sides of the battle would be the result of friendly fire accidents; but that was the fog of war for you. A strange stench spread throughout the ship; probably some kind of coolant, or possibly burning insulation. Probably the odors of blood and burning people were mixed in there, too.

Zuzack and his followers charged through the ship, herding several species of people ahead of them, shooting and cutting down anyone putting up resistance. The security goons and mercs were all but gone by now. There was little doubt who had the upper hand; the story was told by the corpses, fragmentary and whole, that littered the corridors. Very few wore the gray of the pirates' battle fatigues.

Still the magma rifles and blasters pounded away, taking out the last of the resistance. Small fires sprang up as volatiles took hits, and in a few cases even the metal burned; magma rifles weren't exactly subtle, precision weapons. They were made to destroy and kill in as little time as possible. The smoke grew thicker and, combined with the incessant honking of the Klaxons, made it almost impossible for anyone without the right imaging equipment (which of course Nina and Alexa didn't have) to know stem from stern. To make matters worse, the emergency sprinkler systems finally kicked in, dousing the women with water as they emerged from their alcove.

Cursing fluently, Alexa slogged back to the crystal viewport and pressed her face against its chilly surface, holding her breath against the smoke. The sprinklers were starting to put out the fire, so the smoke was dissipating, but it was being replaced with steam. Dammit, the port was fogging up. Rubbing the side of her hand against the quartz, she cleared it off enough to peer through into space. A few escape pods were vectoring away from the transport, only to be intercepted and captured by several small unmanned cutters, which were radio controlled by crewmembers inside the destroyers.

Nina joined her at the port. "Alexa, let's go. We gotta hurry, it's not over yet." She shot Alexa a concerned look.

Alexa stepped back, fingering her bald spot, still pissed at the mercenary she'd killed. She looked at her own ghostly reflection in the port until the steam fogged it over and finally replied. "Yeah, I know, it's just…" She grinned. "You know, I kicked the guy's head as hard as I could, and you wouldn't believe how much I hurt my foot…"

Nina was confused by her friend's remark. "It's just *what*, Alexa?" She laid her hand on her friend's arm, eyes narrowing with concern. "C'mon, now, we need to hurry or we'll lose some of our share. You know how the hairy bast…I mean, *our Captain* gets. He's gonna take all the good stuff for himself." She gently shoved Alexa toward the action, and once she was moving, they both started to run towards the fighting.

By the time they got there, there wasn't much resistance left. The two women moved through the ship with the rest of the pirates, collecting anything of value and gathering up prisoners. They brought their loot to one of the ship's largest rooms, the main ballroom. It was itself a work of art, decorated beautifully in gold and silver, offering the impression of a palace. Like most of the spaces inside the ship, the ballroom was more or less intact; the less damage there was to the ornate rooms, the less damage they'd have to repair later— and the more money the ship would bring when it was sold. Alexa and Nina marked their spoil with small patches that both kept in pouches hanging from their shoulders. When they were done, they hurried away to find more loot.

They avoided elevators, and soon found themselves approaching the living quarters for the first class passengers. Along the way, however, they ran into several surviving members of the security team.

Alexa fired her blaster a split-second after Nina opened fire with hers. The blasts cut down three of the enemy soldiers. After a short firefight, the rest of them took off toward an elevator. Alexa motioned to Nina for her to ignore them, and then gestured towards one of the VIP hatches next to her. Alexa positioned herself with her back next to the hatch, while Nina blew the lock and forced it open. Alexa tossed in a concussion grenade; and once its blast had shaken the walls, they jumped into the exclusive suite with their weapons held ready.

Someone shouted out desperately, "Please, don't kill us!"

There were seven of them, all civilians: a well-dressed man, woman, and boy, and four others, probably their servants. They were down on their knees, trembling, with their hands held high in surrender. There was naked fear in their eyes, something Alexa and Nina were used to. Alexa felt for the frightened passengers, but she hid her own personal feelings behind a cold mask, as Nina did. It was something they both had to do in order to survive in the situation they found themselves in. So neither one of the girls' eyes displayed any emotion or mercy, only hard, cold ice.

The civilian woman covered her face with her hands, weeping openly, collapsing in a trembling ball onto the floor. Covering them with her weapon, Alexa motioned to Nina, who produced several tag collars from a pouch and quickly moved toward the group.

"Spare us, please," the man said, "My name is Af De'Lac. I am a colonial governor from the Florencia Federation."

"Shut up, you annoying toad," Nina said harshly. She locked a collar about the man's neck.

"Don't do this," the man cried, his voice sounding more desperate by the second. "I can make you wealthy. I'm worth millions of Galactic credits. Leave us alone…help us, and you will be set up for life."

"Don't bother Master," one of the servants said coldly. He showed no sign of fear, and stood up in defiance when Nina reached out towards him with a collar. Alexa aimed and fired one round at the man, separating his head from his neck. The head bounced off the ceiling and bulkhead, hitting Nina on her head.

"Watch it, bitch, that really hurt," Nina complained, rubbing her forehead. Alexa only rolled her eyes and gestured for Nina to hurry.

"I beg of you," the Governor pleaded. "Spare me and my wife; you can have our servants..." For a moment there was an eerie silence in the room. Governor Af De'Lac looked around and then continued, "And my son."

Alexa looked at the kneeling man in disbelief, and a sudden anger washed over her. Nina noticed her friend's reaction and stepped between them. "Alexa, let it go, we need them."

"Bullshit!" Alexa whispered threateningly. "That one hit too close to home. Step aside, Nina."

The Governor's wife had stopped crying when she heard what her husband had said, and looked at him now in disbelief. A loud argument erupted as she let her husband know in no uncertain terms what she thought of his base cowardice. Their son's eyeballs seemed ready to pop out from their sockets.

The Governor seemed to shrink down into the floor. "Don't hurt me, don't hurt me!" he wailed. "Take my wife too!"

"I said, *shut up*."

Nina kicked the man hard in the face, causing a stream of blood to jet from his nose. That shut him up: his eyes rolled back, and he slumped to the floor unconscious. The boy cried out, and the woman screamed and wept even louder. Nina never took her eyes off Alexa, and didn't stop staring until she had calmed down. She glanced threateningly towards the rest of the prisoners. "You shut up too, or you get worse."

Alexa stood there watching the prisoners with professional detachment, letting Nina affix the slave collars to the rest of them one at a time. The servants didn't appear discomfited—they were probably used to being chattel—but the boy and woman looked as if they might faint when the locks clicked home. When Nina was finished, she nodded to Alexa, who activated the collars from her wrist computer. Each of the five hostages who were still awake immediately passed out.

"Should have done that right away," Alexa mumbled.

The two young pirates proceeded down the long corridor, capturing fifteen more VIP prisoners and about twice as many servants. When they returned to the first suite, they noticed a small group of male pirates attempting to remove their slave collars. Nina shouted, "What the hell are you doing, you bastards?"

She and Alexa knew exactly what was happening. Stealing from each other was the worst thing any pirate could ever do, but it happened all the time. Nina glanced at Alexa, who gave her a hard look back. Even though the two were still teenagers, their looks could have turned a blue-white star to ice.

A small, ugly pirate with large flapping ears turned around with an angry grimace on his face and shouted back, "Mind you own business, bitch, and we'll mind ours." His comment was supported by laughter from the other four pirates with him.

Nina tilted her head and looked at the pirate questioningly, then shot him in the face. The head exploded over his friends, who only stood there staring, stunned from shock. Alexa raised her own gun and fired—but nothing happened. Cursing, she dropped it immediately and yanked a small cord on her sleeve, sending one of her elbow blades flying into the group of claim-jumpers. It hit one in the gut, and he went down immediately.

One of the pirates leaped forward before Nina could react and slashed at her gun hand with a machete, sending pieces of two fingers flying. Nina screeched and dropped the gun, then grabbed her injured hand, looking more angry than upset. Alexa dived onto one of the pirates and bit down hard on his throat.

A high-pitched squeal overrode the sound of the fray, drilling into the eardrums of the battling pirates. They all stopped fighting immediately and looked toward the hatch, rooted to the deck in fear. In the doorway stood a huge man, a boson's pipe in his mouth: Zuzack, the Captain. "What's going on here?" he demanded.

Nina held onto her bleeding hand and attempted to stand at attention while giving a brief report. Alexa spat out part of an Adam's apple and wiped a sleeve across her bloody mouth. Before Nina could get more than a few words into her explanation, Alexa blurted out, "We were protecting our investment, Captain! These prisoners have our collars, and Lebba and his friends attempted to remove them, sir!"

Zuzack looked suspiciously at Alexa, and then at Nina, who nodded vigorously. He turned cold eyes to the surviving group of male pirates, now pared down to two. "Is this true?"

The men shifted, uncomfortable. The Captain walked up to one of them, then glanced down to where a tool set lay on the floor, next to one of the prisoners. It was clearly marked with Lebba's sigil. Zuzack smiled at the pirates and said, "Weapons, please."

Lebba and his surviving helper, sweating profusely, meekly handed over their various guns and blades to their Captain, who stalked over to where the girls stood, nodded, and said to Alexa, "Carry on, my dear."

Nina and Alexa walked up to the last two pirates and cut them down with their own knives. Neither dared resist; they died helpless, staring at their Captain with horror.

The Captain smiled like a proud father at the two young girls. "Ah, I should have known that the two of you would have gone for the VIP section, while the rest of the idiots went to the dock and the cargo hold to make their claims! Now get back to work. There's much more that needs to be done."

He gave each of the girls a hard slap on their buttocks. Alexa and Nina saluted their Captain as he left the stateroom ahead of them. They struggled past a clutter of Zuzack's personal bodyguards and staff officers, most of whom smiled approvingly at the girls. Some of the older pirates even made some positive remarks about taking care of thieves.

When they were gone, an officer who looked like a skinny, furless rat with an unnaturally large nose walked up to Zuzack and reported, "Captain, the ship is under our control. Major Grotech also reports that we can fly this ship with no problem. The Captain apparently surrendered at the bridge."

"Good! Have all prisoners assembled in the main ballroom; the ones in the coolers can remain with the ship. Then have a prize crew take command and follow us later. By the way, I would like a word with you in private, Hughes." Zuzack motioned to his guards and other officers to remove the unconscious prisoners in the suite and then to give him the room. When they were alone, he turned to

Hughes and said casually, "My friend, next time we ram a ship, you'd better have the shield coordinates right."

Hughes opened his mouth as if to say something, then intelligently thought better of it when he saw the way the Captain was looking at him. He started to tremble, but the Captain only motioned for him to continue.

"Captain. Sir. Umm, to calculate the velocity and match trajectory while closing in on a ship while both ships are firing is extremely hazardous and difficult." Voice wavering slightly, Hughes said, "Again, sir, I must recommend that we stop ramming our intended targets and go back to the old method, where we used infiltrators and hijacked the ships. The slightest error when calibrating the shields on a target ship while traveling at superluminal speeds..."

Zuzack gave his lieutenant a warning look. "Whatever, Mr. Hughes. We will stick to the ramming-and-boarding method. All that infiltration crap takes too long, and time is something we don't have." He walked over to a large crystal viewport on the far wall of the suite and looked out into space and down at his own ship, the *Bitch*. "This tour has taken too much time, and we must hurry back to my brother—or there will be hell to pay." Oddly enough, a tear trickled down Zuzack's hairy dark face when he mentioned his brother. He kept looking out into space, making sure Hughes wouldn't notice the tear. With his back still turned, he motioned with one of his large muscular arms for Hughes to move on. *Brother, I miss you so*, Zuzack thought, while peering into the Big Dark.

TWO

THE girls hobbled along the large balcony that encircled the ballroom. "Look! Look at this shit, Alexa!" Nina held up her left hand, displaying only three complete digits. She looked more pissed than hurt, which made sense, since Alexa could see an emergency pain-block bracelet wrapped round her wrist.

Alexa smirked. "You always put your fingers where they don't belong. That's why you keep losing them." She shook her head when Nina thrust her hand toward her.

"They grow back. Eventually."

Alexa rolled her eyes. "Yeah, and what if they didn't? What if the Ancestors hadn't fixed that before they first headed into the Big Dark?"

"Then I'd be in deep shit, wouldn't I?" Nina muttered around a couple of pain pills. An emergency p-block never lasted more than a few minutes. "Now, are you gonna fix 'em up, or not?" She waggled the stumps at Alexa.

Shaking her head, Alexa removed a first aid pack from a pocket on Nina's right leg and began to wrap the damaged hand. Nina winced, and Alexa commented, "Be cool, it's only a few fingers. Have Doc do a cloning stim later."

Nina sniffed, "Well, actually, the right term would be *regenerate*, because cloning is only when you... *Fuck*, that hurt, bitch!" Alexa ignored Nina as she administrated the first aid. When she'd finished she looked at her friend with pride. "All done. And damned well, if I say so myself."

Nina sighed. "Thanks. You know, if I keep this up, I'll have more regenerated parts than originals."

"And what's your point? As long as you have your original head and brain you're fine, right?" Alexa smiled at her friend—but she still looked sad.

Nina was biting down hard, obviously trying to ignore the pain from her hand; and in her eyes, Alexa could see the shadows of a sadness that mirrored her own. But all she said was, "Right."

Nodding, Alexa injected Nina with a hypo from the pack, then dosed herself with the same drug. Both shivered and smiled, their eyes glassy, as the drug hit their systems. Once they felt they could go on, they continued out onto a second level above the ballroom, and smiled as they headed toward a very wide spiral staircase. By then, the sounds of fighting had more or less ceased, and someone had silenced the alarms, too. The lights kept flickering on and off, like distant heat lightning, but at least it was normal-spectrum; someone had turned off the yellow warning lights.

As they swept out onto a landing, Nina glanced at her companion and said, "Where's your blaster?"

Alexa's cheeks turned red, and she frowned. "Um, don't ask. I'll get a new one later. By the way, Nina, do you have any more charger mags? All of mine are useless...must have charged them wrong or something." Nina nodded and tossed Alexa a couple of power charge magazines with her good hand.

"You're welcome," Nina mumbled back as she checked her own weapon for any damage. She glanced up and let out a snort of amusement. "Look. The Twins from Hell." She gestured toward two female aliens who appeared, at first glance, to be identical to each other. Both wore battle fatigues like Alexa and Nina, and carried enormous magma rifles. Their purple skins were stippled with small yellow dots, and they both had long, prehensile tails. At the moment, those tails secured a young prisoner between them.

"Mohama and Miska, what do you have there?" Alexa called.

"Just a young brat," Miska replied haughtily. "Thinks it is Oman like the two of you, but it has a pale skin."

"We figure we could kill some time until General Assembly," Mohama added happily. "Care to join us as we ravish him over there?" She nodded towards a secluded area.

"Sure!" Nina grinned. She moved close to the prisoner and yanked up his head. "He's just a boy," she exclaimed. She started to fumble between his legs. When she found his private parts she looked at him, impressed. "I'm in." She glanced at Alexa. "What about you?"

Alexa rolled her eyes and said firmly, "I like my men past puberty, thanks." The boy looked at her pleadingly for help, but Alexa deliberately misinterpreted his look and said, "In your dreams, kid, in your dreams." Wasn't her responsibility to protect little lost boys.

"Still waiting for your knight in shining armor?" Nina smirked.

Suddenly irritated, Alexa stopped and turned around. She walked back to her friends and glared at the prisoner. "How old is he?"

"Who cares? He's as tall as we are, and check *this* out." Miska sliced through the boy's trunks with her razor-sharp nails, exposing his privates. Alexa raised her eyebrows but failed to whistle, given her missing front tooth. "Hell, he's still too young. He'll explode before we can have any fun with him."

"Not if you do that nerve thing you so happily brag about," Nina mused, while looking over the boy and licking her lips.

Alexa shook her head and said, "It's just waste of time. Besides, he's obviously an Orchid Oman, since he's been circumcised. His end nerves are ruined, and that would block the impulses from his sexual nerve."

Nina insisted, "But you could give it a try?"

"He better be worth it, girl, or you'll be out of power batteries for the next galactic year."

Everyone but Nina started to laugh, including the victim. The victim! Nina stuck out her tongue at Alexa and the twins.

The girls went wild around their young trophy, and hurried him away toward a small, secluded area behind a staircase while they danced around him and tore off his clothes. The boy's eyes grow larger and larger as the four girls informed him what each one of them would do to him. He didn't really look that scared; it was obvious, in fact, that he was quite excited. They hurried towards a hatch near the staircase, leaving a long trail of equipment and clothing behind them.

But their fun wasn't to be. Suddenly, unexpected, the bulkhead erupted with a deafening roar right beside them, tossing them all head-over-heels from the pressure wave and filling the air with debris and billowing smoke. The boy's body acted as a shield, protecting the girls; Miska and Mohama fell back, with the boy on top of them. Nina fell down the stairs and Alexa slammed hard, head first, into a bulkhead, losing another tooth.

After a dizzying moment she looked up, holding her head in both hands as she cursed with a bloody mouth. She was disoriented, and she could feel blood oozing out of her ears. She tried to get back on her feet and into the fight, and then time stopped.

She looked up into a pair of dark blue eyes staring down at her. There he was. The knight—*her* knight.

Ever since Alexa had been sold to the pirates at the age of ten, she'd had only one dream: To be rescued by a knight in shining armor. That dream was silly, and it hadn't really lasted long. Once she'd turned fifteen she'd been adopted by the Captain as his daughter, and automatically received second crew shares. Now she was looting for her freedom, to get enough credits to manumit herself. She hated piracy with a passion, but she had no choice in the matter: so she dove into the life with a vengeance. Still, every time a shot was fired, her heart clenched and her soul was forever scarred. She knew she had to leave this horrible life, or she would end it herself.

Alexa stared, paralyzed, at the most handsome young man she had ever seen—and she let her guard down in the process. An iron-hard fist struck her in the face, followed by another in the gut. She went down like a poleaxed sheep, crashing into the bulkhead she'd just crawled up from and breaking her third tooth of the day. She hit the deck in a still heap, dead to the world.

A dozen young men and women, all dressed in light blue formal uniforms, charged out of a hallway armed with slug-throwing handguns and blasters. They quickly removed the girls' weapons, and made sure they stayed unconscious for a while with their own version of the pirates' slave collars. Then they began to advance against the pirate positions in two-by-two formations. Unlike the pirates, who had been reveling in their victory and were shocked by the unexpected attack, the newcomers were very organized, very professional, and very well-disciplined. They fired short, controlled bursts and advanced fearlessly against their enemy, who substantially outnumbered them. Their facial expressions were invariably ironclad masks of hatred.

It was a suicide mission, and they all knew it. But they didn't let that stop them for a moment.

When Zuzack realized what was happening, he cursed and bellowed, "Alarm! Nastasturus!"

The word send cold chills down many of the pirates' spines, and confusion erupted among them.

Zuzack stood at the center of the ballroom shouting out orders to his pirates. "Get them, lads and tramps, give them all you got, and don't damage them too much! They're worth more alive than dead!"

Laser and magma bolts rained down like a hailstorm all around, but Zuzack just stood there as if he were immortal, displaying no sign of fear. The pirates advanced, unorganized, and several of them were killed or injured from the effective fire laid down by the cadets from the Nastasturus Federation. Lieutenant Hughes grabbed his weapon and aimed it at the oncoming threat, but Zuzack only laid his large hand on his lieutenant's shoulder and said calmly, "Fewer crew members means more spoil for the survivors. Remember, we're done in this sector and heading home." Hughes gave his Captain a strange and questioning look, and after a few moments he lowered his weapon and smiled uncertainly.

The fight was bloody but short, for the Nastasturus soldiers soon began to run out of ammunition. At that point, Zuzack ordered his troops to charge in and capture them alive. The pirates swarmed the cadets, and the hand-to-hand fighting was fierce.

One of the pirates aimed her rifle at one of the cadets' backs and was about to press the trigger when her head was separated messily from her body. Zuzack wiped his sword on her quivering form and snarled, "I told you, fools, I want them all alive!"

Zuzack gestured towards his third officer, Major Grotech, who snapped out an order through his helmet communicator.

A moment later, four huge lizard-like dogs charged from the boarding tube into the civilian ship. The Tilters rushed the young cadets before they noticed the new threat from behind, and it was all they could do to fend off the huge animals. Meanwhile, pirates approached with net-throwers, discharging the weapons when they got within range and capturing several of the cadets that way. The Tilter dogs themselves spat a web-like substance that immobilized the remaining cadets, and suddenly it was over.

Alexa and Nina helped each other to their feet, and supported each other as they picked their way through the cadets. They stopped long enough to kick a couple, but not too hard, so they wouldn't piss off the Captain too much. The twins Miska and Mohama followed angrily, after they noticed the bloody emasculated mess their fun-toy had become. Along the way, they took back their weapons from the captured cadets.

"What a waste," Miska growled. "The poor thing could at least have been allowed to die with a smile on his face."

Alexa ignored her; her attention was elsewhere. There he was again: her Knight. No shining armor, though. He was a young man in his early twenties, with short dark brown hair, his face bruised up from the fight. Knight or not, he needed to be taught who was in charge. She smirked. *Time to break him in.* Then her gaze snagged on his deep blue eyes, and an odd weakness seemed to overcome her. *Dammit, knees, don't you mutiny on me now!*

Alexa kicked towards his face, coming as close as she could without actually touching him, and lisped through her broken teeth, "Anybody ever told you it's not nice to hit a lady?"

"You are no lady. You are a whore and a pirate." He said it through clenched teeth, a menacing gleam in his eyes.

Alexa glared down at him, frustration and anger roiling inside her. Bastard. Her long-lost knight had made her feel weak, something no male was allowed to do. This was no way for a knight to treat his damsel in distress. She aimed another kick at the young soldier's pretty face, and her toes struck the wall hard when he jerked his head away. Pissed, her foot throbbing, Alexa lost her cool. Knight or not, it was time to kick some serious ass. Literally. She was about to kick him again when something snagged her ankle from behind and, to her horror, lifted her up in the air upside-down.

Hanging helplessly, she twisted around to see what had her. The large saurian woman holding her up shook her head, the razor blades woven into the ends of her long dreads clinking and rattling. The saurian grunted, "Cap'n said no damage, Brat."

"Let me down, Myra, or I'll turn you into a pair of *boots*."

Hissing in laughter, Myra tossed Alexa over her shoulder and smacked her buttocks a few times. "Now, now, my little princess, you are no longer a member of your Royalist Clan. You will obey, or Cap'n will have his way with you—again."

Alexa started screaming and protesting, her legs kicking holes into the air and fists punching Myra's back hard. The saurian barely noticed. "Like hell he will, you lizard bitch!" she screamed. "Like hell he will! Let me down, I'm warning you! I mean it, Myra, you'll be the start of the next fashion statement to sweep the galaxy—and dammit, stop spanking my ass!" She was not going to put up with this crap. Imagine, being treated like this in front of her knight!

But the more she struggled and shouted threats, the harder the smacks fell on her firm, unprotected buttocks. A few of the pirates standing nearby started to laugh at the display. Instead of breaking up the fight, they started cheering Myra and Alexa on.

But soon the cheering stopped like someone had cut it off with a switch, and so did the spanking. A large, strong hand grabbed hold of Alexa's dreadlocks, pulling her head back, interrupting her complaints.

"You again. Let her go, Myra," Zuzack ordered. He held Alexa up by hair, with her legs kicking several feet from the ground. It hurt amazingly badly, so she shut up. "Now, young lady," Zuzack growled, "you will obey me, or I'll sell you—but only after the entire crew has had their way with you. Is that understood, Brat?"

Alexa looked at him in horror. She tried to nod as she grabbed onto her hair and the Captain's long, muscular arm in a futile attempt to stop the pain and pressure from her scalp and hairline. She felt more than heard the sound of tearing flesh near her newly-acquired bald spot, and she realized that if she didn't respond quickly, she was about to lose her whole scalp.

"Yes, Captain, I swear I will never do wrong again, I swear!" Alexa shouted sincerely. She didn't plead or ask for any mercy, even when he gave her a little shake. Dammit, would she lose all her hair? She ground her teeth. Well, be that as it may. She would at least be alive, and it could be fixed. But she felt sure that if she begged for any mercy, she would die for sure—or worse, be scalped alive.

Zuzack stared at Alexa, and there was madness in his eyes. The ripping sound of Alexa's scalp giving away turned him on, apparently. Well, she knew that other people's fears turned him on more than sex did. But there could be, no fear in Alexa's eyes. She bit down hard on her lower lip, preparing for the excruciating pain that would soon follow, when her entire scalp and all her hair would be lost forever. She figured Zuzack would never allow her to have it regenerated. He and most of the other older pirates treasured their battle scars almost as much as any normal treasure.

To her amazement, Zuzack's expression changed and he begun to laugh, as he put Alexa down very slowly. Then he was patting her on top of her head like some animal. "Kids!" he roared. "That's my little princess! Be nice, and I might reclaim you as my daughter again!"

Zuzack laughed hard, and bore the look of a proud father as he walked over to the Nastasturus cadets. "You boys and girls better be officers from wealthy families or Clans," he told them brightly, "because if you're not, you will be sold off as food. Hell, I might just let you have dinner with some of my crew later." He laughed loudly, rubbing his large belly. The cadets only stared back at him hatefully—except for one, who was trembling and covering his face, trying to conceal his tears from his friends.

Zuzack ignored the whimpering young cadet, his eye caught by another young man with red hair who stood out from the rest and glared defiantly at him. More hatred radiated from the redhead than from any one of the other cadets, or even any of the prisoners in general. "I take it you're the leader of this little group?" Zuzack asked coolly.

The young cadet didn't answer; he just continued to glare at the enormous pirate Captain with defiant eyes. His stare made Zuzack feel a bit of unease; but hell—no fear, no fun. He walked up to the cadet, grabbed his arm, and pulled him to his feet, ignoring the boy's struggles.

"I don't like the look in your eyes, boy. I think it's time to teach you and your fine friends a valuable lesson in manners and respect toward your new owner."

Zuzack looked more or less human—but he wasn't, not entirely. He smiled and opened his mouth wide, lifted his tongue, and a barbed feeding tendril flashed out with lightning speed. It struck the cadet in the left eyeball, and before the kid could even feel it, had yanked out his eye and disappeared back into the Captain's mouth. The cadet dropped, screaming, blood oozing from the black hole where his eye had been. He screamed and cursed, threatening the pirate and all his followers with vile fates that he had no means of carrying out.

After crunching up and swallowing his prize, Zuzack assured the prisoner, "I know what you're thinking, lad: that we'll clone it back. But we won't. I see by your insignia that you're a cadet pilot. Well, you can never pilot a craft with only one eye—at least, not a military craft. By the time you reach a safe port, it will be too late to clone it back...if you make it back alive, that is."

Lieutenant Hughes sidled up to his Captain and whispered, "Sir, with all due respect, he is worth more intact."

The Captain pulled Hughes aside and whispered, "Listen, Lieutenant, they're all officer cadets. Remember last time we had some, and what they did to my old ship? The damages and the loss of good fellow pirates' lives weren't worth all the trouble. Not again! This time, I intend to make sure they don't start anything funny."

"But what if he is worth a high ransom, or top dollar in the slave pits?"

"Don't worry. If he is, then we'll fix him up as good as new. But if he's just an everyday cadet, or no one of importance, then..."

"What do you intend to do, Cap'n, if I may be so bold?"

Zuzack leered at Hughes and murmured, "Wait till supper." He turned back to the prisoners. "In the meantime, put them on the slave blocks, just in case they get creative." The two pirates looked at each other and began laughing.

The prisoners were rounded up like cattle, and most of the pirates gathered with them in the huge main ballroom. There were over three thousand people present, and at least half of them were prisoners. The prisoners, exhausted in mind and body, sat and lay down on the floor. Many of them were injured, and most were bruised from the fight. Some of the prisoners were in shackles, but most were not. What they all had in common was the collar each had around his or her neck, engraved with a number or sigil that represented the individual pirate or clan who had claimed the prisoner for further trade.

Zuzack snapped out an order and the wall on the far end of the ballroom peeled back, revealing two large airlocks flanked by wide viewports. No doubt they had been used to load large items and passengers directly into the ballroom. Visible through the ports were the long barrels of the anti-fighter guns attached to the ship's hull. Zuzack stepped forward and pressed a control on a computer console, and two sets of controls morphed out of the wall. He took up station at one while the saurian woman, Myra, took the other. Both grasped a joystick with a pistol handle, while peering through the port into space.

Two pirates pushed a well-dressed elderly man into the airlock and slammed the hatch shut on his screams. He pounded on the inside of the hatch, and his face, bright red and contorted with fear, was visible through a small window near the top. A pirate turned a knob on the wall, and the old man grabbed his head and seemed to be screaming from pain. A whisper of horror swept through the crowd.

"Pull!" Zuzack shouted out loud.

One of the pirates by the airlock pulled down a handle, and the old man was spat out into space as the remaining air went screaming onto the void. He was still alive, kicking and screaming, as Zuzack and Myra opened fire, cutting him into pieces. During the entire atrocity most of the pirates cheered the events, though some looked on with less enthusiasm. Bets were made, and money, jewelry and prisoners exchanged hands.

The crew began to chant, "One more, one more."

The Captain looked at Myra, who shrugged, and then pointed at an old woman wearing a dress that would have cost a normal person a year's salary. "That was your old man, wasn't it?" Zuzack asked innocently. The woman, crying silently, simply nodded. "I take it would be to cruel of me to part two loved ones."

For a long moment no one spoke; then the old woman lifted her head high and said proudly, "Do what you will, monster."

Zuzack gestured sharply, and two pirates moved on the woman. In seconds they had her shackles off, and had forced her into the airlock; the entire time she fought as hard as her husband had. Her face twisted in fury, she pounded on the port so hard that her fist left smears of blood across the thick crystal.

The pirate crowd had a frisson of extra amusement when a little boy leapt up off the ballroom floor, escaping the clutches of his mother, and rand toward the hatch shouting, shouting, "Grandmother, grandmother! No, NO, I'm coming!"

He reached the door and tried to open it as the pirates roared in laughter; when it became clear he had absolutely no chance of succeeding, he, too, pounded hard on the glass, his face a mask of fear and pain. His grandmother mouthed "I love you" from the other side of the port.

Zuzack grabbed the boy from behind. "What is this, a mutiny?" He smiled at the young boy, reveling in his fear. "Say goodbye to your granny, lad. PULL!"

The old woman shot out into the darkness and Myra opened up, cutting her into pieces with .50 caliber slugs.

Zuzack turned to his jolly crew and hollered, "Enough! Start processing the prisoners. Never mind cleaning this old ship of anything of value and supplies—we'll do that later. We'll have our regular auction over any unclaimed spoil when we return to base, so finish up here as quickly as you can." He turned to his officers. All saluted him and nodded; they needed no further details or instructions. Everyone knew what needed to be done.

The crew cheered their Captain and their success and then went back to looting the ship, despite their Captain's orders. The officers and the more experienced pirates concentrated on processing the prisoners.

Zuzack held up the young boy who had just lost his grandparents. The boy tried to hit Zuzack, but to no avail. Zuzack crowed with delight. "As for you, my little mutineer, I'm going to have me some *fun* with you." Zuzack tossed the boy over his shoulder, laughing, and walked down the corridor toward an empty stateroom. Soon, a hatch clicked shut behind them, and the boy's horrible screams cut off.

TWO starships hurtled through space, leaving debris and bodies floating behind. The first ship was the *Bitch,* an old, modified destroyer—class vessel from the trading wars that could carry a crew up to three thousand. The *Bitch* had been upgraded and repaired several times, and far more weapons had been attached to her than were normally used. When she was underway, the cannons and missile turrets were lowered back into the deck, and hatches covered their emplacements.

The *Bitch* was followed by a vessel ten times larger. It was a more modern vessel and quite beautiful, except for some hastily repaired hull damage. She was the *Bright Star,* a vast Transport Cruiser that could handle over twenty thousand passengers in comfort. Five thousand were active at any one time, while another fifteen thousand people were stored in the coolers. The crew was—had been—about fifteen hundred strong, and less than two hundred were security and officers.

The coolers made the trip inexpensive for the people who chose to ride that way; they were frozen in stasis and basically stacked like cordwood in the hull. On the *Bright Star,* four types of berths were available: First Class, Diplomatic, Second Class, and Third Class, which were the coolers. Nearly all the money was made from the first three classes; the cooler travelers were just gravy. Most Civilian Transport Cruisers were owned and operated by The Federated Merchants (T.F.M.) or The Commercial Traders (T.C.T.). The Federated Merchants happened to own the *Bright Star.*

THE *Bitch* was as busy as a kicked beehive. Most of the crew was repairing the ship, while others were busy locking down and guarding the prisoners, now that they'd been processed and selected for the different types of Blocks. Males were parted from females; different species and families were also selected into different blocks.

The slave block was the preferred tool of slave traffickers and prisoner transporters throughout the galaxy; it made transporting unwilling humanoid cargo a lot easier. A smaller version was a very popular toy item among children on several worlds; they used it when they played games like Traders and Slaves, or Prisoner and Warden.

To Zuzack's surprise, Alexa and Nina volunteered to take care of all unclaimed prisoners—something most pirates couldn't care less about. Alexa did it to keep herself near her fallen knight. With help from Nina, she removed his uniform and placed him on a block, sitting him gently down on a bench. They put his ankles onto two half holes in the center of the stock device, and his wrists on the sides at the same level. The upper part of the stock was placed on top, locking him down. When they were done, they pushed a button on the stock, and air filled the rubber bladders lining the arm and leg holes, rendering the wrists and ankles immobile. Alexa attached a controller to her sleeping knight's neck—it logged information about the prisoner's health status into a computer built into one side of the stock—while Nina lowered the bench. It was now impossible to escape without help.

After they'd finished with Alexa's knight, they did the same thing with the rest of the Nastasturus cadets, though perhaps less gently. Later, they moved on to the other unclaimed prisoners. For some of the larger aliens they altered the block, aided in their work by colorless little androids.

THREE

THERE were tall mountains. He could fly, and thought surely he would soar over the peaks... and then he fell screaming toward the ground and then into it, deeper and deeper, as everything turned darker.

There was silence.

He stood at the top of a mountain, holding a young boy's head in his hands, and stared at it. It stared back at him. The mouth opened as the head tried to speak, but it couldn't; it was dead. The young boy could only look down at the head in his hands. A head without a body, looking back at him with a guilty and wondering expression. "What have I done?" the boy asked himself.

From the background came a faint keening sound; and then there were drums. The peal of a horn filled his ears, and he realized that he was surrounded by the sounds of warriors fighting a fierce battle: the clash of steel, gut shots, the muffled whump of artillery, the screams of the wounded.

His gaze wandered across the battlefield and affixed on two figures. One was male, the other female, and they fought side-by-side with a singular passion.

There was a bright light, and a wave of searing, excruciating pain passed through his body. He screamed and lost consciousness. When he awoke, his head was lolled to the side; and he saw a young boy lying face-down on a table, with several horrible creatures standing around him. The boy screamed out from fear and pain.

The white light blinded him again and something moved inside of him, his rectum jolting with pain as something was forced inside. It seared all his nerves with an electrical jolt. Meanwhile, millions of needles were stuck into his skin, and each caused a different pain than the last.

Everything turned dark.

The sky was filled with a vast black cloud, and bloody rain turned the ground a ghastly red. Quaking with horror, he realized that the roiling cloud formed the features of a horrible beast; and as he watched, a great wound of a mouth opened and thundered, "Find me and bring me back. Bring me back, find me, and you shall find the truth."

Was it the monster speaking—or someone else?

One person knelt at the center of a battlefield littered with millions of dead, surrounded by tongues of fire hotter than those of Hell. "Father and Mother, forgive them not," the figure prayed. "All of them knew what they were doing. Awaken, awaken young one, it is time..."

Two dark eyes stared at him from the clouds, and for an instant a crown of laurels flashed above, on a noble brow. Then the boy became aware of the stench of the battlefield, and the unbearable miasma filled his nostrils, and...

---——oOo——---

ALEC woke up with a splitting headache, his vision blurry, and was almost overcome by the stink of urine and excrement. He tried to focus his eyes, but that just made the headache worse. That, combined with the horrible reek, made him vomit—and dammit, that didn't help either.

When he tried to focus his eyes next, all he could see was a dark blur. He heard people crying and moaning around him, begging for help, food and water. Some were screaming. What had happened? Had there been an accident?

When his eyes finally focused, he noticed that he was sitting in a crouched position, with his ankles and wrists clamped into four padded holes in front of him. He couldn't see his hands or feet, but he could feel that they'd removed his gloves and boots.

It was uncomfortable as hell, but he could bear it, he thought. A second later, he was hit with an intense cramp, and suddenly understood the screams.

That was when he realized his neck was all but immobilized in some sort of collar that was attached to the wall behind him. He wore some sort of pale tunic and that was all. Every time he moved his neck, he felt a little jolt of electricity surge through his body. He tried to scream, and the mask that covered half his face gagged him so that only a muffled noise left his lips. He started to panic.

A cramp in his leg muscles made him spasm, and it hurt so badly that he screamed again and lost control of his bowels. He panicked some more and started to struggle against his bounds, but it was soon clear that his efforts were in vain. He was stuck.

"The neck controller is programmed to do that so that you can learn your first lesson in submission," a young female voice explained in a friendly tone. She sounded more like a grade-school teacher than a malicious pirate.

Tears in his eyes, Alec looked up towards the sound of her voice. The neck controller attacked him, causing his entire body to shake even harder; he bit down hard on the soft rubber gag-ball stuck in his mouth. Fortunately, his bowels were empty now, so he couldn't embarrass himself further.

He looked up again, after his recovery, and he saw her. Despite his predicament, he stared in shock. She was the most beautiful woman he had ever laid eyes on, bar none. Her black hair was twisted up in dreadlocks that hung straight down to the middle of her back; but what particularly captured his attention were the warm doe-brown eyes. She seemed a bit apprehensive, yet stared at him with the curiosity of any young woman who sees something she likes and wants.

Everything that Alec saw was perfect until she smiled at him, displaying a dark gap in her smile where several teeth were missing. He blushed, embarrassed to be sitting half-naked, in a pool of his own waste, in front of such a beauty.

She ignored the smell and pushed a button. The gag fell from his face and was winched up into the ceiling. Alec trembled and shrank back like a scared animal; he hated himself for it, but couldn't help the reaction—it was automatic. He tried to catch his breath and relax in an effort to maintain a little dignity and demanded, "Where am I, and who are you?"

"Doesn't matter," the young woman answered in a neutral tone. She stepped closer to the stock, and looked at Alec with a calculating expression on her face. "Not bad. I might just buy you myself." She tapped her fingers on her lips. "Can you cook?"

Alec spat, and hit the girl in her face. At first, she looked taken aback; then disappointment flashed across her face, followed by rage. Pursing her lips, she spat back in *his* face. They stared at each other for a long moment and then, astonishingly, both burst into laughter.

"What is going on here?" A deep, throaty voice demanded. A tall saurian woman clumped up next to the human girl, looked over the scene, and taunted her. "Fraternizing with the cargo, Alexa? Wonderful!"

The girl muttered, "Idiot. Now he knows my name, *Myra*."

"Big deal. What do you think he's going to do—write you after he's sold?" The lizard woman flourished a thin cane in the air to punctuate her remarks, then laughed cruelly and smacked Alec smartly on his exposed hands and feet. It didn't hurt much, but the strike caught him off-guard and his body jerked involuntarily—so the neck controller hit him like a sledgehammer. Without the gag, his scream echoed through the cargo hold. Myra snickered. "That shit gets me every time. Did you see his face?" She laughed as she patted Alexa on her back and moved on.

Alexa looked after Myra, fury writ large across her face, then turned back to Alec, who was trembling like a scared rat and coughing up blood. "Um, sorry about that, I'm truly am, I never wanted..."

"You *will* be sorry, pirate. You *will* be." Alec looked up at her with hooded eyes.

Just then Myra's voice came over the intercom: "Stand by for cleaning." Alexa looked at Alec, shook her head, and walked away. A moment after the hatch slammed closed, a series of sprinklers began to shower the room with powerful streams of water from all directions. The filthy runoff drained out through gridded holes in the floor.

"You always have had a way with the women," a weak voice said over the hiss of the sprinklers, barely audible.

Alec strained to look to his left without moving his head, but he could barely see the speaker, who sat right next to him. "Andrew, that you?"

"Who do you think it is, your mom? 'Course it's me. C'mon, Alec! Get your chin up and show some damned dignity. Ever since we got captured you've behaved like a fresh recruit."

"Watch it, pal, I can still beat the crap out of you. If I could get loose." It wasn't an idle boast; Andrew Bow was several inches shorter than Alec, if as impressively muscled. He was from the capital world of the Nastasturus Federation, Tallas. His family was wealthy, members of the Royalist hierarchy, and he would one day inherit his father's title as Baron of the Three Lakes. If he survived this, of course. His voice had a rather high pitch and could sometimes be annoying to the people around him—but he was loyal and knew how to keep a secret, which resulted in him having the dirt on all his friends. Not that he would ever use it. He could talk to almost anyone about anything, and was overall a likable guy.

"How you holding up?" he said now.

Alec answered, "Lovely, and you?"

They both laughed; it was bitter, but a laugh nonetheless. Andrew said, "Man, she's one hot little pirate, isn't she?"

"I guess she is, but that doesn't change what she is, now, does it? Vermin is vermin." Alec glanced sideways at the blurry figure of Andrew. "Where are the others?"

"Dunno. I just woke up when that gag was removed."

Someone behind them on the slave block said, "We're here. This is Sal...I'm behind you, along with Mat and Tech. Dunno where Jack is."

Sal had been born on the backwater planet of Zuma, but his family had been raised to the level of Elite citizens for distinguished service to the Federation, and therefore lived on Tallas now. He was a wheeler and dealer, and if money had an odor, he could smell it. Like Andrew, Alec, and Tech, he was an Oman, and his family belonged to the Presidential clan. They were very wealthy, and unlike most of their fellow Elites, had worked their way up from scratch. Their main wealth came from communications; they own several satellite production and research companies.

Mat belonged to the Herrier species, and he and his family were also Elite citizens of the Nastasturus Federation. They were not considered especially wealthy, but his family had belonged to the Superior Senate for more than ten generations, which meant that they never had to work and their offspring were born into retirement for all eternity. This was one of the highest honors under the Nastasturus regime. Mat was the only volunteer in their squad.

Tech was a citizen of Tallas, where he had been born, and because of that he automatically belonged to the Elite. Most of his family, except for his mother and older sister, had disappeared on a deep space voyage before he was born. He'd lost his mother when she left him with her sister on a search-and-rescue mission and was never heard from again. When he got older, Tech had sworn never to stop looking for them until he knew for certain exactly what had happened to them. His interest in pirates and abductions had made him into a fanatic on the subject.

As for Jack—he was the squad leader, and no one knew him well, beyond the fact that he was a cadet in the School of Military Intelligence. That meant he had to belong to the Elite, since only they were ever recruited into military intelligence. As for his species, everyone assumed he was a standard Oman, but it was hard to tell. He might well belong to one of the hybrid or transgenic races.

Andrew demanded, "Anybody see what happened to Jack?"

"Last I saw of him, he was taken away by a couple of pirates," Sal answered.

"Missing an eye," Alec added dryly.

"Ugh." Andrew was quiet for a moment, then: "Anyone seen Major Nesbit or any of the girls?"

Alec muttered, "Nesbit's an officer, so they wouldn't keep him here. The girls must be in another area." What he didn't want to say—but couldn't help think—was that they were probably being gang-raped right about now.

Sal cut in, "The major could be dead for all we know."

Mat spoke up for the first time, in that rough voice of his, "Wonder what happened to him. Did anyone see him once the attack started?"

Like his crew, Major Thore Nesbit was an Elite citizen. He belonged to the Royal class, was extremely intelligent, and very well respected among his family, friends and foes alike. His full name was actually Nesbit Thore Af Hornet, and he and Alec shared a secret from the others: they were cousins.

No one replied to Mat's question about Major Nesbit. Raising his voice in anger, Andrew yelled out loud, "You bastards, you will all *pay* for this!" His shout was interrupted by an electric zap as the collar kicked in, causing him to gurgle and spit blood.

A voice from an intercom warned them, "Any more lip out of any of you and you'll be gagged again, boyos. Now shut up!" Alec tried to whisper something, but a mild tingling from the collar made him stop. From the intercom came, "That goes for whispering too."

None of the cadets had anything more to say after that; they dared not even sob. Alexa stood behind pillar a dozen yards away, gazing toward Alec and his friends in their barbaric slave blocks. There was a deep sadness in her eyes, but her tears were concealed by the water pouring from the sprinkler system.

Hours turned into days, and days into weeks. Alec and his friends lost count of time. The lights never dimmed, so they had no idea of the ship's daily cycle. People came and went at all hours, and they slept whenever they could. Their misery was horrible, and the cramps were regular and agonizing. From time to time, pirates came down to taunt and tease them; and every time, Alec's friends screamed and cursed while threatening the pirates with the most painful, undignified deaths they could think of. Alec didn't. He remained subdued and kept a low profile, slumping in a submissive posture, taking the pirates' taunts without saying a word. It took everything he had to do it; he *wanted* to be defiant, but he *needed* them to think he was beaten. They'd get theirs.

Most of the time Myra and her guards kept the pirates in check, but once a pirate managed to get too close. He looked Sal, Tech and Mat over with an evil smile on his face. The pirate's name was Gor, and he reeked from alcohol and cheap drugs. Grinning maliciously, Gor removed his oily black shirt, revealing several scars and a bar code tattooed onto the right side of his chest, along with the Nastasturus Unicorn symbol. He murmured into Mat's ear in a low, threatening voice that everyone in the block could hear: "Look what your beautiful Federation has done to me, you bastards. You invaded my world and turned me and my people into slaves for your mighty army." He spat in Mat's face.

But Mat didn't even flinch. Instead, he glared at the pirate in contempt and said calmly, "And now you are a traitor and pirate scum," in his gravelly voice, before spitting in Gor's face.

Furious, Gor slapped a button on the side of the slave block, and the seats on the device folded down. The bars holding their arms and legs in place didn't. Their wrists and ankles snapped like dry twigs; but the crackle of bones fracturing from the pressure was overwhelmed by their loud screams of pain. Gor roared with laughter, his mad eyes never leaving the three prisoners as they hung from the stocks in helpless agony. When he moved over to Alec and Andrew's side, he stared at them with a cold glare, nothing human left in his eyes. Alec swallowed, a chill running down his spine.

Suddenly an alarm sounded from the slave block's life support system—but it was nothing near as loud as Myra's curses as she rushed into the hold, trailing both a guard android and medical android. The guard android quickly slid between Gor and the prisoners, as the medical android plugged an arm into the slave block, accessing its records and returning the bench to its original position. Myra arrived, her face flushed bright green, and slammed Gor into a bulkhead. "What the hell are you doing, you useless fuck!" she screamed. She shook him until his teeth rattled. "Answer me, before I have you skinned alive!"

Gor shouted back, almost incoherently, "Their evil federation put me and my people through hell! It's my right, it's my..." He gave out a mad scream and flung himself on Myra, who was so taken by surprise that she crashed to the floor with Gor on top of her. He grabbed one of the short but heavy leather whips from her belt and yanked it away; it had a wicked-looking hook at the end. Before Myra could react Gor leaped up and slashed away at Alec, tearing away part of his left eyebrow. Alec screamed as blood gushed down his face, obscuring the vision in that eye...but he never moved a centimeter, lest the collar activate.

Myra smacked Gor off his feet with one huge hand, sending him crashing into the two Oman guards who had just arrived to subdue the altercation. All three crashed to the deck, and shortly Myra was on top of them. She shackled Gor and subdued him with a hard punch to his face.

"Take this crazy fool and throw him in the brig," she ordered, "and have Lieutenant Hughes charge his account for whatever credits this mess is gonna cost by the time the butcher is finished with them. And get her down here ASAP."

Some of the crew had already started to attend to the injured prisoners. Andrew, the only one who wasn't injured, growled, "The butcher?"

Myra rolled her eyes. "The medical officer, dear. Did you think this little medical andy would be able to fix you up all by itself?"

After the attack by Gor, the Nastasturus cadets received better treatment. Even the Captain himself came down to see them—but he was only making sure that his cargo remained intact and undamaged. He looked with pride on his prisoners. Most of them sat staring back at him, still defiant—except for one of the young prisoners, who was slumped in his stock with downcast eyes, and seemed almost to be whimpering. Zuzack shook his head in disgust and contempt, then loudly told the android guard to secure the slave block to prevent any unauthorized access.

After that, Alec and his friends were allowed to talk to each other without any punishment. Probably every word they said was being recorded, but they talked anyway; somehow it made the long hours go faster. Still, time crept by very slowly. They were attended once a day by a medical android, which impersonally clamped a large hose to their mouths and force-fed them a grayish paste manufactured to satisfy the needs of all known vegetarian and omnivorous sentients.

That didn't mean it was appetizing. The stench of the paste reminded Alec and his friends of something that had died and lain in the sun for several days. More of the paste was hurled up rather than swallowed, but the android didn't care; whenever that happened, it would just force more down the victim's throats until a satisfactory amount had entered the biological system.

After Gor's visit, Sal, Tech and Mat were taken away for a few days to be healed by the ship's doctor. Soon enough, they were returned to their places in the slave block. Alec's eye was a mess. The physician had just frowned at his injury when she saw it, then slapped the skin back and spat on it as she rubbed on a dollop of white lotion that had burned like hell. By the time Sal and the boys returned, Alec could no longer see out of that eye, and the wound was terribly infected, oozing pus and a clear serum. His brow burned with fever, his head a solid mass of pain. From time to time he lost control and began to scream, and his friends tried to calm him with soothing words. Most of the time, though, they treated him with contempt.

Once a day they were showered clean by the sprinklers and, sometimes, water hoses wielded like weapons by bored pirates. The water was recycled, tasteless stuff and didn't include anything like soap or disinfectant, so though it sluiced their bodies clean, it didn't really do anything about the smell. It was cold, too, and when it dried it left them tormented by an itching sensation all over their bodies.

During one of these cleanings, a high pressure stream hit Alec's wound, opening it up. He woke up from a dull sleep with blood and pus pouring down the side of his face. He didn't scream this time, even though it was agonizing, and he had stopped making any noise at all long since; he was simply too beaten and exhausted. All he could do was carefully turn his head away, ever so slightly, and try to protect the injury from the water jet.

He noticed a faint scent of flowers, as of perfume, and looked up. For the third time he saw the young and very attractive pirate, Alexa, standing before him.

She wore a pale gray coverall decorated with dark stains, matched by smears of grime on her face. No matter; she still looked astonishing. She had braided her long black dreads and fastened them in a messy curl on the back of her head. Distantly, Alec noticed that she was shifting from one foot to the other, looking very nervous.

Alexa looked up towards the second level, where Myra was sitting behind a large tented window inside a small guard tower, observing the VIP cargo room. They nodded at each other. Myra looked down at her left hand, upon a beautiful necklace made of bright, shining stones, and smiled as she thought, *Young fool in love. Ha!*

Alexa approached Alec with something shiny in her hand, and he wondered, dully, if this was the end. But she passed the thing over the side of his head and it started beeping; some kind of med scanner? She cupped his chin in a firm hand, and he tried to pull away, only to be shocked by the collar; and she started as if it had been she who was shocked. She dropped the medical instrument, but was able to snatch it out of the air before it hit the ground; Alec was impressed. Then she brushed her hair out of her face, and gave Alec a puzzled look, mixed with a bit of disappointment.

"Please relax," she said softly. "I'm not going to hurt you, really." When Alexa took hold of his chin this time, gently but firmly, he made no resistance. She began to fold up Alec's eyebrow back to where it should have been, causing him to pant and shudder in pain. She hesitated for a long second before continuing. "No painkiller. Sorry," she murmured as she lifted the skin flap back to its original position. She clicked a switch on the medical instrument and aimed a warm, bright beam at the injury while holding a white cotton swab under it, removing the scab carefully, sopping up the blood and pus as it came. She leaned over a bit and got closer to his face, a grim expression on hers.

Alex, trembling, became aware of her strong, feminine scent, and somehow it relaxed him. She was too close for him to see anything but a golden blur with his good eye; the black-haired beauty was either wonderfully tanned or had a natural dark bronze skin tone. He slumped, and began enjoying her sensitive touch on his bruised body.

When she was done she stood up and leaned back with a concerned expression, examining her work. She apparently decided that he needed more work with the medical instrument, so she grabbed the injured region again—not nearly as carefully as he should have. Alec emitted a quiet snort of pain. Alexa stopped and whispered, "Whoops!" Then she leaned forward and started the process over again.

Alec muttered back, "Who are you calling 'whoops"? Let me out of this shit, and I'll give you whoops."

She ignored his confused remark and snapped, "Hey, you, please try not to shake so much. You're making the wound open again."

After that, Alec stared straight ahead and remained silent. Alexa continued her ministrations for a few more minutes before she straightened and pronounced with satisfaction, "There you go." He noticed that she was standing with her fists clenched, pushed into her sides, and vaguely wondered why. She tilted her head to the side. "It's not perfect, but at least you can use your eye again. It'll leave a small scar for all your girlfriends to admire."

"Don't have any girlfriends," Alec mumbled.

"Perhaps you don't like girls," Alexa responded.

"Of course I do, I love girls, I..."

"Always put my foot in my mouth," Andrew interrupted softly, and he and his friends in the slave block shared a moment of laughter. Even Alexa smiled, a little.

Alec blushed a little; his head was already clearing up. "Thanks, bonehead," he grumbled at Andrew.

"You guys always this nice to each other?" wondered Alexa.

"Only at times like these," Sal replied.

"Great, look what you've done. You woke up all of the bastards," Alec whispered.

"Sorry. Are you *jealous* now?"

"Jealous about who, you? Ha!"

Alexa looked at him icily—and perhaps with the tiniest bit of disappointment—and then started to gather her things up into a small box.

Tech whistled and sang out, "*Id*-i-ot!"

Alec looked at Alexa, puzzled, as she began to walk away. "Oh, hey, wait a minute, please. I'm sorry," he croaked.

Alexa turned and looked back at Alec. "Sorry for what? That I'm a pirate?"

"Well, yes, that. But, but..."

Alexa nodded angrily, and then she hurried away.

"Way to go, bonehead," Mat rumbled.

"Wait, wait, I want to thank you," Alec shouted, as she disappeared into the depths of the dimly-lit hold.

"Told ya. You always put your foot in your mouth," Andrew observed, followed by another round of laughter from Sal, Tech and Mat.

"Shut up!" Alec shouted. But he was angrier at himself then he was at his friend's comments.

Now that he felt half-human, he could talk to his squad mates again; it had been a while. Days, he figured. "It's about time they got you some treatment. I was getting sick of all the pissing and moaning," Sal teased.

"Yeah, but at least it was entertaining," observed Tech.

Andrew said, "Especially compared to the delicious, gourmet meals we've enjoyed on this somewhat wild but absolutely free cruise. I have to say that's gotta be the worst part...and I must add that..."

"What the hell did you just say about the food?" Alec demanded.

There was a brief silence, and then everyone but Andrew began to laugh. Andrew muttered in a falsetto tone, "Barbarians! Do you *really* like this shitty food? Uncultured ruffians!"

This time, they all laughed. No matter the hellish predicament they faced, the team simply enjoyed each other's company. But the laughter invariably masked nervousness, shock, and despair.

Myra relaxed inside the security tower, listening to a classic Oman opera while examining the necklace with pleased eyes. Occasionally she listened to a word or two of the young VIP prisoners' conversation, but she really had no interest at all. She glanced down at Nina, who was kneeling between her legs, pleasuring Myra with her tongue while caressing the lizard-woman's thighs and using one of her index fingers to depress a small tentacle next to Myra's three navels.

Nina smiled at Myra, who flexed her back. She was about to explode in an orgasm—but just before she did, an explosion jolted through the ship. Nina stopped what she was doing and looked up, surprised, but Myra only forced her head back towards her achingly moist alien cave.

The entire ship shook as another explosion rumbled through the ship, and this time it couldn't be ignored; the two women tumbled to the floor as the lights flickered and went out, plunging them into blackness. An alarm sounded as yellow emergency lights flickered to life.

From an intercom a loud voice exhorted, "Battle stations! Repeat, battle stations! We are under attack!" The voice repeated itself several times in several languages.

Alec and his friends cheered when the ship rang like a bell and the battle stations alert went out. Sal shouted, "I told you guys they were coming for us, didn't I?"

"I hope you're right," Mat said doubtfully, "but don't get your hopes up until it's over."

Within minutes, every able-bodied crew member was manning his, her, or its battle station. In the weapons bays, gunners plugged themselves into the tracking systems of the laser cannon emplacements, chain guns, and missile turrets that broke the sleek lines of the hull. A half-dozen pirates manned each weapons bay, some providing tactical information while others offered fire support and kept the ammunition coming. When the last team member leaped into position, a protective electromagnetic shield flickered into place over each station, betrayed by a cool greenish haze, and armored bulkheads locked into place to protect the occupants. The overhead lights flickered over to red; and as the orders were given to fire, the rapid stutter of chain gun fire echoed through the entire ship. The *Bitch* shuddered occasionally as missiles vectored away toward their attackers.

Those attackers happened to be two small frigates, flying at maximum battle strike speed, heading straight at the *Bitch* in an attempt to intercept the larger pirate vessel. They fired their chain guns and lasers as well as launching missiles, but they were faced by a vessel five times their size, whose own weapons were now beginning to open up at *them*.

Zuzack sat in his throne on the command bridge, shouting out orders to his officers and crew. "Shields up!" he roared. "Helm, evasive maneuvers! Engage the enemy!"

The tactical officer shouted, "Sir! With the shields up, we'll lose a third of the power to the engines!"

"Too late!" Zuzack shouted back. "We have to take them head on!" He glanced at someone who stood in the shadows behind him, wearing a shade-cloak that effectively concealed his or her identity. The mystery person looked back at Zuzack, nodding in consent.

The firefight was short but fierce, and there were several explosive impacts on the destroyer's hull before the pearly light of the shields spread to cover the entire hull. The frigates, ignoring the captured *Bright Star*, redoubled their joint attack on the destroyer. The shields deflected or reflected the weapons fire, like water off a duck's back, as with a few bursts of maneuvering thrusters the helm brought the *Bitch* about and brought their main weapons to bear. As lasers and particle cannons belched their deadly light, turrets spat missiles into the fray, and a dozen unmanned drone fighters launched from the forward fighter bays.

The fighters bore down hard on the first frigate. Zuzack, who had over sixty years of experience fighting in space for both the Florencia and Nastasturus Federations, sounded very confident when he gave the order for all weapons to fire, and to concentrate at the nearest target. The frigate all but dissolved under a series of bright flashes, finally splitting in two before the pieces were vaporized by secondary explosions.

As Zuzack was ordering that all weapons fire was to be directed at the second frigate, it veered away, dropping into sprint mode and disappearing into high warp. After the tactical officer declared local space free of hostiles, Zuzack ordered him to lower the shields and proceed with all possible speed in the opposite direction of the frigate. "Damn, that was a close call," the Captain mused. "First Watch Officer, take us away from this system, and find a calm place where we can stop and make repairs before we end this campaign and head for the Rock."

Realizing they were on their way home for the first time in months, the bridge crew cheered their Captain; he leaned back into his comfortable command throne, enjoying every moment of it—or trying to. At that instant, someone put a hand on Zuzack's shoulder, and the huge pirate began to tremble. Sweat poured down his hairy dark face, and he turned around to look into a pair of burning eyes. The bridge crew fell silent, and stared at the Captain in horror.

A whispery voice, almost loving in its intensity, emerged from the shadow-cloak. "You did well, pirate, but now let's move on. More urgent matters await us all."

ALEXA headed toward the VIP Prisoner section, smiling and nodding at everyone she met. She was in a good mood for once. Along the way, she ran into Nina, who immediately tried to turn and head in the opposite direction. Alexa was able to snag her arm before she could.

Nina whipped around to face her, a sick expression on her face. "No, no, no! No way in hell! Never again! Never! Myra stinks, and is..." Nina paused, swallowed hard, and continued. "I don't want to have to think about it. It turned me off sexually for a galactic decade, at least."

Alexa escorted Nina down the hallway with a firm grip while addressing her in a motherly fashion. "Now dear, don't be like that, what are sisters for?"

"Technically we aren't *real* sisters, and besides, I'm no longer your servant but a third level crew member, so..."

"Details, my dear, details. So if I can get you a chance with that dude Zaxor that you said you like, *then* would you do it next time I ask?"

Nina wrinkled her forehead and drummed her newly-repaired fingers on her lips. "Zaxor? How would you...?"

Alexa leaned closer and whispered, "Guess who has the watch down on the VIP deck...right now?"

Nina's eyes brightened, and the two girls hurried down to the cargo room, singing and laughing, forcing a few of the other crew members to jump aside, cursing, as they barreled through the corridors.

When Alec saw Alexa again, he couldn't help but feel relieved. He'd never admit it out loud—not to his friends, not to the raven-haired beauty before him, or even to himself—that he had missed her and been very concerned about whether or not she'd survived the attack days before.

Alexa noticed his expression and the dark circles under his eyes and she teased, "Awww, were you worried about me? Did you miss me?"

Alec was at loss for words. Dammit, he'd always had problems with his expressions betraying his emotions. He opened his mouth to deny it when a voice next to him whispered, "This is the part where you say yes."

He turned his head as far as he could and glared at Andrew, who was grinning.

"Would you like for me to gag him?" Alexa asked innocently.

"Would you, please?" Alec said, staring at Andrew, who had decided to look at the ceiling—hunting for an escape hatch, maybe.

Alexa looked over her shoulder towards the guard tower attached to the far wall. She smiled when she saw Nina on top of young Zaxor, riding him like no one had ever been ridden before.

Alexa bit her lower lip, looked around, then quickly picked up a sponge and dipped it in a bucket full of soap solution. Without a word, she started to swab away the grime and blood on Alec's face. After a long moment she stepped back, eyed the scar on his left eyebrow, and let out a small sound of relief.

Alec noticed that this Alexa took her duty very seriously, and she did everything she could to avoid embarrassing him. He was surprised when she began to whistle softly while cleaning him…and as she leaned closer, he could smell her faintly floral perfume. He felt ashamed by his filthy appearance and current situation, and begun to blush.

She noticed it, but kept cleaning him. When she transferred her attentions to his stomach, he tensed a bit; she glanced down, inhaled sharply, and moved quickly to where his hands and feet protruded from the stock bar. Now it was her turn to blush, which he found bemusing. A pirate, blushing?

Well, it was obvious *why* she was blushing. He cursed under his breath, and glanced down at his "little bastard." It was fully erect, straining hard as a rock and high as a mountain.

"Sorry about that," he whispered between his teeth, while trying to concentrate and make his "little bastard" shrink. It was like trying not to think of green elephants.

"Why?" Alexa replied, looking innocent. "At least it proves one thing for sure."

"What's that?"

"I turn you on."

Alec looked at her blankly. No use telling her that the wind would have turned him on right then. "What's your name?" he finally demanded, though he knew it well enough.

Alexa looked at him and answered, "Pirate, remember?"

Alec let out a short cry as she dragged one nail across the bottom of a foot. "Oh, dear. Ticklish?"

"No!" he exclaimed.

She gave him a quick tickle, and Alec bit down on his lip. Alexa stopped, looking a little disappointed. She walked over to his free side, leaned over, and suddenly gave him a small peck on his ear. Then she breathed into it, "I have traveled through endless parsecs of space and oceans of universe just to find you. You are the most beautiful man I have ever met, and one day I will be your bride and queen, while you shall be my husband and shining knight. Nothing can ever come between us; and if anything or anyone attempts to interfere with our everlasting love, then together we shall conquer the universe, so that our many children may live in peace."

She stopped whispering, caressed his cheek, and stood up suddenly. She looked at him with a serious expression. "Now, young man, get some rest—and don't you go anywhere, now." She gave him another quick kiss on his ear, and another on his cicatrized eyebrow. Then she looked Alec in his eyes, lifted up his tunic, and barked, "Down, boy, down!" With that, she covered him up and walked away whistling.

Flabbergasted and embarrassed, just stared straight at the nearest bulkhead for a long moment. Then he looked down at "the little bastard" and whispered, "Traitor."

FOUR

THE *Bitch* and the *Bright Star* exited the jumpgate one after the other, set a new course, and plunged into another jumpgate in the same transit cluster. When they emerged this time, Zuzack ordered a new course set for a large asteroid conveniently located just a few million kilometers away. As they approached the asteroid less than an hour later, the ships were met by several drone fighters, which took an escort position around the *Bright Star* and led the way into a massive bay that opened into the interior of the hollowed-out asteroid. Meanwhile, the *Bitch* settled into orbit around the asteroid.

When the *Bright Star* reached its new berth inside the Rock, the prize crew slid it carefully into position between two other ships: a cargo freighter about twice its size, and a liquid materials freighter about four times larger. A shuttle with the skeleton crew from the *Bright Star* soon lifted from the cruise ship and joined up with a small frigate class ship. The two vessels left the asteroid and rendezvoused with the *Bitch*.

By then, most of the pirates had gathered in the main cargo hold, and they greeted and cheered the crews from the shuttle and the frigate while bragging about their success. After things had settled down a bit, the main hatch slid aside and in walked Zuzack with his senior staff. He had dressed for the occasion in a dark blue coat with gold piping on the collar and sleeves. Around his massive waist was a black leather belt with several blinking instruments attached to it. A large holstered gun and several knives balanced the weight on the opposite side. His long black hair had been tied back and braided into several tails, each decorated at the end with teeth from a different sentient species. Around his head he wore a dark blue scarf; his uniform was of a slightly darker blue, his knee-high boots black and polished. He dripped with jewelry.

His staff were all armed, and each one was dressed much like their leader. As they entered the chamber, the crew began to cheer their leader. Zuzack took it all in like a flower takes in sunlight; he loved the flattery of his crew.

There were some pirates, numbering about 200, who didn't share their fellow comrades' enthusiasm; indeed, most looked at Zuzack with disgust. Almost all were female, and all of them had gathered in a loose knot away from their Captain's biggest fans. From the looks of it, Myra was their leader. Among them were Alexa, Nina, Miska and Mohama. None of them wore any sparkles or jewelry; instead, most were dressed for combat.

Alexa herself favored a loose, white open blouse, tight black pants and black boots. She held a matching waist-tight black jacket over her shoulder. Around her hips was a thin black belt with a round silver buckle, and she was armed with two guns attached to holsters on either side, along with knives thrust into her boots and waistline. The injuries sustained in the last battle had been healed, and she smiled dryly, revealing all her brilliant white teeth.

Nina was dressed with a cream-colored tunic and gray leggings, all overtopped by a long brown coat. The coat was decorated with dried bloodstains and several scalps deriving from as many sentient species. Various bulges under her coat suggested the presence of various unknown weapons. Miska and Mohama still wore their space combat fatigues; and regular hand blasters, similar to Alexa's, decorated their thighs. Their thin, muscular tails twitched like dangerous serpents behind them. From time to time, they snapped them like whips.

Zuzack glanced at them, his expression unreadable, and jumped up on a large crate that had been placed in the center of the room just for this purpose. He wanted to look over his crew—or rather, down on them—and be heard. He stood there, raised his hands dramatically, and smiled, cheered by the sound of his happy crew egging him on. Then he stopped smiling and lowered his arms, glaring at the defiant group of mostly women off to one side. They glared back. Zuzack made an extravagant gesture with his arms, signaling to his crew to be silent while he turned his eyes away from the women. It took a moment before silence reigned in the audience chamber.

Zuzack loved the knowledge that he had the power of life and death over almost three thousand pirates. He stared down at them, trying to look them all in their eyes, looking, perhaps, for any traitors. He made sure all of them knew that he was their only and ultimate leader. He avoided turning his gaze towards the defiant group of mostly female pirates. Just as he took a deep breath and was about to launch into his speech, he noticed that one of his men was leaning against a pillar with his eyes shut.

Zuzack's eyes narrowed to thin black slits. A female pirate who stood next to the sleeping man gave him a nudge with her shoulder; but by then it was too late, because a millisecond later the sleepy pirate's head exploded, splattering the people around him with gray matter and gore. The rest of him slid quietly to the deck. The female pirate stared, aghast, at what was left of her companion. Her entire front was covered with brains and blood. She looked towards Zuzack, who was holstering one of his blasters, angrily mumbling something about laundry.

Zuzack said loudly, "Well, that means more spoils for me...the rest of you...us...whatever." The only response was nervous laughter from a few of the older and more experienced crew. Zuzack grinned widely, revealing his fangs, and shouted, "My fellow brothers and sisters! We have had a long and successful campaign in this sector, but now it's time to divide the spoils, head for a neutral trade station, and sell it!"

The crew let out a roar of happiness and anticipation, and again Zuzack gestured towards the onlookers, demanding silence. He went on, "The spoils will be divided according to my...*our* tradition, and the rules you all agreed to when you joined up. Now! Since there were a few mishaps with the first catch, and Myra's crew blew up the spoils before we could get to them..."

Myra interrupted Zuzack, and her tone was anything but polite. "Hold on, now, it wasn't our fault that some idiot targeted the fuel tanks. Besides, you know very well that shot was fired from the *Bitch* while I and my lassies were floating through space."

There was an uncomfortable silence in the hangar, and all the pirates looked first at Myra and then back at Zuzack, who looked like he was about to explode. He moved his hand toward the gun at his side, and Myra did the same. Everyone standing between them began to move away, leaving the two huge pirates staring at each other across a wide expanse of steel deck. Sweat pooled on Zuzack's brow and began to slide down his face in fat, greasy drops; if the lizard woman showed any signs of apprehension, none could read it. Finally Zuzack's murderous expression morphed into a false smile and then he said, "But Myra, my dear, if you would let me finish, you wouldn't have to interrupt me, now *would you!*" The last words were shouted, and in response all the women standing around Myra drew their weapons simultaneously and aimed them at Zuzack.

Perhaps half of the pirates in the room didn't move a muscle; the rest drew their weapons and covered Myra and her girls. Zuzack looked the room over calmly; he hadn't yet touched his weapon. He was canny enough to realize that that would have been a death sentence; and though Myra's crew would also most assuredly die in any firefight, it was obvious that he had less support than he had expected. He swore a silent oath about what he would do to anyone who had not supported him in this.

Zuzack's second, an old pirate named Grotech who affected a white uniform dressed with medals and decorations from a lost time, touched his elbow and said in a low voice, "Relax, my liege." Raising his voice, he called out, "Stand down, people. You are all hardened cutthroats, and some of the best warriors in the universe. We cannot fight among ourselves. Let's not ruin everything we've worked for because an old bitch like Myra demonstrates lack of discipline. You, Myra! You and your crew have been assets to all of us, but if you don't respect the Captain, then you and your tramps will have to fight all of us."

Zuzack made a gesture with his gun hand and added, "Everyone, just put away your weapons." The pirates exchanged glances; but it wasn't over, as the chill in the air attested. Zuzack looked to Grotech with deep appreciation and took a shaky breath, deciding to give the short speech instead of the longer one that he had rehearsed together with Grotech for several hours. "Let's divide the spoils!" he shouted. The hangar bay filled with a loud cheer as the crew responded with gusto.

Representatives from the various pirate gangs and collectives hurried towards a rank of tables where Grotech and several officers had placed themselves. All of them carried clipboard comps, and dove into the negotiation process with the officers over the unclaimed spoils. Several pirates congratulated Zuzack; he jumped down from his perch and grabbed several pirates by their forearms, returning their greetings. All the while he kept an eye on Myra as she muscled her way through the crowd towards the negotiating tables, apparently ignoring Zuzack.

Alec woke from a fitful sleep as several pirates banged their way into the VIP cargo hold and started hosing down the slave blocks, giving them their first good cleaning in weeks. A one-eyed pirate shouted orders at them, and Alec gathered that his subordinates were supposed to scrub everything down as well as possible and then remove the slave blocks from the hold with their contents intact, healthy, and presentable. After they were more or less clean, Alec and his team were removed from the cargo room, along with five other slave blocks. Over a hundred slave blocks filled with people were left behind.

As the six slave blocks were rolled through the ship, the one-eyed pirate walked up to each of the slaves and checked his or her health status. He noted that one of the prisoners at the end of a slave block had unaccountably died; no matter. He pointed at the dead prisoner, and two other pirates removed the dead man's body. They opened a disposal hatch in the deck and dumped the body into it; it would be recycled or jettisoned at the next opportunity.

The supervisor made a whistling sound as he made a mark on his computer pad, then gestured the procession onward toward a different hangar. Alec and his friends looked around unobtrusively as they went, memorizing as much of the ship's layout as they possible could.

They reached a large docking bay filled mostly to capacity with fighters and shuttles of different sizes and types. As he heard a mechanical grinding start up, Alec craned his head to the left (thank God the electronic restraints were shut off for the trip!) and watched as two vast hangar doors start to slide open. The flickering greenish light across the gap betrayed the presence of an electromagnetic containment field. He could see thousands of pirates in the chamber on the other side, but couldn't hear anything; the shield muffled the sound from the adjacent area. They were heading towards what appeared to be a hatchway piecing the bulkhead next to the shielded hanger door; half a dozen laser beams crisscrossed the hatchway, indicating that it was a death trap for those who tried to cross it. The deadly beams flickered off as he watched, leaving a faint ozone stink permeating the hangar. The guards rolled the slave blocks through the hatch, and suddenly Alec and the other prisoners could hear the full-throated roar of thousands of screaming throats.

After the spoils had been divided and logged into the pirate representatives' clipboards, each returned to his or her group and began the next level of spoils division. Each pirate had his or her individual comp-pad, like the clipboard comps but pocket-sized. As the groups began squabbling among themselves, Grotech sidled up to Zuzack and reported, "There was some hard bargaining, but we came out on top."

Zuzack murmured, "How much more?"

"Five points, and three percent over our original half lot. It would have been more, but it's more or less impossible to trick that old bitch Myra, or that sneaky little Crow bastard Sate."

"You have done well, brother; don't you worry about Myra and her little tramps. I'm sure we can come up with something. Now: let's begin the auction for unclaimed spoils."

"Captain," Grotech said cautiously, "You realized that we still need Myra and her crew? They're the best spacewalkers we've ever had."

"Don't worry. Now, let's get going."

Grotech waved the chrome hook at the end of his right hand toward Hughes, who hurried up to him. "Lieutenant! Start auctioning off the leftover spoils, and get the slave blocks down here." Hughes nodded, raised his left arm in what was supposed to be a salute, and pressed a button on his belt.

Several pirates emerged from the adjoining hangar, guiding carriers stacked with heavy chests and boxes filled with clothes, jewelry, medical supplies, and equipment. They were brought up to a spot before Zuzack's location, whereupon Hughes whistled sharply to get everyone's attention. He shouted out, "Lovelies! It's time to auction off all the leftover spoils that no one has claimed!"

The pirates surged forward with happy cries as Hughes held up a beautiful red silk dress. He barked out a price, and the auction took off. The officers started to hand out syringes, pills, and flasks of alcohol from the common shares to anyone who wanted it—and most did, accepting the gesture with wild smiles on their faces. It was at this point that the slave blocks were brought in and lined up on a ramp behind Zuzack and Grotech. The one-eyed pirate and his team had covered the slave blocks and their contents with sheets, concealing their contents.

The auction just a few meters away was taking its time, and the pirates were becoming rougher and louder. A few minor fights broke out, but the secondary officers put an end to most of them quickly. Then someone pulled a knife, his victim fell down bleeding, and before long some of the pirates were betting on the fights, the auction forgotten. Just as things began to spiral out of control, Zuzack stepped back up onto his perch and raised his hands high. The crowd begun to calm down, except for some creative swearing from a few individuals. Zuzack patted his holster meaningfully and stared at the troublemakers, and soon there was a complete silence.

"Thank you! Thank you, everyone. Now, for the second-best thing we've all been waiting for." Zuzack leered. "It's time to auction off the last remaining lot: the unclaimed slaves." Again, the entire crowd screamed its approval.

Zuzack stepped to the side of the first block as Hughes took his place at the center and removed the sheet. The pirates stop cheering; the slave block contained only an older couple. Hughes announced, "Here is an Ambassador from Florencia and his ugly wife. They will assuredly have a fine ransom. We will begin at one hundred thousand credits for both of them."

The block was moved forward on the platform at the end of the ramp for everyone to see. A serious silence settled over the crowd. A few of the older and more experienced pirates began to shout out their bids, though most of their compatriots watched with dulled expressions and a decided lack of interest.

After the old couple was sold, another block was brought up and the covering whisked away. "And here," Hughes explained, "we have the Ambassador's children. Three daughters, ages nine, twelve and seventeen; and two sons. The youngest is seven—and lo and behold, the oldest is seventeen, and he is a twin to his sister."

The Ambassador's wife began crying hysterically as their block was led away by the man and woman who had purchased them. The Ambassador screamed at his new owners, "Please listen to me, I beg of you! Don't let them separate our children from us! Buy them, and I promise we will compensate you, I swear!"

The two pirates looked at each other, then shook their heads simultaneously and moved on as the ambassador shouted out his protests. His wife had fainted.

The pirates launched a spirited bidding war for the ambassador's children, several demanding that the twins be sold as one lot. Hughes looked at Zuzack, who nodded his head in consent. The bidding continued, and Nina put in a bid for the twins. She asked

Alexa for a loan, and her friend agreed; but Myra outbid them, and the twins ultimately went to her.

Alexa shrugged. "Sorry, but I couldn't go higher."

Disappointed, Nina replied, "I know. But those twins, combined with the Governor and his family that we captured earlier..." She sighed heavily. "I just thought it could be our ticket out of here. But I also know that you have your heart set on that soldier-boy."

The third block was brought up on the podium and the cover whisked aside. The crowd went wild when they saw the contents: ten beautiful young girls wearing only white thin tunics—and wet ones, at that. The poor girls on the block stared at the pirates in horror, and some began to cry and whimper. Hughes began his spiel: "Here we have ten lovelies from the infamous world of Marengo. They are all virgins belonging to the Oman species: we have different types, as you can see, from dark to pale in different levels. These ladies belonged to a wealthy family, and are trained in the art of seduction. We think they can be worth a great deal of credits, and can sell them to you individually or as a lot. The entire lot begins at thirty thousand credits; are there any bids?"

There was an eerie silence in the room for a long moment, and then the pirates begin to boo Hughes, demanding that the girls be sold separately and at a lower starting bid. Again Hughes looked at his Captain for his consent, and again he gave it. A spirited round of bidding began, and in the end Hughes was offered much more than he had originally requested. When the bidding was over, the new owners demanded that their slaves be released immediately and handed over to them. The poor girls were removed from the block, and the ship's chief physician injected them with a stimulant that would enable them to walk after so long in the stocks. Once the Doc made sure that the girls could walk, they were handed down to their respective owners, kicking and screaming as different hands passed them on over the heads of the crowd. The pirates thought it was a hilarious spectacle, clapping their hands and chanting as the slave girls screamed and fought for their freedom.

One of the beautiful slave girls was passed over a three-eyed pirate, who took the opportunity to pull her down to the ground and tear off her clothes. The poor girl gave out a horrifying scream—which cut off in mid-shriek as she watched the triocular pirate fall in two lengthwise halves, sliced in two from crown to groin by a single sweep of a monomolecular blade. The body fell in a bloody mess onto the floor, and a monstrous pirate kicked it aside and stepped forward to tower over the Oman girl. He was over nine feet tall, with four arms and a black exoskeleton. In his hand was a giant ax, with a long shaft and a blade twice the breadth of an Oman's head. Everyone in the room fell silent.

The huge pirate stared at Zuzack on the podium and snorted out, "Thief...My price, no damage!"

Zuzack just nodded his head. The crowd returned to the normal shouting and screaming, ignoring the body parts on the floor. The young slave girl attempted to cover herself up with her torn tunic. Seeing that it was inadequate, the large alien with the axe handed her his own mantle. She looked at him in disbelief, wrapped herself in the fine cloth, and fainted.

The fourth block up for auction yielded ten young Marengo boys, all in the same age group as the girls, all with the same background and training. They were quickly sold off to pirates both male and female, and received the same brutish treatment as the girls had. They fought for their lives, but were quickly subdued by their new owners.

Hughes sidled up to Zuzack and whispered, "I think most of the crew has spent what they have. Shall we give them more drugs and booze and wait with the last lots, or shall we continue?"

Zuzack looked pleased and replied, "Let's finish it up."

The fifth block was moved into position. Hughes took a deep breath and then he shouted out, "Now, for the next lot: five officer cadets from the Nastasturus Federation!"

As the slave block containing Alec and his friends was pushed into position, he did everything he could to look as miserable and submissive as possible, refusing to meet any pirate's stare. His friends, however, elected to be defiant. They sat up as straight as they could, presented cold, proud faces to the crowd, radiating disdain for the pirates as Elite citizens of Nastasturus.

Andrew managed to whisper to Alec through his clenched teeth, "You're a disgrace to Nastasturus, us and your family."

There was relative silence in the hangar until someone yelled, "What status?"

Hughes answered, "Elite! They are all Elite citizens."

That meant huge ransoms, very likely. A grumble ran through the crowd, as pirates cursed because they'd already spent most of their loot on the previous items auctioned off. Another pirate shouted, "There was supposed to be six of the males. I saw six of them at the fight!"

Several pirates muttered and nodded their heads in agreement. Zuzack said mildly, "He is in the infirmary, and he is mine. That's final." There were some mumbles among the pirates, but no one dared to complain out loud or make any challenges against their Captain.

Hughes began with Andrew, and he was sold to Zuzack almost immediately. No one dared to seriously go against the Captain when he was bidding. The next prisoner up for bid was Alec. Hughes glanced at a clipboard comp and then grabbed Alec by the hair, forcing his head back.

"Here we have a fine young officer cadet, similar to the last, but this one has darker hair—and look!" Hughes pulled open Alec's eyelids and a hovering probe focused in, revealing a dark blue eye on a huge monitor behind him. There was silence for a moment, and then, from the back of the crowd, someone shouted, "He's a Silver Guard! A freak!"

The very term "Silver Guard" sent a murmur through the crowd. Scowling, Zuzack stepped up to Alec, grabbed hold of his head, and stared into Alec's eyes. Then he glanced at Hughes and muttered, "Are they real, or are they faked...clones?"

"They are real, my Captain," Hughes affirmed. "I had Doc take a look at him, and she concurs."

Zuzack looked down on the thin female alien who served as his chief medical officer, and she nodded in consent. "They are real, and I would like to buy him, so I can remove the eyes and study them."

Zuzack snorted and gestured to Hughes to continue. In the background shouted someone, "He's evil! Cursed! Toss the bastard out an airlock!"

Another voice shouted out, "It's gotta be a fake! There haven't been any dark blue eyes in any Oman species since they removed the DNA from the base stock after the First Universal War—and that was ten thousand years ago!" Doc glared out over the crowd and replied calmly, "You are all wrong. There is no curse attached to the Silver Guard trait. And dark blue eyes may be very rare in Omans, but they do occur. In fact, they're becoming increasingly common, especially in Omans from the two Federations. Your own superstition is only proof of your lack of intellig—"

She was cut off short as an empty flask hit her forehead dead on, and she went down in a heap. Most of the pirates laughed. Someone shouted, "Bad karma, bad luck! Toss it out and away!"

Zuzack shook his head in disgust, gesturing to a couple of fellow officers to help the bruised Doc to her feet. He approached the edge of the podium, raised his arms high, and shouted, "Nonsense to all of you! That Silver Guard shit is all a bunch of hocus-pocus. You don't want to bid, then don't. Hughes! Sell the slave off."

An ugly mutter ran through the crowd as many of the pirates openly expressed their dismay. They looked on with hateful, frightened expressions at Alec as the bidding got underway. Many of the older pirates, though, knew better than to let superstition get in the way of commerce. They appraised him with interest, and started checking on their available funds.

Hughes began the bidding at fifty thousand credits. There was some minor commotion and then Alexa shouted out loud, "I'll take him!" Everyone turned and stared at her.

"Fifty-five thousand," Doc called irritably, dabbing at a cut on her forehead with a bloody rag.

Alexa returned, "Seventy-five thousand!"

The Doc looked angrily at Alexa, and shouted back very firmly, "One hundred thousand."

The crowd followed this development with eager anticipation, anxiously awaiting the outcome. After a long moment with no answering bid from Alexa, Doc walked over Hughes to claim her price.

Alexa shouted desperately, "One hundred and fifty thousand credits!"

Nina smacked her own forehead with the heel of her hand, rolling her eyes. Doc swung around, shot a hateful glare at Alexa, and pointed two fingers in the air. She screamed, "Two hundred thousand!" Looking pleased, she smiled poisonously at Alexa before turning her attention back to Alec. Alexa glanced at her computer pad and shrugged, so Doc turned towards Hughes, who was just about to close the deal.

Zuzack looked at Alexa, and for a split second he looked sad, almost fatherly. With a clear voice he bid, "One quarter million!"

Doc's expression twisted into a mixture of surprise and hatred. She locked eyes with Zuzack's in disbelief, and opened her mouth as if to say something she might have regretted. Zuzack just gave her an evil smile, a smile that told Doc the bidding was over—or else. So she bowed her head submissively and forced a dry smile, admitting that she had lost. The crowd cheered on their Captain as the winner, and the bidding proceeded on the other three male cadets.

The sixth and final slave block up for bid that day held six young women about the same age as Alec and his friends—the female cadets from the Nastasturus Federation squad. The crowd went wild, and the bidding was extraordinarily spirited. After they were sold off, Zuzack addressed his crew.

"Fellow pirates! Now for what you have all waited for most. Let's finish a hard, long tour in space with an even harder and longer party!" He gestured in the air with both his large, hairy arms and two hangar doors swung open, revealing another large area already prepared for a victory celebration with plenty of tables, chairs, benches, food and drink for all. Hundreds of slaves and service androids stood in serried ranks along the walls, ready to serve and guard. There was a rush as the pirates ran for the best seats in the house.

Alexa wasn't among them. She looked down at her boots, feeling hopeless and miserable, then looked up as Nina placed her arm around her to give her some comfort. Nina pointed at Zuzack and complained, "Look at him. That bastard only bought him to piss you off."

Another female pirate with short red hair and very pale skin, dressed in a red skirt and vest, joined them. "I bet he had it all planned with Doc, so they could get the price up," she snarled.

Nina looked at her in surprise. "Think so, Tara? But why did the Captain buy him, if that was the case?"

Tara looked at Alexa and sneered. "Because he and everyone onboard knows that this little tramp has been down the VIP section every time she's had a chance. She likes to stand in the shadows, staring at the Silver Guard slave. Don't you, love?" She smiled cattily at Alexa, who blushed deeply. Tara purred, "C'mon, Alexa! You can still buy him, but I don't think it'll be worth your while. Just ask the Cap'n. He knows you'll pay anything for the boy. But be careful, or he will surely claim your soul—and more if he can."

Alexa looked up with teary and excited eyes. "You think I can still buy him?"

Tara glanced at Nina meaningfully, and both of them shook their heads in bewilderment. "What's so special about him?" Nina demanded.

Alexa shrugged. "It's hard to say...do you remember me telling you about the strange dreams I've had? Somehow, it's him. He's the one I told you about in my dreams, the one riding the great warbeast."

"Romantic fool," Tara sneered, rolling her eyes. Nina did the same.

"Screw you both," Alexa muttered, pushing herself between them and heading towards Zuzack. From behind her Nina shouted, "Be careful, or you'll end up the Captain's own private odalisque!"

FIVE

ALEXA ignored Nina and pressed on through the crowd. All around her, pirates were still bartering among themselves, ignoring the raucous party in the adjacent hangar. Business was business, after all.

When she finally got up to the podium, Alexa walked up to Hughes and asked, "Where's the Captain?"

"He's where I'm heading, over at the officers lounge. You think we're gonna eat with *that* scum?" He nodded towards the hangar where most of the pirates were celebrating with food, drinks and their slaves. It looked more like the beginning of an orgy than anything else.

By then, most of the pirates had stopped bartering and had joined the party, where a few of them had started gambling. Some of the young men and women from Marengo were put up on top of the tables and sold again, while some were made to dance to music that bellowed from the loudspeakers scattered across the hangar. Several of the slaves had been put into boxes or tables with only their heads sticking up through a hole; male or female, they were forced to perform oral sex on pirates of many different species and genders, while their owners charged their customers a stiff fee.

A few—again, male and female alike—were tied to tables or strapped into pillory devices for the pirates to abuse as they would, sexually or otherwise. Their agonized screams and whimpers regularly punctuated the buzz of conversation, background music, and loud song-competitions as drunken pirates did their damnedest to wring some enjoyment from the occasion. It wasn't longer before some of the pirates came together in small groups to bet on how long their slaves could endure the torture.

More drinks and food were served up, and many of the pirates, true to form, were soon passed out in their own filth and mess. As they got deeper and deeper in their cups, scuffles and several genuine fights broke out, and some pirates were injured before they died down, because no one was there to bother maintaining order. At one point, a group of pirates started tossing knives at one of the pilloried slaves, a young Marengan boy, betting on who could get a knife closest to him without killing him. That ended when one woman planted her knife in the center of the young man's chest. "Oops," she said disingenuously. This pissed off the owner, who turned bright red and smacked the female pirate upside the head. Their personal fight soon turned into a brawl—and it wasn't long before their fellows were betting on the outcome.

Elsewhere, the 17-year-old twins were being forced to have intercourse on a tabletop, while a large circle of pirates cheered them on. The slaves didn't seem to mind too much. Some of the older pirates sat quietly at a nearby table watching the action, being serviced under the table by their own chattel.

At another table, a male slave crouched on his knees with a rope clenched between his teeth as another slave—prodded at knifepoint—penetrated him from behind. The rope in the kneeling man's mouth was attached to the trigger of a gun affixed to the chair facing him. He made a loud keening sound as he was penetrated, and on the second thrust, he couldn't bear anymore and shouted out his pain, letting the rope slip from his mouth. His eyes widened

PIRATES | 75

in horror as he realized what he had done—but that expression lasted only a millisecond before it was wiped from his face by the crackling discharge of the energy gun. The slave behind him stepped back, covered with blood and brains, shrieking.

A small ugly alien shouted to the slave, "Why are you stopping? The bet was to see for how long you could keep going. Back to work, dammit, or I'll lose my bet—unless you want to be a female when we're done with you." The small pirate gestured with a knife towards the slave's groin. With a look of horror and disbelief, he stepped forward and tried to go on.

---oOo---

SICKENED, Alexa hurried away from the hellish scene, the sound of the pirates' ecstasy echoing in her ears. She ended up on an elevator with Hughes, who looked at her with irritation and announced, "You're not allowed on the Officers' Deck."

"Mind your own business, and tell the Captain I'd like a word with him."

"Suit yourself, tramp," Hughes replied, smiling darkly. Just as the elevator doors started to close, a pale hand was jammed between them and they bounced open. Nina jumped inside and joined them.

Nina looked at Hughes and said brightly, "Hey there, you little shit!"

"Be careful, you tramp, or I have your—"

"My what, you scaly-skinned dumbass? You couldn't have any of me if you were rich as the Emperor of Narris."

Alexa glanced at Nina, trying to hide a smile. By now, Hughes was trembling in anger. "You just wait and see, bitch. One of these days you'll regret mouthing off to someone important like me."

Nina was about to respond with another cheeky remark when she felt Alexa's elbow in her side. Nina glanced at Alexa, who shook her head slightly. They both faded to the back of the elevator, putting Zuzack's lieutenant between them and the door. Nina made a funny face and stuck her tongue out at his backside, while Alexa tried to stifle a giggle. At that instant, Hughes's head spun 180 degrees—Nina had forgotten he could do that—and he grabbed her tongue with his whip-thin tail. He whispered threateningly, "I warned you. Now let's see what you taste like."

Nina stared at him in horror, her eyes watering from pain. She had to stand on her toes when Hughes lifted his tail, threatening to tear out her tongue.

A short, sharp blade wielded by Alexa suddenly licked out and sliced off the end of Hughes' tail. His head spun back into its original position and he emitted a high-pitched scream; this time, he was the one in pain. His tail whipped around the elevator car, splattering the wall with rosy blood droplets. Nina spat out a small piece of his tail and wiped her mouth on her forearm—then she and Alexa laughed hysterically, till their eyes filled with tears and they had to lean on each other to remain upright. Hughes spun to face them, glaring for a moment, then held his maimed tail in one hand and stared at it with sad eyes.

When the doors opened a second later, he glared at them again, dropped his tail, and limped out of the elevator car with as much dignity as he could muster—which wasn't much, as he managed to kick his damaged tail with his right foot as he went, emitting another loud squeak. Cursing, he grabbed it in one hand and stomped into Zuzack's wardroom.

Nina and Alexa leaned on each other, laughing so hard they could barely see straight.

The elevator doors had opened up into a large, exquisitely-appointed chamber that reminded most viewers of a conference hall, except that the bulkheads were decorated from the floor to the ceiling with all types of loot. Zuzack sat behind a long table at the center, flanked by his senior officers. Two tables along the sides of the wardroom provided seating for a group of lower-ranking officers; they were all attended by several tunic-clad slaves. The mood here couldn't have been more different from the debauched revelry in the hangar below.

Needless to say, Hughes' interruption and bleeding tail quite captured the officers' attention. They looked stunned for a long moment, even Zuzack; but when Hughes managed to trip himself up with his own damaged tail, falling hard to the floor, the room erupted with laughter. Alexa walked in, followed by Nina, both still giggling and wiping away tears. Alexa surreptitiously slipped the razor that had damaged Hughes back into its arm-sheath.

Trying to school his face into the proper serious expression, Zuzack looked at Alexa and Nina, wiping away his own tears of mirth. "Your party's downstairs. What you want?"

Alexa straightened her back and answered boldly, "I want to make a trade, Cap'n."

"We're done trading for the day. Another time, perhaps."

"I will give you my governor family lot, the slaves I took during the prize capture, for the blue-eyed soldier."

Zuzack frowned. "Ha! An interesting offer, but no thanks!"

Maintaining her cool, Alexa added, "And one hundred thousand credits."

Grotech leaned over and whispered something into Zuzack's ear. Zuzack smiled, then replied, "Tell me, Alexa-girl, is he really worth that much to you? You realize that the ransom from the Governor alone can pay off your contract, and you can move on, free at last. I thought that's what you wanted, especially after you left us and joined up with Myra's bunch."

Alexa looked into Zuzack's eyes as she walked towards him, kicking the bruised Hughes aside as she went. He jumped back, cursing Alexa and all females in the universe, to the vast amusement of Zuzack and his other officers. When Alexa reached Zuzack's table, she looked down at him and proclaimed, "You once said that I was like a daughter to you, right?"

"A daughter with certain...perks," he said lasciviously.

"But a daughter, yes?"

Zuzack looked uncomfortable. "What are you trying to get at?" He looked at Alexa suspiciously.

The other officers looked on curiously as Alexa gathered her courage. She knew that she couldn't come across as weak; Zuzack and his staff hated anyone who was weak, and wouldn't hesitate to take advantage. She continued, "When 'adopted' me, Cap'n, you made a promise that you would spoil me for life. I demand that you spoil me for life *right now* and give him to me!" She crossed her arms and glared at him stubbornly, somewhat to his surprise. The officers in the room seemed amused by the spectacle caused by the little female Oman, who only stood there patiently, arms crossed and tapping her left foot, waiting for his response.

Finally he growled, "That was before you joined Myra and her bitches."

Alexa shouted angrily, "Joined them, bullshit! I'm your inside girl—I thought you *knew* that." She hopped over the table and landed in his lap; the officers laughed, and Zuzack looked puzzled and a little amused. Alexa grabbed one side of his braided mustaches and stroked his beard, putting on an innocent face. "You *did* make me your daughter—with perks—and I'm sorry I haven't been around… but you see, I've been so busy infiltrating Myra's crew, becoming your best fighter pilot, and training my little friend Nina here."

Zuzack smiled. "Ah, yes. Nina the little nymph, the slave I gave you as your servant—the slave you turned into a pirate."

"Just like you turned me into one, Daddy dear. But her credits still belong to me. She's not free or anything."

Zuzack placed one of his large fingers over her mouth to silence her. "Are you going to make the soldier boy one of your personal crew, and a pirate too?"

"No no no! I just want a little toy, to practice on for my membership."

The last words she whispered into his ear, breathing heavily and massaging his chest. She caressed his large bat-like ear with her tongue. Zuzack grabbed her by her shoulders and stood up. He was almost twice her height, and he looked down into Alexa's eyes with a fatherly concern. "My little flower, have you finally grown up and become a woman? You think you are ready to join our fellowship?"

Alexa looked up at him with a serious expression, "Yes, Father."

Zuzack melted; all anguish and concern left his expression and was replaced by a delighted smile. He embraced Alexa, who almost disappeared in his huge arms. Nina looked on without revealing her thoughts, as the other officers raised their cups—the cups made from the skulls of Omans and various transgenics and aliens.

Zuzack escorted Alexa to the center of the room and proclaimed, "Hear this! My adoptive daughter Alexa has asked to become a member of our clan for life. As your Captain and leader, I accept this and ask for your votes in the matter, as the law requires." He looked at his senior officers one by one, his stare meeting theirs in frank appraisal. In response, the officers either drank from their cups, or they poured the fluid within onto the deck. Twelve drank; five spilled their wine. Doc glanced at Hughes, who sat muttering in a corner, and nodded her head. Zuzack pronounced, "Hughes' vote is not required. The majority have voted for Alexa."

Zuzack let Alexa go; she stood at attention before him. "You know the procedure?"

"Yes, Father."

"You know what you must do?"

"Yes, my Father and Captain," she said stoutly. "I shall prepare him, and when we reach Home Base we shall dine on him; and his entire brain shall belong to me so that his strength shall be mine, and forever after I shall drink from his naked skull."

Zuzack looked at her with pride and declared, "So it is written, and so it shall be done, to prove that you are the ultimate survivor in this brutal universe." He took a knife off the table and made a thin cut on her right cheek. Then he kissed the small bloody cut, leaving his lips covered with her blood.

The rest of the officers who had voted for Alexa walked up one-by-one and gave her the same blood-kiss. Then it was the turn of the remaining five, those who had voted against Alexa. From his refuge in the corner Hughes smiled evilly, because he knew what was to happen. Without warning, the first of the nay-saying officers walked up to Alexa and punched her hard in the face, breaking her nose with a sick *crack*. The next kicked her in the ribs; and then the other three moved in, each taking a single brutal shot at her.

By the time it was over, Alexa was on her knees, spitting blood and checking her teeth. She looked up as one last officer walked up to her: Hughes. He lifted his own skull cup towards his mouth, as if to vote Aye; and then, his evil grin broadening, he pulled it away and poured the contents on the deck. Grinning viciously, he kicked Alexa hard in the forehead and she fell backward, stunned. Hughes spat on her and took his place at one of the tables, handling his tail with great care.

Groaning, Alexa pushed herself up off the deck, stood shakily, and looked them all in the eyes one by one. She ended up locking eyes with Zuzack. "The next time I am in this wardroom," she stated around a mouthful of blood, "we shall dine together on the Silver Guard soldier; and at the end of the night, I shall drink from his skull, which will be my own until the end of my life."

Zuzack nodded, satisfied, and looked at Hughes. "Sign over the blue-eyed male Oman to my daughter."

Hughes asked stiffly, "What is the price?"

"Her governor family lot...and one-quarter million credits."

Alexa looked at Zuzack in disbelief.

Zuzack said dryly, "My little flower, after all, I'm a pirate," with a gleam in his eye. She nodded stiffly, and Zuzack escorted Alexa and Nina to the elevator. He held on to her arm like he was a father walking his daughter down the aisle to her groom.

In the background, a port irised open in the floor, and a table rose up into the center of the room. From the center of it protruded the shaven and oiled head of one of the Nastasturus cadets, a wooden block shoved between his lips as a crude gag. As the doors of the elevator slid shut, Alexa and Nina heard his muffled screams, and the laughter they aroused from the pirates surrounding the table.

Jack blinked, bewildered, as the bright light opened up in the ceiling, and the odd torture device he was strapped into lurched upward. He'd woken in the darkness just a few minutes before, his body confined, his mouth full of something hard that tasted of wood. What the hell was going on...?

When the thing he was strapped into clicked into place and came to a stop, he found himself surrounded by pirate officers holding cups made of what looked like the brain-pans of men and other sentients. Given the lack of depth perception due to the loss of his left eye, it took him a moment to realize that he was strapped into a kind of table, with only his head protruding above the surface. Panicking, he jerked his head around, and saw that, across the room, the massive pirate leader was ushering two women into an elevator. Suddenly he knew what was about to happen to him, and he started screaming against his gag.

THE elevator doors slammed shut, and Zuzack turned to stare at him with eyes that held not a sliver of humanity. The other pirates had the same look in their eyes as they approached the table, with looks of anticipation on their faces. They all stopped in front of a white circle that circumscribed the table, about one meter out. Each was holding a tool with a knife at one end, and a combined fork and spoon at the other.

The ship's medical officer stepped over the white line to the table, and leaned over to appraise him. "My recommendation, Captain, is that we each take only a small piece for now, and then put him on the grill. If you want him to be alive for as long as possible, we'll have to bring in the life support table."

"Let's do it, my dear Doctor, and let's see how long this Elite citizen will stay with us and entertain us," Zuzack replied, drooling. "But for now, let us have a little appetizer."

Doc yanked the block out of Jack's mouth; then, before he could say a word, she made a single professional slice with a laser scalpel, removing half of his tongue and cauterizing the wound in the process. As he howled, she tossed the piece of him to Zuzack, who swallowed it in one gulp. The other officers looked on jealously as she carefully eased her way around the table, making a perfect cut along the top of his skull. With a quick twist she removed the crown of his head and placed it front of Jack, with a chilling smile. She stepped back, revealing his brain, then made a quick slice across his meninges and peeled them back. The pirates oohed and awed in anticipation as Jack screamed.

Moving carefully, precisely, Doc carved off several thin slices of Jack's brain, and deposited them on a silver plate held by a slave, who looked on with a dull and empty expression; she herself had long since been pithed. The slave took the silver plate and walked around the table, so that the pirates could help themselves to one piece of brain each.

Jack's face had gone slack and he had pissed himself— whatever she had done had caused him to lose control of his bodily functions—but inside, he was all but insane with horror, disbelief and pain. A strange gurgling sound came from throat as he saw, from the corner of his eyes, a kind of metal cart slide into the room through a side door. There appeared to be several medical instruments attached to the sides—and on a shelf underneath was a brazier containing red-hot coals.

Jack was one of the lucky ones. What was left of his brain shut down when he saw that, and he didn't have to endure the horror any longer.

SIX

ALEC found himself back on the block, with only one of squad-mates with him. Andrew sat with his back towards Alec's, and hadn't said a word since the auction.

"I take it you're jealous of some of our friends right about now," Alec whispered.

Andrew stirred. "What do you mean?"

"From what I've been hearing, you could be getting to know some of the male pirates more...*intimately*."

There was a long silence; then Andrew snapped, "To hell with you, Alec. I don't know what you're talking about."

Alec smiled humorlessly. "Or worse, some of the females."

"Fuck off."

"I don't know what the big deal is," Alex continued. "No one cares about crap like that anymore. So what if someone likes males, females or both?"

Andrew said angrily, "One day I'm going to be your superior officer, pal, and I'll make you eat those words."

"We all know you like males more than females, Andrew."

"You do, huh?" Andrew sounded surprised. "And when did you find out?"

"First time you opened your mouth."

Andrew snorted. "Go fly into a red sun, fool."

They were quiet for a while, then: "Did you hear Mat's scream?" wondered Andrew.

"Who could miss it? Did you see what they made some of the girls do?"

"No, I turned my head away. I don't care how much training we've received, there's a limit. I...I didn't really believe these pirates were as bad as they told us in Academy, but they're worse."

"Yeah." Alec sighed. "Let's hope and pray that we can maintain our own dignity until our last breaths."

"Agreed, but coming from you...the way you've been behaving is a surprise," Andrew said slowly.

"It's called *acting*, nimrod. I've got a plan."

Alexa half-ran down the corridor, Nina following behind and cursing her for ruining her new coat. "You had to cut a piece off the little weasel's tail inside the elevator, didn't you?" she complained.

"I can let him rip out your tongue next time, girly," Alexa snapped, increasing her speed.

"Oh yeah, there *is* that." Nina lunged at Alexa and grabbed her shoulder, bringing them both to a halt. She blurted, "Look, Alexa, you're my best friend, and I have to say this: you shouldn't even be thinking what you're thinking."

Alexa glared at her. "And what am I thinking?"

Nina looked over her shoulder, making sure that no one could hear them. "That governor and his family could have been our ticket out of here, and now you want to become a full member of the Blood Order. Girl, I thought you loved that Silver Guard guy—and now you're going to eat him? What the hell is *wrong* with you?"

Alexa looked at Nina, startled, and said quietly, "Good gods, you couldn't have gotten it more wrong if you'd tried." She shook her head, then turned and began running down the corridor towards an elevator bank. Once they were inside and the doors had slid shut, Nina looked sidelong at Alexa and said, "Y'know, I love to eat my boys too, but then I don't really mean *eat* eat, but eat as in..."

Alexa grabbed Nina by her coat collar and thrust her against the wall. Her face just inches from Nina's, she whispered hoarsely, "Wake *up,* Nina! Do you really think I'm going to *eat* him? I'm no cannibal. Even if we paid Zuzack he will never let us leave alive." She let go of her protégé and stepped back, glaring, and said in a low voice, "Trust me. The Silver Guard is our ticket out of here. Just please do your job, I beg of you."

"I hope you know what you're doing," Nina sighed, looking more doubtful than ever.

"I did when I freed you, didn't I, bitch?"

Nina stepped forward and hugged Alexa hard. When she disengaged, she said, "Okay, I trust you. You're the only family I ever had, after all. Now, hurry back to your quarters, and your "maid" will soon be there with your catch."

---oOo---

ALEC was nodding off when he was rudely awakened by a sudden shower of cold water.

"Wakey, wakey! Wake up, lover boy! Your new mistress and owner are waiting for you." When his eyes cleared, he saw a dark-haired woman standing in front of him. "I'm Nina, Alexa's buddy. Now, I'm gonna let you lose, okay? But let's be clear about this: if you give me any problems, I'll use this."

She held up a wide silver collar, which she slid around Alec's neck in a single fluid movement. Once it was in place, she stepped back and pushed a button on a remote control. Alec jumped in his seat as a bolt of electricity jolted through him. He cursed under his breath, and Nina muttered, "Yes, yes, I know I'm a bitch."

Moving quickly, she injected Alec in his arms, legs, and back with a medical hypo, and suddenly, he felt very drowsy. Nina took the opportunity to hit the button to release him from the stocks, then gave a signal to a medical-andy in the background. The android moved forward and picked up Alec bodily, and held him up for a few moments until the drug began to wear off a bit. Once he was able to stand without any assistance. Nina made a gesture with her hand and Alec began to limp slowly forward, in agony from his sore, atrophied muscles. Nina escorted him toward an elevator seemingly made entirely out of glass.

While they walked, Alec tried to memorize as much of the ship as he possible could. He was already basically familiar with this type of ship from countless hours of military training—it was of a type used throughout the inhabited galaxy. When they reached the elevator, he leaned back against the glass wall and closed his eyes.

When the doors slid open again sometime later, they headed into a cargo hold filled with several large shuttles crated in storage. Nina shoved him along, and soon they reached a docking bay and got into a small capsule attached to a maglev rail on one wall. Alec looked around carefully, noting the presence of several dozen unmanned fighters hanging from the walls and ceiling; netted into various cargo niches were a number of smaller civilian space vehicles. Then the capsule doors shut, and they accelerated into motion.

Nina and Alec changed into another capsule several minutes later, and they moved forward, towards what Alec expected to be the bridge area. Alec looked at the woman sidelong, thinking, *It's like she's showing me the entire ship...what's that about?* When he tried to strike up a conversation, Nina just raised her left arm, showing him the remote control to his collar. He got the message and remained silent.

One thing Alec noticed about the ship was that she was filthy and stank; but nonetheless she ran smoothly, and there were even signs of order and organization here and there. They met very few people along the way, and Nina proceeded with a sort of arrogant confidence. Eventually, they came to an unmarked hatch that Nina keyed open with her handprint, and the first thing Alec noticed when he was prodded into the cabin beyond was that the foulness that pervaded the ship was gone here; instead, the air was perfumed with a delicate floral scent. His eyes widened. Nina noticed his reaction, and for the first time she smiled. "Female quarters," she explained, sounding a little cocky. She directed him to the last hatch on the right side of the corridor, just before a sealed blast door, and pressed a small button on the hatch frame.

———————oOo———————

ALEXA glanced at her wrist computer as she hurried down the corridor; she now had less than an hour to get ready for her knight. She cursed Myra aloud for making her unexpectedly clean the filters on her fighter. "What does that big lizard know about engines?" she grumbled. She glanced at the comp again and picked up her pace.

When she breezed into her quarters a few minutes later, she looked around and let out a heavy sigh. It was pretty obvious that there was no way she could adequately prepare the place for a night of hot romance in less than an hour. Loot and other crap was stacked all over the place, from the comfortable L-shaped couch in the tiny living room to the little table in the galley cubby, and dirty clothing was scattered all over. Well, hell.

She rolled her eyes, and then she attacked her own mess. She tossed most of her belongings into one corner of the room, piling it higgledy-piggledy together in a small mountain of clothes, weapons, jewelry, and various equipment she'd liberated from the *Bright Star* and its unfortunate predecessors. Then she glared at it, hands on her hips. "That didn't help," she snarled, feeling a little thread of panic worming around in her stomach. She drummed her index finger on her lip, then suddenly yanked a large tapestry off the wall and covered the mess with it. That just left the ugly, scarred section of bulkhead that the tapestry had been covering. She'd forgotten about that blaster accident. Well, hell again. She fingered a button on her wrist comp, and a little cleaning android charged out of its alcove like a happy little puppy, whistling and singing. The android started trundling around, vacuuming up debris and dusting every surface it came across. A closer look at the andy made her realize that it, too, was filthy; she hadn't used it in a long time. She just rolled her eyes and gave up on the living room, deciding to head into the galley. It was separated from the living room by a hell-bead curtain.

As she approached the curtain, the cleaning android zoomed in front of her and stopped to vacuum, causing her to stumble over it. She aimed a kicked at its backside, cursing; it reacted only with a happy little beep, then hurried away. Alexa remembered, now, why she hadn't used the little shit for a long time.

In the galley, she began preparing a substantial meal of mostly vegetarian dishes. When she checked the wine cabinet, to her dismay she found only three dismal bottles of red. About a dozen little sticky notes were posted on the inside wall of the cabinet. She took one note and read: *"Dear Lex, just borrowing a bottle, love Tara."* She removed a few more notes and read: *"Sis, in need for some nice wine, love Nina."* And so on. She noticed that most of the notes were from Nina. *You little horny-toad, you haven't been yourself since I introduced you to Zaxor...taking my best wine, you slut!* Sighing, she decided to make the best of things and went back to her meal preparations.

---oOo---

WHEN she was done in the kitchen she hurried into her bedroom and started trying to pick up some of the mess, booting the clean-up android aside as she went. She glanced at the clock. Oh, dammit! She tore off her clothes, crashing to the deck, hard, when she got tangled up in the legs of her jumpsuit. She checked her teeth; everything there, thank goodness. She grinned, and crawled into the bathroom on her hands and knees.

When the hatch slid aside, the first thing that caught Alec's eyes was the beautiful woman standing in front of him. Her white mother-of-pearl teeth set off her burnished bronze skin when she smiled. Her lips were perfect, and her shining black hair was braided in a strange fashion, looped around her head and garlanded with starflowers, which filled the room with their intoxicating aroma. She wore a beautifully thin, black-and-silver scale dress bearing a strange fractal pattern unlike anything Alec had ever seen before. Its perfect fit and tightness revealed her slim, well-shaped, muscular body to her advantage, and made it clear that not one ounce of fat ruined his vision. Her nipples, standing tall atop the most perfect breasts he'd ever seen, stole most of the scene, pressing as they were against the thin metallic garment.

She made a welcoming gesture and stepped aside. "Come in. Make yourself at home." Somehow he stumbled inside, drinking in the sight of her as he did. Her wiry arms, toned with well-defined muscle structure, were held behind her back; she stood with her perfectly-shaped legs together modestly. The dress covered most of them, but a faint breeze from an air intake rustled the hem, revealing a few more inches of perfection. He glanced down, and saw that she was barefoot, her feet buried in a thick rug, toes curling. He looked up to meet her mischievous smile and noted, distractedly, that she wore no jewelry or make-up to distract from her perfection.

The second thing that Alec noticed, and the only thing that could possibly take his interest away from the hottest babe he'd ever seen, was the heady scent of the first decent food that he'd smelled in weeks.

Nina looked at Alexa, who nodded brusquely for her to leave. Nina held up the remote for Alec's collar, and placed it on a small shelf next to the entrance. Then, giggling under her breath, she overdid an attempted curtsy, bowing exaggeratedly toward Alexa. Then she smacked her lips loudly, causing Alexa to smile.

Alec turned around and looked at Nina, who until then he'd almost forgotten, as she backed out from of the room, half laughing. The last he saw of her before the hatch closed was an image of her falling on her ass, entangled in her own legs, still laughing like a fool. When he turned back around, the vision was standing before him, just a few paces away. She stepped with the grace of a panther and goddess, and extended her arms towards him in a welcoming gesture. Was this Alexa...?

Alec turned red as he realized that he stank and wore only a torn rag. Alexa noticed his shyness; she took his hands into hers, and leaned up toward him, giving him a quick peck on the cheek. Then she stepped back and looked into his eyes. "Welcome to my home. I hope you have had a nice journey."

He smiled drily and glanced towards the galley.

"Not until you're cleaned up," Alexa said, taking his arm and escorting him to toward the tiny bathroom. Completely overwhelmed, Alec was content to allow the dark beauty to lead him. He looked around as he went—never hurt to remain alert, no matter how aroused and hungry he was—and noticed the odd, meters-high lump hidden under a big tapestry in the corner. He wondered about it, but not for long.

When they reached the bedroom door, he stopped. A huge round bed took up most of the room's space. Unlike the rest of Alexa's suite, her bedroom was clean and well-organized, with several soft stuffed animals arranged next to the bed's pillows. Behind the bed was another curtain, concealing what he assumed was the hatch leading to her bathroom.

He shrugged and allowed her to lead him into a typical head for this type of vessel, except that a round bathtub big enough for two dominated the center of the room. It was filled with bubbles and flowers. A dim light emanated from the bulkheads, combining with the steam in the room and the flickering light of several candles to send dancing shadows in all directions.

Alec ignored the bathtub and headed directly towards the mist shower. He stopped and turned towards Alexa, who looked back at him, seemingly puzzled—or was it curiosity? He glanced at his tunic and made a small inquisitive sound. Blushing, Alexa turned around, and Alec skinned off the tunic, tossing it aside. Alexa turned back around as he entered the mist shower, and was able to enjoy his muscular stern view before he shut the frosted-glass door.

When Alec finally stepped out of the shower stall, after a very long, well-needed shower, he allowed himself to be dried by the head's hot-air jets and misted with a faint clean-smelling scent. He realized suddenly that he had no clothes, and that there were no garments for him to cover himself with in the bathroom. He looked past the bedroom area towards the living room and saw his uniform hanging next to the entrance, perfectly pressed and cleaned.

He heard a soft voice singing, and for a second forgot the dangerous situation he was in. He walked, naked, to the living room, as arrogantly as he could. But that didn't last very long, as he saw that the beautiful young woman was sitting on the couch in a kneeling position, shining one of his black boots.

She noticed him standing behind her, looked up, and stopped polishing the boot before placing it next to the other. Alec moved towards her, but she slid sideways, her back toward him. Her outfit made a faint metallic sound as she stood up. Alec hurried to his uniform and climbed into it, studiously ignoring her, then walked over to where his shining black boots sat in front of the couch. He sat down to pull them on, then turned to look at her. She was watching him with a faint smile on her face. When she realized she had his attention, she gestured toward the coffee table, which was spread with a variety of food and drink, and slid forward off the couch, to kneel before one place setting.

He quickly took his place on the opposite side, next to an old clay bottle that he imagined held some kind of wine. His knees sank deeply into the carpet, protesting their treatment of the last few weeks; but at the moment, his joints were the least of his concern. "Thirsty?" she asked solicitously, her voice low and musical.

He nodded, so she poured some clear liquid into a silver cup—loot from somewhere, he imagined—that she then handed to him. He sipped it; when he realized it was water, cold and delicious, he emptied it in one breath. He placed the cup on the table carefully, and she refilled it. Alec drank deeply again, and then fell on the food like a madman. Though there seemed to be no meat at all, it was without doubt the best food he had ever eaten. He crammed steaming breads into his mouth, followed by steamed vegetables both commonplace and exotic, following it with something red that came in kernels on a cob. She watched him, obviously amused, and handed him bowl after bowl filled with different types of food.

———oOo———

ALEXA herself was ravenously hungry, but hers was a hunger no mere food could ever sate. She licked her lips; it was all she could do not to drool as her knight, who had no table manners at all, devoured the food. Well, she supposed he had an excuse; weeks of nutrient paste could leave anyone wanting. She didn't care about his lack of manners; he was exquisite. She bit her own lips and moaned under her breath as she undressed her knight with her eyes.

Alec stopped eating and looked up, realizing suddenly that he was behaving like a pig. He controlled himself, sitting up straight; and when she reached for the clay bottle, he intercepted it and said, "Please, allow me." He filled her cup and then his own before saying, in a steady voice, "I'm grateful for your treatment of me, but I hope you understand my resentment towards you."

"Resentment? Why?"

He looked at her, bewildered that she could be so dense. "Until a few weeks ago, I was a free man. I was on my way home from eight years of military training to celebrate my graduation with my friends when you and your pirate buddies attacked. You killed some of us and enslaved the rest, strapping us into those horrible slave blocks. We were left to rot in our own filth, tortured occasionally, fed nutrient paste that makes shit seem edible...and you have the gall to ask why I might be a little *resentful*?" He was all but shouting as he said the last word.

Alexa leaned forward, propping up her chin on her folded hands, listening intently as the young man raved on.

"Not to mention that you *auctioned us off* like livestock among yourself, and GULL only knows what horrible things your friends did to mine at your so-called party."

He stopped to catch his breath.

She smiled brightly and said, "Oh, that."

He looked at her, astonished; and for the first time—though certainly not the last—he thought, *She's insane.* "Is that all you have to say for your actions?" he demanded.

She shrugged. "I'm not defending myself. But if it makes you feel any better, I'm not proud of being a pirate. I was never given any other choice. They took me when I was a kid. Like you, I'm a slave."

"I'm no slave!" Alec shouted.

Alexa rolled her eyes and frowned. "Why of course not, Your Highness, you're free as a bird." She stared into his eyes. "My friend,

I might have a few more privileges than you, but it doesn't alter the fact that my freedom is severely restricted—*just like yours.*"

She launched into her life story as Alec stared, flabbergasted and amazed.

"...And my guess is that my sisters felt threatened by me for some reason. Why, I'll never know; I wasn't special or treated special or anything. I was just the youngest out of seven or eight. Don't remember much about them though..."

He tore off some bread and leaned back into his cushioned seat, listening intently.

"...and then when Florencia started cracking down on the slavers..." she paused and shrugged again. "Hundreds of pirate clans banded together and started hitting the shipping and passenger liners, taking everything and everyone they could get their hands on. My siblings and I were on our way to school on the capital world, and, well, they bartered me for their own freedom. I was sold within days. Later Zuzack's clan seized me from my owners, and that's how I became part of this crew."

Alec realized that the young woman in front of him must have endured more than he could ever have imagined. Despite his own predicament he felt a bit sorry for her, the more so when he realized there was a tear trickling down one lovely cheek. She ignored it, maintaining a proud bearing, and related to him her recurring dream of a pale Oman, Alec himself, riding a war beast; and by his side, riding a beast even larger and more magnificent, was she.

Alec nodded and asked bluntly, "Can you help me get off this ship?"

She stared blankly at him for a long moment before finally nodding. "Of course. And I want you to take me with you...along with some of my friends. We're like sisters, and we have a good plan."

"So why do you need me?"

Alexa looked at him, seeming faintly puzzled. "Well, first and foremost, we belong to each other and with each other, I think." She blushed at her confession. "Second, my friends and I need citizenship in your federation. You can get it for us."

"And how do you know that?" he challenged.

She looked at him solemnly. "I can feel it. Correct me if I'm wrong."

Alec nodded slowly, "I can't, but my father can. Do you know who my father is?"

She shrugged. "Someone important, is all I know. Only the most Elite clan would have allowed the Silver Guard traits to express without rooting it out of their DNA." She glanced down at her food, which was barely touched, and looked back into his eyes. "I know all this seems weird to you, but if you can help us, then we can help you. And if you don't want anything to do with me, then...you can stay here as my guest until we leave. That is, if you still want to get away?"

"Of course I want to get away," he said in a low voice. "But we need to rescue my friends first."

"No!" she snapped. "That would be impossible. We'll need to steal the Captain's private emergency shuttle, and it's designed to handle maybe three or four people. We might be able to get as many as eight people inside, but that's it."

"I will never leave my friends behind," he stated flatly.

Alexa rolled her eyes. "I understand about your honor and service traditions, but know this: first of all, some of them are already dead, maybe most. That's just the way it is. The fight's over for your friends, at least for now. But once we're free, we can help you buy them back. It won't be long before Zuzack heads for a New Frontier station to sell off all the loot, including the slaves."

Alec listened intently, ideas forming in the back of his mind.

"Or Zuzack might head back to his clan's headquarters," Alexa continued. "His brother Horsa is head of the clan, and I and some of the other girls—like Myra, the lizard woman..." She waited for his reaction, but it never came. "Well, he has something important, and his brother wants him to return ASAP. If he does that, then it may take over a year before we can escape if we don't move now. If I'm lucky, I might be able to pay for our freedom, but that would only include you and me. I can't leave my sisters behind. So as you can see, we're in the same boat."

Alec interrupted her, "How old?"

"What?"

"How old were you when your siblings sold you?"

"I was going to be ten years old that year."

Alec looked at her with sad eyes. He realized that in front of him sat a victim and a survivor, not just a pirate—which was something they'd never taught him about at the Academy. He picked up a napkin and leaned forward to wipe away her tears, but she jerked her head away. He looked her in the eyes and reached for her again; and this time she allowed him to dry her tears. When she looked up, he stood next to her, holding her small hands in his much larger ones.

"I never thanked you properly," he said.

He pulled her up, and she allowed him to take control. He kissed her gently on her soft, warm lips, sending a shiver down her spine. She pulled her head away and looked at him, and in that instant nothing else mattered to either of them. Their lips met again, sending electrical volts straight to their sexual centers. "If you help me escape, then I'll owe you my life," he whispered into her ear.

SEVEN

ALEXA drank in his masculine scent as his hard, cold lips turned warm and soft against hers. Those lips parted and their tongues met; and then the entire universe ceased to exist for either of them. They belonged to each other. They embraced, becoming as one. Their breathing and the pounding of their hearts merged to form a mystical rhythm unlike anything either had ever experienced; they allowed themselves to fall into the beat, and it overwhelmed them. Time and place no longer mattered.

He gently pushed her away; her body protested and she moved closer to him. He grinned, then took their silver cups and filled them with the black wine from the clay bottle. She looked at him curiously as he handed her a cup and said, "For us."

She replied, "Forever."

They each took a sip, eyes focused on the other.

Alec stood up and pulled her gently next to him. He was more than a head taller than she, and when he reached down to kiss her, he held her arms tight in a strong grip down along her sides.

She relinquished control to him. His hold hurt her a little, and he fumbled some, but she was in another place and time—and the only thing she felt was love. She closed her eyes and leaned her head towards his to meet his lips with hers, tiptoeing to speed up the process. But the kiss never came, and she looked up, surprised; but she immediately closed her eyes when she felt him nibbling, kissing and caressing her neck. She tilted her head to the side, making her neck more available to him. She didn't notice that her body was trembling, but she was starting to feel faint.

He gripped her chin with his strong hand and forced their mouths and tongues to meet, first very roughly; but the longer they kissed, the more gentle it became. When both of them caught their breath, each made a lustful sound, too primal to be articulate, and again their lips met. Without knowing when or how it had it happened, Alexa noticed that she was pressed against the wall. He pulled her arms above her head and interlocked her wrists in one of his large, strong hands, making her first feel a bit insecure and panicky—obviously the brute didn't realize his own strength—but when their lips again met, she surrendered herself totally.

He lifted his right knee and moved it between her legs; and while his left hand was extended above their heads, holding her wrists, he moved his right hand along the side of her face with a soft and gentle touch. As they kissed, his fingers moved in slow circles down her neck. He moved his hand to the open circled area in her scaled dress that revealed naked skin and her pert belly button, and began caressing her soft skin with small circular motions.

Breathing harder, she let out a brief giggle. He teased her, easing a hand up the cool metallic dress to touch one her nipples. When his touch got more insistent, he jumped and stepped back, letting go of her, looking at the little cut on his finger that was oozing a drop of blood. He'd cut himself on one of the scales. She smiled and moved towards him, interlocking his head in her arms, squeezing her elbows towards his neck. She kissed him first gently and then harder—and now he was the one surrendering.

"You didn't expect me to be that easy, did you?" She smiled seductively at him.

She pushed him away, still holding him firmly. She looked at him and him at her. He raised his cut finger to display the blood trickling down his knuckle, and raised his eyebrows questioningly. She snapped at his hand as fast as a snake, biting down on his finger with her mother-of-pearl teeth. He grimaced in pain, but when she put his hurt finger into her mouth and began to clean it with her tongue while sucking hard, he lost it.

Like a raging storm, he tried to pick her up in his arms; but that only resulted in more cuts from the metallic scales of her dress. He put her down with a frustrated expression as she giggled, enjoying her power over him. She took his hand then and led him like a little schoolboy towards the bedroom, quietly humming an ancient tune from a distant world.

She turned him with his back towards the bed, and gave him a small push. Grinning, he fell onto his back, but quickly struggled up to a sitting position as she began to undress him. She unzipped his uniform jacket and dropped it on the ground next to her, then gently bit off his shirt buttons. The shirt seemed to float through the air a moment later as it landed on his jacket.

With a gentle touch she kissed his shoulders, chest and stomach. Then, without saying a word, she knelt and removed his shining black boots and the stockings underneath, kissing the top of each foot, allowing her tongue to slide around one of his big toes, making him groan. Finally, she loosened the belt buckle and removed the belt, then bent and bit off all the buttons along the fly. Then she slipped off his trousers; and before he had a chance to grab her and pull her down to him, she moved back, tossing his pants on top of the other garments.

She began humming a more seductive song as she slowly stepped backwards, removing the long cord that had been restraining her hair. A shiny, straight fall of black cascaded down her shoulders and back, almost to her buttocks. He stared at her, astonished; the dim light made her look like a goddess. She touched a hidden catch on her hip, and the metallic scales of her dress started to fall away, a few at a time, leaving a trail of sharp metallic flakes behind her on the deck as she sashayed forward. When the last scale had fallen off, she spun around and began to slowly dance towards him, very seductively, still softly singing.

Alec sat up in horror as she scuffed through the scales in her naked feet, leaving thin lines of blood behind them as she danced forward. When he looked at her face, he saw that she had responded to the pain not at all, her dreamy expression unfazed as she continued singing and dancing towards him, gloriously nude. He realized that she was performing some sort of ritual, and felt a frisson of fear—fear mixed with arousal.

He extended his arms towards her as she reached the end of the bed. She ignored him for the moment, placing her feet, one at a time, into a small dish half-filled with a clear, thick liquid. The bleeding stopped immediately, leaving the cuts on the bottoms of her soft, white soles barely noticeable.

She moved seductively into the bed, and when he tried to meet her, she slid away smoothly as an eel and pushed him over onto his stomach. She straddled him, sitting down naked on his buttocks; he could feel her warm skin, satin-smooth and flawless, on his own.

She poured an oily liquid from a small bottle onto his back; it emitted a fresh scent like nothing he'd ever smelled before. Then she started to gently massage him all over; her soft, gentle touch—with the occasional tickle—quickly sent his skin into goose bumps, driving him toward the brink, but he endured and enjoyed the moment. He wanted to cry out and beg her to grab hold of him, but something held him back.

Soon, he was drowned in thousands of small kisses all over the back half of his body, from the top of his head to the bottom of his feet. She didn't miss a spot; and from time to time she used her tongue, knowing that he was about to explode. When she lay full-length on top of him, breathing into one of his ears, he turned over suddenly. Catching her off-guard, he pushed her down and tickled her, then stilled her laughter with a deep, passionate kiss.

She allowed him to have control for the moment, apparently enjoying the hard press of his groin against her stomach. But soon she pushed him away and got up onto his stomach, perching there while ignoring his erection, which was poking her buttocks and lower back insistently. She had to force him down several times to keep him in place. He was bewildered by the thoughtful expression on her face, wondering what she had in store for him.

She tapped one of her index fingers on her lips, thoughtful, ignoring his quizzical expression. That was about the time that he noticed that his wrists had been bound to the bedpost with a soft, shiny black cord; he'd been so caught up in the moment that he hadn't noticed her do it. At first he panicked and tried to buck her off, but was prevented from doing so by her strong legs.

She bent and sang softly into his ear; and even though he didn't understand the words, they made him relax and settle down—at least, as much as any young man could in a situation like this one...

She rubbed the oil on his front side, taking special care not to touch his erection. She kissed him and nibbled on his nipples as the oil dried, breathing into his ear teasing, whispering promises about what she was going to do to his mind and body. She teased him by scratching him near his most sensitive region, and from time to time she gave him a brief tickle. When she kissed his feet again he jumped and almost kicked her; and before he knew it, a soft velvet scarf had shackled his ankles tightly to the bedposts.

Alexa noticed that her poor "victim" was about to blast off, so to speak, so she moved her face toward his hard-rock member and started to blow softly on it. When her warm breath touched the tip of his sex, he groaned; but she refused to touch it. She knew that he could explode at any second if she wasn't careful. Quickly, she slipped her hand forward and pushed hard on the nerve under his scrotum to prevent him from releasing his warm white love juice all over her.

His sharp sound of disappointed frustration, mixed with surprise, made her giggle. She looked at him with a mischievous smile and stretched out beside him, so that she could look at his strong, muscular body for a while. She was sure that it seemed a very long time for him; he wanted her so badly that she could see that it hurt. Sweat glimmered from his muscles, and his face glistened with it.

Alec had no idea how long time she teased him, how many times she brought him to the point of climax but then prevented it; all he knew was that the strain was starting to hurt him, and every time she did it he felt faint. He had no idea that it was possible to stop an imminent ejaculation that way. The pleasure was still there, but the pain that had started to grow along his spine was becoming debilitating. Sweat poured down his face; and when he felt her tongue playing with his testicles and her fingernails tickling his buttocks, he all but went nuts, struggling so hard against his bonds that he was afraid his heart would burst.

She ignored him completely, prodding the nerve for what seemed eternity before she rose up and took a firm grip of his erection. *Finally,* he thought, relieved. Wrong!

Alexa moved the boy's foreskin up over his aching glans and held it there. She then started to move it up farther. The sensation was incredible, until he realized that she wasn't going to pull his foreskin *down*. She kept stretching it upward, until she noticed that her victim was about to pass out.

Now was the time...

She released his foreskin, immediately slid her warm lips over his erection, and at the same time let go of his release nerve. In her hungry first gulp she took it all the way down to the base of the rock-hard shaft, still tugging down his foreskin with her fingers. His warm fluid exploded into her mouth over and over again, and no matter how much she swallowed, half of it dribbled from her mouth all over him and her. She used her tongue, licking it all up with a ravenous appetite.

She moved her head around, sideways, up and down, while playing with her tongue along his hard erection, milking him dry. When he begged her to stop, she only smiled and started sucking him harder. One of her fingers eased inside his anus and began massaging his prostate, while the other massaged his release nerve from the outside.

He screamed and moaned, which only turned her on more; and she didn't stop until he was fully hard again. Without any hesitation, she placed herself on the best seat in the house, impaling herself on his thick shaft. This time, she was the one who exploded right away. She had skewered herself on her knight's spear, and they were a perfect match.

She cried out in ecstasy, climaxing in wave after wave, almost blacking out with the pleasure of it all. When the best was past she collapsed over him, still feeling him thrusting into her from below. She gasped in surprise when a hand grabbed her hair, yanking her head back. Cords trailed from his wrists; he'd managed to tear them off. He turned her around and pushed her roughly down onto the bed, then bent over and removed the scarf from his ankles.

Both of them were panting and gasping for air as he climbed atop her and thrust his way inside. She wasn't ready for him, and the position and his size hurt her a little—but the passion he triggered more than made up for that. Both of them soon exploded in hard orgasm; and when they came out of it this time, they embraced and held each other quietly as they rested. Then they went back to touching each other tenderly all over, and it wasn't long before lightning struck again. Like a raging storm, they made passionate love.

Whenever Alec thought it was over, that he no longer could perform, her sensitive touch brought him back to life, turning him into a ravening caveman who couldn't get enough. At one point, it got so out of hand that they rolled out of bed; so he lifted her and pushed her forward into the bulkhead separating the bedroom and living room, and as he penetrated her from behind like a wild beast, thrusting hard, she cried out aloud.

Alec immediately stopped and turned her around, embracing her tightly. "Did I hurt you?"

"No, fool, you just made me the luckiest woman in the universe!"

"You're so beautiful," he said, running his fingers down the curve of her cheek; and then he was at a loss for words. They kissed again, and then they slid down to the deck, where she grabbed his erection and impaled herself on it, gasps of pleasure demonstrating how much she loved it. They moaned loving words as they both climaxed again, one after the other.

They trembled together, staring into each other's eyes as sweat poured down their bodies. When they finally calmed down, he took her into his strong arms, carried her to the bed, and laid her down on a big, thick pillow. He knelt beside her; she extended her arms towards him, and again they embraced.

After he climbed back into bed he laid there looking up at the ceiling, still breathing heavily; she had curled up next to him, with her face on his chest, and fallen asleep. A lock of her raven hair touched his nose, tickling it irritatingly, but he didn't want to move in case she woke up. A million and one thoughts were going through his head at that point, and he was totally dumbfounded about what course of action to take.

Should he take this murderous pirate as his bride—or should he kill her?

EIGHT

ZUZACK stood quietly, looking at the people ranged before him. Even though nothing in his posture or expression revealed his inner thoughts and emotions, his eyes did. They were filled with a fearful anticipation. He sighed in relief as he watched the object of his fear duck through the shuttle hatch, and the hatch iris shut behind him. When the shuttle lifted from the docking shelf, it felt like a huge weight had been lifted off his shoulders.

The shuttle moved slowly through the pale green force field into the Big Dark, and accelerated away at an incredible speed as the matter-antimatter drive kicked in. Satisfied, Zuzack walked away with a concerned expression, both his arms behind his back, looking down and thinking hard. Had he known it made him look like a very large and confused child, he would have stopped immediately.

"What now, Captain?" an officer asked Zuzack.

Zuzack glanced at him and replied, "We'll continue as planned. I suppose my brother has to wait a bit longer." Zuzack didn't even notice when the officer stood at attention and saluted him. He was far too concerned about other things, and left the officer standing, confused, in his wake.

He headed down to engineering, passing several crewmembers along the way; most of them gave him a false smile and a quick, sloppy salute. He ignored their lack of decorum; as long as they would fight and die for him, he didn't care much about military tradition. He went past several different cargo bays, ignoring the moans, screams, and curses from the prisoners inside. He was used to it all.

He finally entered the engine room, where he met with his chief engineer, a small, stooped creature named Zozo, who lovingly tended the six main engines with watchful eyes. Zozo had been with him from the start, and was intensely loyal; she was, in fact, the only being Zuzack had ever confided in. Even though she was an officer, she hardly ever intermingled with the rest of the crew, preferring to remain in her beloved engineering chambers; and Zuzack couldn't remember if she'd ever left the *Bitch* since he had taken it. Her only interest and ambition was to run a perfect machine. Zuzack looked at her, pleased, as she ignored him, tapping with all three arms on the comp pad before her. She'd started out with six arms, but over the years she'd lost one in an explosion and the other two to gambling.

Back then, gambling had been her biggest weakness; but for some reason, since they'd transferred to this ship, she hadn't bet a single centicredit on anything. Zuzack suspected that was the reason why she was so alienated from the crew—but then again he didn't really care, as long as the ship ran without any mishaps.

"Do you have what I ordered you to make?" Zuzack asked her. She didn't even bother to look at her Captain; she just left off typing with one hand and reached towards a small wooden box lying on a cluttered table, her arm stretching out to about three times its normal length in the process. She handed the box to Zuzack.

He frowned when he saw the box, but his displeased expression brightened when he opened it. "Ah, she's going to love it. Thank you, Zozo!" He turned and left the engineering room.

Zozo looked up and stared at her Captain's retreating figure, perplexed. She'd known Zuzack for seventy-five universal calendar years at least, and never once before had he ever thanked her for anything. As he turned a bend in the corridor, she shook her head and returned to work.

Zuzack walked down the corridor smiling, making an odd breathy sound he probably thought approximated a whistle. Any crew members who passed him saluted sharply, their surprised looks tinged with suspicion. Zuzack, happy? Who was this stranger, and what had he done with their Captain? Their eyes followed as he moved on, ignoring them.

One of the pirates muttered to a comrade, "What's up with him?"

"No idea, but I't kinda scared, me. I never seen the old bastard smile, ever. Not a happy smile, anyhow."

Zuzack entered the bridge, still "whistling" happily. Everyone in the room stopped what he or she was doing, and looked at him in confused suspicion. He plopped down into the command chair. One of the officers made a short snorting sound, and everyone returned to their respectively duties.

Grotech brought a computer pad to Zuzack and reported, "Here are the latest reports, Captain."

Zuzack glanced at Grotech irritably—that was more like their Captain—and gestured the reports aside. "Later, Grotech, later." Nodding, Grotech set it on one of the mini-desk platforms attached to the arm of the chair. Zuzack opened the wooden box in his lap, smiled, and then snapped the lid shut hard, making Grotech and several other nearby crew members jump. Zuzack noticed that, and his smile broadened. "Where is my little bird?" Zuzack demanded. Grotech looked at him with a questioning expression. "My little daughter?"

Grotech lifted his eyebrows, his bulging oval eyes protruding oddly far from his flat face. "Um, which daughter, sir? At last count you had adopted 367 of the female crew."

Zuzack growled, "Alexa. Where is Alexa? About this high." He held out his large hand, demonstrating Alexa's height, and continued sarcastically, "Black hair, very pretty, a foul mouth that should be regularly cleaned with soap!"

Grotech nodded in understanding. "Ah, *that* one. A moment, sir." He stepped over to his workstation and hit a few keys, then looked up at a monitor displaying a large blueprint where a single white light pulsed. He reported, "Your, ahem, *daughter* is in her cabin, Captain." He looked over and saw the Captain's fist flying toward his head, and that was all he remembered for a while.

"Jackass," Zuzack muttered. He glanced at a nearby crewman and ordered, "So fix him up." The crewman hurried to the bleeding Grotech as the Captain got up and left the bridge, now even happier than before, tossing the box in the air and catching it repeatedly.

ALEC felt like an emperor as he lay on his back, naked on Alexa's bed, still trying to catch his breath.

Alexa hurried in from the kitchen, holding a bundle of grapes in one hand. She dove on top of him and landed on his chest, causing Alec to lose his breath again. She laughed as she ripped a grape lose from the bunch with her teeth. She leaned forward and fed him the grape from her mouth, then kissed him. She repeated this "feeding" procedure over and over again, then placed the grapes on his chest and leaned her head on her hands, while digging her elbows into his rock-hard abdomen.

"You're killing me," he complained jokingly. Grinning, she lifted herself up, picked up the bunch of grapes, and started throwing them one at a time toward his mouth. He managed to catch one, but to her amusement, the rest bounced off his face. Finally he said, "Please, let me rest for a while, m'lady. It's not possible for me to continue."

She gave him a puzzled look and stopped throwing the grapes, then looked down at his chest and, with her forefinger, made small gentle circles around one of his nipples. She avoided his eyes; she was completely focused on "studying" his chest.

Alexa said, "I noticed that you have a circle around your neck. Is it some kind of tattoo?"

"Tattoo?"

"This thing." Alexa raised a hand and ran her finger along a thin bright line, barely visible, that circumscribed his neck.

"Oh, that. Oddly enough, that's just a birthmark."

Alexa had begun to bite and kiss Alec's right ear. Now she stopped and breathed into it, "Birthmark? No, that's a..."

She stopped in the middle of her sentence, moving back towards her original position as she felt his heart pumping faster and his loins growing harder. She looked up at Alec, giving him that most innocent expression that only a young woman can produce.

He rolled his eyes and grabbed her by her waist, sitting her down on the bedside as he scrambled off the bed. He knelt in front of her on the floor as her face took on a mischievous look. She lifted her feet and put them on his shoulders, indicating that she wanted him to kiss them; he ignored that, though, and moved his head in between her legs. It wasn't long before she was moaning in ecstasy.

A loud electronic squeal interrupted her pleasure. "Shit!" Alexa snarled, bouncing up off the bed (careful not to hurt her lover) and hurrying to the computer on her desk, slamming her hand down on a key.

"Did I do something wrong?" Alec wondered, licking his lips.

Nina's voice erupted from the intercom, filled with what sounded like concern and fright. "Alexa! Let me in, quick! Zuzack's coming."

Alexa spat a curse, and clicked the lock override on her console. Nina charged into the room as Alexa and Alec hurried to get into their clothes.

"No time for explanations," said Nina, looking for the remote control she'd left on the shelf at the entrance.

Alec and Alexa hurried into the living room, and Alec asked, 'What's happening? Who is Zuzack?"

Alexa answered, "He's the Captain...*No!*"

Before Alexa could stop her, Nina had pushed a button, activating the thin silver slave collar Alec still wore. He choked, grabbing at the collar as he fell to his knees, dropping his towel.

—◦O◦—

ZUZACK was more or less singing as he hurried down the hallway to Alexa's quarters. He passed a couple of female pirates and slapped one of them, hard, on her rear, sending her crashing into the wall. She glared at him angrily and, when she knew he couldn't hear her, she cursed roundly.

Zuzack found Alexa's quarters and pushed the entry button, but nothing happened. He pushed it again, and still nothing happened. What was going on in there? He glared down at his boots, thinking, and then shouted for Alexa to open her door. A moment later, he started to pound on the door. Some of his happiness had begun to evaporate by then, leaving only frustration. Just as he'd determined to smash the hatch in, it opened—and in front of him stood a smiling Nina, half naked. "Sir?" she asked innocently.

Zuzack looked at her and frowned. "Move it, you sniveling little shit," he told her, shoving her aside. He stepped into his daughter's quarters, and his eyes widened at what he saw.

Obviously unconscious, the prisoner hung from manacles fastened to the ceiling, stark naked. Alexa was busy carving on his muscular chest with a sharp knife; by the looks of things, she'd been at it only a few minutes. When she saw that Zuzack was watching, she stepped away from her victim, smiled at her father, then turned with lightning speed and tossed the knife at the prisoner. It hit him just beneath the shoulder-joint and stuck there; he barely twitched. A trickle of blood oozed down his chest.

Alexa looked at Zuzack, then crossed the room, picked up some leather strips, and started to wrap her hands with them. When she was done, she looked up at him irritably and growled, "You're interrupting my exercise and my preparations for the ceremony."

He noticed that there were bloodstains on her unbuttoned white blouse, which barely covered her fine breasts; and her tight, black knee-high shorts clung delightfully to her delicious curves. She wiped sweat off her brow with a forearm before shoving a mass of black hair out of her eyes. "What?" she demanded.

All this turned Zuzack on tremendously. He looked at Nina, who was barely dressed in a diaphanous white gown, and then back at Alexa. Zuzack grinned, grabbed Nina, and tossed her very roughly towards Alexa. The hatch slammed shut behind them, and his smile broadened.

Zuzack looked like an enormous child seeking approval as he held the wooden box out to Alexa. He had to bend down to maintain eye contact. She smiled mischievous as she approached Zuzack and reached for the box.

"Ah, ah," He warned, raising his long arm in the air, forcing Alexa to tiptoe and jump for the box. He stepped to the side, concealing the box behind his back. Alexa put her hands on her hips, tilting her head to the side and giving him a sly smile.

"It's for me, isn't it?" she demanded.

"Have you been a nice little female?" Zuzack asked, still keeping the box out of her sight.

Alexa replied, "Always."

He walked around her suite, behaving as if he were inspecting it. He leaned into the bedroom and noticed the mess on top of the bed. He raised his nose into the air and sniffed deeply, wrinkling his eyebrows. With a sudden angry expression he turned around, glaring at Alexa; but his expression soon melted to one of surprise.

She and Nina were foundling each other, kissing very passionately. He walked up to them, smiling. They stopped kissing, but Alexa kept her arm around Nina's for a long moment before drawing away and walking over to the unconscious prisoner. She started dancing around him like a kickboxer, delivering roundhouse and snap kicks to his body as if he were just another punching bag. Zuzack looked on with a stunned expression, then quietly sank down on the couch. After a few minutes, Alexa turned to Zuzack and started to walk towards him—when she heard Alec moan.

Without even looking, she delivered a roundhouse kick to his head, snapping his head back; a tooth spun out of his mouth, and a fine mist of blood sprayed onto one bulkhead. As the prisoner passed out again, Zuzack smacked his knees with his ham-sized hands, laughing until tears were trickling down his face.

"My little bird! You're using him as a punching bag. Who would have known? You truly are a mean little pirate." "The meanest, and soon I shall drink from his skull," Alexa vowed, "and become a full-fledged member of this clan."

Zuzack stood up and grabbed her by the shoulders, looking down into her blood-splattered sweaty face with a father's pride. "And I shall marry you, my little bird, and together we shall become the most feared pirate couple..."

Alexa finished for him, "...in the universe, Father."

Zuzack tossed his head back and laughed merrily.

Alexa heard Alec moan again, and looked desperately at Nina. "Shall I gag the bag?" she asked laconically. "I'm tired of hearing him whimper."

Alexa nodded sharply, so Nina roughly gagged the prisoner with a wooden pole with ropes attached to the ends. She tied it hard behind his neck when she noticed him starting to come to.

"Now, Zuzack, what have you brought me?" Alexa wondered.

Zuzack grabbed her and pulled her down onto the couch with him, where she perched atop one of his large knees. Nina sidled up next to them with a curious expression on her face.

Zuzack handed the wooden box to Alexa, then looked on in eager participation as she opened it up to reveal an odd-looking high-tech surgical instrument. It had a bone handle, inset with a small metallic plate. A few buttons and three small wheels were also inset into the handle, which tapered into a short metallic arm tipped with a thick, round metal plate.

"Oh my!" Alexa shouted happily, while Nina blew a short whistle. Zuzack smiled at their reactions.

"I took it from a slaver over fifty years ago...well, only the handle, actually. It's made of some type of horn from a creature called a cornius. I had Zozo build the rest, and now it's your first Marker."

Nina interrupted, "A cornius! Aren't those the creatures that the Silver Guard rode on thousands of years ago? I thought they became extinct, along with the Silver Guard, at the end of the war on the Blood World?"

Zuzack shot her a puzzled look and said, irritated, "Who cares? It's worth a ton of money, and almost impossible to find. And no, those things were called K´droges or something..." He shook his head.

"A Marker, I have my own Marker!" Alexa said proudly. She looked at the tool with teary eyes. "Does that mean that I'm free now?" She looked at Zuzack with a searching expression.

Again Nina interrupted. "No, no! You still have to go through the ritual. And actually, you're not supposed to receive your own Marker—or should the correct word actually be Brander?—until you pass all the tests, and..." Nina never saw the back of Zuzack's hand before it hit her on the mouth, sending her flying over the couch.

"I couldn't wait to give it to you," he explained to Alexa. "I've been so exited since you declared your intention of becoming a true member of our Order. I honestly thought I'd lost you to Myra..."

Alexa looked at the tool in her hand and turned it on as Nina got up, clutching her bloody face and cursing like the pirate she was. The flat end turned red as it heated up, and then white. She pushed one of the buttons, and several sigils and numbers morphed into existence on the flat end of the brander, shimmering in the tremendous heat.

Zuzack observed her intently. "If you can keep a secret from the other officers, then I will let you practice branding on your punching bag—as long as you slice off any piece of flesh with a burn mark before the ritual. We wouldn't want anyone else to know."

Alexa eyes widened in horror, but she quickly put on a smile, "You mean, now?"

"Of course, my daughter and future wife, why not?"

Alexa looked down at the tool and mumbled, "I don't know if I'm ready for that—"

Zuzack interrupted her, grabbing her wrist very hard. "I *insist*, dear."

Alexa stood up quickly and strode over to her "punching bag," shooting Nina a quick glance that begged for help as she went. But Nina only looked back at her in horror, shrugging infinitesimally.

Zuzack saw her expression and ordered, "Come here, you. I want to make sure that there are no more interruptions from you. And bring some wine and some of that new drug...and turn on my favorite music. Hurry, you useless cow!" He unzipped his pants, releasing two enormous erections with a loud sigh. Nina looked at him with horrified disgust...until she realized that his evil eyes were staring back at her. Then she scuttled into the galley. When she returned to the living room, she held the clay bottle of black wine, several smaller silver bottles, and a syringe gun. A horrid arrhythmic drumming sound was issuing from hidden wall speakers.

Zuzack gestured towards the bottle, and Nina, trembling, handed it to him. He bit off the clay neck with his sharp teeth, and spat out the pieces before taking a long swig of the contents. Then he set it aside and yanked Nina down in front of him. She knew what she had to do, so she lowered her head, her expression dull, and began to perform orally on one of Zuzack's erections while massaging the other.

"Proceed, my little flower!" Zuzack shouted to Alexa as he took another chug from the clay bottle, burping in ecstasy.

Alexa turned her head away from them with disgust.

"More music, and make it louder and faster!" Zuzack called to the room computer. "And more humidity! Less light!" The room dimmed immediately as the drum tempo sped up, and a faint white mist begun to pour out of the air vents.

―――――oOo―――――

WHEN Alec finally came back to consciousness and managed to focus his eyes, he saw the most beautiful woman in the universe standing in front of him. She was saying something in a low voice, but it made no sense. "I...no...you...th...lo...y...sor..."

He couldn't make out the words—and then he didn't care, because he felt a horrible pain on the right side of his chest that burned straight through his skin and muscle, directly into the bone. He screamed like a lost soul, struggling against his bonds; and instead of the pain decreasing, it got worse, until it felt like every cell and nerve in his body was being crisped in his own private hell. His eyes bulging, he stared at Alexa's bewildered, teary face and tried to speak—but he passed out before he could.

NINE

THE beast was climbing. No, it was flying...it was gone...no, it was not real. The cloud was blue and the sky was white and a second dark line emerged.

He fell back into the cave and there were fires; they burned away his flesh until all that was left was a screaming skeleton.

The monster laughed as it tore into his flesh with its sharp fangs, devouring him alive.

The boy shouted out for help, but no one was there to help him. Instead, everyone he knew stood around him, looking down, laughing at him as they ate parts of his body.

The head of the young boy was placed on a pole, and two black birds landed on his skull and proceeded to tear one of his eyeballs from its socket. The birds took off then, fighting for the eye. The remaining eye stared back at him.

"Awaken; awaken, and you can hear me. Listen to me, listen to my words, for I am you and all of you are I, but no one listens. Awaken, and I shall return...bring me back. Bring me back. Awaken, and remember *what all souls remember but dare not face. Do not hide from yourself... awaken, and step forth from your shadow and into my light. For the two of us are one. Awaken and thunder..."*

A large beast stood on its hind legs, and from its head came an alarming sound, echoing inside the boy's brain. The sound increased; and it wanted to get out into the open. It wanted to return; it knew it was alive.

On the egg was an eye; and the egg was growing, even as the eye was shrinking.

The monster was back, and its concubines pleasured him. The most beautiful female in the universe, his love, was pure evil. With malice, she laughed as she bit down onto his flesh, tearing it off his bones. Her laugh was as clear and delicate as crystal, and she taunted him as she chewed on his raw meat, while blood dribbled down her alabaster chin.

He screamed, but there was no sound, for he no longer had a tongue or even a mouth. The pain struck his heart like a lightning bolt and ended up inside his hands, and then there were more drums.

THE drumming sound and the strange odor struck Alec like a tornado as he swam back to consciousness. He felt nauseous and faint. He had an incredible headache, too, but its intensity paled in comparison to the severe pain in his wrists and chest. He blinked and tried to focus, but it only caused him to feel dizzier and drowsy, so he closed them, tight. His heart was pounding like a jackhammer, in unison with his quick, labored breathing. Millions of needles were pricking his fingers and hands, and a similar feeling, but hotter and more continuous, flamed from his chest.

He couldn't feel the ground anymore, and wondered if he were floating in the vacuum of space, dead or worse. He clenched his eyes more tightly shut in a desperate attempt to exclude the pain, but the strange drumming stole his concentration, and he opened them again. This time he could see, somewhat. He tilted his head back and looked up, noting without emotion that his hands were tied together over his head, attached to a rope that was bolted to the ceiling.

His hands were a mass of mottled white, bluish, and purplish flesh, and seemed to have swollen to twice their normal size. When he shivered, the pain in his wrists and arms intensified; and it was so bad that it temporarily numbed the burning sensation in his chest. He was breathing even harder now, and realized he'd hyperventilate and pass out again if he weren't careful; so he tried all the techniques that he'd learned at the Academy to calm himself. Eventually, as the pain in his chest began to return with a vengeance, his heart rate and respiration began to slow. He turned his head to orientate himself, and that's when he realized that he had died and gone straight down to the evil Red Land of Amarada, his people's version of Hell. *Not a dream after all,* some part of his mind whispered.

A huge hairy demon sat naked on the floor in front of him, guzzling wine and laughing as two women pleasured him sexually. Each had a long, black phallus in her mouth, hungrily attacking it with her lips and tongue while massaging the monster's round, hairy belly. As he watched, their sweaty and naked bodies—which were festooned with torn rags that might once have been clothing—dropped to the ground, and they changed position, facing Alec on their hands and knees. The monster moved up behind them, positioned himself, and began thrusting.

Their ecstatic moans repulsed Alec. Their bodies were covered with blisters, bruises, and long, deep contusions, all fresh; their hair was greasy and messy. As the monster thrust, and they started screaming in mingled pain and pleasure, they lifted their heads, displaying their faces to him.

Alexa! No, No, NO! It can't be, it can't...

Alec's life flashed before his eyes, from the moment of his birth to the present...including the dreams, the strange, violent dreams he'd had ever since he could remember, all of them nightmares. The attack, the slave blocks, the torture, the auction, and the beautiful goddess that he had sworn to himself he would worship for eternity. His childhood, family school, friends...A strange time before his present life, which he didn't understand but still remembered parts of.

He remembered everything—and then it stopped. Time stood still. Alec thought of nothing more; no pain, no despair, no anything.

His eyes turned dry, dead, as they focused on another pair of eyes, those belonging to the love of his life.

She stared back at him and smiled, as she emitted a loud moan of pleasure.

This is all wrong, he thought, and then he listened to the voice coming from inside him. *Who or what are you?* he asked the voice, but it didn't answer him. *I'm going mad. I'm losing it,* he confessed to himself.

Welcome back... the voice responded.

———o○o———

ALEXA let her mind go blank from the effects of the gas that she and Nina had inhaled, splitting an entire bottle between them; she could only feel joy and pleasure from the drug, and all her responsibilities just faded away. The animalistic drives that the drug had teased out of her mind made her welcome each and every hard thrust inside her vagina; she came closer and closer to climax. But still...something felt wrong, very wrong. She didn't know what it was, and she lost her concentration. She looked up at the beautiful man hanging before, smiling at him.

My treasure, my treasure and my beloved knight, she thought. She tried and failed to blow him a kiss, even as her sexual partners intensified their activity, and she was caught up in the feedback loop of pleasure between the three of them. The more she watched the young man, the more she desired him; the wilder she became, and the louder she screamed out from joy and lust.

His beautiful dark blue eyes gazed at her with love... or so she thought. But she began to feel a vague sensation of unease; somehow, all this was wrong. Suddenly she felt faint, and a headache begun to creep up from nowhere.

"No, no, NO!" she cried out, trying to slide away from the demon penetrating her.

Then someone was forcing a plastic mask over her nose and mouth; soon Alexa felt the headache vanish, and a wonderful sensation of wellbeing flowed over her, increasing her sexual appetite and lust for more.

Zuzack bellowed out his pleasure, laughing out loud as he ravished the two young hot vixens from behind. They lustfully endured his attentions, responding with a ravenous appetite that fed his own. No matter that it came from the drug.

Nina screamed in ecstasy as she removed the facemask, tossing it aside; the empty cylinder clattered against the deck. She began laughing uproariously as she sailed suddenly through the air, bouncing to a halt on top of the big bed; Alexa landed beside her, both of them having been tossed there by Zuzack. Nina stopped laughing, grappled with Alexa, and began kissing her furiously as the Captain straddled her from behind. Alexa moaned as he thrust both his rods into her, filling both her rear orifices as full as they'd ever been. Nina was on her back below her sucking on her tender nipples. The combined sensations from pleasure and pain sent her body into convulsions, and her own screams echoed in her ears.

At the same time, however, she could hear the faint, soft voice from within telling her that this was all wrong.

A small hand forced her face down and she recognized the hot, damp odor of Nina, who was rubbing Alexa's face between her legs. Alexa gagged and attacked Nina's clitoris with her tongue while she massaged her own breasts, feeling the long black snakes of her master withdrawing from her. He then penetrated Nina just inches from her face. The sight of it turned her on even more.

She gurgled happily and reached over, snatching a syringe from the bedside table. Somehow, Zuzack had had the presence of mind to bring it with him. She laid it against his dark, hairy erection and pushed a button. A loud roar from behind told her she had done well.

SOMEHOW, Alec was hanging on. Despite the countless hours of rigorous physical and mental training in one of the galaxy's tougher military schools, he had been slipping down toward death for some time now. But now something else gave him strength, an inner power that filled his life essence to the brim and demanded to exit into the unknown.

He forced out the gag and stretched his head towards the small knife protruding from his left shoulder, ignoring the shouts and screams of pleasure coming from the adjacent room. He opened his mouth and snapped at the knife, trying to snag it with his teeth; but he could not reach it. And so he despaired; tears poured down his face as he thought of the beautiful woman who hours before had declared her love for him, rutting with the demon who was her Captain.

But Alec listened to the little voice inside him, and made another attempt; and this time he bit down hard on the poly-alloy handle. Ignoring the throbbing pain, he was able to wrench it out of his flesh with a savage twist of his head.

He took a deep breath through his nose, mentally preparing himself for the agony that was sure to come, and slowly pulled himself straight up until his head was facing his shackled wrists. He eased down his chin until the sharp edge of the knife blade was on the length of rope just above his ruined hands, and began a sawing motion that soon had him swinging back and forth. The pain from his swollen hands was incredible, throbbing down his spine, making him want to scream. But he dared not. Something powerful inside him made it possible for him to go on. Was it love? Hate? For the moment, he neither knew nor cared. His frustration, and his sudden hatred for the people in the next room, made him go on.

He didn't know how long it took him to get free; but when the strands finally parted and he fell to the carpet, the beastly show was still going on next door. He rolled aside and looked up, hoping beyond hope that no one had heard the thump as he hit the floor. The loud noises from the three lovers made Alec smile, though it wasn't a very nice smile.

He started to saw at the knotted rope connecting his wrists, with the knife still held in his mouth. He cut himself several times, once quite badly, but didn't let it bother him. This was about survival.

When his hands were finally free, he pulled the severed rope away with his teeth, and looked hard at his poor hands, realizing that they were all but useless. He remembered seeing a first aid kit in the galley, and began to crawl away in that direction, as the pins and needles of returning circulation began sending new agony into his hands and wrists.

It took him a while to get there, find the kit, and fumble it open with his teeth and insensate hands. After he had clumsily applied what first aid he could from the hypos and nano-paks, he massaged his hands and wrists with an ointment that settled warmly into his muscles and bones, easing the pain and allowing him as near to full dexterity as he was going to get, short of them healing completely.

He could still hear Alexa, Nina, and Zuzack having a good time in the bedroom, but he managed to shut it out. His survival instinct took charge of his actions, and he let it; all he wanted was to survive and escape this hellhole. When he'd done all he could, he stumbled to the cooler, removed a bottle of cold water, and downed it in a single breathless gulp. He could feel his hands starting to tingle in a pleasant way as the medication and nano-machines started healing them, and looked down to see that they'd lost their hectic purple hue, approaching something near normal. He was starting to feel human again. He stretched his neck and shook himself, then began moving his arms in long circular motions. His wrists and shoulders still hurt like hell, but the first aid was working its high-tech wonders. He wasn't perfect, and knew that he'd need to have a med-tech look them over in the near future; however, they would do for now.

Suddenly, he realized that the suite had fallen silent; the sexual revelry was apparently over for now. He flattened himself against the galley's bulkhead, cursing himself for not noticing sooner, and eased into the living area. The three in the bedroom showed no signs of leaving; *Probably exhausted*, he thought with revulsion. As he moved with a stealthy silence through the suite, he noticed several syringes and canisters capped with facemasks scattered around. He picked up one of the canisters; it was almost full. His face grim, he dialed it up to maximum dosage and quietly entered the bedroom—and found himself staring into Alexa's eyes.

Alexa smiled as she looked into the eyes of her shining knight, who finally had come to rescue her. She leaned towards him with glazed eyes and a dull expression, making a seductive gesture with her arm, but he simply ignored her.

She blinked, bemused. Why was her head echoing? What was her knight doing with that drug canister...and why was he beating up on poor Nina and her Captain...? Wait...what was the Captain's name again? Oh well, it didn't matter; she hated him anyway. She loved her knight.

She gave Alec a loving smile and reached out for him. He grabbed her arm, spun her around, and tied her hands behind her back with a strip torn from her best stain sheet. She turned her head and looked back at him over her shoulder, giggling, and slurred, "My my, I knew you were kinky after all, my knight...come and tie me up as hard as you can, and have your way with me..."

That's as far as she got before passing out.

Alec shook his head, tying Alexa's ankles together before pulling them up behind her and tying them to her wrists. He didn't want to hurt her, but he had to ensure that she was secure. Alec had given Zuzack twice the maximum dose from the bottle, which was enough to knock out a horse, so he was snoring away peacefully; but it hadn't been so easy with Nina, and he'd hurt her more than he intended. Somehow, as he was struggling with Zuzack, she'd woken up and demanded her fair share of the drug. She'd tried to yank the canister out of his hands, so he'd been forced to punch her out. Alexa, on the other hand, was as high as a kite and needed barely a whiff of the gas to put her out.

After Alec secured all three pirates, he began to tear Alexa's suite apart, looking for weapons, clothing, medical supplies, and anything else he might need to rescue his friends and get back to civilization. He found his clothing, but all the buttons were gone—thanks to Alexa's lovemaking technique—so he was forced to pin them together as best as he could with safety pins and brooches he found in Alexa's bureau. He pulled a loose tunic on over his uniform to disguise it, then started to sort out the weapons on the living room table. There were several knives, three projectile pistols of various calibers, a magma rifle, two particle-beam blasters, and a variety of grenades and other bomblets. Not to mention three separate med-kits. He was surprised that the Captain allowed his crew to maintain such personal armories, but all the better for him. He was rechecking the equipment when he heard the harsh voice behind him.

"So, have you had much action, boy? You look kinda young to me."

Alec turned towards the bedroom, his face hard and cold as Antarctic ice. The Captain lay in the doorway of the bedroom; he'd apparently rolled himself off the bed and wriggled his way to where he could see what was going on, because he was still trussed up tight. Even from where he crouched, Alec could smell the reek of alcohol, filth and drugs that rolled off Zuzack in waves.

Alec looked at him with contempt, and then turned back to his task.

"You'll never make it," Zuzack assured him.

Alec remained silent and continued his preparations, until he noticed, from the corner of his eye, that Zuzack had started to struggle against his bonds. Suddenly incensed, Alec stood, walked up to him, and kicked him in his face. The one intact fang left in his lower jaw broke off, giving him a matching pair once more.

Zuzack spat out blood and tooth fragments, and despite his predicament, let out a horrible laugh. "Are you going to kill me?" he asked.

Alec went back to the table, and began to check the weapons again. He couldn't carry all of them, so he had to make some hard choices.

Zuzack was apparently feeling a little uneasy. "What're you going to do with me?" he demanded. Obviously, he didn't give a damn about Alexa and Nina. That was about par for the course among these pirates. Annoyed, Alec turned back to him, holding the largest knife in his hand, and gave Zuzack a chilling smile.

"Wait, wait." Zuzack was trembling now; maybe it was a reaction to the drug overdose, maybe not. But his eyes were filled with fear, and sweat matted his pelt as Alec paced toward him, holding the knife at the ready.

Alec leaned down towards Zuzack and grabbed hold of his braided beard.

"No! No! Wait! For all galaxies in space, wait!"

Alec smiled as he sliced into Zuzack's face with the tip of the knife. The big alien yanked his face away, looking horrified, and started to weep. Alec was caught off guard for a second; then a powerful wave of disgust flowed through him. He straddled Zuzack's chest and pulled the ugly face closer. "Can't take your own medicine, hey?" he sneered. "You're not afraid to dish it out, but when payback comes, you're nothing but a big baby, I see." He spat in the Captain's eye.

"I beg of you, don't!" Zuzack bawled. "Money, treasure beyond your imagination, women, men, whatever pleases you! It's all yours!"

Alec stopped for a long second, pretending to think; then he lifted the knife once again and carved a line along the curve of the pirate's cheek. Zuzack screamed, "It was I who captured the *Black Moon*!"

Alec stopped, for real this time.

"So you have heard about the *Black Moon*," Zuzack said, his voice quavering. "Its holds were filled with tritonium silver, more than you can ever imagine, enough for any man to become an Emperor."

Alec looked at him, puzzled, and asked curiously, "So why haven't you become one?"

"It's all yours, all of it, take it and let me live!"

Alex shook his head. "You're just trying to buy a little more time for your miserable soul. The *Black Moon* is a legend. It's time to die, pirate."

Zuzack was desperate. "No! It's here, here on this ship. On my soul, I *swear* it's here, and I know a way for you to take it and leave, and no one but you and I would ever know." Zuzack looked triumphant and hopeful, as if he believed that he'd bought himself some more time; he saw the cadet, once a frightened slave and now a self-aware killing machine, hesitate.

It didn't last long. Alec smiled and started to cut again.

Zuzack panicked. He spoke very fast, knowing he was about to die, tossed in everything he had... "My brother recently got his hands on several maps, almost all of them fake, as usual—but one is a genuine map to the treasure everyone has looked for. It is a time map, and I know that it's genuine because I've found more than twenty tritonium silver bars by following its lead. Take them and the map. I beg of you, spare my life, you can have..."

Once Alec had listened intently to the large pirate spill his guts, he thrust a rag into Zuzack's mouth. Then he grabbed him by his long hair and dragged him from the bedroom into the living room, a task that took a while, given Zuzack's size. Alec was stronger than the average Oman, but by the time he'd gotten the pirate where he wanted him, his hands were throbbing again and the pain in the right side of his chest was well-nigh unbearable.

He prodded Zuzack with one foot, and the pirate spoke. "In my quarters are the tritonium bars...and, and the map. There is more treasure...all you have to do is follow the instructions, and go to one place after the other..."

Alec listened to the cowardly alien as he opened up like a book, and then asked laconically, "And how would I be able to get from here to your quarters, and later off this ship? What about my friends? Moments after your crew learn that you're my hostage, you cease being their leader."

Zuzack frowned. "So, ah, you do know something about our ways."

Alec glared at the pirate, and said, "I have the benefit of a very good military education, pig. And a man learns fast when he's in your hands. If that's your answer to my question, then what use are you?" Alec leaned forward with the sharp blade, placing the point on Zuzack's neck.

"Listen, you cold-blooded little bastard!" Zuzack screamed. "We can get to my quarters through a secret passage between here and there. Then you can take my private shuttle—it's made for galactic travel for two. Your friends...even if you could save one or two of them, which I highly doubt since they are no longer under my control, they're spread all over the ship by now. Think! Not even with me as a hostage running around with you...you can never save them. Besides, the *Tramp* is only equipped for two people. Please listen to me."

Alec stood up and drummed his fingers on his lips, looking down at the trembling creature Zuzack had become... wondering if he was faking his fear, as Alec himself had.

Zuzack interrupted his reverie. "Hell, I'll even throw in the two sluts over there." He nodded his head towards the bedroom area, and had gall enough to smile.

Alec was pretty sure, by then, that Zuzack was faking at least some of his terror. He leaned close to the pirate, and whispered, "This is what we will do." He outlined his plan, and after a few protests—and a few painful cuts—Zuzack nodded his head in consent, having apparently decided that Alec would, in fact, take him with him to his own quarters. Alec nodded, and foraged around Alexa's quarters until he found the remote that controlled his slave collar. After using the remote to remove it, he walked back to Zuzack and, to the pirate Captain's horror, he placed the collar around his neck and locked it down.

"Now, my hairy fat friend," Alec pronounced, "I'll know where you are at all times. And it'll keep you in line, I'm sure. Hell, you know how it works, right?"

Zuzack nodded, looking a bit gloomy.

"Good, because if it looks like I won't make it back, or if you do anything I tell you not to, I'll turn it up to maximum and reduce your head to a little greasy spot. Now, after I return, we'll take care of that shuttle of yours. Got it?"

Zuzack looked at Alec with a dark and miserable expression. Alec continued, "I've given you my word of honor that I will not kill you while I'm on your ship. I realize your word may not mean a lot to you, but mine is everything to me; believe that or not as you choose. But if anything goes wrong, then that commitment means nothing. Are we clear?"

Zuzack blinked and nodded, so Alec turned away to check and double-check the girls' bounds. After giving Zuzack the same treatment, he dosed them all with the happy gas from a nearly-full canister and gagged them hard. Before he left Alexa's suite, he opened a panel in the bulkhead and proceeded to reprogram the locking/lighting protocol to his liking. Then he took a deep breath, slipped out into the dim corridor, and shut the hatch behind him.

TEN

HE wore one of Alexa's embroidered tapestries around his body to hide the array of weapons he'd attached to his belt and thrust into various pockets and folds of his uniform. He also wore a wide bandanna around his head in a poor attempt to conceal his identity; but it was basically all that he could do, given what he had to work with, and it only needed to work for a few moments. He hurried down the hallway towards the hidden hatch that Zuzack had told him about, and was somewhat surprised when he found it. He checked it over carefully before he opened it and did the same after he had it opened. Then he looked down at the remote control in his hand and smiled, thinking, *No, he wouldn't be that stupid.*

He entered and closed the hatch behind him, then moved swiftly through a long, narrow passage until he reached an old lift shaft, exactly as Zuzack had promised. The platform took him up several floors and then jinked sidewise, then went up several more floors and went sideways again. It stopped in front of a small, unadorned hatch. Alec stepped down from the platform and entered the code Zuzack had given him into the lockpad. The hatch slid aside and Alec stepped inside the small office on the other side, ducking his head; Zuzack must have had to double over just to get in there. The lights flickered on, and he stood quietly in the hatchway as he looked around and got himself oriented. The little office was plain and boring, hardly the place he would have expected Zuzack to keep his secret things hidden in; but then, maybe that was the idea. Nodding sharply, he entered the office and, just as Zuzack has said, quickly found the tiny secret compartment hidden in the left rear leg of the plain wooden desk. When he thumbed it open, several different types of computer chips fell out onto the deck. He carefully wrapped them in his bandana and thrust it in a pocket.

There was a hatch in the far wall that opened in what appeared to be Zuzack's quarters. Alec was surprised by how clean and small the place was. Shrugging, he fiddled with the light controls on the terminal set into the wall of the chamber, causing the lights to flicker and change color from dim red to dim green; this elicited an electrical blue-white flicker from one of the deck plates. Removing a hatchet from the armory attached to his belt, he walked over to the deck plate and smashed it hard with the hatchet. The false plate shattered, exposing a hollow space beyond. He removed a flashlight from his belt and shone it down into the hole, revealing a large hold that he suspected wasn't located on any blueprints anywhere.

He let out a whistle when he saw what was in the hold: it was stacked with treasures of all kinds, from holocarvings and rare animal hides to stacks of gold, platinum, and other precious metals. He shone the light around the room's corners, and soon found the tritonium bars. They were neatly packed in two small boxes, ten in each. Alec looked around for something to put the boxes in, and saw a stack of folded cargo sacks in one corner.

Luckily, Alexa had had plenty of rope in her quarters. Grinning, he attached a length to Zuzack's bedpost—which was bolted to the deck—and let himself down into the treasure trove. He grabbed a sack from the stack in the corner and, working fast, stuffed all the tritonium bars and a few other light, valuable items into the bag. He didn't dare get too greedy; he could carry only so much. Then he shinnied back up the rope into Zuzack's office, where he untied the rope, coiled it, and put it away. He was bloody well ready to get the hell out of there.

But he realized that there might be more to find, so he calmed himself and took the time to go over the Captain's quarters inch by inch. It's wasn't long before he found a cylinder-shaped container hidden in the bedstead; he opened it and found even more map chips inside. Nodding to himself, he slid the cylinder into his loot bag—and heard a faint sound behind him. He turned slowly, gun at the ready, letting the bag slide down to the floor.

In front of him was large curtain. He'd mistaken it for a wall tapestry covering the bulkhead, but from the way it was rippling, there had to be an opening behind it. He lifted one edge slowly; and when he saw what was inside the adjacent room, he choked—and lost everything from his last meal.

He fell to his knees, skidding in his own mess, gasping for air. The world seemed to recede, and he felt numb. When he finally managed to raise his head and get back to his feet, he looked his friend and squad leader Jack straight in his only eye. Jack's mutilated body was strapped to an odd-looking table. His head was forced up in an unnatural position, so that he could look over what was left of his body.

The top of his head had been removed; it was a raw mess of red and gray tissue, and Alec could see that part of his brain has been removed. Elsewhere, Jack was in even worse shape; how he was still alive, Alec couldn't fathom. In many places, his flesh had been torn away so that his skeleton was plainly visible. Part of his rib cage was missing, as were his genitals, ears, nose, and all his fingers and toes. Several tubes ran into his body, feeding him various types of liquids, and a respirator kept him breathing.

So the rumors were true: this pirate clan cannibalized some of their captives, and kept them alive while eating them. A wave of pure revulsion passed through him. How could any reasoning being eat another sentient?

Heart in his throat, Alec walked over to Jack, staring—and Jack stared back, his eyes filled with pain and horror. Clearly, he knew what was happening. He made a guttural, gobbling sound, and Alec carefully removed the gag that tightly bound his mouth, as a bit binds a bridled horse's. Alec swallowed hard as he saw that half of Jack's tongue was missing, and what remained appeared to be badly burned. But Jack still he managed to choke out a few coherent words: "...kill me..."

Without hesitation, Alec crouched and yanked the power cords of the life support machines out of the wall. Jack's face turned pale, and the life in his eye quickly faded out.

Alec leaned forward and gently kissed Jack's forehead. "Brother in arms, I shall remember you. May your soul find the everlasting peace and honor that it deserves." Alec stood and gave his dead friend one last salute.

Then he stood there, staring long at the horrible display, and started to tremble.

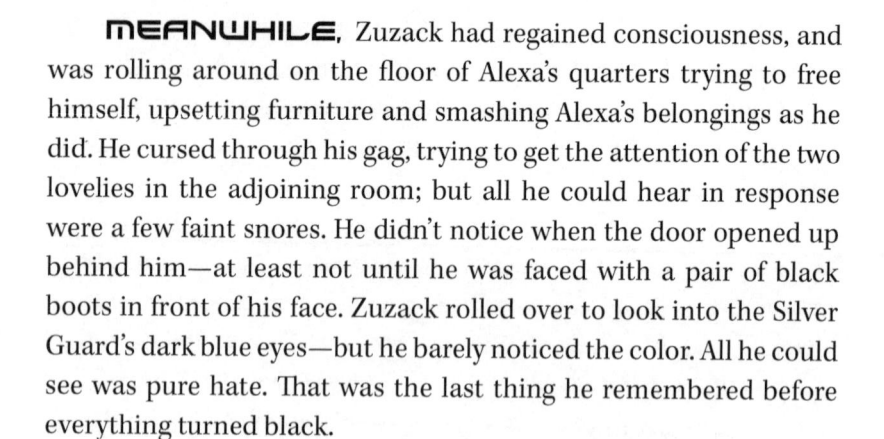

MEANWHILE, Zuzack had regained consciousness, and was rolling around on the floor of Alexa's quarters trying to free himself, upsetting furniture and smashing Alexa's belongings as he did. He cursed through his gag, trying to get the attention of the two lovelies in the adjoining room; but all he could hear in response were a few faint snores. He didn't notice when the door opened up behind him—at least not until he was faced with a pair of black boots in front of his face. Zuzack rolled over to look into the Silver Guard's dark blue eyes—but he barely noticed the color. All he could see was pure hate. That was the last thing he remembered before everything turned black.

ALEXA *stood alone on a high rocky shelf, wearing a white gown. One of her ankles was shackled to a chain attached to the mountainside. On a ledge below her crouched a huge beast-like thing; it was black and hairy, with an ugly short snout. Smoke trickled out of that snout.*

Ignoring the dragon, she gazed out across the sunlit countryside. In the middle distance, the clear, sparkling light reflected from a suit of shining tritonium silver armor, which was worn by the most beautiful and perfect man in existence.

The knight charged the big, hairy beast. But the beast-thing only laughed as it tossed its huge head back and vomited a stream of fire at her. She was engulfed in flames, and it hurt like hell...

ALEXA screamed as the exquisite pain in her left buttock jerked her back to consciousness—or she tried to, anyway. Even though she shrieked at top of her lungs, very little sound got past the gag in her mouth, beyond a thin, muffled keening. Her eyes tearing, she choked against the gag and tried to reach up and untie it—only to discover that she was trussed up like a prize pig, her hands tied together and tied to her ankles.

As she struggled, trying to free herself, she was able to pull her legs back enough to notice that a thin cord looped around her neck and attached to her big toes was strangling her. She stopped struggling immediately and curled her legs forward towards her head, easing the pressure around her neck. Her back was strained to the maximum, though, and the pain from her torso made her vision blur. She turned her head as much as she could—a few centimeters at most—and saw Nina's wide eyes staring horrified into hers; her friend was in an identical predicament.

Something hairy and dripping was hanging above them; and when she raised her head, she could see that it had Zuzack's face. But something was missing; it was a sunken parody of itself, the eyes blank pits. That's when she realized that Zuzack had been scalped—but, well, more than that. Not just his hair, but his entire face had been peeled off, skin, hair and all.

She heard a harsh whining sound, and after a herculean effort, managed to roll over toward it...and almost became ill at what she saw. Sitting on the floor against the bulkhead, bound in a cocoon of ropes from shoulders to feet, was Zuzack. His entire head was a blank red mass of muscle tissue, blood vessels, and exposed nerves;

around his neck was a precise surgical cut, showing where his assailant had started with the overall face-peel, leaving the rest of his body intact. It looked almost as if he were wearing a red knitted hood of some kind. She turned her head away, not sick exactly, but not as triumphant as she had thought she'd be once Zuzack finally got his comeuppance.

Then her knight was there, lifting her up into a kneeling position, still forcing her to bend back her head. In his right hand he held her marker, its head glowing bright orange. She could feel the heat on her face, though it was almost a foot away.

"You said you wanted to be my everlasting soul mate, and together we would conquer the universe," Alec said bitterly. "Ha! And all this time I believed you."

To her horror, Alexa began weeping; not from the pain her bounds were causing or from the burning sensation on her left buttock where she had been branded, but from the bitter pain she felt from having to betray her love. That love was about to come to an abrupt end, one way or another, because she couldn't tell him why she'd done what she'd had to do for all of them to survive.

Her everlasting love, the sole love of her life, was standing right there, so close and yet still so very far away. She'd never cried like this before, not even when her beloved siblings had sold her into slavery to save themselves. Maybe it was because her heart had never broken before. She lowered her head against her bounds, trying to strangle herself.

"And all this time you were planning to have me for *supper*. Your Captain told me everything, whore."

When Alexa heard this, she lifted her head again, trying to scream through her gag while shaking her head. Then she saw Alec's dead Silver Guard eyes, and she knew that she would die. She closed her eyes as the tears dried up, surrendering herself to her destiny.

Alec stopped talking. He stepped back, feeling faint; it seemed like a red mist was fading from his mind, as if he were coming back to himself after some horrible purpose had taken possession of him. He looked around, bewildered, and in a sudden rush, everything he had just done came back to him. He felt a little sickened by his actions, but less than he might have expected just a few weeks ago; after all, everything he'd done had been justified. However, what he'd been about to do next hadn't been, necessarily.

He looked at Alexa, and saw that she was deliberately straightening her legs, so that the cord tied around her toes was pulling tight the noose at her neck. Nina was crying helplessly, trying to worm her way towards Alexa. Alec took a deep breath, and really *looked* at his two helpless victims. A voice somewhere deep inside told him, *You're a soldier...perhaps a killer. But you're not a murderer.* With that he drew one of the knives at his belt and sprang forward, cutting the strangling cords on both of the girls.

He looked at them with sad eyes, then knelt by Alexa and combed her raven hair with his fingers. "For what it's worth," he finally whispered, "I think I did love you." He removed the gag, then sat up and tossed a knife on the bed next to her. "Help my friends, because I cannot."

Alexa coughed and spat, trying to catch her breath. By the time she did, he was out the door and gone. Finally she shouted harshly. "Wait! Wait...I can help you! *I love you!*"

But it was too late. Her knight had left her.

Alec never heard her last words. He was moving fast by the time the hatch slammed shut, weighed down by the weapons though he was, hurrying back towards Zuzack's secret quarters. When he reached the hidden opening to the suite he made a sharp right, plunging through what appeared to be a solid bulkhead. It wasn't; it was an air-tight nano-wall, and it let him right through with only a slight scratching sensation as the tiny bots it was composed of dragged at his skin. He found himself in a cylindrical chamber with rungs bolted to the wall. He scrambled up the ladder and spun open the pressure hatch, then climbed through. He was in Zuzack's personal shuttle.

After a quick inspection, he started prepping for take-off and spun up the engines. While they were rumbling to life, he took the time to return to Zuzack's office, where he'd stashed the bag of loot. He rushed it into the shuttle and made ready to leave; but as he was donning a pressure suit, a wicked smile grew on his face. There was quite literally a king's ransom down in the treasure room; might as well take as much as he could carry. He emptied the bag's contents into a locker, then raced back into the pirate Captain's quarters with greedy eyes.

When he entered Zuzack's suite, he saw someone else leaning down, peering into the hole in the floor.

Grotech heard footsteps behind him, and looked up to see a person he didn't recognize. Senses honed by more than a standard century as a pirate, he knew immediately that something was awry. He slapped a control on his wrist comp, then spun, a huge knife in one hand and his particle-beam blaster in the other.

Alec was taken aback at first by how quickly the alien reacted, but he was able to dive to his left, so Grotech's first shot went wide, gouging a hole in the bulkhead instead of him. An alarm started to groan as the pirate rushed him, and Alec fired the pulse gun that he'd kept hidden under the bag as a precaution. The pulse hit the pirate in the chest, making him bounce back as if he'd run into an invisible wall. He crashed to the deck, unconscious.

Too bad pulse guns were meant for non-lethal crowd control rather than combat, Alec mused.

The bulkhead irised open just to Alec's right—another freakin' hidden door—and Alec tossed a fragmentation grenade into the middle of the right group of guards as he dove toward the nano-wall behind them. The guards never knew what hit them. The grenade *was* meant for combat, and it intermingled the body parts of all four men quite nicely as it exploded.

None of the grenade fragments made it through the nano-wall, though some of its concussion did, causing Alec's ears to ring. He dove back through the nano-wall, hitting the ground on his shoulder before rolling smoothly to his feet. He yanked a hovermine from his belt, twisted a little knob on the side, and dropped it. It rose to chin height and hovered in the center of the room. Alec glanced at the hatch the guards had come out of. It was still irised half-open, and he could hear groans coming out of it; they'd be back upon him soon. He quickly programmed the mine to detect motion and air-density gradients, and set the protection field so that nothing else, from grenade concussion to bullet impacts, would set it off. He set the timer for three minutes; after that, it would detonate whenever it detected any movement at all.

He cursed himself for his greed as he turned back to the nano-wall leading to the shuttle—and that's when he noticed the new doorway on the other side of the room. *Another* secret door? Sheesh! Actually, there was no door or hatch at all, just an archway; probably it had been another nano-wall, disrupted by the grenade blast. Curious, he reset the mine for six minutes and slipped inside.

Here was Zuzack's real sleeping quarters. It was huge, but then so was Zuzack. He immediately noticed that there was a prisoner decorating the far wall, his arms and legs shackled to the bulkhead. Alec recognized him as Nikko Behl, the civilian Captain of the *Bright Star*. Formerly of the Herrarier system, the elderly man had spent his career as a fighter pilot for the Nastasturus Federation. Alec and his friends had met Behl on several occasions, and they admired the old veteran. He'd recently retired to what he thought was a safe job... and now this.

Alec glanced at the wrist comp he'd taken from Zuzack, then glanced at the mine hovering in the center of Zuzack's office. There was time. He hurried to free the unconscious Captain Behl; the old man fell to the floor like a damp rag when he was released, but a quick check of his pulse proved he was still alive. Of course, he'd been tortured. He lifted the old man carefully and draped him over his shoulder in a fireman's carry, then moved as fast as he could out of the bedroom and toward the nano-wall on the other side of the office.

They'd just gotten through when time ran out and the grenade exploded, hurling Alec and Behl to the deck as a residual overpressure wave pushed through the wall. A second later the nano-wall emitted a quiet hiss and failed, falling into an inert layer of dust on the threshold. Alec could hear agonized screams out there, so apparently security personnel had tried to rush the room as he and Behl were going through the wall.

They probably wouldn't try that again for a while.

He tore open a medkit and found a blue self-injector full of stimulant, which he jabbed into Behl's nearest bicep. The old man came around almost immediately, completely aware; his combat training hadn't abandoned him. Alec whispered urgently, "Captain, there's no time to explain. There's a shuttle up there." He pointed upward. "We need to get up there and go. Can you climb?"

The Captain didn't waste words. He gestured at Alec, who slapped a blaster into his hand. Then he turned and laboriously started climbing the ladder. Alec followed, carrying the loot, covering them as a clamor of voices came through the empty archway where the nano-wall had been. Face grim, he removed another grenade from his belt and lobbed it through the opening.

It exploded very nicely.

Then they were through the hatch. Alec tossed a pressure suit to Behl, quickly sealed the hatch, and dove for the controls. He'd already initialized the flight computer and spun up the engines, so everything was set. He jammed down his fist, breaking a glass cover over the emergency accelerator and jamming it down in one brutal motion.

He was pushed back into his seat by a giant's fist as the engines lit off and accelerated them down a long tunnel. He kept his eyes glued to the monitor in front of him as, somehow, the suited Captain Behl managed to pull himself into the co-pilot's seat and strap down, despite several gravities worth of acceleration. His breath echoed hard through their comlink, but he seemed healthy enough.

The tunnel ended abruptly, and the *Tramp* accelerated away from the destroyer into the Big Dark. As soon as they were free, Alec started evasive maneuvers; and just in time, because by then some of the *Bitch*'s weapons had come online, and the lasers and particle beams were stabbing out toward the shuttle. Behl cursed and said calmly, "Hand over the controls to me, son. I've got forty years of experience doing this."

Alec nodded and tapped a few keys, transferring full control to the co-pilot's console. He pulled up the weapons/ops screen, and immediately noticed a tab marked *Anti-Flak*. "Permission to release countermeasures, sir!" he barked.

"Do it!"

He pressed the tab, and a dozen small missiles erupted from the back end of the shuttle. They intercepted a half-dozen larger missiles launched from the destroyer, and interposed themselves when they could between the *Tramp* and the energy weapons lancing out from the *Bitch*. Between Behl's inspired flying and the countermeasures, space behind them was swept clear by a series of explosions. Meanwhile, Behl kicked in the afterburners, and the shuttlecraft rapidly increased the distance between them and danger.

Retrorockets flaring, the destroyer spun on its short axis and headed after the shuttle, the massive engines piling on velocity at a rate the smaller ship couldn't hope to match. Zuzack stood on his command bridge, his face a mask of pain, as the Doc patched him up.

"Stop shooting at that ship, you idiot, its cargo is worth too much to be lost," he growled to his tactical officer. "Use the tractor beam or the grapple!"

The tacco shouted, "Sir, they're too fast! We can't lock on with either!"

Zuzack cursed at the sudden pain as the Doc thrust a syringe filled with a pale green liquid into his neck. As the goop drained into his bloodstream, he muttered, "Of course she's too fast. She was made for me."

He pushed the Doc aside and walked over to the large viewscreen at the forward end of the bridge, and watched the *Tramp* as it disappeared into distance. Briefly, he turned back to the tacco. "Very well. Cease attempts to lock on with the tractor beam or grapple, and make no more effort to fire on the shuttle. There's a tracking system on board; we'll get her back soon enough."

He turned back to the viewer, which now showed nothing but the bright pinpricks of stars. "I'll catch you, soon, very soon," he vowed. "There aren't many places to hide in this region of space."

Zuzack turned around, and for the first time saw his own reflection on the silver shining breastplate worn by Lieutenant Hughes, who stood there facing him with an idiotic grin. It turned out that Hughes didn't need any wings in order to fly. He crashed face first into the Doc, and they both went down in a heap.

ELEVEN

THE limousine sped through an exotic mélange of sculpted parks, sparkling waterfalls, tiny gem-like pools, calm woodlands, and thousands of palaces in various sizes, colors, and architectural styles. The structures stood many kilometers apart, rising up like individual dreams in the exquisite landscape. Small shuttles and hovercoupes passed the limo occasionally, but the traffic was very light, barely enough to disturb the delicate animal life that grazed the greenswards below. Clouds of flutterbirds graced the upper reaches of the airspace, their bright colors sharp against the cerulean skies. Were one to look in that direction, far to the north was a dazzling cityscape constructed of countless enormous skyscrapers, their elaborate designs as varied and competitive as their heights.

The hovercraft came lightly to rest in front of an enormous place constructed of dark green marble veined with convoluted gold designs, next to a large fountain that sprayed water fifty meters into the air. As a wing door in the back of the car slid open, several servants standing next to the fountain hurried forward, only to stop as a curt voice bid them halt. A pair of black, shiny boots hit the marble of the entry court, and their owner stood with a poise that was almost feline in its elegance.

The boots belonged to Admiral Hadrian Cook, the commanding officer of the 11th Galactic Fleet of the Nastasturus Federation. Cook was in his early sixties, though his body was that of an athletic thirty-year-old; he paid plenty to keep it that way, too. The Admiral waved away the servants as he placed his forage hat on his shiny, bald head. His facial expression was carefully controlled, concealing any emotions he might have been feeling; and several battle scars stood out from his pale white skin, reminders that he was a survivor. He could have had them removed very easily, had he chosen to do so. But he wore them, as he wore his perfectly tailored, sharply pressed uniform, with the grace of a king.

Trailed by the servants, he strode briskly up the flagstone walk and climbed the wide stairway to the main entrance. As he reached it, two guards in old-fashioned colorful uniforms saluted him. They might have been ancient Colonial Marines, given their clothing and accoutrements, except for their thoroughly modern plasma rifles. Cook ignored them as he entered the palace, and was greeted by an old man wearing a servant's uniform with a distinctive patch on his chest, informing every one of his exalted station.

The Chamberlain bowed his head and said, "This way, Admiral," while gesturing cordially with one hand.

Admiral Cook followed his escort through the enormous palace, passing several guards and servants on the way. He ignored his magnificent surroundings, moving forward as if programmed. His frustration at having to leave his Fleet in this time of need was tightly reined in, and entirely concealed from any who didn't know him very well indeed.

His aplomb was shaken somewhat when they passed a large chamber, where several people were arguing vociferously. Hearing the upset voices, some of which he recognized, he paused in the entryway as the Chamberlain continued on a few steps. When the servant realized his charge had abandoned him, he stopped and fixed the Admiral with an irritated stare. "This way, Admiral," the Chamberlain repeated firmly.

Eyes narrowed to slits, Cook ignored his escort and strode purposefully into a vast, exquisitely-appointed drawing room. A cluster of Elites were gathered inside, some still shouting as others wept. The weepers were two elegantly dressed women, who sat on individual divans grouped strategically next to a fireplace, surrounded by a score of civilians. The older woman was about Cook's age; she was dressed in a lavish white dress with a décor of green and gold leaves, her gray-peppered dark hair coiled atop her head in a fashion a decade out of date. Her name was Lady Beala Hornet.

The younger woman, who sported loose, long curly blonde hair, was more up to date in the fashion department, but the expensive jewelry that dripped from her neck, wrists, and ankles failed to make her look like anything more than she was: a moderately pretty, very wealthy young woman. Cook recognized her as an Oranii, the daughter of a local Elite business baron and his nephew's most recent squeeze.

On closer inspection, Cook noted the occasional military uniform scattered among the clutter of ornate civilian dress. Elites, of course, of various ranks; along with the civilians, they were offering comfort and support to the ladies on the divans. A short, stocky man in pseudo-military civilian dress paced the floor nearby, cursing and punching the air with a clenched fist.

Several individuals in less-martial uniforms stood apart from the clot of Elites; it took him a moment to recognize them as the local constabulary. He scowled, puzzled, as a tremulous voice shouted, "Hadrian! Oh, Hadrian, thank heavens!"

Lady Hornet pushed her friends away and spread her arms wide, making no move to stand. Cook did his best to erase his frown as he removed his hat and walked over to give Beala an awkward hug; she was family, after all. As he stepped back, the lady fought to compose herself, drying her eyes with a small cloth provided by an attendant.

When she looked up at Cook at last, her face was bleak. In a trembling voice, she stated, "They took him...they took my son." Then her face twisted in fury and she screamed out her frustration: "Those bloody pirates took *my only child*! Hadrian! I want them dead, dead, dead! Do you hear me?"

He nodded graciously. "I hear and understand, milady," he said, careful not to promise anything.

Those words were followed by an explosion of comments and shouts from everyone surrounding Lady Hornet. Meanwhile, Lady Oranii apparently concluded that she was being left too much alone, and that she required more attention than the old hag next to her. She screamed theatrically and cried louder, her face glistening with tears.

At that moment, Cook was reminded of why he had chosen to become a soldier, and wished that he was on some calm battlefield very, very far away from all this civilian commotion. He could make no sense of anything that was said amidst all the shouts and screams. He embraced Beala again, and was just about to say something comforting to her when he heard a cough from behind. He saw his opportunity to regroup and took it. He gently but firmly disengaged himself from milady's arms and, without a word, turned around and placed his cap back in its proper place, on his head.

The Chamberlain was pointing in the direction of the hallway, a tight little small smirk on his face. Cook stepped forward and gave the jumped-up servant a glare that quickly made him spin around and scuttle forward, with Cook following in his wake. The Admiral manfully ignored the cries from the weeping ladies as he left the drawing room and continued his tour through the palace. His mind was a welter of thoughts, most of them personal; he had to force himself to ignore them and focus on his mission, which currently was to report to the Supreme Military Commander of the Nastasturus Federation.

He shouldn't have taken the detour in the first place, dammit.

Five minutes later the Chamberlain paused in front of two huge doors, which slid open at his gesture. Cook swept off his cover, handed it to the Chamberlain, and entered.

"...and that is the last report we have received," a nervous police inspector was saying as he approached. The officer was addressing a huge man's back. Said man stood before a large window, gazing at a floral clock that dominated the park outside. Currently it stood at half past three, the Admiral noted absently. He approached the big man's dais and stopped, waiting until he was noticed.

It didn't take long. The man by the window turned abruptly, his eyes locking briefly with Cook's. Like Cook, he wore a tailored, light-blue uniform with white trousers and shiny black boots. He too was bald; but unlike Cook, he retained a fringe of gray hair. He was in his early seventies.

Marshal Guss Villette von Hornet, the Supreme Commander of the armed forces of the Nastasturus Federation—and Lady Beala's husband—looked as calm as he ever did, as if nothing untoward had happened.

Cook stood at perfect attention, clicking the heels of his spotless boots together. "Admiral Hadrian Cook reporting as ordered, sir!"

"Stand easy, Admiral." Pushing past the police inspector, the Marshal made his way toward the seat of his battered granitewood desk, nodding for Cook to take the visitor's chair. The policeman remained standing.

Hornet said crisply to Cook, "Admiral, are you aware of the fate of the civilian cruiser *Bright Star*, late of the Federated Merchants?"

"I was made aware of it this morning, sir. It was logged as lost more than three weeks ago."

"You may not be aware that my son was aboard. Along with the rest of his cadet squad."

Cook regarded Marshal Hornet with a cool expression and replied, "That is most unfortunate, sir, but what does that have to do with me?"

At first, Hornet looked stunned; and then, slowly, his face suffused with anger and he growled, "Nothing, *Admiral*, except that Alec is your nephew, and *I* need your help."

Cook scowled and snapped, more sharply than perhaps he should have, "Sir, this is a civilian police matter. It shouldn't be, but it *is*. It's all laid out in the Constitution, and if you'll recall your history it's something that the police themselves fought very hard for. I don't like it any better than you do, but the separation of powers is considered inviolable."

"That's exactly what I have been explaining, sir," the police inspector said anxiously. "We are handling this, and we will…"

Marshal Hornet stood up abruptly and smashed a ham-sized fist down on the scarred black surface of the desk. "Silence, the both of you!" He took a long moment to calm down before he eased back down into his chair, and looked at them each in turn. "What you fail to understand is that it is *my son* in danger…and neither of you is married to his mother."

He drummed his fingers on the desk and then said, "Admiral Cook. I need you because of all the senior officers in service, either within the military or the police ranks, you have the best track record when it comes to tracking down pirates. You started out with the Federal Police and spent more than ten years as a Commissioned Pirate Hunter, as I recall."

"Sir! I switched services more than thirty years ago!"

"Protest noted. However, you were the best, and I believe that your knowledge can be of great use to both the FPs and the CPH Authority." The Marshal leaned forward, his eyes blazing. "Moreover, you have a singular qualification that places you at the head of my rather short list of candidates: you are family. It was, in fact, you more than I who inspired my son to join the military."

The Marshal leaned back in his chair and steepled his fingers, allowing a taut silence to grow between them. When he spoke again, his voice was devoid of emotion. "Admiral Cook, you will deploy the Eleventh Fleet to the last known coordinates of the *Bright Star*. You will track down the pirates who took the liner, engage them, and rescue the surviving passengers, including my son. You will not return until your orders are countermanded by an officer with the appropriate authority, or until you are successful."

"The entire fleet, sir?" Cook was stunned. "You want me to take the entire Eleventh, several thousand vessels carrying more than two million crew members, to look for one person?"

"I do not. There were thousands of people aboard the *Bright Star*. Repatriate as many as you can." He took a deep breath and looked down at the desk, his eyes haunted. "I will admit that, yes, my thoughts are primarily with Alec and his squad mates."

Cook nodded. "Well, how many of them are they?" He looked at the police officer.

"Fourteen, sir, including the Marshal's son."

"Fourteen lost cadets?" Admiral Cook repeated.

"Most of them are from very important families, sir, and..."

Cook interrupted the inspector: "And one Dealer has a better chance of finding them than ten galactic fleets will ever have."

The policeman nodded eagerly. "Yessir, that's what I've been saying to the Marshal, sir. Our investigators have already appointed several Dealers to this particular task."

"Are the two of you finished?" Marshal Hornet looked up at the policeman and Admiral Cook with tired eyes. "Admiral, it's not just that I want you to find my son and his mates. Your orders go beyond even finding the thousands of other people the pirates took off the *Bright Star*. I want you to do nothing less than obliterate the pirate clan responsible, to wipe them from the face of the universe. I want to send the pirates in all the inhabited galaxies a very clear message. I also mean to send a severe warning to the Merchants and Traders, making it clear that I will not allow these depredations to continue on their watch without severe repercussions."

Cook's eyes widened. "You cannot mean for me to bring military force to bear on the Merchants and Traders, sir. That might spark a civil war."

"I doubt it will come to that, but I'll do what's necessary to excise this cancer of piracy before it destroys us all."

"At the expense of the rule of law, sir?" Cook asked stiffly, his outrage obvious. "Your orders as they stand would be illegal without the Government's consent. It would be tantamount to a coup d'etat."

Marshal Hornet looked at him calmly. "I will get the Government's permission, Admiral. Even if I do not, I will activate the override clause in the Military Compact so that my order stands for one full year. In any case, the consequences will be upon my head. You cannot legally ignore a lawful order I give you, and I order you to do this."

"And what if I construe it as an unlawful order, which it obviously is?"

"In that case, I would have you removed, broken in rank, and replaced with a more willing officer, Admiral. You would be exonerated at court martial, but almost certainly retired from service, while I most certainly would be hanged."

"I see." The admiral fiddled with his gig line, an uncharacteristic gesture that shouted out his inner turmoil to any who knew him well. He looked up suddenly. "Marshal, even if the Merchants and Traders accede without a fight, this could turn very ugly if we use the military instead of the CPH Authority. It might force a constitutional challenge that could tear our Federation apart, sir. Please reconsider. Allow me exclusive use of the CPH in this, not the military. I can plan the mission and even take temporary leave of absence so that I can lead this expedition. I ask you—no, I beg you—to reconsider."

Marshal Hornet shook his head slowly, his fingers drumming on the desktop. After a long moment, he waved his hand and ordered, "Inspector, leave us."

When they were alone, Admiral Cook continued, "Guss, we don't even know what clan took them—and for all we know, they may be already be dead or sold off. In the latter case, it's only a matter of time before a Dealer finds them and buys them back."

"That process can take years of negotiation," Hornet replied in a tired voice. "Besides, Admiral, we know exactly who took them. There were survivors." He gestured toward the fireplace.

For the first time since Admiral Cook had entered the Marshal's office, he paid attention to the other people in the room. He recognized most of the men and women as high officials in the Nastasturus government, Federal Police, Commissioned Traders, and so forth. Cook's eyes stopped on two uniformed military officers who stood at ease beside the fire, conducting a quiet conversation. As he watched, the younger of the two glanced out the window and laughed. The other man nudged him, and they immediately stood stiffly at attention. When the Marshal beckoned to them, they marched in unison up to the desk and threw perfect salutes. Cook returned them perfunctorily, as did the Marshal.

Hornet made the introductions. "Admiral Hadrian Cook, you know our cousin, Major Thore Nesbit. With him is officer cadet Andrew Bow." Both young men stared straight ahead, still standing at attention.

Admiral Cook looked at them suspiciously. "The two of you got away?"

In unison they answered, "Yes, Admiral!"

"During the attack, I take it?"

Cook noticed that Bow glanced nervously at the Major, who replied loudly, "No, Admiral! We escaped after being held prisoner for three weeks, sir!"

Cook glared at Nesbit; he didn't care for the man, relative or not. Perhaps it was because of his naked ambition, or his popularity among both the military and the masses. Maybe it was because of his good looks; a man had no right to look so beautiful, or to be built so perfectly. Perhaps it was because of his stated sexual preferences; Cook had no doubt that the boy with Nesbit was his current catamite. None of those things cut any ice with Hadrian Cook; despite Nesbit's beautiful face and perfect body, Cook knew that he was looking into the eyes of an experienced killer...or worse, a murderer.

Cook turned slowly towards the Marshal and hissed through clenched teeth, "Everyone. Leave us."

No one moved except for Major Nesbit and Cadet Bow, who looked at each other questioningly.

"Leave us!" shouted Admiral Cook, as he stared at his superior officer.

This time it worked. With the exception of the two young officers, no one waited for the Marshal's consent; they scuttled out the exit and were gone. Nesbit and Bow remained, uncertain of what to do, until Hornet nodded towards the door. They saluted sharply, turned around, and walked quickly out the door, the sound of their boot heels echoing down the hall.

The atmosphere was taut with emotion as the two officers stared at each other. Finally, Admiral Hadrian Cook af Hornet spoke. "I warned you that something like this might happen eight years ago, when you sent Alec away for his schooling."

He glared at his brother, who stood slowly and strode toward the office's north wall, where a huge painting of the founding of the Federation extended from floor to ceiling. He pressed a spot on the ornate frame, and it flashed twice before disappearing, revealing a large wet bar and several computer monitors on a low credenza.

Cook continued, "Guss, I told you it would never work. You should have trained him here, where it was safe."

The Marshal filled two glasses made of vaporous ice with a thick, dark-blue liquid. He attached handles to the glasses, to protect hands from the tremendous cold, and exited the bar. The painted nano-wall faded back into place behind him. Not looking at the Admiral, he gestured with his head for his brother to follow.

They walked out onto a terrace surrounded by lush green growth, and seated themselves on a pair of overstuffed all-weather armchairs. Without a word, the Marshal made a tiny gesture; the balcony doors slammed shut behind them, and the entire terrace started to slowly move upward towards the roof. When it reached the top, it slid sideways along the battlements before stopping inside a large opening in one of the towers, giving the two men a fabulous view of the landscape.

Hornet broke the silence. "I will be brief."

"Thank the stars," Cook muttered.

The Marshal frowned and continued. "Without Alec marrying into the House of Oranii, and strengthening the House of Hornet—not to mention insuring its survival—our clan's future looks dark. Brother. You realize that Nesbit would do anything to marry Michelle Oranii."

"You're referring to the spoiled blonde tramp downstairs?"

"Yes. Her."

Cook snorted. "Right. Nesbit has no interest in anything female."

Hornet shook his head in disagreement. "He does if they can give him status and recognition."

"You're saying he might try to join our House with hers? If Alec is gone, that would give him enough power to claim his inheritance, and immediately ascend to the main branch."

"Indeed it would."

They sat silently for a long moment. Nesbit Thore af Hornet was the child of their sister Lywellyn, dead these two decades. As firstborn of his generation, Guss was the head of the main branch of the powerful House of Hornet; leadership of the clan was by primogeniture, and had been for untold centuries. The clan head's younger siblings automatically became heads of their own cadet branches of the family, hence the "af Hornet" cognomen. Only Guss, his wife, and his eldest child—his only child, thus far—could be considered true Hornets, with all the Elite privileges that implied. Having been born to Lywellyn, Nesbit's privileges were more limited. However, if Alec were dead or incapacitated, Nesbit could ascend to the main branch of the family as the eldest survivor of his generation.

The Marshal took a sip from his ice glass, licking his lips from the cold before he spoke again. "Yes. If Alec is dead, Nesbit is free to marry Michelle Oranii, whereupon he will demand his birthright and be the next person to inherent the House of Hornet. This is something we must prevent at all costs. He is still a member of our House, but he wants to start his own."

Admiral Cook nodded. "And that's the real reason behind your decision to send the Eleventh out to look for him. I understand that, but why give me that order in front of everyone? Now your actions will be challenged by the Senate."

"That's precisely why I did it. If that happens, I'll activate the override clause, so that no one can question any of my orders the first year. After that, of course, I will be forced by the Senate to stand down the order and bring you back home. But it will give you one year to find him."

"What about sending a message to the Merchants and the Traders? Did you say that just for show?"

"Hell no. They've been too lax too long; if they want to keep policing the spacelanes themselves in conjunction with the FPs and the CPHA, they need to do a better job than this. Things are falling apart out there; it's not even safe to take a hop from here to the far moon. It's beginning to look like their organizations are riddled with corruption from top to bottom—that they're actually *allowing* some of these depredations. I won't have that. I expect they're currently receiving that message loud and clear from their representatives. Hopefully, it will frighten them enough to start searching for Alec and his friends."

"You don't think there's any risk that they'll try to sweep certain evidence under the rug?"

The Marshal shook his head. "I don't see that happening, as long as Alec is still alive."

Cook peered at him over the rim of his melting glass, and realized that he'd best finish his drink before it ended up on his trousers. He took a deep chug and smacked his lips. "Guss, it'll still be like looking for a needle in a haystack. A very big haystack."

"I don't agree. Two CPH ships attacked the very same pirates not long ago. They weren't hard to find, and I think we can do so again."

"What class of commission?" Cook wondered, curling his hands around the glass. He stared moodily into the thick bluish liquid inside.

"The latest...the First Class Frigates."

"And how did they fare?"

"They were destroyed."

Cook's hand clenched convulsively; the ice-glass shattered, spilling sticky fluid over his hands and staining his perfect uniform. He rose slowly, ignoring his discomfort, and strode to the railing, looking out unseeing at the landscape. After a long moment, the Marshal joined him at the rail.

Finally, Cook turned back to his brother and commanding officer. "Dammit, Guss, the First Class Frigates are the best the CPH has," he said gruffly. "No average pirate vessel could stand a chance against one of them, much less two. That would require either a fleet or, at bare minimum, a very large cruiser. No pirate known uses a cruiser; they're not nimble enough. Guss, why don't you just arrest that little bastard Nesbit and his lover? This whole thing stinks worse than the ass-end of a bluttercow!"

PIRATES | 151

The admiral lifted an eyebrow. "Arrest him? On what charges, with what evidence? He's a bloody hero. I take it you haven't followed the news lately."

"Me follow the news? That Government propaganda bullshit?"

Marshal Hornet looked at his younger brother coldly and said, "I know we have our differences, Hadrian, but I will not have anyone of my family slander the Federation. Anyone."

Cook nodded sharply. "Of course. My apologies. Now, what rules of engagement must I follow during this little pirate-hunting expedition?"

Hornet chose not to notice Cook's tone. "You are to use your own professional judgment at all times. However, I advise you to avoid the direct use of force if at all possible. Do not destroy anything belonging to the Traders or Merchants."

"What if they're in the hands of Florencia or some other foreign power?"

"In that case, you may consider this expedition an act of defense, and you may engage that foreign power, but only in space."

"And I may use any of my unofficial sources?"

"Details like that don't concern me, Hadrian. Just find Alec and the other prisoners. If you feel that you must, you may ask your Order for help."

Cook gave his brother a puzzled look. "I thought you disliked the Grisamm."

"Professionally, I do. But this is personal."

Cook nodded, and decided to throw caution to the wind. He wrapped his brother in a fierce embrace and said softly. "Let's do it."

Guss whispered, "Just find him as fast as you can. I'll have your orders sent to your flagship."

Cook pulled back and said, "Do you remember that one time when Alec didn't speak to me for almost a year?"

"Of course. What about it?"

"I'll make a long story short. It all started when Nesbit challenged Alec to a game of HoloSquares."

Guss frowned and said, "Yes. That was very embarrassing for me...er, Alec."

"Well, brother, not really. You see, there's something you never knew."

Again, that cocked eyebrow. "What is that?"

"Nesbit made the challenge the day before Alec's tenth birthday."

"Yes, so?"

"The following day, in front of all the guests at his birthday party, he made a bet with me."

"He *gambled*?" Hornet blurted.

Cook rolled his eyes. "Yes. He gambled. He bet me one credit that the game would be over in five minutes. Needless to say, I took the bet. Both Alec and Nesbit were very good at HoloSquares, and I really wanted to see who was best. Well, we both know what happened."

"That we do. It was the one and only time my son embarrassed me in my own house. He lost the game in less than five minutes."

Cook nodded and fell silent for a moment before he said, "I just now realized why he was upset with me for almost a year. I never paid Alec that credit."

"And why should you? The spoiled brat lost the game."

Cook looked at his brother and said coldly, "True, but he won the bet. I was angry at him for doing so, but that was no reason to dishonor myself by not keeping my word."

"Ah." After a moment, Hornet raised his head towards the sky and muttered, "Guess you owe him a credit then."

The two brothers looked at each other, and for an instant Cook thought that his older brother wanted to say something more—something he was hiding. Neither one of them noticed when the balcony began to move back toward its original position.

TWELVE

CAPTAIN Joss Urrack tugged opened the massive double wooden doors; they were ancient, three times his height, but so perfectly balanced that they opened with a touch. Inside was a large stone-walled chamber, hewn from the living rock of the mountain. The chill walls were decorated with thousands of strange-looking animal horns, in various shapes and sizes. Set into the center of the floor was a large, bronze-colored metal disk, with a strange beast carved into the surface. Along the rounded walls were twenty enormous drums; at the end of the chamber was an altar, with musical notations carved into the stone. A very old, dust-covered basket sat in the center of the altar; next to it were arranged a number of ancient artifacts. No one remembered their use.

For thousands of years, Urrack's people had guarded this ancient chamber, which they know only as the Hall of Gall. Perhaps it was a tomb; in any case, they had forgotten what it was, and why they guarded it. They knew only that to do so was important. It had become a custom, part of their culture. It had no religious or political significance; it simply was a tradition, something that linked the new generations of Urrack's people with those that had come before.

Occasionally Urrack wondered: was the Hall in fact a tomb, with the bones of ancient Elites laid beneath the flagstones? Or was it a place his people had used for sacrificial rituals, or perhaps a temple for prayer? He had long since decided that it didn't really matter; ultimately, it was just something that was important to his people.

One thing was certain: the place was creepy. The darkness lay thick as cobwebs across the chamber, and the only light came from torches in sconces along the walls. Powered lighting was not allowed in the chamber, which made no sense to Urrack; surely the torches, with their soot and heat, did more damage than modern lighting ever could. He himself had taken part in the yearly scrubbing of the soot from walls and ceilings.

No matter. All he wanted to do was to get his guard shift over with.

The twenty guards who had accompanied him were lined up outside in strict formation. For two days and two nights, they would remain outside the large wooden doors unless ordered inside. There could be no communication between them, nor could they drink or eat anything until the next guard shift replaced them. Again, tradition. It was an honor for any of his people to stand guard at the Hall of Gall.

This responsibility fell only to select, mature individuals of the very best and brightest, those who had performed something extraordinary during his or her lifetime. That person could be anyone: a scientist, a reporter, a soldier, a factory worker. It was the last thing they were required to do before retirement from seventy five years of service either in the private or governmental sectors.

The torches inside the Hall sparked strange reflections from the engraving on the dusty floor. It would soon be time to put together a work detail to clean the place, Captain Urrack reflected. He had almost finished his rounds and had started for the exit when a wave of cold swept over him, causing him to shiver. Goose-bumps rose on his exposed flesh as he realized that something unnatural was happening—and that thought sent more cold chills down his spine. Something was wrong, very wrong. He turned around very slowly, and saw a strange bluish glow emanating from the altar. There was no power source in the Hall of Gall to generate that light, and yet it was there.

"Guards!" he called loudly, his throat desert-dry.

Without waiting for a response, he cautiously approached the strange light. He noted that the Hall was growing colder as he went, and darker. He glanced at his torch, puzzled. It was as bright as usual, guttering slightly in the draft from the door, and still the room was becoming darker. It was almost as if the shadows were thickening, trying to smother the light.

When he was within a few meters of the altar, the bluish glow vanished. He stopped, then shook his head and squinted. Could it have been his imagination, or the first sign of age?

"Captain," one of the guards said from behind.

Captain Urrack turned and looked quizzically at the two guards who had joined him. Clearly, they too could sense that something wasn't right. He was sure that their disquiet was brought on by the same thing as his: fear, an emotion all but unknown to his race. The guards raised the edged, forked sticks of their Yahariias lances; Captain Urrack nodded to them. Fighting the alien emotion, this fear, he turned back towards the altar—and that's when he saw it. Some sort of pale liquid, seemingly made of living light, now filled the ancient basket almost to the brim.

It shuddered and danced, and that's when the throbbing began.

―――oOo―――

URRACK'S people lived on a well-tamed, tectonically-dead world with no large predators, and little worry from the weather. They had lived in peace for at least as long as the Hall of Gall had been quiescent; they had no need to fear anything. But soon all that would change. From the deep, silent caves at the center of the largest mountain on their world's single continent pulsed a sound no one had heard for ten thousand years. It was felt more than heard, and spread from its focus through the caves into the surrounding valleys, and thence to the open plains and coastal jungles. Every member of Urrack's people, from the least to the greatest, became instantly aware of the throbbing's meaning and purpose. It left no one unaffected; those who slept awoke, and all over the continent people put aside what they were doing and turned toward the Mountain of Gall. What once had been blessedly forgotten now was remembered by the Samari, as something in their collective racial memory stirred, stretched, and raised its behorned head. Drums: drums that brought only one message.

War.

THIRTEEN

NIKKO Behl glared at the monitor in front of him, cursing fluently in his native tongue. Alec glanced at him, eyebrows raised, and Behl immediately switched to Nadjarish, the common tongue that had been cobbled together thousands of years ago in order to facilitate communication after the end of the last, devastating war. It had since become the lingua franca of the inhabited galaxies, the first tongue of thousands of worlds and a secondary tongue for tens of thousands more, in one dialect or another.

After his cursing ran down—and quite inventive it had been, too—the captain growled, "By the way, son, name's Behl...Nikko Behl."

"Yessir, I recognized you, sir," Alec said, just as their small craft shuddered from what appeared to be a glancing blow from a magma blaster. "Alec Horn..." Alec's instinct took over, and he repeated, "Alec Horn, sir."

"Honor making your acquaintance," Behl replied, then cursed fluently as their ship shook again. "Sorry, lad, I get a little emotional when a ship's up my ass, throwing things at me that can hurt."

"No worries, sir, you fly like a Master-Level pilot!" Alec tapped at the weapons panel, releasing a second anti-flak burst.

"Hmmph. That's good, because I *am* one."

Alec looked at him, amazed. "You're a Master-Level pilot? Begging the Captain's pardon, but what are you doing flying for the Merchants?"

Behl snorted. "Well, normally it wouldn't be any of your damn business, son, but since I'm guessing we're going to be spending some real tight quality time together and given the fact that you just saved my life, I might as well tell you. Money."

Alec looked puzzled. "Money?"

"Yeah, that's right, a lot of money."

"But...I'd expect that anyone with a Master-Level at anything would earn a fortune."

"Well then, you don't know much, now do you?" Behl tapped the control panel and peered closely at readout. "Looks like they've stopped firing." His fingers danced across the keypad. "All righty then...navcomp's got a fix, and says we're less than a light minute from a natural jump point. Looks like a wormhole that's lost its event horizon. We hit it right, we can get home. Eventually." He tapped a few keys, peered at the board, and said, "Course plotted. I'm accelerating to 0.5 c; we'll be there in two minutes." Behl sat back with a satisfied look on his face.

It was a long two minutes before the nav alarm went off. Behl roused himself, made a few adjustments to their course, and muttered, "Hang on, son, here we go."

It was the first time Alec had been present on the bridge of a vessel that was allowing itself to be drawn into the hungry maw of a singularity, and for a few moments he forgot about his predicament. Not that the experience was particularly spectacular; the cabin lights and panels dimmed abruptly as the engines sent them on their space-warping approach to the singularity, and outside the ports, all became pitch black. For a few seconds, everything appeared to move in slow motion, and it felt, in the pit of his stomach, as if they were falling down a deep well at enormous speed— which in fact they were.

Then the ship seemed to stop abruptly, jerking its occupants forward. *Must have hit something*, Alec thought, a split second before a bright white radiance flooded the bridge and he was pushed hard back into his crash couch, as if by a giant's hand. He took a deep breath and examined his instruments. They were back in normal space.

Alec glanced at Behl. "That was interesting, sir. Do it again?"

"Ha! Don't you worry, son. Something tells me we'll be doing this a few more times."

"How come it's nothing like this when you're a passenger?"

Captain Behl shrugged. "You have to be at the center core of a big ship or in a little one like this one to get the full experience."

Alec scowled. "The flight simulators at school included nothing like this."

"They should, but they don't," Behl agreed. "But I'm glad I was able to put a smile on that mask of yours."

"Mask?"

Behl tapped a few keys on the instrument panel and looked sidelong at Alec. "No offence meant, son, but the first time I saw you was after you almost blew me up. There was a big boom, the nano-wall died, and suddenly there was this bloody, weather-beaten warrior standing in the doorway, loaded down with weapons. I saw your eyes, and the stare you gave me. Shit, you made that hairy bastard of a pirate captain look nice there for an instant."

"Um, sorry if I startled you." Alec's memory of the rescue was a little spotty, since everything had happened so fast. "You startled me, actually. I had no idea the nano-wall was there…and when I saw you hanging from the wall, well…"

Behl nodded. "Well, I appreciate you taking me with you." He looked around the cockpit and said, after a long moment, "I guess this is that pirate bastard's back-up plan."

"What do you mean?"

"Most pirate captains have contingency plans in place, in case they need to make a quick getaway. Kinda like the ones Admirals have aboard their flagships. This must've been one of Zuzack's."

Alec listened with interest as Behl continued. "The crews have their escape pods and the officers their shuttles to make an escape in, if they have to. Most Admirals keep a pinnace or gig in place, so they can escape if they need to. Let's 'em maintain their chain of command. In this case, the pirate bastard turned a fast scout ship into his personal escape pod."

Alec interrupted. "Isn't this ship a little big for a scout?"

"Yes and no. What we're sitting in is the scout ship itself; it's integrated into a larger transport chassis of some kind. Haven't found the commands that will detach the transport chassis yet, but I'm sure I will if I dig deep enough into the comp system. I bet we'll find a lot of interesting things back there, whenever we get a chance to look. Hell, we might be sitting on a fortune."

Alec glanced surreptitiously at the bag behind him.

"Here, take the stick," Behl said suddenly. He tapped a few controls before Alec had a chance to protest, and suddenly the ship jinked to the left. "Right aft thruster's a little hot," Behl said helpfully, as Alec grabbed the yoke and did his best to get the steering under control.

"I thought you knew how to fly," Behl muttered as rubbed his forehead.

"I do. I did well in Piloting and Nav at the Academy," Alec defended himself. "It's just that..." He stopped talking and focused on the steering.

"Here now, just relax." Behl unstrapped himself, then leaned forward in the microgravity and adjusted Alec's hands, efficiently instructing him how to gain control over the ship. Within moments *Tramp* was back on course, and over the next few hours Behl gave Alec better lessons on maneuvering and flying than he'd ever learned in school. Eventually the older man stretched and excused himself to go to the head. Alec barely noticed when he heard the hatch cycle behind him, but Behl's shout of "Holy shit!" yanked his attention back to reality.

"Hey, now," Behl called, "Don't let me make you lose control of the ship, cadet." His voice reminded Alec of some of his instructors from the military academy. He turned his head to glance at Behl as he entered the tiny bridge; the old man wore a huge grin. "C'mon, let's trade places. You got to see this with your own eyes."

Alec quickly traded places with Behl, who took the yoke with practiced ease, and scrambled through the hatch leading back to the cargo spaces. The first thing he noticed in the hold was a huge bed; on the far end of the small space was a compact pantry, flanked by two open hatches. Alec looked into the leftmost and found a surprisingly neat, well-organized head that was barely big enough to handle someone the size of Zuzack. He grunted and stepped over to the hatch on the right; he found himself facing a short cylindrical hall that jogged to the left about three meters in. It seemed well-enough lit, so he hauled himself inside. He soon found himself in a larger space that was so tightly packed with goods that there was little room left to move around. He grabbed hold of a bar on the wall and pulled himself off the deck, peering at all the boxes and crates strapped to the deck. Several had been jimmied open; he could see that they contained clear plastic containers filled with from food, furs, and alcohol to weapons, money, and jewels. He whistled faintly, and wondered what the hell they were going to do with all that loot.

After inspecting it for a bit longer, he headed back toward the cockpit. On his way back, he noticed a clipcomp hanging on the wall. He took it down and activated it, punching up the single file in memory. It turned out to be a cargo manifest; and as he read it, Alec began to laugh.

Nikko Behl was busily studying star charts on a monitor when a clipcomp was suddenly thrust in front of his face. He jumped and scowled; but then, as he realized what was on the electronic screen, he grinned and started laughing; it wasn't long before Alec joined him. And if their laughter seemed to have a hysterical edge, no one could have blamed them, after all they'd been through.

At the moment, they were traveling with a fortune large enough to buy several planets outright. And not just dinky little pioneer worlds, either.

When their laughter died down, Behl wiped his eyes and looked abruptly at Alec. "Thank you, son. Thank you for saving my life and putting your own on the line."

"Please don't mention it, sir. It's what a soldier does."

Behl nodded sharply. "And did you have friends on the *Bright Star* with you, Mr. Horn?"

"Yessir, my entire squad. Eleven other cadets, six women and five men. And Major Nesbit, of course."

"I remember the Major. Had him at my table a couple of times. A very handsome and correct individual."

"Yessir. He's always correct. Never does anything wrong."

"A gentleman never criticizes his superior officers," Behl snapped.

"Um, aye aye, sir," Alec said formally.

Behl relented. "It sounds like you have some resentment towards him."

"No sir! Well, it's just that he always smiles, and I know from experience that he isn't as perfect as he tries to make it seem."

"No one is perfect. Are you, Mr. Horn?"

"Um, no sir."

Behl looked at Alec with interest. "Something more there. Tell me."

"Aye aye, sir." Alec took a deep breath. "Well, sir, it's like this. Mr. Nesbit and I are related, so I know him fairly well. When I was young and started in a private school, Nesbit was there...his last year. I always got into trouble for certain strange things that happened, and somehow Nesbit always seemed to be linked to the trouble. But..."

"But you could never prove anything?"

"Right, sir. How did you know?"

"Oh, that's easy. That type of character exists everywhere. They're convinced they're nice people, and they get everyone else believing it too. But underneath it all, they're sadists and tyrants. When they get a little power they can't help but wield it, because they love inflicting pain for their own pleasure and material gain. They're pure malice. Nesbit's like that?"

"Maybe, sir," Alec said hesitantly. "He's...Nesbit is smart. First in his class when he graduated. Normally he'd be second lieutenant, but when he graduated he was already a major."

"Ah, so you're a little envious, then."

"Not really, sir. I'm a general."

Behl grinned, shaking his head...but his laughter died a-borning as he looked into Alec's guileless dark blue eyes. Alec continued, "Well, um, officially I haven't received my rank or training, and of course I don't have the experience, but I earned the rank in battle. Actually, it was our graduating battle against forces from Florencia, on one of our newer colony worlds."

"So actually it's only a brevet rank," Behl said, staring fixedly at the nearest monitor.

"Yessir, that's right."

Behl muttered, "Then perhaps the major envies you?"

Alec shrugged. "Doesn't really matter much, except it makes most of my friends envy me, and perhaps my parents proud. I was to be rewarded my new rank at the annual graduation festival on Tallas, upon our arrival. That's long past now. After that, I was to receive the higher level of schooling necessary at the capitol."

"I take it you want to return to Tallas ASAP?"

"Well, yessir, but not right now. First I need to rescue my friends."

Behl shook his head, and after a short silence adopted a more serious and fatherly tone. "You can't save them or rescue them, son. Some of them will be dead by now. You could buy the survivors if you ever found them...and by then, most of them wouldn't be the same people you used to know. But you can never really save them. If they come from important or wealthy families, then there's a small chance they'll be traded or bartered back. Or sometimes the government will buy them back, as long as they've got a lot of money invested in their educations and training."

"You do what you have to do, and I'll do what I have to do, sir," Alec said stoutly.

The Captain smiled. "My debt to you is for life, Mr. Horn, no matter how you see it. If you want to go back right now and take on those pirates head on, you just give me the word. This little bird has a shitload of heavy weapons we can throw at them. But if you want an old man's advice—for what it's worth, General—then we might want to regroup and reorganize ourselves, find some allies, choose our own battleground." There was no disrespect in Behl's voice, only grim resolution.

Alec looked at the old man in silence. "Thank you, Captain Behl. Would you like to hear my plan so far?"

"Does it include action?"

"Yessir, plenty."

"Then I'm in." Behl signed deeply. "Ya know, I was getting pretty bored hauling cargo and transporting civilians anyway. This brings back old memories that I'd love to share with you sometime. But in the meantime, let's hear your plan. I'll let you know what I think as you move along."

Nervously, Alec trotted out his plan, or what he had of it at least. Behl listened with some skepticism at first, occasionally putting in a word or two; but after some time he appeared to become engrossed, and by the time the young officer was done he was looking at Alec with undisguised respect.

Once Alec had finished laying out his proposal, a half-hour later, Nikko Behl spent a full hour picking it apart, telling him what was wrong with every detail. By the time he was done, Alec looked shell-shocked—and all the more so when Behl concluded with, "... but apart from that, it's a pretty good plan."

Alec nodded, swallowing hard. "Thank you sir, but it's obviously not good enough. Do you have any suggestions?"

The grizzled captain scratched his bearded chin. "Think about what I've said. Sleep on it, and present an amended plan to me tomorrow. We need to take the time to get this just right."

"Aye aye, sir."

In the coming days, Nikko Behl and his new protégé spent innumerable hours shaping their plan to rescue the cadet squad and, if possible, the crew and passengers of *Bright Star* from slavery. Over time, they formed a simple plan that seemed it might be effective, at least for retrieving the cadets. Privately, Behl thought it was the absurd to chase down Zuzack and try to find Alec's lost friends—especially after what Alec had done to Zuzack before vacating the premises—but he kept his reservations to himself. He owed the kid his life and his sanity, which had been on the ragged edge of breaking after weeks of intermittent torture. And besides, he too had lost friends and mates, and he craved some payback.

And even if the plan never turned into reality, it was a good way of passing time in the confined spaces he had to share with Alec. They'd ended up in home space, more or less, but many days from a port, jumpgate, or inhabited world, so it was important to keep their minds and hands busy. When they weren't talking about the plan, Behl taught Alec everything he knew about space travel, from jump navigation to EVA. Alec did many things he'd never experienced at the Academy.

They took turn resting and eating in the small compartment behind the cockpit, and Alec used some of his off time to prowl the cargo hold, checking the contents against the manifest he'd found. Everything seemed to match up. One evening as he was rummaging through the loot, looking for the chocolate the manifest said was there somewhere, he called out to Behl, "Sir, why is it you seem to have no interest in the cargo, aside from that Tallasian caviar and such? You realize there's all kinds of loot in there, right?"

"That's right, skipper, and it's all yours. I've nothing to do with it, nor any right to make a claim."

When he heard that, Alec stood up suddenly—too suddenly, as it turned out, because he staggered and cracked his head on the cargo hatchway. Cursing up a storm, he made his way toward the cockpit, wondering aloud why they had to have gravity on anyway. Micrograv had been just fine for the first day or so.

"I heard that," Behl called from the helm as Alec approached, looking at the blood on his fingers.

"If we were at a full gravity I would have brained myself just now," Alec groused.

"Good thing we ain't, then. I told you why I've got it set at a quarter-g, and I know some of your instructors did too. If you're in micrograv too long, your bone chemistry and cell structure will change, and your muscles will turn to jelly...let's just say you wouldn't be able to walk or jerk off for a long time when you got back home."

"Yessir, I know, I was just bellyaching. So, um, what did do you mean about the loot, sir?"

"You captured the ship from a pirate, son, so she's all yours. And even though an intergalactic court might consider me a crew member, or even a Captain with the right to claim a small part of the share, you're still the owner."

"But all this is stolen stuff, sir! I mean, I might have a claim on the tritonium silver that I took from Zuzack, since it clearly falls under the treasure statutes, but I couldn't imagine they'd let me keep all this stuff."

"Hah. For most of that stuff, the provenance is lost, son. And even if we *could* return it to the rightful owners, you'd still get a huge cut and keep this flying tin can. Must say it looks like shit from the outside, but that pirate must know something about engines and avionics, because it's in mint condition otherwise. No worries, Alec. You're young, wealthy, and your life has just begun. I just want to repay my life debt to you."

"Don't you worry, you old geezer, you'll have some of the spoil."

Behl snapped off a precise salute. "Aye aye, sir! Whatever you say, General!"

"Please don't call me that, sir."

Behl smiled as Alec retired to the cabin to sleep.

They also spent a good deal of time learning the weapons systems. The ship carried an ample supply of rocket-propelled targets, which enlivened the long, boring hours. They turned it into a sort of game, a competition that kept them sharp and their minds active. Occasionally, and often without warning, one of them would release a target from its launch bay, and the other would skewer it with one of the forward laser cannons.

Alec was grateful that he'd had the opportunity to spend this journey with an expert spacer. No matter how tough the last eight years had been, and no matter how well he had done, he was still a rank beginner compared to Nikko Behl. He couldn't have had a better tutor in the ways of handling a spacecraft, either. Whenever

Alec sat in the comfortable pilot's seat and wore the helmet linking him to the ship's systems, he felt that he was in control over his own destiny for the first time he could remember.

Behl's voice from the copilot's seat, criticizing, complaining and on rare occasions congratulating Alec on his flying techniques, was like a second part of his own mind.

After the first month in space and several jumps later, Behl informed Alec that he was flying like a professional. Frankly, he was astonished that the kid had come so far so quickly; then again, he'd never had the opportunity to drill someone as much and as intently as he had Alec. The bond between them grew, and rarely did they get on each other's nerves. Behl had long since realized that it was because Alec loved to learn, and because he himself loved to teach.

One day Alec lightly said something that would change Behl's thoughts about Alec forever: "A true Master will always remain a student."

"Who told you that?" Behl asked sharply.

"Not sure, sir," Alec admitted. "Just something that stuck with me."

The captain said no more; he just leaned back and enjoyed the ride.

After that, Nikko Behl had never had any second thoughts about whether or not Alec deserved to be a general. He might be young, but he was a natural-born leader.

FOURTEEN

IT had been over two weeks since the mysterious young prisoner had escaped the *Bitch*, after killing seven crewmen, injuring 13, raping two others, and mutilating the ship's captain. The pirates were in collective shock; they'd though he was a frightened pretty-boy coward, but clearly that had been an act—an act so profoundly convincing that even his own squad mates had fallen for it. Clearly, his Silver Guard ancestry had come to the surface, with all the sly cunning that suggested. Bold defiance hadn't worked for his friends; so he'd acted frightened, submissive, craven. By now, most of the officers and crew had revised their opinions of Alec Hornet significantly upward. Those who hadn't had learned to keep their opinions to themselves; so far, Zuzack had killed four crewmen and one officer who had been too forthright in disagreeing with the Captain.

This night, Alexa lay on her bed sobbing. Nina made an attempt to comfort her, but Alexa pushed her away.

Nina stood slowly, and looked down at her best friend and sister-in-arms, not knowing what to do. She looked around Alexa's suite, noticing that it remained in the same condition as it had been the night of the escape. The place was decorated with broken glass and furniture; bottles, inhalers and syringes were scattered across the deck, and that damned rope still dangled from the ceiling. She looked down at Alexa, who looked like a pale wreck. Her body was desperate for a good washing and some nutrition. "When was the last time you had something to eat?" she asked loudly.

She repeated herself twice, but there was no answer. Nina knelt beside the bed and stroked Alexa's clammy forehead. She whispered, "Sorry I've been away. Captain made me and a few others follow the runaways in our fighters."

For the first time, Alexa stop sobbing. With a faint glimmer of hope in her voice, she asked, "Did you bring him back?"

"'Fraid not. They were long gone by the time we took up the chase, and we lost them after they dived into a wormhole. Zuzack has launched hundreds of probes, scanning for their engine signature and transponders, listening for transmissions. We'll find them eventually."

Alexa buried her head in her pillow and started sobbing again.

"Hey! That's for the better. What do you think would happen if Zuzack got his hands on him? No matter how much he might be worth, Zuzack would have burned him alive."

Alexa kept on bawling and ignored Nina, who stood there scowling, hands on her hips. Finally, she made an exasperated noise, then grabbed Alexa by her ankles and pulled her off the bed. Alexa was taken by surprise at first, but as Nina continued hauling her toward the head, complaining of her stench, she woke from her pity party kicking and cursing. "Let me go, Gulldammit, or I'll tear you into little pieces! Get out and leave me be! You hear me, you cantankerous little harridan?"

"I hear you, all right, and thanks for the compliment—but you're getting a shower whether you like it or not. While you're getting cleaned up, I'll fix us some food. And later, if I can find a friggin' pitchfork, we'll start cleaning up around here. *Capice*?"

"I'll kapeesh you, you flyblown daughter of a diseased whore!" shouted Alexa angrily as she wiggled out of Nina's grasp. She tried to stand as Nina watched, smirking, but began to sway from lack of sleep and nutrition.

Nina saw her opportunity and jumped Alexa from behind. "I'll show you, you stubborn little princess!"

"Wait a...No! NO! Stop that, you bitch!" Alexa protested as Nina pushed her down on her back and pinned her with her knees.

"Who you calling bitch, bitch?" Nina snarled. "I'm not going to stand there and watch my best friend destroy herself over some damned slave. You hear me?"

"Get off me, tramp, or I'll have to pull rank!" Alexa threatened. By then, she'd pulled up out of her funk enough to recover some of her natural guile, and although Nina's weight made her gasp for air, she was able to wriggle away again, causing Nina to pitch backward and smack her head against the bulkhead. Alexa kicked herself free and started to crawl away.

The sudden silence from behind made Alexa turn and look at Nina, who lay there unmoving. "Oh, crap," she groaned. "Hey, Nina! Nina, are you okay?" Alexa crawled back toward her friend, and just as she reached out to check her pulse, Nina opened her eyes with a devilish grin on her face. She leaped up, bowling Alexa over, flipped her face down, and sat on her legs. Alexa was on her stomach, trying to crawl away, her eyes filled with something very like horror. She screamed at the top of her lungs and protested. "NO! No, not my feet! No, it's not fair, bit—"

Alexa broke into laugher as Nina dug her fingers into her soft, pale soles. Nina was grinning as she watched Alexa writhe in paroxysms of laughter, occasionally begging her to stop when she could catch her breath. But no, Nina continued. Alexa begun to cough between her bouts of laughter, and finally choked out, "Stop, stop, or I'm gonna pee myself!"

Nina looked over her shoulder at Alexa, and said silkily, "Will you stop behaving like a spoiled brat and come to your senses?"

"Bitch," Alexa spat in a futile demonstration of defiance.

"I learned from the best, milady—"

Nina's amused rejoinder was interrupted by another voice. "Hey! What's going on here?" snapped Tara, as she looked down on a laughing Alexa and a giggling Nina. Both girls sobered up quickly when they saw that her hair was red. Tara was Hactan, and her mane changed color depending on her mood. At the moment, it was reddish shot with black streaks, the color for anger bordering on rage. They noticed belatedly that she wore battle fatigues.

Tara stood glaring at them for a moment before gesturing them forward into the head, where she turned on the shower. She shoved them both into the shower stall, where they were quickly soaked. They looked up at her like two wet puppies when Tara growled, "Now listen up, you two! What do you think—!" Her harangue broke off with a shriek as, with matching evil smiles, Alexa and Nina grabbed Tara and pulled her into the shower stall. A sputtering Tara tried to talk some sense into them, but she didn't do a very good job. Soon her laughter filled the suite, too, as the three of them began attacking each other as the water poured down. Finally, Tara managed to catch her breath and shouted out the second worse word that could be heard on any ship: "Mutiny!"

By then, Nina was straddling Tara's chest, while Alexa was about to pull off one of her boots. They stopped and glanced at each other. Nina cried back, "I'll give you mutiny, you little..."

As she felt Alexa pull off her sock, preparing to attack her delicate sole, Tara used the last of her breath to shout, "Mutiny! For real! I'm not joking, idiots!"

Nina shot Alexa a puzzled look. Alexa stood and turned off the shower, dropping Tara's boot and a sock on the wet tile. Tara struggled to her feet, complaining bitterly about two crazy little girls who were in desperate need of a spanking. Nina and Alexa helped steady her as she slipped on the soaked deck.

"What do you mean, mutiny?" Alexa demanded.

"Hmmph." Tara wrung water from her mane, which had faded to a washed-out pink. "If you hadn't been locked up in here feeling sorry for yourself, you'd know what's going on." Alexa had the grace to look embarrassed, and Tara continued. "While the rest of us were out scanning space for your darling, that old hag Myra made known her plans to take over the ship...finally."

The girls moved into the living room, still soaked, and Tara cursed as she tried to pull on her wet boot, falling on her well-padded derriere in the process. A moment later they were joined by the rest of the gang, who filed in quietly. The Twins from Hell, Mohama and Miska, were there, with their long, serpentine tails coiled together as usual. Both were dressed for battle, with a number of weapons visible about their persons; who knew how many weren't. With them was young Kirra, a lovely black-skinned Oman whose tight dreadlocks fell down to her shoulders. There were tiny blades braided into the ends of the dreads. She was dressed in a flat black outfit the same color as her skin, and her toned body all but dripped weapons, although there were various bags and pouches in evidence, too. Blonde Zicci stood beside her, an Oman with a slight admixture of Herrier that gave her bronze skin and an exotic beauty that was quite different from Kirra's. Unlike most women on the ship, she eschewed dreadlocks and instead wore her long curly hair in two pigtails, obviously going for that "innocent little pirate" look. She was dressed in a long-sleeved brown tunic and loose trousers that de-emphasized her voluptuous figure, her wide feet thrust into combat boots. Most of her weapons were concealed under her tunic, except for a large magma rifle hanging from her shoulder. She too was wearing several bags and packs. Both Kirra and Zicci looked puzzled at the sight of their three soggy compatriots as they enter the living room.

Tara sat down on the couch, tossing her wet sock away. She pulled on her boot without it, cursing again as water poured out. Then she looked up at Alexa. "Let's get right to business. Because Myra doesn't trust you, Alexa, and because there's this rumor that you're getting ready to join Zuzack's clan permanently, she sent us to find out if you're with her or not."

Alexa looked at Nina and then back to their armed and bedecked friends. "You must be joking. I was buying time, that's all, just—"

"Don't worry," Kirra purred, "we know you'd never join that monster…right?"

"Of course not. As I was saying—"

This time Alexa was interrupted by Zicci. "What side are you on?" the blonde woman demanded bluntly. For a moment, Alexa didn't understand; she sent a puzzled glance toward Nina, who stood by her side with a suspicious expression. For the first time, Alexa noticed several more bags and weapons on the floor. She knew they belonged to Nina.

"Are you here to take care of us?" asked Nina.

Tara joined the other girls. They all looked to Alexa for an answer while ignoring Nina. Jaw set, Alexa snarled, "The only side I'm on is my own, and that of my best friends. That happens to include Nina and you guys. Zuzack and Myra can get married and have a bunch of scaly little brats for all I care."

"And I'm hers...I mean, I'm with her. Alexa, that is," proclaimed Nina.

The assembled pirates released a collective sigh of relief that took most of the tension in the room with it. Alexa nodded sharply and stomped off toward her bedroom, where she began to get dressed in her fatigues. "There's no way that zarky lizard bitch could make it, especially since the Silver Guard prisoner escaped," she called toward the living room. "Zuzack has too many defense systems in place now."

Zicci replied, "Whatever. But we can all get out of here on one of the shuttles. Tara has prepped one for us, and..."

Zicci was cut off by Nina, who snapped, "Are you all brain-burned? We can't take off in one off the shuttles. All the docking areas are locked down so that no one can leave."

"It worked for Alexa's slave," muttered Tara.

"I heard that. He wasn't my slave," Alexa answered.

Nina shook her head and continued. "And it especially won't work since Alexa's knight in shining armor took off. Zuzack has turned on the inner forceshields all over this old tin can."

"This is still our best chance," Kirra pointed out. "I'm sick and tired being locked up here, treated like a second-class citizen. I haven't left this ship in over eight years."

Alexa strode into the living room, strapping on a battle vest festooned with grenades and small weapons. "If we can get the shield down, then maybe we can get away—but we'll get blown to bits before we get a kilometer from the ship. The only way to avoid that is to take out the tracking systems for the missile launchers and the particle beam turrets, and to do that, we have to get into Zuzack quarters and hack into his personal computer files. No. I say we hide out and see which side wins, and then we decide what to do based on that."

Nina opened a cupboard and helped herself to some of the weapons and equipment inside, passing it on to the other women to pack. Meanwhile Alexa keyed open a secret compartment in the bulkhead, and took out a couple of bulging backpacks.

Tara said, sounding hesitant, said, "So you're saying we should hide out like cowards while the rest of the crew does all work?"

Alexa slammed the hidden door shut with a crash. "You tell me, Tara! Tell me what *any* of them has ever done for you, or for any of us, that didn't gain them something?"

Nina cut in, "All they've ever done is forced us to commit murder and all kinds of other heinous crimes while they use us for their perverted sex games. By the holy Gull Itself, who *knows* what they have planned for us in the near future?"

"I doubt it will be much better around here with Myra as Captain," Alexa said, as she checked the charge magazine of her pistol. "And what will happened when Zuzack's brother hears of this? You all remember Horsa, don't you?"

They remembered, all right. When she spoke the name of the most feared pirate in the known universe, each of them reacted as if a corpse had run a chill finger down her spine.

"I know we've all planned to get away someday, and we will," Alexa continued. "I'm just not so sure that this is the right time. Let's stick together and ride out this storm as a team, and maybe the stars will smile upon our faith—and with some luck, we can get away from here in one piece." She looked to her friends for reply; but before anyone found their voice, she said in a low, deadly tone, "Right. What did Myra say you were supposed to do in case I warned Zuzack?"

All of them but Nina looked at the floor, refusing to meet Alexa's glare.

"That's what I thought," Alexa said.

Nina gritted her teeth and said spitefully, "I'm going to skin that fucking lizard alive."

"We would never hurt each other. We're family," Tara protested.

"I know." Alexa embraced all her friends in turn.

When she hugged Zicci, the blonde Amazon pulled away and asked, "Why are you all wet?"

Alexa, Nina, and Tara looked at each other; then, simultaneously, Alexa and Nina pointed to Tara and said, "She started it." Talking over Tara's protest, Alexa said, "So, when is this mutiny of Myra's supposed to start?"

An explosion from the corridor outside answered her question.

FIFTEEN

"**ORDER!** I will have *order* in this Hall of Council!" The shout was repeated several times by the short, stocky woman in red, to no avail. Finally, she clapped her raised hands above her head several times, sending an eerie staccato sound echoing throughout the red marble Hall. As the hubbub died down, she smoothed her gown and took her seat.

Marquessa De La Nosassa La Peck, the First Lady of the Karpatrika Civilian Hall of Council, looked over the room with a displeased expression. She snarled, the teeth lining her long snout making her displeasure with the constant interruptions plain. Realizing that her dander was up, most of the Council members returned to their seats, though a few remained standing, their voices raised in protest. Finally, Nosassa decided that enough was enough. She brought her gavel down on the granitewood podium so hard that the handle splintered, and the loud bang finally made the standing Council members pay her heed. "The next time anyone interrupts, I will have that person removed by the guards!" she shouted.

Eyes glared at her sullenly, but at least she had their attention and they were all quiet. She straightened her back and composed her expression to neutrality before she began her speech. "Honorable Marquises and Marquessas, Senators and Governors, it is abundantly clear that everyone has his or her own opinion on this matter. However, the only opinion that matters is that of God. The time has finally come for the ultimate universal expansion of the Florencian Federation. It is no longer possible for us to remain at peace with Nastasturus, and we all know why! Their heretical lack of faith, their materialistic hunger, their lies, and most of all their own expansion, their so-called 'manifest destiny,' have all become threats to our very existence."

Nosassa paused for any possible interruption. When none came she continued, "Our recourses are failing our God and all His true believers, and this must no longer continue. When the Nastasturans say that their goal is only to help the peoples of the newly-discovered inhabited worlds, we all know that what they are really doing is gathering more species into their fold, so that they can continue to feed their capitalistic hunger. They want one thing, and one thing only..." she paused dramatically before shouting, "MORE RESOURCES! They need more species to ally with them against the true inheritor of this universe, the only true entity in existence." She raised her hands and screamed, "Af De Ma Floda Reltih! GOD!"

Everyone in the room stood immediately, shouting out the One and Only Name.

Nosassa stepped away from the podium and fell to her knees, followed by everyone else in the room, including the hundreds of guards posted along the rows of red marble pillars on either side of the Hall. They all bowed their heads, humming to themselves as Nosassa raised her head and shouted out a prayer. Then she stood up in silence, observing her subjects as they prayed. After a long moment, she called, "Enough! God has heard you! We must proceed; there shall be no more delays!"

As the Council members returned to their seats, she made an imperious gesture. The floor in the center of the room irised open, lifting a huge holoprojector into the light. It flicked on, displaying a complex three-dimensional scene encompassing several galaxies. Pastel colors indicated the domains of the various political entities in the known universe.

The Council members focused their attention on Nosassa. She took a deep breath to calm herself, then spoke in a clear voice: "God has spoken! Three steps we must take to accomplish our goal of complete universal expansion. First, we shall make the entire galaxy of Herica ours by excising the cancer of the Nastasturus Federation, exterminating all sentient beings claiming allegiance to that diseased entity. We shall continue this cleansing until the remaining species finally submit themselves to the One True God!"

Her words were followed by scattered shouts of agreement. Nosassa made a gesture of silence, then said, "Second, we will deal with the thieving Merchants and Traders in the galaxies of Yaharra and Sabaza. Once they too have been purged and brought under our control, we will commence the third step, universal expansion from here to eternity!"

As Nosassa spoke, the three-dimensional display indicated with arrows how the process would play out, staining the galaxies the bright red of noble Florencia. When the entire map was red, the holoprojector snapped off and retreated into the floor. Nosassa gripped the podium and faced her people with a calm and confident expression. Most of them looked at her with excitement, though there were a few skeptical faces visible.

"I sense that there are those of you who are in doubt," Nosassa declared in a low, threatening tone, but still loudly enough for all to hear. "Have some of you lost faith? If that is the case, then I suggest some time spent in temple is in order, so that your souls can be purified and cleansed. That way, when you travel and become one with God in the afterlife, there can be no infection." She looked at the silent councilors before her. "Perhaps I was wrong..."

At that moment, Ambassador Governor Ramses De Shatz got to his feet and faced the podium. Her face dark with frustration, Nosassa gestured for him to speak.

"My faith is in God, and only God!" Ramses declared. "I say this so that there shall be no misunderstanding." He locked his eyes with Nosassa's; she nodded her head for him to continue.

"The three steps are the only direction we need. And for them to work in our time...we need an act of God."

The meeting dissolved into chaos, as people—Council members and guards alike—shouted imprecations: "Traitor! Unbeliever! Sinner! Unholy!"

Nosassa slammed her hands on the podium, and several guards stepped forward in unison, their heels clattering menacingly on the hardened marble. Everyone sat down, with the exception of Ramses.

In a voice trembling with suppressed emotion, Nosassa said, "Would Ambassador Governor Ramses De Shatz care to elaborate on this delicate matter?"

Ramses straightened his back and tugged down the front of his crimson robe, which was adorned with a yellow line along the length of each arm, the symbol of his station. "Honorable followers and appointed ones," he intoned. "For over ten thousand years, we and our ancestors have stood here and said the same things; and in consequence, many times have we expanded God's belief and might. We are expanding by the Word of God; and when I say *Word*, I do not mean by the force of God's almighty priesthood and its warriors. Yes, it is a slow process, but we have proven over and over again that we cannot force the only right way of thinking on the lesser intelligent beings. And it is indeed the only right way. But their rude manners and animalistic behavior are not to be taken lightly. Their barbarian ways cannot be met with a military force. We can better educate these lost souls by the Word, not by a show of force."

Several consenting shouts followed these words.

Ramses continued, "And even if we must end our temporary peace with Nastasturus, who then shall lead our forces to war? No second Marquis De La has been appointed by the One and Only God for over a thousand years, and by right of tradition, only a second Marquis De La can bring God's holy angels to the battlefield."

There was silence as his audience considered these words, heads swiveling from Ramses to Nosassa. After a long moment, Chancellor Rock Belim of Handover stood up and announced, "I demand a voice of challenge!"

Nosassa gestured with her left arm towards Belim.

"My home planet is in a desperate situation that requires desperate measures. We *must* be allowed to expand. Handover is vastly over-populated, our resources are fast diminishing, and the atmosphere has degraded to the point that it is almost unbreathable. As I understand it, many of the Florencian worlds are facing similar crises. For our survival, we must be allowed to expand immediately."

Ramses interrupted. "I understand that, but expanding into the zones containing worlds where the dominant species haven't yet achieved spaceflight is against all intergalactic law, even for us. It is wrong, and the result is always the same, war and revolution and..."

Rock Belim cut him off, his voice choked with emotion. "Handover is already suffering a revolution led by rebels supported by Nastasturus! It is Nastasturus that *already* has abrogated our peace treaty."

Several Council members shouted out their agreement, while others protested.

"You have no evidence to back that claim," shouted Ramses, who was now trembling from anger and frustration.

"Since when does the Hall of Council require *evidence*?" Belim demanded righteously. "All we have to demonstrate is that a species does not know of or believe in the One True God. If that is the case, then they are open for us to...re-educate."

Nosassa raised her eyebrows and snorted, causing Belim to incline his head in her direction in a gesture of apology. "What I meant to say, my esteemed colleagues," he said in a more neutral tone, "is that it benefits the inhabitants when these worlds are opened for re-education by our peaceful and loving regime. Besides, Omar is a strategic world that will benefit us in our crusade to spread the Word of God."

Belim took a deep breath, and Ramses was just about to continue his point of view, when Nosassa interrupted both of them. "Enough! The second Marquis De La has been awakened!" she declared, the import of her message rooting all the councilors in place and sending cold chills down everyone's spine, including her own.

"When does he or she arrive?" Rock demanded after a brief pause.

Nosassa stood and looked toward the enormous doors, easily 20 meters high, that brooded on the wall opposite her. Within seconds, the attention of everyone in the room had been diverted toward the doors; and a few seconds after that, all of them became aware of the sound of marching footsteps approaching the doors. The all held their breath as the doors swung silently open, allowing the bright rays of the local sun to probe the red chamber.

A dozen guards, all dressed in bright silver armor, marched inside in perfect formation, as outside, dark clouds blotted out the sun and cast the Hall of Council into gloom. There were gasps throughout the hall, and someone muttered, "Oh my...it can't be..." Someone else finished the sentence: "...the guards of silver."

There was dead silence as the reborn representatives of the most feared and infamous Elite warriors in history, thought extinct these hundred centuries, entered the room. They lined up in a precise row, facing the podium; whether they saw Nosassa no one could say, as their rounded helmets were blank-faced, lacking eyes slits or any form of decoration. Indeed, their armor gave the impression that it was a part of them, and perhaps it was. No clumsy, bulky old-fashioned armor for these knights; theirs was smooth and fluid, almost as if were their skin, and it lacked traditional joints; like skin, it flexed at knee and ankle, shoulder and neck when the Silver Guards moved.

The room seemed to darken further as a thirteenth person, twice the size of the average Oman and cloaked in gray, entered the room. Whoever it was, he or she moved with a lethal stealth and the grace of a god; but the great head was bowed, and none could see the face.

Rock Belim sat down hard as Nosassa said in a calm voice, "My fellow believers, allow me to introduce to you the one and only... Marquessa De La Hoff."

Someone in the room shouted, "But, but, she is dead! The Marquessa De La Hoff died over a thousand years ago!"

The grim figure raised its head and cast aside the gray cloak even as the great doors behind her slammed shut. At the center of the floor stood revealed a very tall, slender woman, her alabaster skin offset by hair the deep black of starless space. As she turned to face the assembly, her thin lips quirking in a smile, that hair writhed as if alive. The black holes of her eyes seemed the pierce the Council members to the core, their dead stare flaying away pretence to reveal the cores of who they were, each and every one. That seemed to amuse her, for her smiled widened unnaturally, revealing what appeared to be hundreds of sharp little teeth, the teeth of a ruthless, obligate carnivore. She spread her arms wide, as if presenting herself for their pleasure; and it immediately became obvious that what they had taken to be part of her raiment was, in fact, bands of pale, loose skin that stretched from her forearms to her hips, forming what appeared to be batlike wings. They made her appear to be twice the width she actually was.

Hoff half-curtsied for her audience, releasing a self-satisfied hiss as a thin forked tongue swept out to clean her teeth. Her posture and body language provided an impression of authority and power combined with danger. It was hard to tell her race; most likely she was a hybrid of Oman and some sort of reptilian species—Omans would mate with anything, given half a chance—but her skin lacked scales. Her face bore a stern and yet friendly look that was clearly deceiving; her manner, and her dead eyes, exposed her for what she really was. A killer.

She smiled towards each and every person, then looked toward Nosassa, who was the only person in the room who dared to directly meet her stare. Nosassa was the only one that knew the truth: Hoff had not been awakened by anyone or anything. She had awoken on her own, and had been very startled, almost frightened, when she had done so.

Nosassa spoke to Hoff as if they were all alone. "The Silver Guard was rendered extinct!"

Hoff wriggled her body, giving the impression that various portions of it were under independent control...as if those parts were moving and sliding about, even as the aggregate was remaining still. To the normal eye, it was a nauseating sight.

Nosassa continued, "And that for a very good reason..." She whispered the last words, sweat trickling down her face.

The beautiful and lethal creature before Nosassa hissed back, "What once was is not what now is..." She spat a wad of something like thick, black saliva; and where it struck the floor, the marble blackened and began to smoke. "We rested, we did. Not die, we did." She emitted a long sibilant hiss, followed by, "Now back we are, to feed we come, on all we will."

The Marquessa De La Hoff emitted a short, almost girlish giggle, then turned and started for the exit.

"Wait!" commanded Nosassa, as she hurried after Hoff. She stopped behind the fey woman-thing, who was twice her size. All who saw her do so had to admit her sheer courage, while also decrying her foolishness. "Please, wait. We must talk; we must plan and organize..."

"We organize nothing." With lightning speed, Hoff spun and had her by the throat, as the Silver Guards formed a semicircle around the tableau, facing everyone in the room. The regular guards, still standing by their rows of pillars, dared do nothing; they merely looked at their commander with concerned expressions.

Nosassa looked at Hoff calmly, not displaying any of the fear she must have felt. After a moment, the tall woman let out an amused snort and let Nosassa go. She brushed her long fingers over Nosassa's cheek, and said, "Talk *we* shall not. Talk *you* shall. Gather us strength you will; feed off strength I will."

Nosassa blinked nervously as she said, "You are talking about funding your armies."

"Yes, yes. Rest is over; no more we sleep; now we hunt, so that others may sleep—some for a while, others for eternity. Talk we must not, talk is over, no more talk, if one talks one cannot feed. Feed one must or sleep one will. Your time to talk has made Florencia a dying nation. No more talk; let us feed or we will never thrive."

She removed her pale hand from Nosassa's cheek, and licked off a sheen of lavender blood. Nosassa lowered her stare, touching her cheek; when she brought her hand away, it was smeared with blood. Like a vampire bat, Hoff had cut open her cheek without her even noticing. She looked up at Hoff, her anger showing now; Hoff was smiling charmingly.

Nosassa murmured in her in her deep threatening voice, "You are not above me, you slavering beast. We are the same, you and I—or should we pay our God a little visit?"

There was nothing in Hoff's posture or expression that revealed whether or the threat had gone home. She only nodded towards Nosassa and whispered back, "Talk then we will, later..." She turned away again, as if to go.

Completely disregarding her audience, Nosassa demanded in a harsh whisper, "Tell me why you have returned, Hoff. You and I know the truth. Tell me as your equal."

Hoff bowed her head, her back still turned. Then she tilted her head and said in a low voice, "I do only two things in life: I serve God, and I conquer. You had your time. Now the time is mine."

Hoff glided out of the room, followed by her faceless Silver Guards, leaving Nosassa alone in the center of the Hall. The massive doors slammed shut in the warrior woman's wake, their clatter followed almost immediately by a loud crash of thunder from outside.

SIXTEEN

THE concussion from the blast swirled through the *Bitch*'s cramped corridors like a hurricane, sending anyone upright flying. After a brief lull, pierced with the screams of the wounded and dying, both sides regrouped, and a hell of laser and magma fire filled the corridor.

It wasn't going well for the mutineers, who had repeatedly been forced to retreat toward the stern of the ship. At first they were able to withdraw in orderly fashion; but when a troop of guard androids joined the fight, the retreat turned into panic. The adamantine hides of the androids were all but impenetrable to standard weapons, from magma bursts to laser and particle beams. A plasma cannon might penetrate, but Myra's mutineers had none of those. The androids waded into the fray, slicing pirates in half and relieving them of their limbs with near impunity; none of the ancient laws that would otherwise have protected the pirates have been programmed into these andies. Before long the corridors of the good ship *Bitch* were awash with blood and ichor in all the bright hues that life had allowed for throughout the inhabited galaxies.

Myra knew, by then, that it was over. She had gambled and lost. The opportunity had arisen to lead the crew in open revolt against Zuzack when the scans had revealed that there had been tritonium silver in Zuzack's stolen personal shuttle, loot that had *not* been shared with his crewmates. He had defended himself by first denying any knowledge of any tritonium silver; and when Mira proved him wrong by showing him what the scanners had revealed, Zuzack had begun to sweat and had changed tactics, claiming that that he was keeping it safe for his brother, the infamous Horsa. But that lie had been the straw that broke the camel's back for Myra and her followers; and when she cried mutiny, twelve hundred souls had joined her, sparking a battle royale which now appeared to be winding down.

When Myra saw the battle androids bearing down on her people, she cursed Zuzack silently. She and her co-conspirators had had no idea that Zuzack had battle androids hidden aboard the ship. Had they not been there, the mutineers might have had a chance; now they were being cut down like unarmed children in the face of the androids' overwhelming power.

The saurian and several of her cronies took cover in one of the bigger observation lounges and prepared for another attempt to take the brig. That was when she noticed, through the huge, curved duraglass port, that several shuttles and runabouts had detached from the ship. As she watched, several blurred into near-light speed, no doubt headed for the nearest jumpgate. Some of her "loyal comrades," trying to save their own asses.

As a smallish shuttle was exiting the docking bay, the green atmospheric shield shimmered over to red—and the shuttle exploded. The explosion made the entire ship shake, and discouraged further flight that way.

ALEXA and her friends had barely left her suite when they were accosted in the corridor outside. They had no idea which side attacked them; they didn't bother to introduce themselves first. Rolling her eyes, Zicci tossed a small grenade at their attackers, while Kirra opened up with a mini-gun; the attackers didn't last ten seconds. Alexa shouted for Nina and the others to start retreating down the curve of the corridor, bringing up the rear.

A hatch at the end of the hallway opened, and several pirates charged through under cover fire, harangued by a voice in the background that Alexa recognized as Hughes'. A magma blast struck Nina on the left shoulder; she looked comically surprised when she raised her arm and nothing happened, because the arm was no longer there. It was on the deck, twitching, still grasping her machine pistol so hard that it was triggering off the occasional round into the ceiling. The wound had been cleanly cauterized, so there was no blood. Cursing, she grabbed the pistol from the hand at the end of her detached arm, and started firing at her attackers.

Meanwhile, Tara's weapon had run dry. She threw it at one of the advancing pirates and launched herself into the air with a perfectly-aimed roundhouse kick—except that her target ducked, and as her flight continued, from out of nowhere came a better target: Hughes' face. Her boot flattened his nose and drove him to the deck. She yanked the laser pistol out of his hand and shot him through the chest, then turned the gun on the next pirate she saw. Not realizing Hughes wore body armor under his jacket.

The rest of the girls continued to blast anything that approached; Alexa, Zicci and Kirra still had a little ammo, though it was running low, but Miska and Mohama had long since emptied their weapons and had been reduced to defending themselves with knifes and, when they could, striking lethal blows at their enemies with the bony blades on the ends of their tails.

Nina's adrenaline soon ran dry and she slumped to the deck, her weapon clattering to the steel as she went into shock. When Alexa realized her plight, she cried out and charged down the corridor to help her friend. By then, Tara was tangled up in a close-quarters, hand-to-hand fight with several pirates, and their mad melee brought them between Alexa and Nina just as one of the other pirates, a tall Oman who had more than a little alien blood, banged Tara on the back of the head, dazing her. Alexa stopped long enough to put two rounds into the bastard, who screamed as his intestines poured out from between his fingers.

"*Look out!*" shouted Zicci as the ceiling opened up and several Tilter dogs leaped down into their corridor, spraying immobilizer webbing in all directions.

The battle was drawing to a close; Myra could hear the sounds of fighting receding, as her people were driven back, killed, or captured. So when one of the walls of the observation lounge imploded, she and her followers were ready; screaming at the top of their lungs, they were charging at the pirates on the other side before the debris had even thought of settling. Myra emerged from the dust cloud to meet Zuzack's horribly disfigured face. The two huge beings crashed together and began pounding on each other as all around them people died, smoke and dust billowed, and medical androids milled around like lost souls. Zuzack and Myra had long since lost their weapons; they fought each other with fingers, teeth, and determination, in a colossal wrestling match of unprecedented viciousness. Myra shoved her fingers towards Zuzack's eye sockets, even as he bit off a huge chunk of her ear.

Myra felt her right side tingle and go numb as a stun beam from one of the guard androids caught her a glancing blow. She fell to the deck, her former Captain on top of her—just like the old days. In a supreme effort of will, she managed to push him away and spun around, looking for a weapon of any kind to use against Zuzack. She noticed a dropped blaster and crawled toward it as best she could, sensing Zuzack close behind.

She'd only been brushed by the stun beam, so the effect had largely dissipated by the time she reached the weapon and spun around, squeezing the trigger, to no avail; the charge was dry. She cursed and hurled it at Zuzack, who was no more than a few meters away, then turned and dove into the thick pall of smoke behind her. A few steps brought her to a clear corridor, and she raced down it, followed by the sounds of pursuit and screams of rage from Zuzack.

For a little while, she believed that she might make her getaway—until she caught sight of something hurtling toward her from the corner of her eye. The next thing she knew, she was laid out on her back on the filthy deck, looking up at Lieutenant Grotech, who flashed her a chilling smile while wielding the firewhip in his hands with consummate skill. Somehow, she found the strength to lift her head, and saw that Grotech was gleefully slicing sections off her legs with the whip; he'd already gotten up to her knees. That's when he flipped a switch on the firewhip and let her feel the pain. The sounds of the mutineers around her throwing down their weapons and appealing for mercy was drowned out by her screams, which were driven more from the horror of what awaited her than from the exquisite agony Grotech was visiting upon her.

"Grotech! Round them up and have Zaxor's team secure the rest of the ship, and tell Hughes to get me a damage assessment ASAP!" Zuzack shouted. "And where *is* Mr. Hughes?" he demanded. He kicked a detached head on the floor aside, spraying blood on anyone who stood in the way.

"Here, my Captain, I'm right here."

"Where have you been? I told you to get Alexa and her friends to help us, and I didn't see you or them anywhere during the battle! Where were you, and where is my beloved little girl?"

Hughes looked dumbfounded as he tried to explain, "Um, Captain, I must regretfully inform you that Alexa and six of her friends must have joined Myra and the mutineers, because when we arrived they attacked us, killing eight of my men…well, and a few of my tramps, but who's counting?"

Zuzack grabbed Hughes by his neck and thrust him into a bulkhead; Hughes gasped for air, pawing at Zuzack's enormous muscular arm. "My princess was about to join up with the Clan!" Zuzack roared. "She would never revolt against her future family! Never!"

"I swear. I swear on the Holy Gull!" Hughes choked out. "I swear it to be true, ask any of my men!"

Eyes wide with rage, Zuzack tossed Hughes aside like a rag doll; the rat-like transgenic crashed to the deck, hands clutched to his throat as he shot a hateful glare at Zuzack's backside. Zuzack approached Hughes' surviving squad, who were, to a man, too afraid to meet his gaze.

"*Where is she?*" he hissed.

Hughes stood, regaining some of his courage. "Captain, she is in her quarters with the other mutineers we captured."

Without a word, Zuzack stalked down the corridors, trailed by Hughes, until he reached the Women's Quarter and swept into Alexa's suite. He found his adoptive daughter and her friends bound and gagged on the deck in the living area, guarded by three Tilter dogs. As the dogs paced around them, hissing and slavering, he looked around and noticed that there were a number of backpacks and bags stacked neatly against a bulkhead. Two other pirates stood near the galley, emptying bottles of wine into their gullets.

Alexa tried to catch Zuzack's eye, but he studiously ignored her. After assessing the scene, and then glaring at the women for a long while, he reached down and tore off Alexa's gag, his face a mask of anger.

Alexa shouted, "Whatever that rat bastard Hughes told you, he's lying!"

"Shut your hole, traitor!" the brave Hughes shrieked from behind Zuzack's back.

"We were attacked and were fighting off the mutineers down the corridor when this idiot attacked us from behind! He should have assisted us, but NO! We had no choice but to defend ourselves!"

"That's as may be, but why were you and your lovelies packed for a long journey?" Hughes sneered, glancing at the luggage bags stacked against the bulkhead.

Zuzack looked at Alexa, wrinkling his forehead, waiting for an answer.

"Standard procedure, you dumb shit!" Nina screamed as she managed to shrug off her gag. A medical andy was tending to the stump of her left arm, as she sobbed in pain and shock.

"No standard procedure of ours," Hughes pointed out.

"We thought we were under attack by a CPH ship and that they'd managed to penetrate the *Bitch*," Alexa explained in a cold voice. "As you well know, whenever something like that happens, everyone goes for their important loot, in case we have to abandon ship. Dumbass." She glared at Hughes. "We've always done it that way and always will."

Hughes was about to make another remark when Zuzack raised his hand, gesturing for Hughes to be silent. He looked around the room and back down at Alexa's friends, who were all, except for Alexa, avoiding his gaze. He saw that Nina was casting Alexa an odd look; to his surprise, Alexa answered it with a quick glance.

Zuzack snorted. "You told me you wanted to be part of the Clan, you did. You made me believe in you." He stalked over to the computer console and snapped on a monitor. He pushed a few buttons, and the firefight in the hallway displayed on the monitor. He peered closely, then rewound it and watched it again. When he was done, Zuzack looked up, confused, and glanced at Hughes. "Have the Doctor heal them at once, and make sure they are clean and fresh. If anyone touches any of them, especially Alexa, I will skin that person alive. Do you understand, Mr. Hughes?"

Hughes look as if he had been betrayed, but his submissive bow quickly his facial expression.

"Make sure they are all in perfect health, as we do with all our slaves before we sell them," Zuzack pronounced.

Hughes raised his head, his eyes shining, as Alexa and Nina shouted out their protests. "You can't, Father!" Alexa shouted, her voice trembling.

Zuzack took a shiny new slave collar out of his pocket and leaned down towards Alexa, fastening it securely around her neck. "You were never my daughter, Alexa, just a fuck-toy. And now I'm tired of your lies. Hughes, take them down to the infirmary and have them repaired at once, especially Nina."

"But Captain, we have hundreds of injured brothers and sisters who were loyal to you, and..."

"Indeed we do, but we'll make no money off them, now will we?" Zuzack jabbed a finger at Hughes, then toward the bound women. Hughes nodded sharply, as the Captain turned to one of his combat androids and ordered it to follow Hughes and make sure nothing happened to the prisoners.

SEVENTEEN

ALEC Hornet woke up wondering where the hell he was. Rubbing the sleep from his eyes, he looked over the large, messy bed, which was currently inhabited by two naked sleeping beauties in addition to himself. Both young women were blondes; one of them was clearly an Oman, like himself, while the other—a lanky orange-furred minx with six breasts—belonged to no species he was familiar with. He rubbed his throbbing forehead as he tried to remember what, exactly, had happened the night before. He peered around the luxurious suite he found himself in, and noticed several different styles of bottles and canisters clustered on a nearby table, and several others on the floor. He shook his head, and was startled when a loud buzz came from the direction of the door.

Alec pulled himself up from the bed, removing a thin pink blanket from one of the blondes, who made a murmuring sound as she turn over and went back to sleep. The bell kept ringing. He moved towards it, attempting to conceal his private parts, and that's when he noticed the color of the blanket. He lost his concentration and stumbled on the end of the blanket, falling hard.

As he got back to his feet, a complaining voice from behind him made him forget about the annoying doorbell, and when he looked he saw a strange and very ugly creature lying on the floor, snoring and scratching itself. The sight brought Alec fully awake, and he looked at the thing in horror; then he shook his head and muttered, "No way in hell. I wasn't that wasted."

The door buzzer reminded him of why he was awake, and he finished wrapping the pink blanket around him. Before he could get there, though, the door crashed opened and in marched Nikko Behl, former Captain on the liner *Bright Star* and, for the last two months, Alec's personal flight instructor. He was grinning widely, and charged into the suite like a tornado.

"Wake up, all you tramps, wake up and get out!" There were some languid motions and complaining voices as the inhabitants of the room dragged themselves awake, too slowly for Behl's liking. "I said wake up, or I'll have you all keelhauled!" Behl shouted, sending a well-aimed kick at the pudgy being on the floor. He snatched up a couch pillow from the sofa and tossed it at the protesting blondes. By then, the alien on the floor had come to, and had begun a long, hard journey on its hands and knees towards the door, mumbling something in a language Alec didn't know. It left what appeared to be its clothing behind; instead going for an odd-looking bag with canisters attached to the sides.

The two blondes leaned on each other as they yawned and grabbed their clothes, if indeed that was what you could call the gauzy strips they donned. Once they were more or less dressed, they toddled over to Alec and began kissing and caressing him. At that point the diminutive alien, who looked something like a cross between a meerkat and an aardvark, cleared its throat and rumbled, "Stop it, girls, he only paid for the one night. Now help old Pulp to her old feet, and let's be gone." When they did, Pulp walked over to Alec and grinned, then reached up and pinched his cheek. She said in a slurred voice, "Listen, kiddo, if you want more, just let us know. You know where to find us." Then she stumbled toward her blonde charges, who ended up having to carry Pulp between them as they finally exited.

Behl tapped a button on the wall, and a large section of said wall folded up into the ceiling, revealing a duraplast window that opened onto the star-speckled darkness of deep space. Alec started in surprise when a sleek little speeder passed the window, just a wee bit too close for comfort. Snugging the pink blanket around his loins, he stepped over to the window and looked out. Near-space was alive with hundreds, perhaps thousands of spacecraft, ranging from one-man speeders to battlecruisers the size of cities. Most were docked to the various rings of a massive space station, with numerous others in the process of arriving or departing. Orbiting the giant space station were several smaller structures of various types and sizes. There was no obvious order, but the traffic appeared to be moving along just fine.

"Nice view, isn't it?" Behl asked, beaming at the scenario in front of them. "New Frontier is one of the larger outposts in the Neutral Zone between Florencia and Nastasturus. I think it belongs to both the Merchants *and* the Traders. God only knows who all those little private stations belong to."

"I don't remember too much," Alec admitted, rubbing his head in a vain effort to diminish a splitting headache.

Behl clapped him on the back, causing him to wince. "Well, whatever you took with your joygirls there, it'll soon dissipate and your memory will come back. Here, have some of this." Behl handed Alec a small pen-syringe.

Alec dialed up a dose and jabbed it into his left bicep. A second later, his eyes opened wide as what felt like a bolt of lightning flashed through him. He trembled for a long moment and then, muttering, "Never, ever again," he tottered toward the head, ignoring Behl's laughter.

When Alec returned, freshly shaven and still damp from his shower, he felt almost human again. He saw a small bundle of clothing lying on the bed, and looked at Behl questioningly.

"General, sir," Behl said innocently, "I took the liberty and selected some clothing from your duffle. We need to hurry, because there's something I'd like to show you." As Alec started to get dressed, Behl asked expectantly, "Do you still want to go forward with the plan?"

"Of course. We'll stay our course and move on, assuming you're still with me."

"No worries on that point, lad. I'm in debt to you. You saved my life, you gave me my dignity back, and on top of that you awarded me with more money that I ever dreamed of having—when you didn't have to. No one has risked themselves for me for a very long time." Behl fell silent, his eyes watering.

Must bring back some bad old memories, Alec thought. Aloud, he said, "Well, sir, let's move on once we've had something to eat. I'm starving."

"No surprise there."

Alec and Behl walked down the wide, lush corridor and came out on a large observation platform five floors up from the first level. The bustling station spread out before them, packed with merchants, traders, and passersby conducting business in the various shops and offices scattered throughout the promenade. When Alec looked up, he could count at least another ten levels above. After contemplating the sight for a few moments, they moved on and caught an elevator down to the main level, where all the restaurants and food courts were located. Large expanses of transparent duraplast separated the businesses, revealing the traffic outside the station. As they passed one window, they noticed a mid-sized cargo ship docking at the main ring of the large station, which appeared to be several dozen kilometers away at least. Behl stepped up to the window and gestured Alec to join him. When he got there, Behl pointed out a beautiful, slim ship, its design ultramodern and its hull gleaming dully in the reddened light of the local primary. "Ah, there she is. See her?"

"Yessir. What type of class is she?" Alec asked.

"Medium frigate class, Marengan design. She's a cargo ship, more or less."

"She looks small for a cargo ship."

"Sure she's small, but she's also very fast, and she's made for transporting exotic materials. At least one of the cargo bays is designed to hold radioactives of the highest ratings. That alone can make a grand profit."

"What about the crew?"

"Twenty to fifty, depending on what you want to transport, but we can easily bunk five hundred hired troops in the holds."

Alec was silent for a moment; and then he asked, "Weapons?"

"Already fitted with some of the best that I know of. However, we can always improve her defenses and weapons at any neutral port that has one or more arms dealers in residence."

Alec looked out at the beautiful ship and said eagerly, "Let's go make a deal."

"Wait, lad. We can't operate her alone. We need a crew."

"Then we'll find one. Surely there'll be some spacers hanging around the station at loose ends, looking for their next berths."

Behl placed his hand on Alec's arm and said, "I know you want to save your friends, lad, and that shows me what a gallant individual you are. But finding a reliable crew qualified to operate that ship *and* willing to go a-hunting for one of the universe's most feared pirates will be well-nigh impossible. And to top it off, finding this pirate will be just about impossible too, as far as I can see."

"Finding him will be the easiest part, I think. I'll admit, though, the crew might be a minor challenge."

"And how will you find him, son? He could be a million light years away or right beside us, for all we know; these pirates can disguise their ships quicker than a chameleon can change colors."

Alec smiled tightly. "Captain, I have something of his, and he will search for me until he finds me." He looked towards the frigate, and his smile relaxed into genuine pleasure. "I know of some people who would gladly join us; all we need is, what, thirty people for the operations crew until we get there?"

"Uh huh. And where is this place, if I may ask?"

"On a mining moon...I think."

"Oh, a mining moon, you *think*. And who does this little moon belong to?"

"Florencia," Alec said tersely. "Now let's check out the ship."

Behl rolled his eyes. "Let me guess: more advice from that little voice inside your head?"

Alec ignored Behl's expression as he muttered, "Yeah, I think so." He peered out at the enormous space station in the distance and all the traffic swarming around it, and abruptly pointed at a cluster of bright motes racing around one of the station's rings. Behl smiled and leaned closer to watch the impromptu race; they could barely see the little speeders at this distance. "How big is this station?" Alec asked, gesturing with his arms towards the station they were on.

"Oh, not so big. It can hold maybe fifty thousand people."

"That's all?"

"Well, yes, this one's mostly just a hotel and casino."

"What about the big one?"

"New Frontier 16? Hard to tell. My guess is in the neighborhood of ten million."

"How can they *feed* all those people?"

Behl looked around for something and then said, while pointing his finger, "You see there? Towards the top, where the large deflector shield is? It's a greenhouse."

"It's huge."

"That it is, and it makes the station somewhat self-sustaining. But I'm sure they bring in kilotons of supplies every day," replied Behl pedantically. "The station functions similarly to some of the larger Ambassador-class cruisers."

"Before now, I'd never heard of trading stations owned and operated by both the Federated Merchants and the Commercial Traders working together," Alec muttered.

"So much for your education," Behl muttered back. He continued, "General, sir, this far out in neutral space they always work together—anything to earn some extra credits. It wouldn't make any sense to compete against each other out here. Besides, it also increases their own safety against the two large federations, the pirates, or the occasional loony who considers himself a warlord. Look over there...and there. See what I mean?" Behl pointed. Alec made out several military frigates and a few destroyers flying in formation, some with Merchant markings and some with Trader markings. He nodded.

The Captain clapped Alec on the shoulder. "Well, let's go and find us a crew."

"Let's find the ship first," Alec replied.

"We've had this discussion before. First we get a crew, and then a ship. Maybe you get the one we've been looking at, maybe you don't. But if you buy a ship and the word gets out that you don't have any crew, just imagine how much you have to pay for their contracts."

"I know, but let's at least make a down payment. I don't want to miss the opportunity to buy that beautiful ship you pointed out earlier."

"You're not going to give in on this one, are you?" Behl sounded helpless, even as he smiled.

"No sir, I'm not."

They hustled through hallways and corridors of the hotel/casino—which Alec finally remembered was called Star-Dice—toward the docking bay. Alec seemed as giddy as a child, and Behl had some trouble keeping up. So did their erstwhile pursuer, who first made his presence evident about halfway along. "Mr. Horn, Mr. Horn, please wait!" The shouts came from a small person with huge ears, a short trunk that waggled back and forth, and what seemed like a very friendly smile that more or less covered half his face. "Mr. Horn, please forgive me." The little man caught his breath between the words as Alec and Behl stopped and waited for him to catch up.

"Yes, um...Mr. Tota, right? How can I help you?" Alec asked dubiously.

Tota bowed his head all the way to the ground, his triple chins wobbling as he chuckled. He was absolutely certain that the young Oman was of the Royal Class or at least a member of a high-ranking clan, and that the older man next to him was his tutor and mentor, educating the young prince for the future—and that both of them were traveling under assumed identities.

The enormous wealth the young prince had deposited to both Merchant and Trader accounts made him perhaps the wealthiest young prince Tota had ever met. Tota had nearly soaked his pants and fainted when he saw the credit reports from the Merchants and Traders, both of which had sent representatives to Tota, asking him to dig up more information on this "secret" prince. Needless to say, Tota had sold bits and pieces of information to both organizations for a minor fortune, educating them about more things regarding Mr. Horn than Mr. Horn himself knew. Some of them were even true.

For example, the prince had lost a fortune the day before in one of Tota's casinos, and insisted on paying not only for his room and food but for the pleasure servants as well, though Tota would have happily given those free to any big spender, as any casino owner would. Landing a "killer whale" like this fellow appeared to be would be a dream come true, especially for Tota, because if he could only get the young master to spend enough of his fortune, he might be able to pay off his last loan to his creditors. *They always pay in cash for these types of adventures, so there are no traces left for their future princesses to follow, getting the young adventurous prince in trouble,* thought Tota happily. Aloud he said obsequiously, "Thank you, young sir, for your time! I have been asked to convey a message... two, actually. The local Key Administrators of both the Federated Merchants and Commercial Traders have requested an audience with His Highness."

"His Highness who?" young "Horn" asked, his face studiously blank.

Tota realized his mistake, and shielded his mouth. Flexing his long, fuzzy eyebrows (they looked like caterpillars who couldn't decide whether to fuck or fight), Tota whispered, "I mean you, Mr. Horn sir." He winked.

"I see." Horn looked at him speculatively for a long moment, then said abruptly, "Mr. Tota, have you heard any news of a missing cruise liner called the *Bright Star*? Disappeared three or four standard months ago."

"No, nothing," replied Tota with a concerned expression, fearing what was coming next.

"You're absolutely sure you haven't heard anything?" Horn demanded. "Nothing about any pirate activity, or anything similar?"

"Of course I have not, sir." Tota flapped his large ears nervously as he shook his head. "No, no, nothing, no, you must not speak of piracy around here, bad karma brings bad business. Perhaps later we will discuss it with the police...yes, that's what we must do." Tota flexed his ears back and smiled; and before Horn or Behl had any chance to comment, Tota burst out, "They are sending their Key Administrators over right away, and they insist on seeing you at once! You must not keep them waiting!"

Behl, who had heretofore remained silent, stepped in. "Are you telling us what to do, you babbling little ear-flapping bastard?"

"Oh no, no, no, no. I would never do that, but sir! No! My deepest and most sincere apologies," cried Tota, as he banged his forehead on the floor in another attempt at a deep bow. "It is just highly unusual, good sir, and they are most powerful and are not used to being kept waiting, and oh, both of them being here will most certainly attract a lot of unnecessary attention..." Tota ran down as he looked around at the crowd and took a deep breath. "I felt it was my duty to you, my worthy customers, to warn you. Going against the advice or wishes of any Key Administrator will definitely put you on the map, so to speak."

Horn looked at Behl, and both of them turned to Tota as Horn pronounced, "Lead the way, honorable Tota, and we shall soon have both Key Administrators off your back."

As the little elephantoid took up point and escorted them, Alec noticed for the first time that they were being trailed by several security guards. He glanced at Behl, who whispered, "I see them." Alec nodded and directed his gaze forward, ignoring the guards.

Tota took it upon himself to be their personal tour guide. He pointed at everything and everywhere as they passed, and Alec and Behl received all types of information. The only problem was that Tota tended to point at one thing while he talked about something else. After a while Alec stopped looking and listening, since it only made him dizzy and confused.

"...And I hope you enjoyed my ladies, I mean, Lady Pulp and the lovelies who were at your service last night. Should you require more of that type of service, never hesitate to ask, for my middle name is 'Customer Service.' Well, my original middle name was Aspha, that name having been given to me at birth by my mother's side of the family, but I had it changed in a court of law for business reasons..."

It was with great relief that Alec and Behl finally entered Mr. Tota's office, where two delegations consisting of six people each were anxiously waiting for them. As they entered, a tall, thin omanoid wearing a severe black suit stepped forward, ignoring the glare of the stumpy being who led the other delegation. "I am Tobbis, local Key Administrator for the Federated Merchants. I would like to introduce—"

Before he was allowed to finish, the squat badgerish woman heading the other delegation pushed forward and said bluntly, "And I am Zala Kend'ss, Key Administrator of the Commercial Traders. We are here to talk." Her outfit was similar to Tobbis'. Despite her fierce countenance and direct manner, she smiled—Alec supposed it could be interpreted as a smile—and bowed deeply.

In the ensuing pleasantries, both Administrators proved to be humble and diplomatic; true professionals, as one might expect in such an important, if backwater, facility. Once the introductions were out of the way, though, they immediately began bombarding Alec with questions. Fortunately Tota, who apparently saw an opportunity to curry some favor with Alec, quickly intervened, earning disapproving stares from the Administrators and their staffs. "My two very distinguished and important friends, I beg you not to unduly pressure our young Mr. Horn, who is perhaps the most important guest ever to have stepped aboard the Star-Dice, if you know what I mean." Again Tota waggled his brows and attempted to wink unsuccessfully, flapping his ears all the while. It was an amusing display.

Alec took the opportunity to walk over to Tota's exceptionally large desk and perch on the edge, crossing his legs and regarding the mismatched Administrators calmly. Using the most patrician tone he could manage—and being the heir of the Hornet clan, that was something to behold—he said formally, "So, Sir and Lady, what is so urgent that it took you away from your duties simply to meet me? I have some delicate business to take care of today, and I must be about it quickly lest it slip through my fingers."

Zala tilted her head to the side and said quietly, "Very well, then, down to business. Allow me to ensure that our conversation is not being monitored or recorded, save by us. Furthermore, I would put a halt to local trade on our end, so that you would not lose your lovely ship." She tapped the keys of her wrist-comp very swiftly.

Meanwhile, Tobbis did the same. "Do not worry," the elegant man said, "Standard procedure." A second later, he said, "There, now. All is secure, and all trades or barter have ceased, at least in the Merchants sectors of this facility."

"And in the Traders sectors as well," said Zala.

Lifting an eyebrow, Alec said, "Why thank you, but that doesn't guarantee me anything, now does it?" He tapped his fingers on the edge of the desk, as the two Key Administrators looked at each in puzzlement.

"The Traders will be sure to compensate you for whatever possible loss you may incur," Zala said.

"As will the Merchants," Tobbis was quick to put in.

Alec nonchalantly waved his hand for them to stop, playing his role of young fop for everything it was worth. "Very well. So what do you want? We start with you." Alec nodded his head towards Zala.

She bowed again. "I wish to welcome you to New Frontier on behalf of the Commercial Traders, good sir, and wish merely to get to know you better, so that we may more efficiently handle your future affairs."

"Very nicely said. I take it that you are here for the same reasons, Mr. Tobbis?" Without waiting for Tobbis to reply, Alec said smoothly, "Thank you very much to both of you for extending us—that is, me—this honor," Alec remarked. He figured it didn't hurt any to "accidentally" toss in the Royal pronoun; after all, he did belong to a Royal clan.

Zala blinked and said, "Sir, you have made some astonishing trades in the last 24 hours, and as a result you have deposited an enormous fortune in each of our local banks. We would like..."

She fell silent, glancing at Tobbis in frank disbelief. Alec had fished a long, silvery metallic object from his coat pocket and was playing with it idly, passing it through his fingers as it were some magician's toy, occasionally letting it pop into the air before snatching it back and beginning again. Tobbis let out a soft moan, even as Zala gasped; and Tota stared wide-eyed and soaked his pants.

Alec affixed a stern look and his face, trying not to laugh, and glared at Tota in mock-disgust. Tota didn't notice the expression and wouldn't have cared if he had; his eyes saw nothing but the silvery object in Alec's hand, which could have purchased his entire station with a substantial amount of change left over.

"Is that... tritonium silver?" wondered Tobbis in a very soft voice.

"Oh, this?" said Alec, sound as innocent as a small child. "Something I found a little while back." He tossed the metallic rod to Tobbis, who caught it nimbly and placed it against a sensor on his wrist-comp. He studied the small display intently, and after a long moment, a strange bubbling sound emerged from his throat. Scowling, Zala approached Tobbis and tugged at his forearm, trying to get him to show her the display.

"No need for that," Alec said loudly. "Here's one for you to inspect." He threw one to Zala, who caught it and could only stare at it for a long moment before she shook herself and pressed it against her own computer's assay sensor. "You want to look at one too, Tota?" Alec sent a third bar flying across through the room. Tota caught it, looked at it, and unceremoniously passed out.

A few minutes later, Alec asked the room at large, "Satisfied?"

"It's real," answered Tobbis in an awed voice. "I...I'm not sure I'm willing to give it back. May I inquire where you got this fr..."

Alec cut him off. "Does it really matter?"

"Certainly not," Zala said decisively. She stepped over to the desk and handed the precious rod back to Alec reverently; Tobbis returned his a moment later. Before Tobbis had a chance to speak, Zala declared, "I believe I speak for the both of us, sir. You will have anything you need, provide it is within our grasp and you can pay for it...which, obviously, you can." Tobbis nodded his head in consent.

"My aide here," Alec made a sweeping gesture towards Behl, "will give you a list of our needs shortly, but for now I would like to go over your list of local spacers for hire."

Tobbis gaped. "Mr., um, Horn, that would be most difficult. There are rumors of war between the two federations, and most freelancers have either been drafted or enticed into service with huge salaries and bonuses. Finding a full crew of spacers would be nearly impossible, and those available would want exorbitant pay."

Zala nodded. "We have over a hundred vessels stranded in local space due to lack of key personnel."

"And what of available properties of, shall we say, a sentient nature? I'm sure many such are available here."

"Let us call a spade a spade, shall we?" Zala said icily. "You speak of slaves. We have perhaps thirty thousand on hand, and I have no idea whether any will fit your particular needs. However, we are expecting a shipment of several thousand chattel soon; perhaps we might be able to find something suitable. Both of us will ensure you are among the first to make a selection, prior to the auction. How many space-qualified personnel do you require?"

Alec glanced at Nikko Behl. "Thirty to fifty, I suspect."

"It is possible we have them. We will have to investigate." She gestured to one of her assistants, who stood in the background, staring at Alec in disbelief. The assistant blinked and spoke quietly into his wristcomp.

"You realize that it's not common for us to engage in the slave trade," Tobbis said smoothly, "but we do have a few independent brokers we contract with. Let me investigate the matter further." He snapped his fingers imperiously at one of his own assistants, who immediately went to work, and added, "Zala, what do you say we work closely on this one? It appears that young Mr. Horn intends to work us against each other."

Alec was surprised by Tobbis' frank statement (he was right, of course) and by the consenting gesture from Zala. Neither seemed to care whether or not Alec had been offended; they were all business now.

Zala looked up and said, just as Tobbis was opening his mouth, "How do you intend to pay, Mr. Horn? We require payment before delivery."

Alec pointed at the two silvery bars as Behl retrieved the third, which was still clutched by the unconscious Tota. Behl had to pry it out of the little man's hands; Tota protested weakly but didn't come to.

Zala and Tobbis both had the grace to look embarrassed as Alec handed over the bars. The amount would purchase or hire the spacers Alec needed thousands of times over. He noted their expressions and said, "Hey, I'm just kidding. Take what you need to get my crew, and then deposit the rest into my accounts. And take a hefty cut for yourselves along the way."

Zala and Tobbis brightened as they tucked the tritonium silver away and then attacked their wristcomps. A moment later, Alec glanced at his own to confirm the deposits, and smiled when he saw the new balances. He could practically buy his own planet now...or at least a decent-sized moon. "Ah, I so love doing business," he said breezily. "Now, shall we have lunch?"

Alec walked out of Tota's office without waiting for anyone's reply, followed close by Behl, who took up position as a bodyguard.

EIGHTEEN

THE face in the mirror was horribly mutilated. A tear trickled down as he watched, and when he blinked, his tears squirted straight out onto the mirror. His tear ducts had been either permanently damaged, or were simply being amazingly slow to heal. The Doctor couldn't yet say.

Stupid bloody quack. Should've had her shot years ago.

Zuzack started at his mockery of a face, feeling very sorry for himself. First this horror, and then the mutiny that had torn his crew and his ship apart. And Alexa's apparent betrayal...he might never recover from that. His slough of self-pity was disturbed by the soft ping of a signal in the next room, alerting him of a visitor. The Captain quickly composed himself, blotting the tears with his forearm and cursing at the prickle of the rough fabric.

That rat bastard Hughes was waiting nervously for him when he opened the door. The transgenic's worn clothing was stained with blood, and he'd been under the Doctor's tender care since Zuzack had last seen him. A complex hook had replaced his left hand, and a metallic plate was bolted onto one temple. He handed Zuzack a large black coat covered with white lines and patterns in a complex design. Zuzack nodded and put on the coat, patting the concealed pockets that contained several different types of knives, pistols, and a few small grenades. He stepped out of his quarters, letting the hatch sigh shut behind him.

Besides Mr. Hughes, several officers and an honor guard awaited him outside. All were heavily armed, and they took up escort position as Zuzack headed down the corridor toward the main docking bay.

The post-mutiny clean-up was still ongoing. Slaves and pirates alike were busily scrubbing the corridors clean of blood and filth, and several side corridors they passed were piled high with stinking corpses. Everyone did their work in silence, and there was an undercurrent of nervous tension running throughout the ship.

Zuzack said roughly, "Hughes, you and Grotech had best have this mess cleaned up by the time I get back."

"Aye aye, captain," the rat-man said meekly.

"How many were lost to the mutiny?"

"Too many, sir. We have fewer than eight hundred loyal crew still standing..."

Grotech, who had just joined them, cut in, "...and half of them are injured. Doc tells me most of them will survive. If we can send some of them to one of the private hospital stations, then most of them should be back in a week or two."

"Do it," ordered Zuzack. "Spare no expense."

Hughes licked his lips with his damaged tongue and said, "Sir, what about the surviving mutineers? You haven't told us what you're planning to do with them."

Zuzack stopped, causing the officers marching behind him to stack up and collide. Everyone looked at him curiously as he turned toward them, a brutal glint in his eye. "We have lost a great deal on this trip," he growled, "even though we still have most of the spoil left, as well as the ships we took." He paused, glancing at his reflection in a nearby port, and took a deep breath. "Killing them would bring me great satisfaction, make no mistake about that!"

he roared. "However," he said more gently, "it would give me *more* pleasure to confiscate their property and sell the traitors on the open market, so we can earn some credits off them. We will soon meet with the Gormé; they always pay the best prices."

Hughes said happily, "So we get rid of them for good, while splitting more loot and earning more money. Genius!"

Zuzack eyed him sourly. "Yes, all the spoil from this campaign will be split among the loyal crew... after my cut, of course."

Everyone cheered Zuzack, and then Grotech asked quietly, "Cap'n, about the cruise liner and the cargo ship. Will they be sold too?"

"Yes, Grotech, we'll sell everything we don't need."

"But that cargo ship could be a valuable asset for us. We could use it to carry our spoil, sir."

"No, Grotech, we can't."

"How is that, sir?" Hughes asked.

Zuzack replied, "We won't need it. Just sell it and all its cargo; it will bring in a fortune. So will the liner, considering that it contains well over eight thousand passengers in cryo-suspension."

The Doc looked puzzled and said, "But, Captain..."

Zuzack glanced at her, smiling thinly. "I assure you, sawbones, we will not need any ship to store our extra spoil in, at least not for a while."

"Why?" she asked.

"Because we are going hunting," answered Zuzack as he began walking away, leaving his fellow pirates standing behind him with puzzled faces. They quickly gathered themselves, realizing that the Captain intended to search for the Oman who had escaped and mutilated him.

"Captain, wait!" shouted Grotech. He loped up to Zuzack, who only began walking faster. "Captain, I implore you to listen to reason. Put a price on the Oman brat's head, but please, don't let him ruin our enterprise."

"I agree, Captain," Doc said breathlessly, as she caught up to them. "With all due respect, please listen to Grotech, sir, if you would. It would be dangerous in the extreme for us to pursue this personal vendetta. I assure you, I know how you feel, and I very much sympathize with you. But it's far too risky, sir, and I doubt the crew will have any of it. There are barely enough of us left to handle the *Bitch* and the prize ships."

Zuzack halted again and looked at her; she ducked her head, but he didn't seem angry, just thoughtful. He shifted his gaze to the stained deck, rubbing his scarified chin thoughtfully. "You don't understand. This isn't about revenge, though I will certainly have that when we find him. What the little Oman took from me is worth more than anything I know of in the universe—and I'm not referring to my face. I mean to get it all back."

Hughes and the other escorts joined them, and to a man, their puzzled attention was on their Captain. He looked up abruptly and said, "Trust me for now, shipmates. You will not lose any credits in this. In fact, you may take my entire share for this run and split it among yourselves and the loyal crew. But there is a catch: for that, you must pledge several more years of contracted service. And don't you worry—should we run across more spoil, then believe you me, we shall take it."

One by one the officers walked up to Zuzack and grabbed hold of his huge right arm, swearing their unswerving loyalty for three more years.

"No, not three. Five more Galactic years," Zuzack said, as he looked each of them in the eye, one by one. All nodded their acquiescence. "Very good, then we have an accord. Hughes and Grotech, make the proper entry in the ship's log and make sure everyone signs off on it. And you, Doctor: I want you to ensure that the best-quality slaves who still live are in an excellent shape before we take them to the traders. They must not be soiled or damaged in any way. Anyone who abuses the cargo before we auction them off, and I mean anyone, will be sold to the Gormé. You, Hughes, find the best auction house in these parts, but leave the Gormé traders to me."

"May I inquire which of the cargo will be sold to the Gormé?" Hughes asked superciliously.

"I will make that decision when we get down to the cargo holds."

Hughes cleared his throat. "You are aware that we can't sell to them any individual who has been frozen for space travel, or who has too many stimmed or cloned replacement parts. The Gormé traders won't buy anything unless it's fresh."

Zuzack walked into a large elevator, cursing as he kicked aside half a corpse that was blocking the door.

"Since when won't they buy frozen food?" muttered Zuzack, as he and his men crowded into the lift.

Hughes said, "I'm not sure, sire but in this sector they only buy fresh. Even if a corpsicle has been revived successfully, they won't buy it if there's evidence the product has been in a frozen state in the past year or so. Might I suggest we find a reputable independent trader for the passengers in cryo-suspension?"

The elevator door opened and Zuzack stalked out, followed by the others. "Very well. Then we will only offer them the ones from the VIP section."

"Does that include, um, your daughter?" Doc asked, immediately biting her tongue when she saw Zuzack's expression.

"She is not my daughter and has never been, for all I treated her like one. I trained her in the ways of the clan, prepared her for the hardships in life, and educated her...and this is how she repays me." He glared at the Doctor. "Put her and her sluttish friend Nina up for sale to the Gormé."

"I wouldn't do that," Doc said quickly. "They're too skinny to make much of a meal for those monsters, so you'd be better off selling them as chattel. Nina for one would make a fine concubine. After all, she comes from a system where the art of seduction is a part of their nature, and she could be pitched as an outstanding pleasure slave, bringing us a lot of credits."

Zuzack thought for a moment, then said decisively, "Very well, sell Nina as a bed slut, but Alexa still goes to a Gormé trader..." He looked thoughtful again, then abruptly changed his mind. "No, the Gormé are too good for her. I have a better idea."

Doc shook her head, as Hughes licked his lips and smiled.

THE *little girl ran for her life. No more than ten years old, she was dressed in the rags of a nightdress, her wet hair swinging wildly in front of her face and blurring her vision. Her brothers and sisters were chasing her, laughing cruelly, murder in their eyes.*

She was hiding inside a closet, trembling and trying to not be heard as she cried. She didn't understand why everyone she loved hated her; and when the closet door opened, she raised her hands in the air and screamed for her mother to help her. But it was her siblings who stood outside the door waiting for her. She covered herself with her arms in an attempt to protect herself.

A strong arm pulled her up, and she found herself staring into an ugly non-Oman face, a female of some sort by the cast of its features; its grating laughter made the little girl cry even harder, and again she screamed for her mother to help her.

She couldn't see her siblings anymore, but she could hear their laughter in the far distance. She was running for her life again, as some slavering, monstrous creature loped along behind her. She was too afraid to look behind her to see what it was, but she could feel its heavy breathing on the back of her neck.

The little girl tried to run, but her legs wouldn't move.

There were shouts and screams, and something hurt. She woke up and looked into the horrible female face, which whispered threateningly, "Will you obey or not? Now tell me your new name, and what you must say!"

The little girl was sitting in a horrible device with her hands and feet stretched out in front of her, clamped between two awful bars, and she couldn't move. She cried for her mother and father, and tears streamed down her face. When she realized that she couldn't remember her parents' names or what they looked like, she began to cry even harder.

The ugly woman nodded, and another being with a grotesque smile did something unspeakable that made the little girl scream in pain. The ugly woman repeated what she had said before, and again the little girl screamed for help.

Her siblings stood in a circle and pointed down at her as they laughed and kicked. The smiling man used a thin cane on the soles of the little girl's bare and vulnerable feet, causing her unbearable anguish. At each lash, the little girl screamed out in horror and pain for her mother to help her, and her voice became ragged and started to fail, even as her siblings' laughter increased.

There was more macabre laughter, and then everything turned black.

―――――oOo―――――

ALEXA woke up screaming for her mother, her feet a throbbing mass of pain. As her vision cleared, she saw the cane from her nightmare, rising and falling, repeatedly lashing down on her tender soles. She was stuck in a slave block much like the one her knight in shining armor had suffered through for those five weeks. She stared in disbelief at the torture device; she couldn't see her hands and feet, but she knew that her giggling tormentor could, and could do just about anything to her that he wanted. She screamed and screamed—not from the pain, she could handle that, but from an outraged sense of injustice, and from the fate she knew she would soon suffer.

Hughes leaned over her as closely as he dared. "Wake up, little tramp. It's time to get up."

He chortled when he saw Alexa's expression, and laughed harder as he stepped back and lashed her feet again. It hurt like nothing had hurt since—

She pushed that thought away and bit down hard on her lower lip, doing everything she could to keep from screaming; but after a few hard strokes from Hughes, she gave in and began shouting out her pain. Hughes leered sadistically as he kept hitting her, harder and harder, drooling in ecstasy. Hughes was in his element, his personal paradise. It wasn't the torture that fed his delirium, Alexa realized; it was just that he was in control over someone else's destiny. No doubt it was all the sweeter because it was she whom he was controlling, a person who had previously been inviolate.

His next stroke was a little high, striking her on the toes; a half-second later something wet and hard landed on her bare chest. She glanced down, and saw that it was the nail from one of her big toes. The excruciating pain that hit immediately thereafter told her it was from the one on her left foot. Hughes smirked and lifted the cane for his next blow—and was suddenly yanked into the air by the collar of his jacket and tossed across the cargo hold.

"Do you have a death wish, you little shit?" Zuzack roared. "Do you *want* me to skin you alive?"

Hughes struggled to his feet and tossed the cane aside. "Erm, Captain, I was only waking her up. Perhaps I got a bit...overzealous. The transport that will take her away will be arriving in the morning, and..."

"Be silent. If you hadn't been so damned loyal during the mutiny I'd have sold you too, idiot, given all the trouble you've caused lately. Get Doc down here to fix this mess up."

Hughes scurried away, his face a mask of fear.

Zuzack walked up to Alexa with a sad and disappointed expression on his horribly-scarred face. He looked at her injured feet and nodded, then grabbed her hair and jerked her head back, staring at her with emotionless eyes. "So that there are no mistakes between us, I want you to know that you are *not* going to the Gormé. I have something better planned."

Alexa glared at him with defiant contempt and spat, "I'd rather be eaten alive than be your whore. I will welcome death."

That got to him, at least a bit; he looked upset for a moment, then threw his head back and laughed. "Oh, my dear, who said anything about death? You will be eaten all right, fear not; and you will be alive while they do it, but... well, let me say this. As a child, I'm sure you heard tales about the infamous Sun Shadow, otherwise known as the Black Lady? Of course you have; who hasn't? She's infamous for her artistic creations.

"No, no, my dear, I'm not speaking of the old horror stories that parents tell their children to make them eat up their suppers...but believe me, for what it's worth, she *does* really exist, and soon you will meet her. So who said anything about *death*? The Black Lady doesn't waste her property that way." Zuzack laughed at Alexa's puzzled look. "Hell, I might just buy some of her artwork. Now, that's irony for you. I would probably have to pay a hundred times more for you as "art" than she'll buy you for as raw material for her next dinner party...or should I call it 'art class'?" Zuzack guffawed, clutching his stomach as his eyes filled with tears of mirth. He only laughed the harder when they started squirting in all directions out of his damaged tear ducts.

Alexa couldn't ignore the pain caused by her uncomfortable position and the beating, but that didn't stop her from laughing herself at the sight. Immediately, Zuzack stopped laughing, and glared at her with an expression much like that of a wounded dog. Then his features twisted in rage, and he step forward, his hands clutching at her throat.

"Go ahead, *Father!*" Alexa sneered. "I told you the truth about what happened back in that corridor, but as usual you'd rather believe that that little rat Hughes—even though he'd stab you in the back in an instant if he thought he could get away with it. I have nothing left to live for, so go ahead, do your worst."

"If you kill her, we might have another mutiny on our hands," the Doctor warned from behind him, "considering what she's worth."

Zuzack glared at Alexa, his eyes narrowed, and turned to face the Doc and Hughes. He took the cane from Hughes and turned towards Alexa; then, with lightning speed, struck one final, brutal blow on her soles. The cane broke. Alexa emitted a short scream before she passed out.

Zuzack handed what was left of the cane to Hughes, who stared at the fragment of supposedly unbreakable granitewood in disbelief. "You may heal her now, Doctor," the Captain said. "Hughes, my fine little rat bastard, you're coming with me. Oh, and Doctor, don't waste any pain medication on her."

The next time Alexa awoke, it was from a dreamless pit of unconsciousness, and her rude awakening was an electric shock. She jerked her head up and leaned back on one of the crossbeams of the slave block, holding back her tears while trying to get comfortable. She had once promised herself that she would never, ever end up in one of these horrible devices again; but here she was, just ten years after making that commitment to herself. Well, she thought it was ten years; she wasn't sure exactly how long it had been since her siblings had sold her. For months after that, though, she had been stuck in one of these horrible devices, forced to learn several new languages and never given any respite except when she was being "tutored in pleasure techniques"—a euphemism for rape, until she gave up and learned to accept it. And after all that "schooling," she never even got sold. Instead, Zuzack's pirates had attacked her owners, kidnapping her and many others; and for some reason, they decided to keep her, while some of her compatriots were sold again...or suffered worse fates.

She frowned at the thought that according to intergalactic law, she was actually considered stolen merchandise that someone, somewhere, still owned. Thinking about that plunged her into a black pit of depression, and she went deep inside herself for a while. When she came to again, she was whispering, "Hear me! Hear me, my love, save me, please save me!" Oddly enough, she felt better; not good, that was impossible in her situation, but more serene and willing to wait for him, come what may, until he found her again. That newfound love had awakened something inside her that she thought had died, and made her feel hope like she never had before.

Of course, he was just a dream.

NINETEEN

AT that moment, Alexa's dream was enjoying a very exclusive lunch with his new "friends" in a private restaurant on one of the minor New Frontier satellite stations. The entire ceiling of the restaurant consisted of a near-invisible electromagnetic shield; otherwise it was open to space. Alec had received more false smiles from a wider variety of species during this dinner than he had in his entire life before this. After all, the Key Administrators and their associates were all as much politicians as businessmen.

Nikko Behl had refused to dine with them; instead he stood in the background, eyeing the proceedings as he continued to play the bodyguard. As for Tobbis and Zala, both played their roles as the perfect hosts to perfection; and indeed, their actions and conversational tactics were so well-coordinated that they functioned almost like some long-married couple. It was clear that whatever they were, they were used to working very closely. *Wonder how often they've broken their corporate rules for their own personal gain,* Alec thought sardonically.

During their time together so far, Tobbis and Zala had provided Alec with valuable advice about the local trade system, and which traders he should avoid. At first, the latter made Alec somewhat suspicious; but when Zala noticed this, she explained to Alec in a motherly fashion that whatever he traded in, she and her college Tobbis would still get their fair share, as long as the trade was conducted in or near New Frontier. Alec decided not to put too much thought or suspicion into anything they said, because he realized that his limited education in economics only made him more confused after listening to them. Both Zala and Tobbis reminded Alec of his teachers from school; the only difference, of course, being that those instructors were uniformly masters of war. But then again, perhaps the Key Administrators were too, in a way.

The only time Alec was stonewalled was when, near the end of the meal, he enquired about pirate activities in the sector. The smiles dropped away suddenly; Tobbis and Zala began to look uneasy, and after a brief moment of silence both of them realized that lunch had taken up a little too much of their time. In a sudden rush, they excused themselves graciously, and Tobbis said that he hoped to see Alec soon at one of their famous Asteroid games. Alec promised to attend one of the games as soon as he possibly could, and Tobbis, Zala, and their entourages filed out.

Nonplussed, Alec spent a few more minutes on his wine and dessert before tossing aside his napkin and standing up. Gesturing to Behl to follow, he walked to the pay kiosk and discovered that the Administrators had already comped the meal. Shrugging, he and Behl headed toward the shuttle bay, where they caught the express shuttle to New Frontier 16 itself.

As they approached the enormous station, Behl chose that moment to begin going over some points about what they needed to purchase, and when they would meet with the owners of the frigate they had been admiring earlier. Alec didn't listen; he was taken aback by the sheer size of the central station, which he was peering at through the viewport in frank astonishment. From a distance, of course, it looked big—but not as enormous as it seemed now that they were right next to it. When Alec realized its tremendous size, he could do nothing but stare.

The shuttle soon slid into a massive docking bay, and eased itself down onto a docking shelf set aside for VIPs. As they left their seats, Behl looked at Alec and said, "All right, Your Highness, snap out of it. What are your plans now?"

Alec was at first taken a bit aback by the comment; then he noticed Behl's mischievous smile and made a typical royal gesture and replied, "All in good time, thou good and faithful servant, all in good time."

They laughed and stepped out of the shuttle into a wonderland of ships that made the grand Nastasturus naval shipyards on Tnegral seem puny. What Alec saw amazed him. The very chamber they were in was larger than many moons, and it was literally jammed with hundreds of spacecraft, some in motion, many docked. He saw everything from one-man jitneys, consisting of little more than an open framework and operated by space-suited figures, to Galaxy-class colony ships bigger than cities. He'd been on large vessels ranging in size from heavy scouts to passenger liners like the *Bright Star* to enormous Omega Cruisers—but of course he'd never stepped foot in one of these notorious trade stations, which dwarfed them all by several orders of magnitude. So flabbergasted was he that he stood rooted to the spot, and failed to notice as Behl walked away, still talking. He came to himself when the exasperated man called. "Alec...Alec! Your Highness! Are you listening?" Alec gathered himself and hurried to Behl's side. The old Captain seemed to ignore the wondrous sight spread out before them. No doubt he was accustomed to such things.

"Sorry, sir," Alec said sheepishly. "I've never seen anything like this before."

"Eh, you'll get used to it. Once you spend a little time in a place like this, you'll be amazed by how much it shrinks on you, and it won't be long before you miss the wide-open spaces of your homeworld—or any habitable world, for that matter."

Alec and Behl took a pneumatic train to a lower level, then disembarked. Alec was taken aback yet again when he looked up and saw clouds floating in the artificial sky. After a long moment, Behl nudged him. "Something, ain't it? Those are real, by the way. The place is so big it has its own weather. Even rains sometimes."

Shaking his head, Alec followed the Captain over to a pair of conservatively dressed beings who Behl introduced as Lady Fuzza and Captain Zlo of Marengo, the capital of the interstellar nation that styled itself the Sun Empire.

"I was taught that Marengo was populated by Oman-descended peoples," Alec said quietly to Behl, while greeting Lady Fuzza. This lady was by no means Oman or near-Oman, and she didn't have the appearance of a transgenic, either; like her companion, she had a crest of bright feathers, no obvious ears, and her skin resembled gray peach-fuzz. Lady Fuzza heard his less-than subtle remark, but seemed not to be bothered by it; indeed, she tossed her head back and laughed.

"Don't believe everything you hear, my noble little Oman," she said warmly. "There are so many different species on Marengo. We've been a multi-species society ever since the Long War and the expansion that followed. It's just that our...chief exports tend to be omanoid. You Omans and your descendant races are so very adaptable."

"Please, milady, forgive my ignorance; I hope I haven't offended you."

Again Lady Fuzza threw her head back and laughed, then reached out with an elongated arm and squeezed his shoulder. "My dear, no one is offended. It takes much more than that to offend old Lady Fuzza. Now tell me, young master Horn, what do you know of Marengan craftsmanship insofar as ship design is concerned?"

"Not much," Alec admitted.

The Lady nodded and made a grand gesture; the air before them immediately shimmered, revealing the frigate that he had admired from the observation port back on Star-Dice. It was sleek, black, and aerodynamically designed, proving it was as much at home in an atmosphere as in deep space. At a distance, it had seemed a bit fragile, even spidery; it seemed very much otherwise now, hovering with a deadly grace that caused Alec to take a sharp breath. Up close, it seemed enormous.

They all moved onto a nearby hover pad, which took them up and around the ship while Lady Fuzza and Captain Zlo extolled its virtues. Alec listened with only one ear, content to drink in the sight of the extraordinary vessel. Behl interrupted them over and over again with sharp questions, but both of the Marengans were happy to respond to everything he asked.

Eventually they stopped near the bridge, and Captain Zlo said, "As you may know, we Marengans aren't particularly sentimental, so we never gave this ship a name; it retains its original designation of *K-13*. This ship is one out of six hundred once commissioned in the Marengo fleet. Because we recently upgraded our navy to the latest generation of warships, they have all been decommissioned, and now civilians may own them. Everything is more or less standard. Well, standard as we are used to on Marengo; I believe most other cultures would find them luxurious. Of course, we have up-graded all living quarters to civilian tastes."

Behl asked, "Any cloaking device?"

"No, no cloaking device. As I'm sure you know, cloaking devices are illegal for civilians to own in most sectors. What you saw here was furnished by the station. However, the ship does have an excellent stealth system; this class was built more for scouting than combat."

"Now, let us take a look inside," said Lady Fuzza. She directed the hover plate to land at its original position beside the frigate.

The *K-13* stood on five huge landing struts. When Lady Fuzza gestured next, a vertical crack appeared on the fore side of one of the legs, streaming white light. Panels slid aside to reveal a cramped lift, which took them up into the ship's interior.

Over the next few hours, Alec and Behl were shown all the ship's copious amenities, and Alec was struck by how fondly both Lady Fuzza and Zlo spoke of the *K-13*, despite the famous Marengan lack of sentimentality. It was clear that they loved the ship, and Alec wondered why they wanted to sell it. When he asked them that point blank, both sighed deeply. They looked at each other, and for the first time there was apprehension in their eyes. After a long moment, Lady Fuzza said quietly, "We have no choice. My Captain and I have been waiting here for our contracted cargo, two hundred tons of crystal-silver, for months now. We put almost everything we owned into that order, and already had several buyers lined up, at an colossal potential profit."

Zlo confirmed, "The profit would have been more than enough for us to pay off our loans on this ship and order our next cargo. After that, it would have been all profit. But our cargo never showed up. The cargo ship apparently was destroyed or taken by pirates."

Alec and Behl glanced at each other; neither said a word.

Behl quickly changed the subject. "Crystal-silver. That's why one of the cargo holds was built with extra radiation protection."

"Indeed, and of course we installed plenty of extra defenses to protect our cargo," added Lady Fuzza with pride. She smiled, a bit sadly. "Unfortunately, we did not bother to insure the full value of the cargo, given the lack of piracy and natural hazards in this sector. But if you purchase the *K-13*, gentlemen, we will have enough to pay off our debt and to purchase tickets back to Marengo, and from there I don't know what will happen. There will be a few upset investors to deal with, of course, but I expect we can handle that when the time comes."

"What will happen to your crew?" Alec asked.

Captain Zlo shrugged. "They will travel back with us, of course. We owe them that much."

Behl kindly asked for a moment alone, and gestured to Alec to follow him to the other side of the cargo hold they were in. Lady Fuzza and Captain Zlo withdrew to the corridor outside, making no obvious attempts to listen in on their conversation. After a moment of muted argument, Alec and Behl stepped out into the corridor where Lady Fuzza and her Captain awaited them. "I have a suggestion," said Alec, and then reconsidered. "Or better, let's call it a business proposition."

Both the Marengans looked at him with a mixture of suspicion and interest.

"Milady, you're asking one hundred million credits for the *K-13* as is, correct?" She nodded, whereupon Alec played one of the hole cards Behl had furnished him with: "You realize, of course, that it is possible to find a similar vessel of this class for less than half that price, brand new. In fact, it is not very difficult."

Lady Fuzza seemed about to interrupt; but when Alec noticed this, he made a small motion with his hand, and Lady Fuzza allowed him to continue. "Though I doubt that there are any more of these Marengan ships for sale in this sector."

Alec paused to allow Lady Fuzza to speak. "We won't sell for any less, and we have had several buyers looking at her already."

"And a few more after you," Captain Zlo cut in.

Alec smiled as he said, "But here's what I'll do. I'll pay you two hundred million credits. One hundred million up front, and another one hundred million once we're done with the ship, one standard year from now." He grinned at their astonished expressions and he continued, "And to top it off, you can take back your ship at that time—or whatever's left of her."

The first of the two Marengans to regain his composure was Zlo. "What's the catch? We won't do anything illegal."

Lady Fuzza peered at Alec through slitted eyes as she echoed, "Yes, what is the catch? For that price, you can buy a full-sized cruiser."

"That's not what I want. I want your cargo frigate. I need something small and fast, with a high carrying capacity. Most cargo ships aren't built for long-haul intergalactic travel the way this one is, and certainly don't have the arms and armor the *K-13* does. I also want to hire your crew for the duration. It will be dangerous work, and the pay will be commensurate." Alec took a deep breath, placed his hands behind his back, and began pacing the deck in front of Lady Fuzza and Captain Zlo.

Behl paid them no attention; he was looking over various aspects of the ship, making rough measurements and entering data on a clipboard comp.

After a long moment of pacing, Alec came to a decision. He looked up at the Marengans and stated, "We are going hunting."

"Explain," the Lady snapped.

"Hunting for what?" asked Captain Zlo simultaneously.

"Pirates."

The word hung in the air for a long moment, the only sound being Behl muttering to himself and tapping on the keys of the clipcomp. Scowling, Lady Fuzza finally said, with notable hostility in her voice, "Mr. Horn, it was a... pleasure, and now we must ask you to leave us. We do hope that you will find a ship more suitable for your needs."

"Please, allow me to finish—"

Captain Zlo cut Alec off. "I think not. As my partner here just said, leave us."

"Your cargo, the two hundred tons of crystal-silver. It was on a deep-space cargo ship called *C-5,* correct?" Behl said quietly, looking down at the clipcomp.

That got their attention. "How did you know that?" demanded Lady Fuzza.

"Because the very same pirates who took your cargo captured the cruise liner I was captaining."

"Impossible!" blurted Captain Zlo. "No pirate activity has been reported in this sector for the last twenty years! That's why we and our investors choose this region of space to trade in."

Behl nodded laconically. "Sure, and since there's no piracy in the sector, you don't need any piracy insurance, right? If a ship and its cargo were to go missing with no further explanation, it couldn't be pirates. And since the ship is never seen again, you can't claim natural disaster or accident, so the administrators of this trading facility don't have to reimburse your insurance claim anyway. At least I think that's how it reads on your contract here." Behl held up his clipcomp in front of them.

"Where did you get that information?" Lady Fuzza asked hotly.

"Never mind that. Now, look here." Behl pushed a few keys, and the display changed. "In the last five years, which is as much data as I can access, three hundred and seven ships have been reported missing in this sector. That's not unusual for a region of space as large and active as this one. Now, what's interesting is that not even a molecule of one of those ships or a farthing of its cargo has ever been recovered, and there have been no piracy investigations at all. That's why this sector is remarkably free of piracy—nobody looks for it, so it doesn't exist. Self-fulfilling prophesy. And also, not a single one of the insurance claims for these ships has been paid out, since all of them are still reported as missing, and the standard ten-year loss assumption clauses have never been activated."

Without saying a word, Lady Fuzza took the clipcomp from Behl and studied the display. Captain Zlo joined her, and Alec could hear him whisper, "I warned you of this three years ago, you and the investors. But did you listen?"

Lady Fuzza handed the pad to Captain Zlo, otherwise ignoring him. "We shall make an official report to the Key Administrators about what you have discovered, sir. But my decision still stands."

Behl rolled his eyes. "Milady, that would be unwise."

"Are you threatening me?" she all but shrieked, in a tone in which anger warred with disbelief.

Alec held up his hands in a placating gesture. "Of course not, milady! Perhaps my friend's comment was rather indelicately put. *We* pose no threat to you. But think it through. New Frontier controls nearly all the trade in this sector, for thousands of light years all around. They guarantee that local traders are safe from piracy...and yet ships still disappear at an alarming rate.

"And if you haven't already guessed from what Captain Behl just told you, we ourselves were taken by pirates not too many light years from here. We escaped from them only through an unusual, convoluted series of events, like something you might see in an adventure vid. Clearly, then, piracy *does* occur in this sector—and it is impossible to believe that the authorities are unaware of it.

"So," Alec said, taking in their suddenly frightened faces, "who do you think could possibly have enough political and pecuniary power to conspire like this and profit?"

After taking a deep breath, Zlo said, "You say you escaped from pirates. Why should we believe you?"

Alec pulled a shiny crystalline mass out of his pocket. "Does this look familiar?" He tossed it to Zlo.

Zlo's eyes widened. "By all the gods and demons! Crystal-silver!"

"You might want to check the registry number, but I think that might be one of yours."

The Marengan traced the figures limned onto one facet with a shaky finger. "I do not have to check. I recognize the number, and here is our house's trading sigil."

"Could it be faked?" the Lady demanded.

"I do not think so, milady, not easily. It is holo-embedded into the crystal itself, and that could have been done only when it was recrystallized for transport." He looked up at Alec suddenly. "Where did you get this?"

"I told you. We were captured by the same pirates who captured the C-5. We stole a ship when we escaped -- belonged to a nasty piece of work named Zuzack. Among other things, there were ten kilos of your crystal-silver in the cargo hold. No idea what happened to the rest. The pirates still have it, I guess."

Lady Fuzza swallowed hard. "We would like to recover it. But our hands are tied. Of course, we must follow both galactic and intergalactic law regulating these things—"

Captain Zlo cut her off. "I don't think those laws apply out here, especially not if the Key Administrators are involved." He slammed a fist hard into the wall. "When the Empire and the federations hear of this, they will send their fleets to crush these villains."

"And that will benefit you how?" Alec asked. "I admit that it might bring some satisfaction for you personally, but will it compensate you financially?" He looked at the Marengans. "On the other hand, if you join my friend and I, you might achieve both personal satisfaction *and* financial enrichment."

Behl said, "Captain, we need you and your crew to serve as officers. Mr. Horn and I will recruit security personnel for any actions we undertake. All you need to do is run the old girl while we do the fighting." He offered his hand to his Marengan opposite.

"If I decide to join you," Zlo said cautiously, "And I said *if*, I personally will be involved in whatever happens, no matter the danger." He clasped Behl's forearm, and Behl reciprocated. He glanced at Alec, who nodded firmly.

"I would like to join also," Lady Fuzza said stiffly, "but unlike Captain Zlo, I have no military background and I'm far too old. However, I am no coward, and would help you in any way I can."

"Perhaps," Alec said slowly, "you should return to Marengo and alert the proper authorities as to what's happening here. This needs to be shut down as soon as possible. And perhaps you could have them deliver us a letter of commission, to make things legal."

Lady Fuzza grinned suddenly. "You don't need a letter of commission; under intergalactic law, you have the right to pursue the pirates for one year after the attack. However, you must offer physical evidence, and I doubt your word alone is proof enough. Though the crystal-silver might be."

"Or not," Behl put in. "They might think *we're* the pirates. And we haven't got the time to clear everything up legally."

Alec looked at him grimly. "I think I have an out. It's considered an act of war for any armed force to engage in hostilities against a member of any Elite clan owing allegiance to the Nastasturus Federation. In the event a senior official becomes witness to such hostilities in the first person, then that official has the duty and responsibility, in the interests of the Federation, to take immediate action and report to the proper authorities." Alec finished with a laugh while the others looked at him, perplexed. "Besides, I might have some evidence that will interest your Emperor." He winked at Behl and said, "Ha, see there, you old bastard? I did learn a thing or two in school."

Lady Fuzza looked at him doubtfully. "So, you are from Nastasturus? And you are one of their senior officials?"

Behl laughed. "You're damn right he is. Believe it or not, the little shit is a brevet general, and the moment he was attacked he became an official general officer in the armed forces of Nastasturus. Bet that bastard Zuzack didn't know that."

Again, there was silence. Zlo finally asked, "Are you Lord Hornet, the boy general who ended the seven-year conflict on Casaba last year?"

Alec didn't answer. He stood turned slightly away, his hands behind his back, gazing out the viewport. His thoughts were elsewhere.

Behl answered for him. "In person," he said proudly. When Alec cocked a bemused eyebrow in his direction, the captain grinned and said, "Didn't take too much brain-sweat to get from 'Horn' to

'Hornet,' son." To the Marengans he pointed out, "He also managed to escape from the notorious pirate Zuzack the Cannibal himself—after he flayed off the bastard's face for him. Not to mention the fact that he rescued and saved my life along the way."

Alec turned around and looked the two Marengans in the eyes, one after the other. "Do we have an accord?"

Captain Zlo walked up to Alec and grasped forearms with him, and a moment later, the Lady did the same. In unison, they said, "We do."

"Then let's go to work, shall we?"

"May I say something first?" asked Zlo. "It is a tradition on Marengo that whenever a new bond is made, no matter what the reason or with whom, we make a toast in blood to strengthen that bond. We then share a first supper together, which I believe is especially apropos here, especially what lies ahead. Are you game?"

Alec looked at the small prick on his right thumb, which stung a bit. He rubbed it and considered the unusual ceremony that he, Behl, Lady Fuzza and Captain Zlo had finished earlier. The blood ceremony itself was a minor formality, in which the participants had a small needle inserted into a finger and trickled a little blood into a wine bowl, which all of them drank from after all had contributed. That hadn't been particularly appetizing, but the dinner that followed had been fabulous. Both Alec and Behl were amazed at the high quality of the food from the *K-13*'s galley.

Alec had guessed that Lady Fuzza wanted to demonstrate the nature of the ship's services, and if that were the case, it had been an effective demonstration indeed. He glanced at Lady Fuzza from the corner of his eye as she walked next to him, with the natural grace of a queen, down New Frontier's endless corridors. During the last few hours, they had bonded and gotten to know each other quite well as they toured the recesses of the ship that he hadn't already seen, while Behl and Captain Zlo went over the engines and weapons systems centimeter by centimeter.

At the moment Alec and the Lady were headed towards a holding area for chattel offered up for sale by the local slave traders. Lady Fuzza seemed as serene as ever, but Alec was somewhat apprehensive about what they might find. They were escorted by two of Lady Fuzza's security personal, Pier and Wolf—Omans dressed, like all of the K-13's crew, in dark blue coveralls and black boots. The weapons holsters on the black leather belts were empty, as weapons were not allowed inside the station proper. Both men were quiet and deadly-looking, with scarred, weather-beaten faces, evidence of hard action in the past.

Alec thought, *A smart soldier has no scars*, something that they'd taught him at the Academy. He wasn't sure about the validity of the statement, though he'd been forced to argue for it in more than one paper. Eying Pier and Wolf, he rather thought that neither of them would have agreed with him. Like the other security personnel Captain Zlo had hired, they were former career military who had decided, as so many soldiers did, that they'd rather work security than retire among civilians. Alec suspected they loved their work more than the paycheck they got from it, and they'd already made it clear to him that they had no compunctions about taking on the pirates they'd be chasing.

In fact, the entire security team had all enthusiastically and without hesitation jumped at the chance to hunt pirates when the idea was presented to them, and Alec rather thought that most of them would happily do it for more than the one year he had proposed. Most of the other crew felt similarly.

"A minor question," Alec said suddenly.

"What?" Lady Fuzza asked.

"What's the name of this station?"

"Most of us just call it New Frontier, dear, but I think its official name is New Frontier 16. Not very imaginative, I realize, but adequately descriptive. I believe there are about two hundred similar stations co-owned by the Federated Merchants and the Commercial Traders, and I think there are over a thousand more that are owned individually by one or the other. And of course, there are all the neutral ones."

They continued their journey through the massive space station, followed closely by Pier and Wolf, who had decided to glare like mad at anyone crossing their path. They left behind a trail of bewildered and upset people, but no one dared accost them.

TWENTY

THE 185 capital ships of the Nastasturus Federation's 11th Galactic Fleet—and all its thousands of frigates, cruisers, and supply vessels—were in the process of forming up at the sector's primary jumpgate, an exercise that took many hours. Meanwhile, several thousand sleek androids were busily deploying large metallic spheres around the event horizon of the stripped-down black hole, in order to increase the size of the opening and thus enable the entire fleet to go through at once. That was ultimately safer, and would use less energy, but it took time.

Admiral Hadrian Cook af Hornet stood on the main bridge of his flagship, *Unity 1*, observing the construction at the jumpgate. "Magnify Section A-10," he grunted, and a section of the image jumped into view and clarified, showing several androids moving away from one of the spheres, which was now glowing Cherenkov blue.

"Looks like the gate will be ready within minutes, Admiral," said a younger man as he stepped up beside Cook. He wore a Lieutenant Admiral's stars on his epaulets.

"Indeed, Mr. Busch. And how goes the deployment?"

"All ships are in place and report ready, sir."

"Excellent. Once the androids have returned to their respective ships, you may order the fleet to advance."

"Aye aye, sir."

Less than an hour later, the fleet moved with lethal purpose into the enormously-expanded jumpgate. Once the last ship had entered, the hundreds of metallic orbs that had expanded it followed, allowing the gate to shrink back to its normal size.

The fleet emerged thousands of light years away, on the edge of the sector where the *Bright Star*, the *C-5*, and scores of other ships had recently disappeared. Once they arrived, they scooped up the dozens of probes that had been launched through the gate earlier to test the waters and warn of any danger. None of them had found a thing.

Admiral Cook reclined in his command chair, reviewing reports and making notes on a clipcomp. Eventually he handed the pad to a waiting lieutenant, who saluted and quickly carried the pad back to the Intel section, a massive room divided into quadrants where hundreds of busy officers manned instruments and computer consoles. Once the lieutenant was gone, Lt. Admiral Busch swung his chair around and raised it to the same level as Admiral Cook's. "You sure about this?" Busch asked, as he glanced from his own clipcomp to his commanding officer.

Cook looked at him and replied, "I am. I believe it can speed up our search." Busch nodded, and allowed his seat to return to its original position, on the command deck below Cook's. He finished up at his station and, after saying farewell to Cook, turned to leave the bridge, followed by several officers.

Before he could reach the hatch, Cook called, "And Mr. Busch, remember: if you make contact with the enemy, do not engage until I arrive with the main column."

Busch nodded and saluted smartly. As he turned to walk away, Cook said quietly, "Good hunting, son."

Busch left Cook standing alone before a large window, as he and his entourage hurried down to the docking bay where his personal shuttle waited to take him to his own flagship, *Endeavor 4*.

Soon thereafter, Cook intoned into the battle communication system, "Stand by for split. I repeat, stand by for split. Second Battle Group, First Section will alter course per standing orders. When you receive the new coordinates and orders, execute when ready. I will join you and assume command later."

On *Endeavor 4*, Busch leaned back in his seat after relaying the order, and gazed at a computer screen as the 25 ships of his section altered course and proceeded perpendicular to the main fleet. He muttered quietly, "I still don't like this, sir. It seems unwise to divide our forces before we know what might lie ahead of us."

Cook listened attentively to his old friend's advice as it was relayed through his earbug, smiling faintly. "Trust me on this one, Alistair. I think it's better we use the Second for acting point. We wouldn't want to scare anyone we might run into."

"You're the boss," Busch answered, obviously unconvinced.

Cook smiled, but made sure none of his amusement was audible in his voice. "After we translate through the next jumpgate we'll be very close to the last reported location of the *Bright Star*. Make sure you launch several scouts, and have your ships group in a defensive position. I'll wait here with the rest of the column."

From the earbug came Busch's voice, "Hadrian, I *have* done this before, you know. By the way, what's on tonight's dinner menu?"

The twenty-five capital cruisers slipped silently through space, visible only by the way they occluded the distant stars, and plunged into the jumpgate before them. When they emerged from the other side, they dispersed in different directions and began scanning nearby space. One of the larger cruisers, the *StarRay 7*, moved immediately to the last reported position of the *Bright Star* and launched four smaller destroyer-class ships to investigate. Each of the destroyers, in turn, launched a pair of frigates, which darted into space with a lethal grace, like hounds intent upon finding their prey. Meanwhile, the other capital ships launched hundreds of probes and drones of their own.

Aboard the *Endeavor 4*, Lt. Admiral Busch gazed at the monitor displaying the positions of all his ships and probes with a look of satisfaction. Before long, they'd have every single nook and cranny of this sector covered. The hunt was on.

Hadrian Cook's face bore its own look of satisfaction as his command chair was pulled back into an adjacent room through a pair of hidden doors. The last thing Busch heard in his earbug through the link was, "The fleet is yours."

Busch thought, *Rest, my friend. Something tells me you're going to need it before this mission is over.* He directed his own command chair to a higher position on the command deck, just as his monitor bleeped and presented him with an urgent new message. Sighing deeply, he reluctantly contacted Admiral Cook.

Cook had just removed his jacket and was lying down when Busch called. "What is it?" he growled.

"Good news, Admiral," Busch announced, triumph in his voice.

Cook grinned, his fatigue forgotten. "I'll be right there."

ON the opposite side of the inhabited universe sat another person with a much less-satisfied expression, a person who most people thought—or rather *hoped*—was a myth. And of those who know of his existence—from rich to poor, citizen to leader—most would deny his very existence. He was the very personification of malice. Soldiers from both Nastasturus and Florencia used his name when referring to attacking each other: "Let's drop a *Horsa* on them..." or "Let's go *Horsa* on their asses." He was the most feared pirate in the known universe.

Horsa was Zuzack the Cannibal's older brother.

He sat in his ornate chair—he refused to call it a throne—facing his "family." He was an impressively tall man who appeared to be thin because of the long coat; but all who knew him realized that he was as muscular as he was smart, which was to say *very* on both scores. Not an ounce of his weight was fat, unlike his brother Zuzack. He was an intelligent, lethal killing machine with the perfectly-shaped body of a young man in his prime, which was especially remarkable given that he was almost three hundred standard years old. His skin, once a lustrous black, was now a pale-gray from lack of real sunlight, and his long blond hair was braided and dreaded, and wrapped around his body in strange patterns. His fangs were coated with a thin layer of hard tritonium silver, and at the moment his long, thin fingers were combing through the thick mustache that graded into his long, white beard. On his surcoat was embroidered his clan's crest, an exploding planet. The clan was called *Wulsatures*, which meant "Armageddon" in a long-dead language.

Horsa had taken Zuzack under his wing when their parents had been killed a long time before. Their brothers and sisters in the Clan had wanted nothing to do Zuzack, because his mother was not theirs; this angered Horsa, and he had them summarily executed for discrimination and greed. He had taken it upon himself to act as father to his infant brother, and it was he who had named Zuzack.

Horsa had trained and formed Zuzack into the perfect loyal killing machine. In the decades since, Zuzack had won fame as a pirate leader almost equal to Horsa himself. Meanwhile, Horsa ruled his clan with the skill of a politician and with the strength of a dictator. His love for his clan superseded anything, and he considered all its members to be his family. But the only one among them that he could trust was Zuzack himself.

Horsa preferred to keep the male pirates working separately from the females, but each Captain was allowed to make his or her own decision on that matter. Today, this was a policy Horsa regretted. There were nothing but problems when the sexes came together, in his opinion; hence, marriages.

He glared at the message on the monitor in front of him in cold disbelief. The message had been sent encoded by means of a highly-advanced algorithm, making it next to impossible to decrypt by anyone who might intercept it. Only he and Zuzack had the key.

Horsa trembled as he read the message again, and his trembling increased, the rage threatening to overwhelm his self-control, as he read it yet again. His pale eyes concealed his thoughts, but his body language could no longer conceal what he was thinking to his lieutenants, who were sitting against the far wall of the semicircular room, facing him in the center. Normally, Horsa kept iron rein on his emotions until it would most benefit him to release them; that made him extremely unpredictable to any friend or foe. The fact that he was visibly losing control at the moment frightened some of his officers almost to the point of fainting.

Horsa read the message one more time:

> H.
> Good news: Went and picked up our package. The map was real. I succeeded in making a first pick-up; many more to come. Everything was there.
>
> Bad news: I have suffered mutiny (Myra's crew) and need your assistance; also, someone stole the pick-up.
>
> I will be at New Frontier 16 in a few weeks.
>
> Your brother, by our blood and for our blood.
> Z.
>
> PS. They also stole the map.

Horsa was just about to explode when he realized how quiet the room had gotten. With an exaggerated gesture, he snapped off the monitor and sat brooding for a long moment. *The loss of the package is bad, but the loss of the map is far worse,* he mused, as he shifted in the uncomfortable chair, which was upholstered with the skins of his enemies. He ground his teeth together, thinking about the content of the message, and drummed his thin fingers on the seat's arms, beating out the tattoo of an ages-old battle call. His love for his brother was the highest emotion Horsa knew, yet he cursed himself for not going with Zuzack when he retrieved the map and tested its veracity. Then again, there were so many false treasure maps out there... who would have known that this one was real? The *Black Moon*'s cargo was the biggest lost treasure in history.

The *Black Moon* was a Croll Battle Cruiser, from a past age when Marengo had been the capitol of what was then the largest superpower in the known universe. The ship's true name was unknown; "Black Moon" had actually been a code name for a large convoy of over four hundred battle cruisers that had vanished between two jumpgates thousands of years previously.

The primary mission of the convoy had been to escort several tons of tritonium silver and countless other megatons of loot to the treasure vaults of the Marengan system. The materiel was plunder that Marengan armies had liberated from hundreds of systems during the Second Universal War, which was just then winding down. Ever since, there had been thousands of rumors of what might have happened to the Black Moon fleet, but they were only speculations: natural disaster, mutiny among the crews, a meteor storm, alien attack, and hijacking. In any case, the ships and the millions of people who crewed them had never been seen again. In time the loss of all that treasure, which would have served to replenish the depleted coffers of a nation wearied by war, had led to the downfall and dissolution of the Marengan Empire. Marengo became just another backwater, renowned only for its Oman chattel.

There were as many false maps purporting to lead to the Black Moon treasure as there were rumors, and annually thousands of treasure seekers were swindled out of their savings by con artists and grifters plying their trade. This was especially the case whenever a new species entered the intergalactic community. Millions of people had looked for the treasure, and millions more would do so in the future. Governments large and small had thousands of scientists and treasure hunters on the job at all times, scanning the universe for the long-lost treasure which, if the original tallies were right, might be enough to buy half a galaxy.

Horsa was the only living creature who knew what had really happened to the Black Moon convoy, and he had secretly sworn that he would take that secret with him to his grave. Not even Zuzack knew; all that Horsa had taught Zuzack was how to retrieve parts of the treasure from time to time—assuming the latest map they had acquired was real.

The map itself had been constructed by a mad genius. The treasure was apparently spread across numerous systems in the various inhabited galaxies, and the coordinates changed occasionally. The map provided a new set of coordinates whenever a cache was located, but one had to go to that specific location and collect the treasure to receive it the coordinates to the next cache.

When Horsa himself had seen this map for the first time he had had his doubts—but he and others had studied for hundreds of years, and once in a while he or his brother would travel and search for the treasure. Horsa had not expected that it was the real thing. He wished now that he had made a copy, but the catch was that it had been impossible to copy completely. Anyone could copy the *appearance* of the map, but not the advanced holographic functions and computer programs, at least not without activating a virus that would render the map useless.

Horsa had recently been too busy ruling his huge clan to bother with the map, and lately matters had become worse, in the form of a fierce rival clan led by a woman called Ogstafa. That's why he'd stayed home and let Zuzack go a-Viking alone.

He snorted in disgust. *My brother should never have intermixed the sexes within his crew*, Horsa thought. *It never works, and now my map might be in the hands of* females. Now he had to lead a damned rescue mission, at a time when he didn't care to leave the clan leaderless for a second.

In normal circumstances, a specially-built probe would launch the map and the other special treasures back to Horsa's stronghold if it happened that Zuzack's ship was boarded. Over the decades, this had happened several times when the two large federations cracked down on piracy, and more than once the greedy Brakks of the Federated Merchants and the Commercial Traders had attacked as well. But Horsa had been forced to come to his brother's aid only once, when the Marengan pirate hunters the pirates called "Predators" had struck. The Predators were the most feared and effective pirate hunters in known space, as impossible to bribe as flying through the core of a sun.

What Zuzack didn't know, and Horsa did, was that a Predator was hidden somewhere onboard New Frontier 16. This was something Horsa's intelligence crew had known for a while, and they kept a close eye on the quiescent Predator while reporting to Horsa alone. The pirate chief received the messages by a transceiver implanted in his skull, but never sent the replies from his headquarters. He was all too concerned that someone might pick up his clan's present location if he did—and besides, as much as he loved his clanmates, he didn't trust them. They were pirates, after all. Instead of breaking his transmission black-out, he did what most military organizations did when they wanted to maintain true secrecy: he used scouts and couriers.

Horsa's closest followers were all within the same age cohort as Horsa, more or less, but they were from many different worlds. Male, female, and otherwise, all were as physically scarred and bedraggled as only centuries of regular battles could make them—and all looked up to Horsa with the same respect as children look up to their parents or a hero, as a leader whom they worshiped above all else.

This day, they were silent as Horsa stood up abruptly, looked them over with fierce pride, and proclaimed in a voice like basso thunder, "Gather the Clan. We are going to war!"

TWENTY-ONE

THAT evening, Lady Fuzza took Alec on a tour of the enormous New Frontier 16. Alec was overwhelmed and occasionally baffled by what they saw. While he'd become accustomed to the huge spacecraft bays down below, he hadn't expected the station proper to be dominated by a huge, hollow space built thickly with skyscrapers, where millions of people lived, worked, and played. The artificial skyline, with the pale sky arching above, made it seem as if they were outdoors on the surface of a planet. Alec was impressed; he'd never seen anything like it before.

By then, it was clear that Lady Fuzza was taking a liking to Alec, and treated him almost like a favored child. She seemed surprised at how naïve Alec was in some ways, despite his exalted background, and was curious about his past; but whenever she moved in on the subject, Alec always found a way to change it. After several attempts, she gave up on her quest to find out more—at least for the present.

During their ambling, they entered a large mall crowded with all types of businesses, markets, food courts, restaurants, entertainment areas, theaters, magical shows, small casinos and so on. They encountered beings from hundreds of worlds: some Oman and omanoid, a variety of recognizable transgenics, and many beings more alien in shape; some walking, others running, a few flying. Most seemed to be enjoying themselves, laughing and otherwise displaying their pleasure. There was a general air of jollity. There weren't many blatant police or security personnel visible, but Alec did notice several metallic orbs gliding high above the crowd, their sensors no doubt recording everything.

Lady Fuzza paused before a bistro and invited Alec to share breakfast with her, while they worked on a strategy to hire—or, if absolutely necessary, purchase—pilots and able spacers. While they waited on their food, she educated Alec about the space station they found themselves resident on, which she had visited numerous times in the past. It turned out to be more than just a space station: it and its attendant substations were more of a fleet of traveling arks. Twelve million citizens and investors had been traveling for over twenty years at sub-light velocity toward a new system in the neutral zone between the Florencian and Nastasturus Federations; when they arrived, they would settle the system's uninhabited worlds and start their new lives. Even though Alec had read all this before, he listened to the Lady intently; he enjoyed hearing her singsong voice.

"They will travel for another fifty years before they reach their destination," she pointed out. "They would ordinarily have taken just fifteen more years, but were unable to make a vital jumpgate insertion a few years ago due to tensions between the Federated Merchants and the Commercial Traders, the primary investors in both the space station and the colony system."

They danced lightly around the crew issue. Neither Alec nor Lady Fuzza believed that they would have any problems hiring soldiers or security personnel for their coming expedition. But earlier that morning, during their first official staff meeting with Behl and Zlo, both Captains had expressed their doubts that they would find any loyal personnel suitable for their purpose. Most private soldiers were pretty tough, but many drew the line at hunting pirates.

Breakfast consisted of one huge fried egg divided between the two of them, and some strange fuzzy substance that Alec had left on the plate. Lady Fuzza ate hers with relish, laughing at Alec and saying, "You don't know what you're missing, young man." After paying the surprisingly reasonable bill, they wondered on, and a few moments later passed a uniform store. Lady Fuzza looked at it thoughtfully, and suggested that they order new uniforms for the existing crew. Alec liked the idea. When they went in, he allowed the Lady to make the selections, as she seemed to have more interest in the subject than he ever would.

After a spirited round of bickering, Lady Fuzza handed a small computer pad containing information about the existing crew's species, body shapes, and sizes over to a sales clerk. Meanwhile, Alec had noticed a shoe department on the other side of the store, and he walked over and started whispering to the cobbler. The shoemaker looked at him with interest, and after thinking for a bit, nodded in consent.

"I think we should let them send down a representative to take the proper sizes, don't you?" asked Lady Fuzza from behind him.

Alec looked at her and smiled. "Certainly, milady, whatever you think is best." He turned back towards the shoemaker, "Do we understand each other?"

The cobbler nodded. "Indeed, sir. I'll admit it's an unusual order, but once I have the sizes, they will be ready in three days."

Lady Fuzza noticed for the first time that Alec held a small concealed packet, wrapped in brown paper and plastic, which he handed to the shoemaker. When the man opened it briefly, a foul odor filled the room. He closed the packet in a hurry and nodded to Alec.

After another half-hour's walk, they reached a large market area where slaves were being auctioned from a podium in the center of a large amphitheater. The display itself was impressive: the place was decorated as an old harbor village from thousands of years ago, during some world's medieval era. To bring more verisimilitude to the scenario, all the people working with the slaves were dressed in clothing and armor from that specific era. He noticed several non-functional but impressive-looking slave blocks lined up against one curving wall, where grinning tourists of several species were having their pictures taken while pretending to suffer in durance vile. Kids were running around laughing and having fun.

Alec ground his teeth but said nothing. If the Lady noticed his discomfiture, she made no mention of it.

From one side of the town square came the sounds of a busy casino. A series of artificial springs divided the large area into small islands, and there were numerous small businesses recessed into alcoves in the walls of the amphitheater.

"Think we can buy any soldiers here?" Alec asked tightly.

"Here? No, we're on the Merchants side of the station. For that, we need to go over to the Traders side."

"But what about that over there?" said Alec, gesturing at the ongoing slave auction.

Lady Fuzza laughed lightly. "Oh no! Believe it or not, that is just for fun, dear. People can sell themselves or their family members for a short time, and sometimes a tourist can buy someone for a day or two. The tourists from Nastasturus are fascinated with the slave trade, and because it's forbidden there, they like to play pretend. Sometimes you might see a celebrity sold off. Most of the time, it's for a good cause."

"Buying a celebrity?"

Lady Fuzza looked at Alec and said, "You only end up having lunch with them, or something like that."

"Oh." Alec sounded almost disappointed.

"Some of the people sold are actual slaves, but only for a short time. They have to be returned, and they can't leave the station. For example, if you want a massage expert, a tour guide, or a sexual partner, you can "pretend" to purchase them for a while. There are some people who actually sell themselves repeatedly. Look at the young men and women over there."

Lady Fuzza pointed at about a dozen youths of various species. "They are all prostitutes, of course—freelancers who do not work for a sponsor, the station administration, or any of the casinos. They can only sell their expertise this way, and many prefer it because they get to keep all the money they acquire. Less taxes, of course. The administrators don't care for any kind of outside or independent sex trade within the station, but of course they know it's impossible to control everything, so they allow this instead. See? Everyone's happy. I guess you could call it entertainment." Her voice remained light, but she looked disgusted by the display. Alec definitely was. He made to move on, but Lady Fuzza caught his arm. She was pointing at a program she had purchased earlier.

"Look, Alec dear! In less than an hour, the Traders will auction off nearly two hundred renegade soldiers and sundry other slaves at Market Eight."

"And where is Market Eight?" wondered Alec.

"Come along, dear." They made their way to a public tube-train station, passing several markets along the way, one selling fresh produce and another packed with speeders and hoverjets. A third market must have contained over ten thousand youths, who bounced around as a musical group played atonally from a round dais floating above the crowd.

Alec and Lady Fuzza were forced to take a detour once they left the train—there was some kind of noisy demonstration going on—so by the time they finally reached Market Eight, the auction had already started. Lady Fuzza shouted, "Hurry!" as she and Alec fought their way through the crowd. "We must sign up with a Trader," she explained as she raised one arm and made a complex signal with her hand. Within a minute several different secretaries, representing different traders and brokers, surrounded them. After they contracted with one, several security people cleared a path for them to get onto a hovercraft, which lifted them serenely above the crowd.

They joined several other hovercrafts berthed along a large wall. Alec had no idea what was going on, but he studied the scene carefully, mind wide open. He had been particularly impressed when he'd seen the Lady negotiate with the Trader and her secretary, and was curious to see how she handled the chaotic scene below, which seemed to make little obvious sense. All that was clear to Alec was the overwhelming miasma of despair that had settled over the slave blocks like a dark cloud, though it seemed that no one else noticed or cared.

After several long hours, Lady Fuzza managed to purchase the contracts of 118 beings with qualified spacer and security backgrounds. Oddly, Alec felt giddy as a child in an amusement park. Not from the purchase of other sentient beings—he prayed his parents would never find out—but because this would be his first real army. Building and creating a private army was something all young Elite cadets from Nastasturus dreamed of doing. To be able to explore new worlds and conquer them, so one's name would be remembered by history...that was something that fueled every cadet's fantasies.

A commotion erupted as the purchased spacers were removed, one by one, from their blocks. By then Captains Zlo and Bell, along with the ship's officer corps, had arrived to process the chattel. With the aid of medical androids provided by the Traders, the ship's doctor examined and passed the slaves one by one while Zlo and Behl looked on critically. Once passed, they were lined up and placed under guard by the security personnel. Most seemed depressed and subdued; a few looked more defiant.

Alec stepped up onto a large crate in front of them, and looked over his new army with great pride. He took a deep breath, then began a speech that he had rehearsed many times during his life—though modified, of course, for the circumstances. He was incredibly excited that he could finally use it in reality, instead of just practicing it to the flowers in his mother's rose garden.

"Fellow sentients, please attend!" He paused briefly to be sure that he had everyone's attention, just as he'd learned in a speech class a few years back. Then he continued. "Once you were free beings. Now you are slaves, chattel, with no rights whatsoever." His voice boomed out over the crowd, and the defiant slaves all scowled and shook their chains. The others just seemed to shrink into themselves a bit more.

Behl and Captain Zlo looked at each other with concerned expressions. Lady Fuzza just smiled, saying proudly, "I gave him a little advice, I did."

Alec continued, "Once you were proud and free. Now look at you. You have nothing: no home, no family, no money. That ends today."

There was a painful silence, in which the enslaved spacers hardly dared to breath.

"As of this moment, each and every one of you is manumitted. You are again free beings."

Now they all had his attention, even the beaten-down ones, and their eyes shone with hope.

"With these words, I would like to invite you to join a new family: mine. You are free to reject me; indeed, you are free to do anything. But I ask you to hear me out before you do.

"I suspect most of you, if not all of you, were captured and sold into slavery by pirates." There were some assenting growls from the former slaves. "Well, I have a proposition for you. Will you hear me out?"

The spacers roared with one voice: "YES!"

"I too have a score to settle with the pirates of this sector," Alec said quietly, so that the spacers had to strain to hear him. "Particularly with the clan of a creature named Zuzack. He captured me along with several thousand other people on the passenger liner *Bright Star,* out of Senoj in the Nastasturus Federation. Yes, in this very sector of space, despite official claims that there is no piracy here. Captain Behl and I managed to escape, but I left people I respect and love back on that pirate ship—and I mean to get them back. You are invited to take part in this mission, not least in order to get some of your own back. You will also receive adequate food and board, medical care, and weapons to get the job done—and you will get a share of whatever we take from the pirates."

He looked over the silent crowd of spacers. Behl and Zlo were working their way down the rows, removing shackles, collars, and other fetters that some of the people had borne for years. Many were rubbing their scarred and chafed skin, and some were weeping with quiet joy. A few appeared stunned, as if they were unable to believe what had just happened to them. Alec nodded and raised his voice, tears stinging his own eyes. "Now, my friends, each of you is free to walk away as of this moment. I promise that. But I would very much appreciate your assistance in this matter of vengeance and justice. If you join with me for this one mission—that is all I ask—you will be common soldiers, and I and these people you see here will be your superior officers. However!" and he raised his voice to a shout, "I consider myself no better than you, and to prove it, each you will each be paid a bounty of ten thousand credits each, right now!"

Now the Captains were walking down the rows and handing out debit cards to each of the former slaves. When they were done, Alec continued, "Gentlebeings, there are no strings attached to that card you just received. Consider it an apology for what you have had to endure. You are free to walk away right this moment. But if you stay with me, if you help me crew my frigate, you will receive another forty thousand credits exactly one standard year from today, and forty thousand more for every year you serve with me." There was a collective gasp from the mass of former slaves. Forty thousand credits was roughly equivalent to four year's pay for an able spacer.

"I won't lie to you," Alec said grimly. "It's dangerous work. You may die. But it will be worthwhile work. If you come with me, all I ask from you is your experience, your devotion, and your loyalty. Just for this one mission, however long it takes."

"Are we really free?" interrupted a large fellow with branched tentacles for hands and a serrated beak that looked deadly. Before Alec had time to answer, a pale omanoid shouted out, "Can we really do what we want?"

Dammit, the rosebushes never interrupt, Alec thought. He gestured for silence, and the former slaves looked up at him with great curiosity, and what Alec thought was respect. Even those that had previously looked cowed seemed eager and hopeful.

"I only want free people working with me," Alec said, a little exasperated. "Of course you're all free do what you want, and…"

Alec's words was drowned out as one hundred and seventeen former slaves ran for their freedom, shouting out their joy and waving their debit cards in the air, leaving the crazy young Oman on his crate completely flabbergasted.

Behl muttered to Lady Fuzza with a puzzled expression, "What did you tell him?"

"That's not what I told him to say," Lady Fuzza said stiffly, shaking her head in disbelief while muttering something about all the money Alec had just wasted.

Behl and Captain Zlo were still in shock, and couldn't believe what they had just witnessed. At that moment, one of the *K-13*'s security officers walked up and asked if he and his crew could go. Behl shook his head without answering, still staring at Alec, who was still standing on the crate, looking pleased with himself. There was a small, stocky being, parti-colored in gray and white, still standing and looking at Alec while picking its nose.

"Well, at least we have one volunteer," Alec announced proudly, and jumped down the crate to embrace the little being. It immediately began trembling with fear. Alec tried to calm it down, but the little creature started to scream out something in an unknown language. "Get me a translator android," shouted Alec, as he let go of the little guy. A hovering orb flew up and over Lady Fuzza's head, brushing her crest, and settled down to the little being's level. Alec walked over to his senior officers and said, "I know what you're all thinking, but remember, we need volunteers or we'll certainly have a mutiny on our hands." He glanced toward the little piebald fellow. "Is the translator done?" he demanded.

Behl nodded his head and said, "Yep!" The little spacer was hobbling away as fast as its bandy legs could take it, clutching its debit card tightly.

"Perhaps Captain Behl and I should go and try to buy or recruit some more crew, while the two of you go to that VIP auction?" recommended Captain Zlo, unable to conceal his disappointment.

TWENTY-TWO

ABOARD a Florencian border station several light years distant, the Commander pondered a message from one of his spies. After considering it for a while, he roused himself, handed the encrypted datapad to a waiting officer, and said, "Lieutenant, take this message to Admiral Jonas Nass of the Ninth Galactic Fleet at Handover. See to it that it's delivered personally. It's urgent, but I don't want to send a transmission, in the event someone might intercept and decode it."

The young courier looked at him curiously, and her commander said, "It appears that Nastasturus is preparing for something. One of their Galactic fleets has entered the neutral zone a few light years away from New Frontier."

The young lieutenant saluted her commander, and then immediately hurried away to a waiting shuttle.

ALEXA woke up from a very long dream of pain to the depressing reality of more pain. Every muscle she possessed ached, and the leather cords wrapped around her fingers and big toes offered an agony all their own. She was strung up spread-eagled, naked, with each of her fingers and big toes tied individually to a large, magnetized metal hoop atop a small hovering podium.

A mechanical orb flew around her, taking measurements; from time to time, tiny lightning bolts speared out to test her nervous system. Sweat poured down her muscular, flawless body; her hair was soaked, and stuck to her head and shoulders like glue. Every time she moved her head, she felt faint. She was thirsty and her tongue had swollen, making it difficult to breath. She was panting harder and harder just to get enough oxygen to survive.

Alexa had no idea how long she'd been strung up like an animal ready for skinning. When she looked up and saw her fingers, she wanted to cry. They were swollen and dark purple, almost disfigured. She couldn't see her own feet, but knew that her big toes wouldn't be a pretty sight either.

She noticed for the first time since she'd come to the four guards standing by an entrance on the other side of the chamber. All were looking at her with hungry eyes, their expressions dull with lust. She wanted to snarl and scream at them, but just then the orb moved in front of her and stole her attention. Alexa made several futile attempts to butt the flying medical andy with her forehead, but to no avail. The orb had examined her for a very long time; for how long she had no idea, but every time it fired its tiny lightning bolts at her vulnerable body, she twitched. It didn't hurt but it tickled, and that was something Alexa hated above anything else. She remembered how she and her best friends—and even her siblings—had all gotten into tickle fights, and for a second she forgot her dangerous predicament...until the orb zapped her again. Being tickled was her biggest weakness. From their expressions and laughter, the guards seemed to enjoy her torture.

Alexa emitted a short, hysterical scream—and then she laughed, more from her ridiculous situation than anything else. She kept laughing and shouting every time the orb zapped her, first in the tender skin under her arms and then down across her stomach and navel. As she writhed and giggled under the torture, she didn't notice as several people filed through an entrance she couldn't see.

"It is happy?" asked a soft-spoken, surprised female voice behind her.

When Alexa heard the voice, she immediately stopped giggling and strained to look over her shoulder. Something cold touched the back of her neck and trailed down her spine, giving her chills and ridging her skin with goose bumps. Something was touching her with its nails or claw tips, she thought, and she was afraid she knew just who, or at least what, it was. Alexa bit down on her lower lip, trying her best not to laugh. The nails moved on over her buttocks and behind her right leg, and she noticed a faint hissing sound, there on the very edge of audibility.

That's when she began to feel strange and afraid. Her skin turned ice-cold, and there was no longer a tickling sensation from the touch. She began trembling like she had never trembled before when the hissing ceased, and the thing behind her emitted a laugh of pure, poisonous malice.

At that moment, Alexa was the more afraid than she'd ever been in her life.

She lowered her head, closing her eyes, too afraid to even cry. The only sounds in the room came from her chattering teeth and from her fast, heavy breathing. Her trembling was using up all her physical energy. She felt something touching her chin, forcing her head up gently. Alexa opened her eyes, and screamed in pure horror.

In front of Alexa stood the source of many dark horror tales, the boogeyman of all boogeymen, except it was no man. It was a woman, a woman whose name was used as a metaphor for some of the most dreadful deeds in the universe. When Alexa saw the monster, she knew instantly that all those horror stories had one thing in common; they were based on reality. She had thought that Zuzack had lied to her about the infamous Black Lady—a legend, a tale to scare children—but she knew now that he had not.

Just as in the stories, the Lady was dressed in a black cloak covering her entire body. Her pale fingers were three times longer than Alexa's, and their skin was stretched very tight across the bones. Her nails were half as long as her fingers, and Alexa could feel her own blood trickling down her back and the stinging sensation from her own sweat when it dripped into the cuts made by those razor-sharp nails.

A motherly and loving voice said something Alexa didn't understand, but the strange sound of the voice made her calm down. A hand touched her gently, comforting, lovingly. Alexa stopped screaming. She mustered her last strength to compose herself, to regain some small measure of dignity and self-respect. Alexa glared boldly at the monster and two lifeless eyes stared back at her, two gaping black pits that held no trace of a soul. Small reddish-gold dots glittered in their depths; they reminded her of hellfire, and the hell of being eaten alive.

The thought of being cannibalized was the worst possible death she could imagine, worse than slow, painful torture, and certainly worse than being burned to death or flayed while conscious.

Alexa knew that she would soon meet her demise in just the way she feared, though, and her natural instinct for survival took over. She began struggling like mad against her tight bonds. She didn't care about the pain in her fingers and toes, or the blood slipping down her wrists as she jerked against the tight leather straps. She snarled defiance at the creature in front of her. Behind the monster stood Zuzack, smiling, and a laughing Hughes. Alexa's defiance deepened to pure hate, and once again, in a desperate effort of demonstrate some dignity, she forced herself to stopped struggling. She looked into Zuzack's eyes and whispered, in a voice colder than the absolute zero of deep space, "I forgive you...until next time."

Her words made Hughes beat on his knees and laugh so hard that tears poured down his rattish face, but Zuzack's smile flickered. In that instant, Alexa recognized in Zuzack something she never seen before: perhaps it was fear. Whatever it was, she didn't care: she gathered her last traces of saliva and spat it at the monster in front of her. But before the spittle reached the intended target, a long white tongue edged with tiny teeth shot out and caught it. With a snorting hiss, the tongue went back into the mouth; the monster just smacked her lips and said in that misleadingly motherly voice, "Oooh, feisty. And she tastes good, too, beautiful and perfect. I'll take her."

ALEC and Lady Fuzza stood in an enormous chamber. The air stank of misery. In front of them stretched several lines consisting of hundreds of slave blocks, holding thousands of prisoners in bondage. There were all types of Omans, omanoids, and transgenics present, along with more alien species of every type in the known universe, and possibly a few more besides. They ranged in age from larvae and toddler to very old. The sentients were organized by species, age, gender, and family in some cases, and further subdivided by special expertise. As the earlier auction had, the scene brought back bad memories for Alec, and he begun to feel faint while observing all those poor people from all their different worlds.

Lady Fuzza noticed Alec's face turn pale and whispered, "If you don't feel well, then perhaps we can do this some other time?"

"No!" he said sharply. "I'm all right. Let's get this over with, before the real crowd gets here." Thus far, only they and about another dozen VIPs had been allowed into the vast room to inspect the "merchandise" prior to the arrival of the hoi polloi. Said commoners waited in their multitudes several levels up, behind large windows and electromagnetic screens: thousands of prospectors and merchants and equally many tourists, staring down at the VIPs in envy. They were all waiting, with eager anticipation, to be allowed onto the floor below.

There was a distinct odor of antiseptics in the room; it reminded Alec of the fresh smell of an infirmary or hospital. Everything was very clean, and the space station provided the slave traders with their own unique slave blocks to enhance the impression made on the buyers. The only thing any slave wore was a thin white shift, the better to show off the merchandise. Towards the center and at the corners of the room were areas with circular platforms, each with one or more slaves attached to a metal pole while the podium moved round in circles. Alec noticed that only very important slaves, such as those with higher education or expertise ratings, the more extraordinary sex slaves—or to use a more politically correct term, "pleasure servants"—and a few so-called "former celebrities" were displayed on the podiums.

A large female omanoid was their tour guide and salesperson. She had pale greenish skin and long yellow hair that was braided into an ornate curl on top of her oval skull; physically, she was very muscular and well-toned. The first impression she gave was of limited intelligence...but then Alec noticed the glint in her eyes, and suspected that she was very experienced and very intelligent indeed.

"I noticed that none of the slaves has been molested or otherwise hurt by any of the guards," Alec said to the slave trader.

She looked a bit baffled and answered, somewhat surprised, "Of course not, good sir. These beings are valuable products, worth many credits apiece. Why would anyone want to damage them? What do you think of us, that we are animals?" The trader shook her head and walked away down the aisle of slave blocks, muttering something under her breath. Alec followed her—but before he could catch up, he noticed several young Oman children sitting in their own miniature block, their hands and feet extended before them just as his had been a few months before. A young, very sad face caught his eye: it was that of a little girl, ten years old, tops. Her innocent expression practically shouted out, *Why, why me, what have I done wrong?* None of the young ones was gagged and Alec thought he knew why: if they dared speak or cry, or worse, make a scene, then they would be punished—perhaps even electrocuted, or something much worse. The thought of it sent cold chills down Alec's spine.

He passed by, unable to speak.

He stopped in front of one slave block and looked at two young girls, whom he estimated were no more than ten or twelve years old. They were giggling and sticking out their tongues at five boys of a similar age on the opposite side, attached to another slave block. The boys behaved as the girls did. Alec thought, *Strange... they let them laugh, but not cry?*

The trader, who had returned to his side, read his mind—perhaps from his body language—and explained, "It is easier to sell a happy product than a sad one."

Alec ignored her remark. Instead, he turned to one of the laughing girls and asked, "What're you all laughing at? What's so funny?"

The little girl tried to wipe her teary eyes with her shoulder but failed. She looked towards the floor in an attempt to hide her expression, and then she replied shyly, as the rest of the children stopped laughing and took up similar submissive postures, "Ollie made a funny face. Master, forgive us. We, we are not spoiled merchandise, and you will be pleased if you buy one or all of us, for we are experts in our field."

Alec looked baffled as he wiped the young girl's face with a handkerchief. "You, an expert? Now, what could such a young person be expert at?"

"We will obey and pleasure you, master. Anything the master wishes from us, we will learn and do."

"They are perfectly bred, and will please you in anything," said a soft voice proudly, "from household labor, to amusing entertainment, to whatever sexual technique you prefer—no matter how...eccentric."

Alec turned around, prepared to jam his fist into whatever face had produced that angelic voice. The only problem was that he found himself staring into a wide red-and-black mottled torso. He had to step back and crane his neck to see into the face that that belly belonged to. It was a non-omanoid easily three times his own size, and he or she was looking down at him with some of the nicest, friendliest eyes he had ever seen.

"No thanks, not interested, perhaps another time." Alec looked straight ahead as he ducked under the being's long legs.

He saw the trader and Lady Fuzza standing some distance away, next to a slave block holding ten prisoners, all women. Alec joined them and said, "Milady, we have been over this section already, and I doubt we missed anything."

The Lady glanced at her handheld computer pad and noted that the trader had just shifted the group from another section. "Not these. They just arrived."

Alec noticed the trader slide a debit card into her sleeve. Alec frowned, and looked over Fuzza's shoulder at the computer pad; then he looked at the slaves. He strolled along the length of the block, and not one of the slaves dared to look back at him. "What are their qualifications?" he asked finally.

"They are all qualified spacers, and several of them are pilots," answered the trader proudly.

Alec walked around the block to inspect the five women on the opposite side. He thought, *Damn, these women look familiar...where have I seen before?* It was with a jolt that he suddenly recognized one, and his mouth went dry. It was that redhead, the friend of the incredible pirate woman who had seduced and betrayed him. What was her name...? Terra? Tara! That was it. Now her hair was a drab brown, but he was certain it was her.

Tara avoided Alec's eyes until Alec said loudly, "Zuzack?"

Tara and the others with her looked up at Alec, horror writ large on all their faces, and then quickly looked down in a futile attempt to cover their mistake. They started to whisper among themselves.

"Trader, I will take them all!" Alec said in a loud voice.

The trader looked up and her face shone in a bright smile, revealing a mouth filled with flat grinding molars. Ironically, she hailed from a species of obligate vegetarians. But then, so did bulls, and look how dangerous they could be...

Her grin failed when Alec added, "And I'll take anyone else who came from this original lot."

"But, but, that's almost two hundred people," The trader stuttered.

"You heard him!" bellowed Lady Fuzza. Alec cast her a quick glance, somewhat surprised by her sudden yell. Then he grinned mirthlessly and stepped up to the cowed Tara. He grabbed Tara under her cheek with a firm grip and forced her to look at him. "Little girl, I *know* you recognize me. I'm the boy who got away. Now, where are Zuzack and his young whore? The one you hung around with, the one with the long black hair? And what about her friend, the one with the tattoo or burn mark on her head? Where are they? Answer! You know who I'm talking about."

"Please don't hurt me," Tara whimpered, looking at Alec in horror.

The trader had overheard some of the conversation; now she approached Alec and whispered into his ear, "We have ways of making them comply, but not here, sir. The auction will start soon and we don't want to demoralize the other products." She straightened and turned towards Tara. "Now answer your new master, or I'll have you sent down to the preparation room. No merchandise traded through me ever embarrasses me, you got that, product?"

Alec's thoughts were a confused, infuriated jumble. Had someone already beaten him to the pirates and wiped them out already? Grimly, he snatched the computer pad away from the trader. She protested, saying something about how only traders had the right and permission to review the manifests—but she stopped talking when she saw Alec's expression.

He looked at Tara, who immediately choked out, "She is not with us. Zu-Zuzack is selling her to the Gormé..."

Snarling, the trader immediately jabbed Tara in the neck with a small metallic device, causing her to pass out. Angrily, Alec grabbed hold of the trader's neck, as Pier and Wolf grabbed her arms and immobilized her. He heard a commotion behind them as station security personnel came running.

"No damage to the goods, eh?" Alec whispered threatening. "And here I'd already bought them. I'd say that leaves you open to criminal charges of damaging another person's property. She'd best not be hurt." He signaled for Pier and Wolf to let her go.

The security guards arrived, demanding to know what was happening. The trader rubbed her bruised neck and stiffly told them that there had been a misunderstanding, as she slid a few debit tickets into their hands. The guards settled down, but warned all of them to take it easy, and then offered to send for a medical andy for Tara. Fuzza declined, and after the guards went on their way, she injected Tara with a small pen-hypo. Tara awoke immediately, looking quite startled.

Alec turned toward the slave trader. "Listen up. These girls are my property now, and if you touch them again or harm them in any way, my friends behind you will tear your flesh off your bones. Understood?"

The trader nodded sharply, glancing at Pier and Wolf; and for the first time, Alec realized that they had concealed weapons, tiny blasters holstered unobtrusively under their arms. They were not unobtrusive at the moment. Alec gave Pier a questioning glance, but the security officer just looked at him with the innocent expression of a five-year-old. Wolf, on the other hand, didn't look innocent at all; he was grinning from ear to ear.

Alec snorted, and gestured to his followers to move out. Behind him were almost twenty slave blocks filled with hardbitten women from all over the inhabited galaxies; and none of the onlookers on the balconies above, or any of those lined up outside the main entrance, knew that they were all former pirates. Someone in the crowd whispered, "Look! There's the young prince," and soon people were passing along rumors at a rapid pace.

"My, my, he must have quite the appetite for the female species."

"They say he's from an old, wealthy family from the Herrier system."

"Hah! He's obviously not a Herrier. My source tells me he is a pirate."

"I was told he's the bastard son of the Emperor of Marengo himself."

"He's a fuel trader. Made his fortune on fuel, he did."

"He must have inherited a fortune."

"Oh no, he's just a lucky gambler, this I know for a fact. My connections at the Star-Dice tell me he's worth..."

CAPTAINS Behl and Zlo were inspecting several crates of newly-arrived cargo when the hangar-bay doors slid aside to admit a long line of hovering slave blocks, escorted by the *K-13*'s security personnel and several inspectors from New Frontier.

Captain Zlo stared for a long moment before blurting, "We are not slavers!" He made no effort to hide his concern and disgust.

"They are not slaves," Alec replied mildly, as he joined Behl and Zlo.

"Then what in hell are they? Lost tourists?"

"Not...exactly." Alec casually studied a clipcomp for a moment, then looked up. "They're pirates. Well, former pirates."

"P-p-p...*what?*"

Alec motioned to Behl, and whispered, "He's here."

"Right now?" asked Behl.

Alec nodded. "At the very least, he *has* been here. He may still be. Anyway, this is part of his crew. They're all women. I don't know what happened yet, but we *will* find out."

Behl grabbed Alec's arm and said, his voice trembling— not from fear, but from hope—"Alec! I must check the auctions to see if I can find some of my former crew and get them back; perhaps some of them can join us?"

"Of course. Take some of the ship's security personnel with you, and take as long as you need. Do you have enough money?"

"After what you gave me, yes, I have more than enough."

"No, sir. Save your money, and charge any purchases to the ship. And now," he said, grinning, "before you take off, there's someone I want you to meet."

Alec gestured to Wolf, who approached carrying a young woman over his shoulder like a sack of meal. "Meet Tara," he said, as Wolf set her carefully on her feet. Her arms and legs were bound, so all she could do was stand there, glaring at them. "Tara was employed by a mutual acquaintance, sir. I'm not sure you ever met her, but she was one of Zuzack's crew."

Behl could only stare in disbelief; Zlo's eyes seemed about to pop out. Alec continued, "When you gentlemen have pulled your chins up off the floor, perhaps you can join me in the conference room. Wolf, put her back." When she was gone, he gestured towards the elevator behind them.

Behl followed, but Zlo stepped up to the nearest slave block. His attention had been stolen by a huge Saurian woman who took up half a block by herself. She was missing both of her legs. When she noticed Behl's attention, she emitted a short cry, then tried for what she thought was a sexy, seductive smile. A giant tongue flicked out and passed over most of her face, making a very strange and un-sexy sound. Zlo was fascinated for a moment, as he might have been by a hovertrain wreck, but then he remembered two things: first, why he had left his wife, and second, that he had a meeting to attend.

Zlo hurried into the conference room, an image of the giant lizard woman flirting with him still in his mind. He shook his head in an effort to make it vanish. He noticed that Alec was now standing over the young woman he had called Tara; she had been unbound, and was sitting in one of the conference room chairs, hiding her face in her hands. Alec hit his hand hard on top of the long table. The bang made the young woman jump in her seat. "Now tell us everything!" he demanded.

Tara looked up with teary eyes.

"And don't you leave anything out," whispered Behl in a threatening voice. "Or my friend behind you will take care of you." Tara pulled her head away from Behl's grip and looked at Wolf, who smiled, displaying a mouthful of brown and broken teeth. Tara started to cry. Lady Fuzza handed her a handkerchief and said in a motherly tone, "Child, please help us, and no harm will come to you. You might just get your freedom back." She gave both Alec and Behl a look of disgust.

Tara trembled and looked thankfully at Lady Fuzza as she dried her tears, and then the words poured out of her like an avalanche. She told them everything that had happened after "Alexa's slave had escaped," revealing how they had been caught up in the failed mutiny and auctioned off as slaves. Ten or twenty of them had already been sold, she said; and from that Alec learned that Nina had been purchased by a frog-like monster. But when Alec asked about Alexa, Tara shook her head. "I don't know, honestly. But Alexa and Nina were on the same block, I think, so you might be able to trace Alexa through Nina." Tara sobbed. "What's going to happen now? Are we going to jail, or are we going to be executed?" She'd barely finished her sentence before she started to cry again, harder than before.

Alec charged out of the room like a tornado, followed by Behl and Captain Zlo. Behl stopped at the door and growled to Wolf, "Keep an eye on her!" Wolf nodded, and eyed the tableau. Lady Fuzza had embraced Tara hard, and now both of them were weeping.

As he stalked out of the hangar, Alec snapped, "Find me that trader, Captain Behl!"

"Aye aye sir, will do." Behl tapped a few keys on his wristcomp, muttered something under his breath, and then said aloud, "She's right outside, actually. Apparently you have a few more documents to sign."

Alec found a very impatient trader waiting next to an empty slave block; it was clear that she was having difficulty hiding her frustration as she tried to finalize the transaction while Alec grilled her about the entity who had bought Nina. When she had a moment to think, she admitted that she did know the creature, and told Alec who it was and how to find it.

Alec smiled tightly at the trader and handed her a 10,000-credit card. "Thank you for the information," he said. She smiled back as she slid the card into her sleeve.

"You should let me go with you," she said. "I can help you with the trade, and they are very dangerous people. You have paid me more than enough, and I would like to make up for my earlier behavior."

Alec nodded sharply in consent, and she looked pleased. "And remember, sir," she cautioned, "whatever you say, *never* use the words 'pirate' or 'Gormé'."

"I understand," Alec replied with some frustration. "And you are sure we have plenty of time to find them before they leave the station?"

"Oh yes, sir," the trader said smoothly. "The special cargo is all locked up. I will find and negotiate with Lady Padda, the woman who has your friend. We go back a long time, her and I, and I don't foresee any problems."

"Very good. Let's get the rest of this cargo into my ship, and then we'll go looking for this Lady Padda of yours. I don't have time for any bullshit, so let's be clear here: this is the amount I'm going to give you, but only if you can get me both of them." He handed her another debit card, which she swiped through her wristcomp's reader. Her eyebrows went up. "Very nice," she noted, "but you haven't activated your transfer."

"That's because I haven't told you what to do yet, now have I? And you haven't gotten me my merchandise yet either." Alec took the trader under her arm and walked away, while making sure no one was listening to their conversation.

Captain Zlo gestured for his security people to begin loading the slave blocks onto the ship. The women were strangely silent, but their eyes held a faint hope that, somehow, their lives were about to improve. Behl walked up to Zlo, followed by Pier.

The Marengan looked askance at Behl. "He's not going to give another speech, is he?"

Behl snorted. "Hell, he'd better not, or we'll be stuck here forever." He looked over the women who were being loaded onto the ship.

Captain Zlo smiled mirthlessly. "Any orders? What we are supposed to do with all these...people?"

"Let them stay where they are. I'm sure we'll have 'em up and running soon."

"Good luck trying to find your friends."

"Thanks, Zlo." Behl ambled off, followed by Pier and two of his fellow security officers, and the little group joined the slave trader and Alec at the door of the hanger. After a quick jawing session, they left.

IT didn't take long before the rumors were flying about a mad Oman who bought slaves and set them free—and to top it off, gave them more money than an average person earned in a year upon their release. The news spread like a forest fire through the entire population of New Frontier 16. Some people thought it a noble gesture, while others considered it a threat to the slave trade. Most people didn't care, and knew that eventually even these rumors would fade. Some individuals, of course, listened more intently than others. One of these individuals was an old woman who called herself Coco Cabelle. Under another name she had been a Marengan pirate hunter—or, as most of her prey called them, a Predator. Coco was currently the head of security for the entirety of New Frontier 16. Her contract was with the citizens of the space station and the infamous Brakks, the leaders of both the Federated Merchants and the Commercial Traders. Coco's main objectives were to secure the space station from any threats, whether natural or unnatural, and to ensure its survival. This also included maintaining peace and order so that the outpost remained financially independent during its long journey.

It had been a long day, and there were hours yet before she could head for her quarters. When she first picked up the report, she looked at it with bored eyes; but those eyes soon widened, and she became quite interested in its contents.

Coco's life as head of security aboard New Frontier 16 was mostly eventless and boring, and she missed her old days hunting pirates for both Marengo and the Brakks. Oh, there had been chances for a little bit of excitement here and there, had she been willing to look the other way in exchange for filthy lucre. But Coco Cabelle was well-known for being untouchable. Not only could she not be blackmailed—her life was a completely open book—but any bribery attempt would result in a speedy expulsion for life from New Frontier 16, or, if she were feeling particularly cranky, a quick death.

Now, this report was something new and different, and she decided to take a personal interest in the situation's development. "I'll take care of this one myself," she declared to one of her officers, who saluted her and then left her office. She frowned as she delved deeper into the report about the young and very wealthy Oman. He had purchased a lot of 118 slaves of various species and had let them all go free. Then he'd taken ownership of a group of almost 200 female slaves, and looked fair to let them go, too. She smiled; good for him! Like all Predators, she loathed the slave trade—and not just because it was the pirate scum's most lucrative sideline, but because she simply believed it was wrong and against the natural order of the universe. She couldn't help raising her eyebrows when she noted the balance on the accounts maintained by the Oman, the result of the sale of several unique and expensive items, including tritonium silver artifacts.

Several different theories began to develop in the back of her mind regarding this young Oman. Might he be a pirate himself? Or perhaps he was a spy or a thief, or even a terrorist sent here to unbalance the outpost's financial system? Might he be a point man for a hostile takeover? He might be a fanatic of some sort; but then again, maybe he was just *nice*. There were a few good people left in the universe. She was completely at a loss with her theories, because New Frontier had never hosted anyone quite like this Alec Horn. She'd never known anyone to buy slaves and set them free; or at least, not this way, and not after giving them each a year's salary. Her astonishment quickly soured into suspicion, and she was craving answers.

A faint sound from her door warned her that someone wanted to see her. Coco avoided using a communicator as much as possible, because she wanted to be able to determine when and how other people could use her time. When she looked up, she saw her second-in-command, Major Lizza, and welcomed the crested Marengan in with a faint smile. The two had worked together for over fifty years before they had retired from pirate hunting and gone to work for the Brakks. "Urgent development a few light years away from us," Lizza reported, handing Coco a clipcomp.

Coco paged through the report, and looked uneasily at her second. "An entire galactic fleet?"

"Yes indeed. We've confirmed that it is in fact Nastasturan."

"Anyone else know about this?"

"I don't think so, but it's only a matter of time." Lizza hesitated briefly, then said, "There is something else."

Coco nodded for Lizza to continue.

"There are more rumors than ever about pirate activities in the sector, and a number of important people have begun to voice their concerns."

"Have the Key Administrators contacted us about launching an investigation?"

"Not directly, but they've made it clear in a roundabout fashion that they want the rumors to go away. They claim they're bad for business."

Coco snorted and pretended to ignore Lizza's last remark. She tapped the report on the clipcomp and ordered, "Take a corvette and find out what the fleet from Nastasturus is up to. I want you to command it personally."

Major Lizza nodded, happy for the chance to get back into action, and left the office. Coco swung her office chair around and attacked her desktop comp.

From the moment she'd arrived at her new post, Coco had suspected that one or both of the Key Administrators were involved in criminal activities, specifically in association with one of the pirate clans. There was no damned way any backwater sector like this one could be entirely free from pirate infestation, not when it was so heavily trafficked. For years, Coco had sporadically investigated anything that might turn her theory into reality. But she had no real evidence of criminal activity, and certainly no proof, that she could connect to either Tobbis or Zala or anyone on their staffs. On the surface, the two were squeaky clean—or at least as squeaky clean as it was possible for mercantile royalty to be. But things smelled fishy to grizzled campaigners like Coco and Lizza, and she had a hunch that something was desperately wrong. Hunches like this one had made her a very successful pirate hunter, and she had long since learned not to dismiss them.

The Brakks who had hired her never mentioned having any suspicions of their own, and they certainly had not directed her to investigate their Key Administrators. However, none of the Brakks had seemed upset—or surprised—when Coco inquired about inside deals between Tobbis and Zala. They denied any such knowledge, but admitted it was possible. "Protect our investment," was all they'd told her. They didn't seem to care how she did it.

So protect their investment she would, in any way she saw fit, as long as it was morally defensible. And for the first time in years, she had a clue that she might lead her to cracking this conspiracy, whatever it was, wide open.

The feral grin she wore as she tapped away on her comp would have chilled the blood of even a demon like Horsa.

TWENTY-THREE

OVER fifty thousand people crowded the spherical stadium, cheering lustily when their favorite team scored again. A moment later the Asteroid players left their chaotic huddle, and took up their hovering positions within the globe-shaped arena. There were fifteen players on each team, and one goal that constantly and randomly changed its position near the middle of the sphere. As the fans waited in breathless anticipation, a new asteroid shot out from an opening in the ceiling, and the players rushed it with great enthusiasm.

The players, both offensive and defensive, were equipped differently, depending on their positions. They resembled astronauts from the ancient days of the First Awakening, when the ancestors of all the Oman races first ventured away from the semi-mythical home world. Most of their uniforms were padding and armor, because the fighting among them was fierce. As one of the offensive players reached for the ball, a defensive player slashed at his arm with a long halberd; the wide, ax-like blade at the end was finely-honed, and penetrated the first player's suit sufficiently to just about take his arm off. Trailing blood, the injured player dropped the ball and dove for an opening in the wall before he could bleed out. A replacement player shot out from another opening, and immediately entered the fray.

The crowd went berserk as the fine red mist settled onto them; they seemed unconcerned about the injured player, so Alec assume that the damage to the man's arm was easily repairable. He'd been informed that organ cloning and stim rejuvenation were common practices in this sector.

Alec and Lady Fuzza sat in a VIP box, with several security personnel standing behind them. They were enjoying the game. Alec explained the rules with an eagerness of a child to Lady Fuzza, who looked on with somewhat less enthusiasm. As the game wound down toward halftime, the door behind them irised open, and in came Captain Behl, Pier, the trader who had sold them the pirate women, and two other people they hadn't met before.

Alec immediately noted the change in Behl. His happiness couldn't go unnoticed. He was grinning as Alec and the Lady stood up, and said grandly, "Allow me to introduce to you, Alec Horn, the *Bright Star*'s First Officer Celestine Brown, and the ship's Chief Medical Officer, Phalaxor." Alec grinned delightedly and made nice with the two sailors as he looked them over. Brown was a well-built woman who appeared to be a Herrier, like Behl, though she had a fluffy tail something like a fox's; apparently she was a transgenic Oman. He could tell from the charisma she radiated that she had a very strong personality, and looked forward to getting to know her better. Phalaxor was a slender non-omanoid of a type Alec had never seen before; he had three legs and two arms, each tipped with three thick digits. His large face bore a camouflage motif in green and brown, and seemed fused into a permanent wry grin, like a dolphin's.

"I'm delighted to see that you found some of your crew," Alec remarked, after welcoming Brown and Phalaxor aboard.

"All thanks to our trader here, who still refuses tell me her name."

"My number is sufficient, and I never get personal with my clients," the trader said dryly.

They were interrupted as another goal was made; thousands of people screamed their approval. Alec gestured for everyone to have a seat, and for the trader to sit next to him. Lady Fuzza gave up her seat and walked over to Pier.

"Any news on the two female pira...um, the merchandise?" Alec asked, his heart sinking as he noted the grim expression on the trader's face.

"I have found one of them," she admitted, "but the other will be...difficult."

Alec looked at the trader curiously.

"One of the items is over there." The trader pointed with a long green-tinged finger towards a skybox opposite them.

"Who is it? I can't see from here."

"I forgot about your poor Oman eyesight, sir. Sorry." She didn't sound sorry. "Here, use these." She removed a small pair of binoculars from the back of the seat in front of them, handed them to Alec, and instructed him on where to aim them.

As he focused in, Alec saw a large box where both of the Key Administrators sat, in the company of several Omans and a number of more exotic races. It wasn't difficult to figure out that the giggling grayish-green lump on one end of the row was Padda. The alien's laughter made her entire fat body tremble in convulsions. Two young and attractive girls—one a slender saurian type and the other a standard Oman with short, dark hair and a prominent tattoo on the side of her head—tended Padda. The Oman was Nina; Alec recognized her immediately. The beast they massaged was so big that the girls seemed tiny in comparison.

Padda laughed so hard that she sneezed, hawking yellowish goo all over the two servants. Nina was covered from head to toe. Once she got over her shock, she spat back at Padda, and punched her in one of her three glassy eyes. Padda laughed even harder, then grabbed Nina like a child and forced her inside a large pouch on her belly. Alec thought that Nina had just been eaten alive, and he leaped up from his seat.

The trader placed her hand on Alec's arm and assured him in a calm voice, "Don't worry, sir, she is only putting the girl away in her womb so that she can teach her a lesson. It's a normal thing they do among her species. The girl will be all right, perhaps a little groggy after...well, I don't think you want to know."

"Buy her. Buy her now," Alec said, agitated.

"If I may say, sir, it would be better if we wait until after the game, or Lady Padda will think that you are desperate and increase the price for the product."

"I *said*, buy her now. It's been several weeks since I got to this Gull-forsaken place. You promised me results, and we can't linger here much longer."

A low voice from behind them threatened, "You heard my Captain. Buy her *now!*" Brown glared at the trader, malice in her dark eyes.

"There is no need for any unpleasantness." The trader's eyes flickered from Brown to Alec.

"As you wish, sir. One moment."

Alec shot Brown an appreciative look as the trader talked into her wristcomp.

Alec kept his binoculars focused on the skybox opposite, having completely lost interest in the game. An assistant or servant of some sort spoke into Lady Padda's ear. The fat frog-woman smiled and laughed, shaking her head.

"Increase the offer significantly," Alec instructed, while looking through his binocular.

Again the servant whispered, and this time Lady Padda looked puzzled. She placed one of her long arms inside her pouch and dug around; a thin, watery gel splattered on one of her neighbors, who glared at her disapprovingly. She finally pulled out a small non-omanoid who panted for air and spat out something nasty at the same time. Padda held him up by his hair towards Alec's skybox with a questioning expression.

"No, not him," Alec muttered, making no attempts to hide his frustration.

Lady Padda pushed her property back inside of her pouch and dug around some more. She pulled out a larger male Orchid Oman who kicked and screamed. "No!" Alec snarled. Again, Padda shoved the alien back inside after listening to her servant, who was chattering into her communicator device. Frowning, Lady Padda reached in and pulled out yet another slave, and this time it was Nina. She held her the girl up her ankle, as she gasped for air and spat out some type of watery gray filth.

The servant whispered something, and Lady Padda laughed, nodding in consent. She then proceed to lick all the slime off Nina as the girl screamed and swung at her with both fists.

"Holly Gull, how many can she fit inside?" wondered Alec, feeling a bit sick. He perked up considerably when the trader informed him that the merchandise was now his.

So focused was he on the spectacle that Alec never noticed that both of the Key Administrators had followed the development with great interest.

---oOo---

THE transaction was observed with even more interest from yet a different part of the arena. At the rear of the SRO section, Coco Cabelle lowered her binoculars, pursed her lips thoughtfully, and walked away with a neutral expression. Two of her assistants followed in her wake.

"Has he made any more inquires about illegal trade?" she asked one of her aides.

"No, ma'am, not him personally," the young man answered respectfully, "but several of his crew and even his trader have made discrete inquiries."

"His trader wouldn't risk her trade-license for any illegal trade, surely."

"Yes ma'am, I quite agree."

"So you don't think he's particularly interested in Gormé?"

"No ma'am, I don't. It appears he's looking for a particular slave. A woman."

She harrumphed. "A *pirate* woman, perhaps?"

The other aid, a crested Marengan woman, cut in, "We believe that most of the slaves he purchased came from the same source, and yes, all of them have questionable backgrounds."

"But they do check out?" Coco asked, passing her hand over an unremarkable section of wall. A hatch irised open, and they entered the lift it exposed, which immediately started to rise.

"Yes, ma'am. All of them were signed off on by Key Administrator Zala."

Coco turned and looked at her aide, hiding her surprise. "A Key Administrator personally signed off on a few slaves?"

"Actually, there were more than two thousand in the bunch she signed off on," the aide said thoughtfully. "But these were the only ones actually placed for sale. The others were retained for what the records note as 'administrative purposes'." He shrugged and added, "It's unusual, but it has happened from time to time."

"Maybe...but not during my tenure on NF-16." Coco scowled. "Any further developments in your research on what might have happened to the *Bright Star*?"

"Nothing as of now," the younger woman replied, "but I'm still looking into it."

The elevator took them straight to the main security office at the center of the huge space station, where they were met in the lobby by Major Lizza and a high-ranking military officer from the Nastasturus Federation. Coco dismissed her aides to their tasks, concealing her frustration at not being forewarned about the newcomer's presence.

Major Lizza made the introductions. "Security Chief Coco Cabelle, this is Lieutenant Admiral Alistair Busch of the 11th Galactic Fleet, Nastasturus Federation."

Coco took a moment to size up the Admiral, who responded by eyeballing her from top to bottom, more arrogantly than she liked. She noted the glee in his eyes, and realized that he was enjoying what she perceived as a particularly tense and dangerous situation. *A killer... The type of killer who shoots first and never asks any questions later.* She'd encountered his kind, on both sides of the law, many times while serving in the CPH ranks.

She did not deign to let her true attitude of him show. "Welcome to New Frontier 16, Admiral. Perhaps we should retire to my office...?"

When they entered her office, Busch sat without being invited. Again, Coco hid her dislike. Major Lizza, of course, waited for the invitation before she sat down at the small round conference table.

"So, Admiral, what brings you here?" Coco asked after a brief silence.

"Our business is our own. However, we expect full cooperation from you and your Key Administrators. Is that clear?"

Since he'd laid his cards on the table in the rudest way possible, Coca felt no further need to hide her opinion of the man. "You should have paid a bit more attention to your diplomacy classes in War College, Admiral Busch. This is not the way to get whatever it is you want. Threats are pointless. You have no jurisdiction over NF-16, the Traders, or the Merchants. Your fleet presence has begun to make people in this sector uneasy. This is neither your territory, nor..."

To her disgust, Coca was interrupted. "Three months ago, a civilian transport cruiser carrying over nine thousand passengers and about a thousand crew members was attacked by pirates a few systems away, well within the region that you people supposedly police. Some of the passengers came from very distinguished families in our Federation. And you *will* cooperate, by Gull, because we believe people associated with your outpost are involved in the attack up to their elbows. No Brakk in the universe can protect you if I discover that this is the case. Is that diplomatic enough for you?"

A strange silence fell; and after a long moment Coca nodded towards Major Lizza, who inclined her head and left the room. Coca pressed a button on her desk, and a force field snapped into place around the conference area. She rose, still silent, then walked over to a bar and poured a couple of drinks. She sat down one glass hard on the desk, causing some of its contents to splash onto Admiral Busch, who ignored the stains and the glass while staring at Coco.

She looked at the glittering force field and took a deep breath before breaking the silence. "Admiral, I will cooperate, but you must understand that I'm more or less alone in this, except for a handful of my people."

Admiral Busch looked at her straight in her eyes. Then he picked up his drink and nodded sharply, while muttering something diplomatically unheard about unreasonable civilians.

Nina felt like a scared child who was about to be spanked by her parents. She was in a spartan office aboard a spaceship of some kind—from what she had seen from the outside, it looked like a frigate—bound head and foot. She stood before a large desk with the back of a large, comfortable-looking chair turned towards her. Whoever was in the chair was busily tapping away at a keyboard, and just as busily ignoring her. She glanced to either side at the two brutes guarding her. One of them was in a desperate need of a dentist, while the other needed to take a very long shower. She wiped her forehead against her shoulder in a futile attempt to remove some of the doughy slime.

"You stink, pirate scum!" the dentally-challenged guard snapped.

Nina jumped when she heard the word "pirate." So they knew... and she knew far too well what could happen to any pirate caught by, well, just about anyone. She could be put in prison for life, raped, abused, executed in a variety of inventive ways—or worse, placed in an arena where she would be tortured to death while thousands of onlookers cheered on her demise. She started to shudder, frightened, thinking that this might be one of the notorious Predators that she had heard so many rumors about—a pirate hunter, someone who had absolutely no pity for those who preyed on the innocent and mercantile alike.

She quickly gathered herself and stuttered, "I-I-I'm no pirate, I'm a, a..."

"Pirate." The office chair had turned around, the man in it correcting her ironically. There was no mistaking who those deep blue eyes belonged to.

"You!" she shouted.

"Release her," Alec ordered, and the two guards unlocked her manacles and carefully stacked them in a corner. When she was loose and rubbing her wrists to restore circulation, he demanded, "Where is she?"

"Who?"

"As if you didn't know. I'm looking for your little friend, the one who was so eager to dine on me at her little initiation party. The girl with the black dreads. I heard everything from your Captain—believe me, he didn't dare leave anything out. Now answer me."

"*Eat* you?" she rolled her eyes. "By all the asteroids in the universe...What are you...?"

Alec slammed his hand on the desk, and Nina jumped.

"That black-haired devil! Give me a name!"

"Ah, you mean Zuzack. He..."

"*No*, Gulldammit! Not *him*, your dear little girlfriend. *What's her name?*"

Nina blinked. "Oh, you mean Alexa? She, uh, she was kind of my owner, and, uh, we got in trouble with Zuzack and he ordered us sold. I, we were on the same slave block at first, but got separated. I sat behind her, gagged. I doubt she knew I was even there."

"Then how do you know *she* was there?"

"Because I heard when Hughes and..."

"Who is Hughes?"

"The rat-lizard transgenic. He's one of Zuzack's officers."

"Oh. That one. Go on."

"I heard Hughes torturing her, and saying what they were... what they were going to do to her."

Nina's self-control cracked then, and she started to sob, then buried her face in her hands. Alec gestured to Wolf, who placed a chair next to Nina and sat her down in it. Once she'd settled down a bit, Nina begun to tell Alec everything she knew. A tiny flame of hope began to grow inside her as she spoke, and she looked up gratefully when an elderly smooth-skinned woman with a colorful crest entered the room, gave her a motherly smile, and handed her a cup of herbal tea.

"I am Lady Fuzza of Marengo," she said gently. "But dear, dear... by the way, what is your real name?"

"Nina."

"Just Nina?"

Nina nodded, looking down at her glass. "Just Nina," she mumbled. "Never had any more names."

"Come, my child, let me help you—and perhaps we can come up with a few more names." Lady Fuzza glared at Alec while helping Nina up from the chair and out of the cramped office.

"You two!" Alec gestured to Wolf and Pier. "Continue drilling and training with the others down below, and let me know how you're progressing later this evening." The two guards nodded, and saluted Alec before smartly turning around and leaving the room.

Behl entered immediately thereafter, and without preamble stated, "We have enough crew now, and considering that a fourth of them are known to be reliable, I think we can leave soon."

Alec gestured for Behl to have a seat in Nina's recently vacated chair, but the captain declined when he noticed what it was smeared with. With a disgusted expression, he continued with his report. "I've recovered almost fifty of my old crew, and all but five have signed on with us. I gave the other five enough money to pay off their contracts, and put them on different shuttles and transports away from here. None of them will talk about what happened until they reach a safe port."

"Good, then we don't have to worry about any pirate hunters competing with us."

"Doubt you'd have to worry about that anyway," said Behl, handing Alec a computer pad. "Moving right along, all the uniforms and weapons have been stored. We've also attached a few larger cannons and missile turrets to the hardpoint installations on the ship. The pirates we bought turned out to be very handy and skillful when it comes to concealing them, but I think we should attach the larger guns in deep space, once we're well away from here. The gunrunner I dealt with told me that the weapon systems, the mines, and the missiles we want are very illegal. Tomorrow we'll begin installing the, um, 'special room' that you asked for..." Behl shook his head and continued, "He says he'll meet us wherever we want."

Alec and Behl spent the next ten minutes going over their plans before Behl burst out, "Oh, hell, I forgot. You have over thirty messages from that little pants-pissing guy."

"From who?"

"That little...you know, our host from the casino."

"You mean Mr. Tota."

"Yeah, I guess that was his name. Tota the little pants-pissing guy, from Gull only knows where."

"I'll look into it later," Alec assured him.

"One more thing. You also have several messages from some tailor who claims your clothes and boots are ready and you should come pick them up. While you're at it, you might consider hiring a secretary."

Alec looked up at Behl with a surprised expression and said brightly, "Why, when I have you?"

Behl left, muttering something about "a spoiled smartass brat."

TWENTY-FOUR

AT that very moment—and much to her surprise, actually—Alexa was being pampered by half a dozen adorable male slaves of various species. They washed her all over with soft sponges, and massaged her shoulders and legs. She lay in a round marble pool filled with clean gel-water, enjoying herself thoroughly. One slave was feeding her grapes and another exotic fruit, while another slave was combing out her long, dark brown hair. Earlier, he had poured on something foul-smelling that loosened her dreadlocks into individual strands. A small waterfall poured into the far end of the rather large pool, and the sound of the falling water intermingled delightfully with the soothing musical strains two other male slaves coaxed from a pair of odd electronic instruments.

The harmony in the room was interrupted when Alexa kicked one of the servants in the face. The rest of the servants immediately stopped what they were doing. Alexa hissed threateningly, "Don't touch my feet."

The servants started to laugh, except for one; and some of them begin to tease and caress her softly. Alexa had never judged a book by its cover, but she knew all too well that her servants had no interest in women. In her disappointment, she let a sigh of frustration. She had noticed that all of them were exceptionally well-endowed; their thin tunics revealed more than enough for her to come to that conclusion. She wouldn't having mind one of them right now. *Or two. Or hell, why not three?* she thought lustfully, and sighed again. Her servants must have read her mind, because they all started teasing her with their caresses.

"My mistress likes her permanent guests to be happy. It does you good," said a gravelly voice from behind her.

"Oh. You." Alexa turned and eyed the short, stocky non-oman woman observing the scene. "What do you want, Sebilla?"

"Just making sure you are relaxed, my dear, and that you get your rest and eat enough. You do need some more meat on your bones; you should really start thinking more about our mistress's dinner guests, and stop being so selfish."

"Whatever." Fuming, Alexa rose from the pool, followed by her boytoys, who begged her to return and play with them. A slave wrapped a towel around her, and then escorted her to a stone table. Alexa lay down on her stomach, and another slave began massaging warm oil into her body. She was rather bored lied on her stomach, but when the masseur started to work her backside, she let out a moan of pleasure. Sebilla looked at Alexa with a motherly expression that an objective observer might have thought was full of nothing but love. Alexa knew better.

"My mistress wants you to be strong and fresh for your special event," Sebilla said sweetly. "Remember, it is a signal honor that you are about to receive."

"An honor, you say. Well, perhaps you would like to change places with me?"

"Oh my dear, now you're just being funny. Old Sebilla would be too stringy and gristly for the mistress's tastes. Truly, it's nothing to worry about. I have prepared hundreds of art products for my mistress. You won't die, dear, or so I fervently hope. It's hard to be sure sometimes."

Alexa clamped down on her emotions and said steadily, as if they were having a regular conversation, "So when will my big event take place?"

"Oh, dear, I must not say. The mistress doesn't want you to be concern about that; after all, you will be part of something not many people have ever been a part of. You should be proud and happy. This is an extraordinary honor, and there will be many famous and important people present on your gala night."

Alexa's skin turned ice cold, and the goose pumps made the masseur stop and look at Sebilla with disappointed eyes. "See what you did? Now we must start all over," complained the masseur. "We just had her relaxed, and now you have gotten her worried again." He made a gesture with his hand at Alexa's back. Sebilla looked at the tiny goose bumps, upset, and hurried away.

Alexa smiled to herself. It had been over a week since she realized that she could postpone her demise—or at least she thought she could—by getting goose pumps or bruises. On several occasions, she had deliberately bruised herself extensively by falling, or had cut herself. Everything had to be naturally healed; the Black Lady (or Shadow Bitch, as Alexa liked to call her) had been very clear on this matter.

All the slaves and servants knew what their mistress demanded, and they took all precautions while tending Alexa. They never left her by herself now, as they had become convinced that Alexa was causing the damage to herself. Whenever she had been caught, she had been told that she had no right to damage someone else's property, and that she should be grateful for not being punished by the whip, or the stick under her feet. So instead of punishing Alexa whenever she did something to herself, a little girl slave was severely whipped—and the last time, the little girl had died. Alexa had been bothered by that at first, but eventually her survival instinct took over. She'd done worse as a pirate, after all. She had decided to keep up with her rebellious behavior. She'd do anything to stay alive for as long as possible.

She had stopped being afraid by now, though, and decided to face her demise with dignity when it came—though she was determined to escape from this hell as soon as she could. She knew that she was aboard a very large spaceship and it was still docked to a very large space station—which one she didn't know—but she doubted that they would begin to feast on her while docked. It didn't matter, though, because she was going to survive and find the love of her life, her Silver Guard knight, no matter what happened—and no matter how long it might take her. She was inspired to survive, and ready to do whatever it took to get away...or if necessary, to kill herself. Perhaps she could find Alec in the next life.

THE Black Lady—Zoris Af Sun was her real name—had taken to observing the beautiful little female Oman from hidden places. Even she was amazed by the little one's *joie de vivre* and crystalline laughter. As a rule, Zoris avoided coming face-to-face with her art projects until she was ready to present them to her guests. She wanted them to be as comfortable as possible, and her presence wasn't conducive to that. From time to time, she cursed herself for having let this one see her in the first place. She was very surprised by how fast the little vixen had recovered after their first encounter. She knew this would be one of her very best art pieces. Too bad it didn't have a lover; a pair in love was always the best material to work with. It completed her work, somehow.

For hundreds of years, she had developed the techniques of her unique style of art to near-perfection. Only she herself, the infamous Black Lady, knew the truth about herself; and every time she was reminded of her once-splendid past, she wept. She might hide in her bedroom and cry for days, sometime weeks. She could never understand why life had been so cruel to her.

Once she had been the foremost physician in her field; but like an animal, her competitors had hunted her. They had stolen her invention, Permafreeze, which allowed individuals to be placed in suspended animation for long-term space travel. Instead of the normal three or six months in a cooler, she could freeze down a person for centuries, without causing significant brain or tissue damage. Her colleges had stolen her invention, damn them, and sold it to Florencia.

Her many different names came from an old fairy tale, centuries old, similar to the tale of the ancient bogeyman. She had used people's fears and superstitions and taken the names as her own. Only a very few people knew the truth about her and what she was about. They were all high ranking politicians, officers, pirate clan leaders and other extremely wealthy individuals. Indeed, most people knew her as a simple if wealthy art dealer; they had no idea about her second identity. She was considered an eccentric collector and trader of antique art from all the known inhabited worlds in the universe.

Zoris wiped away tears as she walked into her private quarters. She hated traveling in space, and couldn't wait until she was home in her own palace, where she could begin working on her next art piece and have her friends over for dinner.

"Inform the captain that I will be resting," Zoris told a servant as she left her observation room. "I don't want to be interrupted." The servant bowed his head submissively and hurried away. She walked along the corridor, drumming the sharp nails of her fingers on the bulkhead as she went, whistling a soft tune of her own composition.

ADMIRAL Jonas Nass gazed with pride at the glorious banner of the Florencian Federation hanging from the ceiling of the command bridge, then turned back to the viewport and watched as his capital ships eased to a halt. The Ninth Galactic from Handover was perhaps the most significant indicator of Florencia's military might, and as always he found it a most impressive, stirring sight as the large battle cruisers formed up into a defensive position. He had just over two hundred and fifty capital class cruisers, supported by thousands of destroyers, frigates, and supply ships.

His fleet faced a force of twenty-five Nastasturus capital cruisers, some ten thousand klicks away. Nass was unworried; his forces outnumbered the Nasties by more than ten to one. Of course, he rather doubted that there would be any fighting; after all, both fleets were in the neutral zone between the two empires. But one never knew what might happen.

When Nass had received word of the Nasties' presence in the sector, he had reported it to his superiors; and within the hour, the president of his Federation, from his office on Handover, had immediately ordered one Galactic Fleet to investigate why Nastasturus would send one of its own fleets to the region. His orders were to observe and avoid contact.

"Admiral Nass!"

The admiral turned to face a younger commander.

"A corvette-class ship from New Frontier 16 has hailed us, and its Captain invites you to meet the station's Key Administrators and to attend one of their formal balls this evening. How should I respond, sir?"

"Tell him I will be there."

"Aye aye, sir, but he insists that you come with him now. They don't want to alarm the civilians aboard the station by letting us use our own ships."

"He insists, does he?" The crafty old admiral knew that this was a custom, and not a trap; and anyway, only a complete idiot would try to kidnap one of Florencia's Elite citizens. "Inform their Captain I'll be docking my shuttle in his bay within an hour, and get me my personal shuttle pilot."

"Aye aye, sir." The commander hurried away to make all the arrangements.

MR. Tota wrapped his arms around Alec's waist, his expression overjoyed, and Alec was surprised by the little elephantoid's strength. Tota was almost crying, and Alec had to push him away gently but firmly. He well remembered the bladder problem this little fellow had whenever he got excited.

"My, my, look at you, young master!" Tota cried. "We have been very concerned since you left almost two weeks ago without checking out!"

"If you're worried about my hotel bill, let me assure you..."

Tota made a dismissive gesture with one stubby arm. "No, no! You have paid me more than I earn in a month. No, it's something else, my dear man."

Alec looked at him speculatively. "Well, that's interesting, Mr. Tota. I've been planning to see you and ask for some help and advice."

"You have?" Tota's face lit up, and his large ears stopped flapping. "About what?" He looked like some odd little dog eager to makes its master happy.

"Well, sir, why don't you start first? Why did you want to see me?" said Alec, while sitting down on a large couch and making himself comfortable. He had a beautiful view of New Frontier 16 from where he sat in Tota's crystal-walled office.

Tota looked suspiciously around the room, then activated an opaque force field, making it impossible for anyone outside to either view or listen in to their conversation. He strolled over and sat down next to Alec, and gestured with his trunk; a small lounge table drifted over to them and hovered in place, extruding a bottle of wine and two crystal tumblers. Alec shook his head slightly, and Tota gave him a sad expression.

The little fellow filled both cups while muttering, "Well, you might change your mind."

After he'd gripped his own cup tightly and taken a quiet sip, Tota focused his eyes on Alec for a long moment and said, "Young master, I regret to inform you that I have been getting numerous inquiries about you from various groups. Most of the time, my staff and I ignore these people. But only a few days ago...well, there was a tragedy. You, see one of the Lady Pulp's girls has gone missing—and the other is dead."

Alec looked at Tota, eyes wide. "The ones I was with that first night I stayed at the Star-Dice?"

Tota stared down at his glass and murmured, "I am afraid so."

Surprised and irritated, Alec snapped, "Are you suggesting that I had anything to do with it?"

"What, me? Do I...? No, of course not! Lady Pulp is very sad over her losses, and frankly so am I, but don't you worry about her—she has many lovelies in her stable, and the police are on the killer's trail. We even have a recording of the incident, I am sad to say, but unfortunately our security didn't get there in time to stop it. But let me show you something, young sir. It has to do with you and your friend the Captain...I think." Tota pushed a button on the hovering table and a holoscreen appeared in front of them. A brief but disturbingly graphic sequence flashed across the screen, showing a huge omanoid and a smaller non-oman interrogating—and then painfully torturing—the orange-furred entertainer he had spent the night with. They were asking about information regarding him and Behl, and she told them all she could—but it wasn't enough, apparently, so they hurt her terribly. Weeping openly, Tota slammed his little fist down on the button. "There is more, but..."

Shaken, Alec demanded, "Who else has seen this?"

"No one but me, young master. I gave the police an edited version. I don't want my best customer to be bothered by the police."

Alec smiled tightly. *Little bastard. It's always about the money.*

As if he'd read Alec's mind, Tota said stiffly, "I'm not interested in your money."

"What do you want, then?"

"Let me answer your question with a short story." Tota took a deep breath. He looked down on the floor and then back up at Alec. "For quite a long time, pirates have more or less controlled this sector, despite official protestations to the contrary. Indeed, people of influence from all the larger local organizations and federations, including our Key Administrators, have been involved in their activities. Those who do not cooperate, or pretend to, either die or disappear. So when I heard rumors about your expedition, to go after and seek the pirates who attacked you, I told myself, 'This I must be a part of.'"

"And why is that?" Alec asked, suspicious—but curious despite himself.

"For two reasons, young master. First, I'm tired of paying our Key Administrators their so-called 'security tax.' It's highway robbery. The second reason is..."

Suddenly Tota leaned towards Alec until his trunk almost touched Alec's face, and hissed, "Revenge."

For a moment, Alec was taken aback by Tota's sudden change from a chittering little blob to a very serious individual, and he said, "Revenge? Why?"

"The love of my life," Tota said bitterly. "My love...she was a slave, and I bought her freedom. Later, pirates killed her—I think," he moaned.

"I'm truly sorry, Tota, but do you really think you should involve yourself with me and my crew?" Alec asked.

"I'm already involved. They have killed one of my employees and kidnapped another. Lady Pulp has been with me for years, and she too wants to see justice done. Besides, you and my loved one have something in common."

Surprised, Alec asked, "What do we have in common?"

"That!" Tota pointed at the faint mark that encircled Alec's neck.

"This? My birthmark?" Alec asked, thinking Tota must be mad.

"It is not a birthmark, young master. Like her, it is an indication that you were once a slave."

Alec laughed sharply. "Mr. Tota, I was certainly never a slave. My father is..." Alec stopped himself, realizing he had almost told Tota his true identity. If that were to become known, he would certain be taken into protective custody and shipped home on the next transport back to Nastasturus.

"Master Alec, you are the son of Marshal Guss Villette Hornet, the Supreme Military Commander of the Nastasturus Federation."

Eyes wide, Alec looked bemused at Tota as the little being handed him his glass. As Alec sipped, Tota continued, "I'm well connected, young sir, but by no means a genius. If I figured out your background, then I suspect someone else soon will—or worse, perhaps someone already has. I doubt that would help your endeavor."

Alec nodded. "Assuming you're right, now what?"

"I once told you I could help and serve you..."

"For money, yes," grinned Alec.

"That was then, young sir, before I knew about your expedition. It is, perhaps, the most foolhardy expedition I have ever heard of, but still, you remind me of a Predator I once knew...you do know what a Predator is?"

Alec nodded again.

"Whenever you asked me or anyone else about the pirate activities in this sector, and even when you and Captain Behl tried to report them, you were given the cold shoulder—just as I was when I arrived many years back. My new love and I was supposed to run this place together, but our ship was attacked. Our captain managed to get us to the escape pods. Unfortunately, my love and I were separated; she was in a different pod, and the pirates took hers and a few others. Shortly after, a Predator arrived and gave chase. I was soon brought here, where I started this hotel and casino as a way to salve my emotional wounds. I have wanted payback ever since. For a very long time, I have conducted my own research in secret, and gathered evidence against both Tobbis and Zala—since I soon realized that both of them had to be in on it."

"What gave them away?"

Tota looked at Alec bleakly and said, "Time. Time gave them away—time for me to do my research. I have looked for my love for many years, longer than you have been alive, and have had scores of bounty hunters and detectives search for her. I've had a standing offer on the trading boards at the slave markets for years, to no result. And then I heard about you, about how you have everyone wrapped around your little finger, looking up to you because of your wealth, and about you purchasing an entire Marengan frigate. Then I hear of you buying slaves and setting them free, because you wanted only volunteers to crew your ship. And you a former slave yourself..."

"I told you, Tota," Alec said firmly, "I have never been a slave..." his voice trailed off. "Oh. You're talking about the time I spent as a prisoner of the pirates. I suppose you could say I was a slave then, if very briefly."

Tota shook his head. "No, young master, the evidence is clear. You might not remember being a slave, but that proves that you once were one, probably as a child." Tota pointed again at the odd linear birthmark around Alec's neck. "I am sure you were, in fact, told that was a birthmark. But birthmarks are never so perfectly straight...and I have never seen one that extends entirely around a person's neck. But I have seen marks like that before, many times."

Alec scowled. "I don't believe it. I've seen the marks left by slave collars—I just freed almost 300 people, after all—and they're thick and obvious. You can barely see my birthmark."

Tota nodded. "Agreed, good sir. Most slave collars will leave a prominent scar if the bearer wears one for more than a few days. But when slaves are freed, they tend to have their collar scars surgically removed. If they are children at the time, no attempt is made to erase the surgical scars using stim technology; it has an adverse effect on their development. Now, it takes a keen eye to note the surgical marks left behind, and mine are keener than most; and seeing as how I operate in a frontier area, I have seen such scars many times. I must say, whoever removed your collar scar must have been an outstanding surgeon, because it is barely noticeable to the naked eye. Of course, my eyesight is extraordinary. But if that is not enough for you, well...look at this."

Tota pushed a button, and metallic shields slid shut over the windows in his office. He stood up in front of Alec, who begun feeling uneasy. He almost stood up himself when Tota's neck, arms and legs started to stretch, his bones creaking and popping as they altered their size and shape. As the trunk retreated into Tota's face, the little man's spine stretched out, snapping and crunching, and he grew several feet taller. Alec's jaw dropped in disbelief.

"Never judge the book by its cover," said Tota, as he settled into his new form.

Where before there had stood a short, stubby elephantoid, there was now a tall, slender omanoid with golden skin, very handsome in an elongated way, at least a head higher than Alec himself. The new Tota's limbs were very thin but well-shaped, his eyes wide, his nose prominent but by no means a trunk, his ears still large, similar to a bat's but tight to his head. Tota's clothes had pooled on the floor beneath him, but this being was still dressed in some sort of thin bodysuit that clung tight to his body, revealing his wiry musculature.

"Look at my neck," he said now, lifting his head to reveal a thin scar very similar to Alec's, though more obviously visible. "My collar scar might not have been removed with the same skill as yours, young Master Hornet, but it *was* removed. You see, I too was a child slave once, and like you I escaped."

Alec shook his head, grinning. He looked at Tota, impressed. "Do you want to join my crew?"

"No! Well, yes, but I realize that I'm more useful here, gathering information that I can pass on to you, than I would be aboard your ship."

Alec nodded. "Agreed. We can always use a spy...and perhaps your station as a base whenever we need repairs?"

Tota nodded, then smiled at him and said, "Your turn. What was it you wanted to say or ask?"

Alec's face was grim when he asked about Alexa and about the odd art dealer who went by the name "Shadow." As he was explaining that he sought the young female pirate since she was Zuzack's daughter and could lead Alec to her father, Tota interrupted him.

"They are not family," he said decisively. "That would be impossible. Most pirates in the local clan, the Wulsatures, are extremely protective of their families and love them unconditionally. She must have been adopted into the clan, or she would never have been sold. When a pirate clan has internal disputes, they tend to fight to the death when settling their differences. If the woman you seek was Zuzack's real daughter, she would never take part in a mutiny; and if for some reason she did, she would have been executed immediately as an aberration."

He gazed at Alec kindly. "Now, about the things she did to you... please don't take this the wrong way, but from my experience talking to pirates from time to time, I've learned that the youngsters they capture are often forced into piracy before puberty. Neither of us can imagine what they have been through to survive, and certainly that colors their behavior. Take my advice if you want, for what it's worth, but it seems to me that you…have feelings for her." Tota raised his hand to stop Alec's denial and continued, "Give her and yourself a new chance to learn to communicate with each other. Listen to her, and then perhaps the two of you can have what was taken away from me and my love. It's unlikely that she or her friends can help you find Zuzack; no pirate captain will let anyone but his most trusted officers know where his headquarters is located, or ever let them have a look at their star charts. But there is another way you can attract pirates, to get them to come to you."

"And for me to pick a spot for engagement?"

"Indeed."

"How?"

Tota smiled and said, "Money, what else? Invent a story about moving your fortune, and you'll soon have several shiploads of happy little pirates looking for you. Now, let's work out a plan for you to be found, and for you to find your love."

"I don't love her," Alec insisted.

"Why, of course you don't." Tota rolled his large eyes.

In the following hour, Alec told Tota what he knew and what he thought he knew about the pirates and Alexa both, while Tota listened intently.

"So you've been running around asking questions about her, have you?" Tota mused. "But you didn't get much useful information, and no wonder. From what you've told me, the creature you're looking for must be Lady Zoris Af Sun. She's the only one I know of who fits your description. I'm not surprised to learn she's a cannibal; some of the more sordid rumors insist that it has become a fashion statement among the idle rich to be invited to Gormé dining events, though not, of course, as one of the entrees."

"What does she look like?"

Tota shrugged. "No one I know has ever seen Zoris's face, as she always keeps it covered whenever she shows up at an auction. Most of the time she works through representatives; but on occasion, she pops up to view a particularly exceptional piece. She is well known for throwing some of the most lavish parties in the sector aboard her exclusive cruiser, which she has named after herself. Key Administrator Zala and Zoris are personal friends. Give me a bit of time, and I can find out about her stay at the station, and whether she's here to make any purchases—or if in fact she already has.

"I do know that there will be a major art auction in a day or two, and Zala always has a large dinner function for important guests and VIPs in general. I'm confident that Zoris will attend. Perhaps I can get you a few invitations; I doubt there will be any problem. However, if you were to purchase one of the more expensive art pieces, then you will be invited for sure. The only problem is that if she has made a chattel purchase, then she won't sell. She never does. You will have to take the girl by force."

"You mean I have to become a pirate to rescue one?"

"No, not at all!" Tota seemed shock. "Eating the flesh of sentient beings is considered cannibalism, no matter the cannibal's species, and as such it is illegal throughout the known universe. If she throws a Gormé dining party, then she will be considered an outlaw. She has been on my list for a very long time as one of the suspects in this whole affair—or should I say, conspiracy. Liberating one of her victims is heroism, not piracy, and will certainly be viewed as such."

"But first I have to prove that she's involved in cannibalism."

"Prove to whom? Your beloved Federation? Half the officials in your government are probably on her guest list. Alec, you're on your own if you want what you seek. Still, your name and your father's stature makes you more powerful than any Key Administrator, another reason I want to work with you. Remember, money can be a powerful persuader; how do you think these pirates can operate almost undisturbed? Why do you think there haven't been any Predators stationed here for years? Why else is there never an investigation when a cargo ship or transport cruiser like the one you and your friends were aboard just vanishes?"

"Natural causes? Equipment malfunction? Crew error?" Alec suggested ironically.

Tota snorted. "Oh yes, so the Key Administrators say. But then, they are the worse pirates in the sector; they might not do the looting, but they certainly benefit from it." His voice hardened. "Let's just form an allegiance, so that combined, we can destroy these vile creatures."

Alec had an inkling that, were he to get much more riled than he was now, Tota might transform from a soft-spoken angel to a hateful demon. He said soothingly, "If we're going to do this, then you need to stay calm, Mr. Tota."

"I can do that, my friend." Tota quickly returned to his original size and rotund shape. "Don't worry about me, Alec; I know how to fool a person or two. Who would ever suspect a short, fat elephant-man who keeps pissing in his pants whenever he's excited?"

They both burst into laughter. As Alec wiped his eyes, he said, "Mr. Tota, I've never been much into art. Will you be my broker? If I give you enough credits, can you make the purchase in my name through my trader?"

"Consider it done." Tota raised his glass in one final salute to Alec before drinking it down.

They spent the next few hours working out a plan on how to communicate with each other, and where and when to meet. Tota pointed out who, among those in power, was trustworthy and who wasn't; but he cautioned that no one could *really* be trusted, given the amount of money involved in piracy and the associated slave trade. He also let Alec in on a few secrets, and Alec took them in with great respect. He realized, for the first time, that there are many people just like Tota, those who wanted to see some justice and compensation for all the unfairness they faced on a daily basis. Whenever Tota returned to the subject of Alec once having been a slave, Alec quickly changed the subject. He didn't believe it—surely Tota was still referring to his time as a prisoner of the pirates—and the whole idea made him uneasy. Tota soon realized that, and dropped the subject to Alec's relief. Alec brought up the problem of finding trustworthy crew, particularly spacers with combat experience, and Tota promised to see what he could do.

For hours they sat and talked, developing the beginning of a friendship. After several bottles of Tota's finest wine, Alec realized that his communicator didn't work inside the protected force field, and asked that it be lowered. When it was, he realized that he had over a dozen messages on his communicator. He left Tota's office quickly, to find Behl, Wolf and three of his other security people arguing with Tota's own security guards.

TWENTY-FIVE

THE two-hundred-ship-long column began to decelerate as it approached New Frontier. Aboard the bridge of the lead ship, a huge intersystem fluids hauler once used to transport water, sat Horsa, leader of the Wulsatures Clan. He was staring into the instruments at the command station, scanning the Big Dark for any possible threat. "Where are the other columns?" he finally demanded.

His first Captain, Slasher, answered, "They should all be exiting from their respective jumpgates within the hour."

Horsa smiled grimly. This would be the greatest operation he and his clan had ever attempted; within a week or two, he would make history as no other pirate had ever done. Not only would he find the thief with his treasure map, but he would also punish the two weasels at New Frontier for not assisting his brother Zuzack. Not least, he would send a clear message to his so-called allies never to cross him.

Horsa leaned back in his command chair and read Zuzack's message over and over again. He had located the thief. Unfortunately, the thief had cashed in some of their hard earned booty, and begun spreading it around liberally. And astonishingly, there was no way to get the money back, not even from the thief! The sniveling Key Administrators, Tobbis and Zala, had excused themselves by informing Zuzack that the banking system had been designed to be impenetrable, the transactions irreversible save at the whim of both spender and receiver—and it was impossible to take the funds from the thief's account without permission. The best hackers in ten galaxies had tried for centuries and had yet to crack it. Actually Horsa knew this; he held accounts himself with both the Merchants and the Traders. It didn't matter who the customer happened to be; the rules were the same for everyone, and that's why both Nastasturus and Florencia kept large monetary reserves on hand with both mercantile groups. Their banking systems were nearly perfect, from a security perspective.

But still, Horsa could not accept that *his money* was being spent by a shitty little Oman slave.

What he had planned was outrageously ambitious, but it was past time he did it anyway. Attacking a large space station like NF 16 was worth the trouble of recovering the map; and a little extra looting never hurt. That no one in their right mind had ever attacked one of these new space stations was something that never troubled Horsa's thoughts. And even if it had, the idea wouldn't have bothered the old pirate much. He was all but blinded by rage.

With over eight hundred ships and almost six million pirates deployed in three separate columns, Horsa felt confident that he could take on the entire universe. A convoy with hundreds of cargo vessels was nothing unusual in space nowadays, as safety in numbers protected against both pirates and being confiscated by one of the two large Federations. However, over eight hundred ships at once would certainly attract the suspicion of at least one of the Federations.

While Horsa was going over his plan for the coming onslaught, he observed a monitor which showed a large destroyer-class vessel battening onto one of the docking arms attached to the hull of his ship. "Finally, Zuzack is here," he growled under his breath, combing his long white beard with his fingers.

A few minutes later, there was a faint sound behind him as the hatch opened. Horsa could smell his brother's distinct musk. He closed his eyes and enjoyed the moment; he loved the scent of true blood. The next thing Horsa noticed was the sudden silence among the crew working the bridge. It was eerie, and Horsa knew from years of experience that such was always a bad sign. He turned his seat and stood up to greet his brother; but his brother wasn't there. This was something else. Oddly, it smelled like Zuzack, and it moved like Zuzack, but it certainly didn't look like Zuzack. This...*thing* had the hairless, scarred skull of some monster out of a fairy tale.

Horsa glared at the creature standing in front of him. It had the odor of his brother and the shape of his brother and it also wore his brother's favorite uniform, but that head... The creature's deformed face was streaked with blood and puss, and something squirted out of its eyes as it took a deep shaky breath.

And then it talked.

"Brother! *Look* at me! Look what it did to me! The little Oman bastard peeled the skin off my head, and then it *pissed* on me. My medical officer says there's no way I can be completely healed, ever, not even with cloning! The monster's DNA has corrupted mine!" Wailing his misery, Zuzack flung himself on Horsa, and began to cry on his shoulder like a little child. If you could call it crying, the way its—his—eyes were squirting.

As for Horsa, his eyes were about to pop out. He stared in disgust at the thing blubbering on his shoulder, ruining his jacket. He knew intellectually that it was Zuzack. No one had a voice quite like his brother's. Horsa had seen worse injuries, and on many occasions he had even inflicted them; he'd been known to skin his own enemies alive, hence the command chair back at his headquarters. But he always showed some mercy, and killed them after a while.

Uncomfortable, Horsa finally laid a hand on his brother's head. It took him a while before he could comfort his brother enough for him to speak again, and even then he had to school his face not to let his emotions show. A greenish gore dripped out from the pit where Zuzack's nose had been, and it left a nasty smear on Horsa's uniform. Horsa pushed his brother away, though not from anger at Zuzack. He grabbed hold of Zuzack's shoulders and whispered, "We shall have our vengeance. I guarantee it, brother." He then turned to his fellow officers on the command bridge while spinning Zuzack around so that he faced them. Then he shouted, "Revenge!"

For a long moment there was complete silence on the command bridge. No one dared to say or do anything.

Horsa turned to his disfigured brother with an icy look in his eyes. "First we shall skin it, and then we shall eat it. We will drink from its skull while we suck on its bones. This I swear to you, my beloved brother." Horsa placed his arm over Zuzack's shoulder and he escorted him away towards his quarters. The two of them needed to be alone so they could morn Zuzack's loss and pain.

A small scout ship followed Horsa's columns at a discreet distance. The pilot and navigator were members of the pirate clan that called themselves the Night-Hunters, and for the last week had been following developments with great interest while reporting back to their leader, Ogstafa.

Ogstafa had just risen to the throne, as it were, by killing her own mother. She belonged more or less to the same saurian species as Myra, but she had no claim to pure blood; DNA from more than a dozen distinct races ran through her veins. She had an unnatural, Oman-like face scabbed by patches of scales that caused a horrible itch and rash. She was always in a foul mood as a result.

From the moment she had discovered that Horsa, her biggest competitor and nemesis, had ventured from his hideout with almost his entire clan in tow, Ogstafa knew that whatever he was up to, she surely wasn't going to miss out on it. She had summoned three more clans to join her: The Black Sun, The Red Knights, and the Sunrays. Ogstafa's coalition easily outnumbered Horsa's Wulsatures three to one. Though the clans hated each other, on rare occasions like this they would ally for a time. Currently, all four clans followed the development from different points in space, maintaining a safe distance from Horsa's convoy and, of course, from each other.

There was no trust between them, of course; you didn't trust a scorpion not to sting you, and of course they were all scorpions, and knew it. All were equally vicious and coldblooded. Like vultures flying towards injured but still dangerous prey, the two thousand ships of the four clans were cautiously closing in from all sides in the open neutral space near the Florencian border system of Handover. Each was electronically cloaked against detection by the dangerous Federation's border patrols, and the crews used all their skills and talent to avoid a statistically-unlikely but nonetheless possible visual detection.

But even in the deep immensity of the Big Dark, it's impossible for almost three thousand ships to remain hidden for long. Many different types of "eyes" belonging to various governments and organizations observed the various pirate fleets with great interest, and even greater concern.

Most of the ships were camouflaged visually as civilian cargo haulers, so individually and even in groups they might not have attracted much attention; but their sheer numbers aroused suspicions, enough that the monitoring systems soon triggered alarms to their respective masters. One of those masters, and perhaps one of the first to become suspicious, was New Frontier's Coco Cabelle. It was her job to be paranoid, so when she coordinated the various reports and signals of large flotillas headed her way, red flags were raised in her mind. She compared the convoy numbers on the screen with the ones on a computer pad, and saw that several of them hade not made any requests to dock or trade. Scenarios ranging from passing convoys to a possible war passed through her mind and were assessed for probability. It didn't take long for her to order a yellow alert for the entire station and to schedule a general meeting for her staff. She also ordered all battle-ready corvettes and frigates owned by both trading groups to return to near-station space and take up defensive positions, an authority she had only in the event of imminent attack. Of course, none of the resident or visiting civilians would know anything about the security upgrade. Wasn't good for the trade.

When Coco reported to the administration about the unusual change in traffic in the nearby systems and open space near New Frontier, the two Key Administrators dismissed it as a threat. Rather, they were ecstatic at what they perceived as a potential increase in commerce. Both Tobbis and Zala were very specific in their orders that her security "paranoia" must not interfere, under any circumstances, with the free flow of trade.

Despite these instructions, Coco ordered her security personnel to General Quarters, where they waited on standby.

Lady Fuzza dabbed at her eyes with a white linen handkerchief as she looked out the window of the sleek little private spaceship. Alec Hornet had bought it for her as a gift while his friend, the short, funny man who derived from no species she was familiar with, had provided her with five crew and ten experienced bodyguards. *Warrior monks of some sort,* she thought as she glanced at one of them. He wore a voluminous cloak, cinched at the waist with a simple rope, that concealed everything beneath it from head to toe. She wondered where he kept his weapons.

Mr. Tota had assured Lady Fuzza and Alec both that these beings were the most trustworthy guards on the station, and they had been contracted for one round trip, not to take more than one full galactic year. Mr. Tota had also convinced Alec to hire fifty more of these odd guard-monks. Alec and Behl had been against it, but eventually they had consented and hired them. *What was it little Tota called them?* the lady muttered. *Ah yes. Ghsnaw, or was it Greshi? Oh well, I can't remember. Tota has so many things on his mind, the poor little creature. Most of the time he just blabbers on.* And after that thought, Lady Fuzza leaned her head back and closed her eyes, while the engines charged up for maximum speed.

It had been a sad farewell with her friend and partner Captain Zlo and the young Oman, Alec, whom she had begun to love like the son she'd never had. He was so full of life and positive energy; she would truly miss him, and she hoped and prayed to her own personal god that they would all meet again.

Lady Fuzza pushed those thoughts aside and concentrated on the job ahead. It would be no easy task, that was certain. Getting a commission to hunt pirates would be a small problem; but to get an audience with the Emperor of Marengo himself in the first place—that would be a major challenge. Once again she went over the plan they had worked out for weeks, and thought of all her connections back home on Marengo, connections that might become useful for the execution of the plan.

Lady Fuzza opened her eyes and glanced down at a small wooden box in her lap that she held white-knuckle tight. Every time she thought of its contents, she trembled. When Alec had shown it to her, she had been stunned at first; and then she had become frightened, and began to doubt herself for a while. But Alec had given her a warm, strong hug, and as they embraced he had whispered in her ear, "If you keep it and take off...well, I won't blame you. Just make sure you deliver the message to the Emperor." At first she felt that he had trampled on her honesty and hurt her feelings, and then he opened the box and she understood why.

"Trust me. By our souls, please trust me." Those were her last words to the young Oman, who had winked at her and smiled. If all else failed, even if she were unable to successfully petition for an audience with the Emperor himself, then she knew that what she held in her hands would open any door.

TWENTY-SIX

ALEC, Behl, Captain Zlo, Tota and one of the monks Tota had insisted of contracting, Frances, sat at a conference table in a room below the command bridge onboard the *K-13*. They had just finished test runs on the frigate's systems, and were reviewing their final preparations before their departure the next day.

With skepticism, Alec asked, "And you're sure it will work?"

"Yes! Yes, of course it will work!" Tota exclaimed excitedly.

Tota was sitting next to Behl, who inched away while muttering, "Hope the little bastard's wearing a diaper." The room went silent after Behl's odd remark, and Alec could sense an uncomfortable tension spreading like a forest fire.

"You so funny! You so funny, my little funny friend," shouted Tota, as he leaped from his seat and jumped up on Behl's lap, showering him with kisses while his trunk whipped him all over. Behl, taken aback by the surprise "attack," fell over on his chair with Tota still acting like a strange little man in love.

"Get off me, you pants-pissing little dragon from hell, or I'll turn you into a throw pillow!"

Tota started to laugh even harder, and jumped up on the table, staring at Alec, who raised his eyebrows while shaking his head. He had become all too accustomed to Tota's sudden outbursts, but he knew too well that it was only a front. Alec said dryly, "If you two lover boys are finished, perhaps we should go over the assault plan one more time."

Behl cursed quietly to himself as he scrambled to his feet and righted his chair, muttering something about "a good old-fashioned keelhauling."

France observed it all with great interest. Very tall and naturally big all over, his heritage appeared to be a mixture of Oman and Sparniac. His skin was black as space, very like his Sparniac relatives, and his dark brown eyes sparkled with experience and intelligence. Everyone in the room knew he was an experienced soldier. He subscribed to the same martial religion that Alec's Uncle Cook did, a belief system that was a constant thorn in the side of Alec's father, Marshal Guss Hornet.

The Grisamm Order maintained a presence in most of known space. No one really knew much about them; the truth of who they really were, what they really wanted, and the main goals of their belief system remained mysteries. The rumors batted around about the Grisamm were not, as a rule, particularly favorable ones. They were considered religious fanatics, because they traveled from system to system preaching their odd pan-sentient creed. They were also known to be skilled teachers in many different fields, particularly medicine, space travel, military arts, and the sciences. Some people thought of them as very intelligent and peaceful. Some considered them a cult; many parents in particular were afraid that they would brainwash their children and take them away.

Both Alec and Behl had been very surprised when Tota had assured both of them that a Grisamm monk would rather die than break his or her word. As he put it, "Once a Grisamm has committed, then it is for life—or until the objective has been achieved." They hated pirates, slavers and totalitarian entities in general. One of their strongest beliefs was that everyone, everywhere, should enjoy total freedom. Enslavement of any sentient species should not be tolerated.

In other words, it hadn't been very difficult for Tota to recruit them. Tota had explained that their hate towards pirates and other illegal activities in general was overwhelming. Alec and Behl had raised concerns at that revelation; none of them had any strong religious beliefs, and in fact, as Nastaturan Elites, had been educated to believe that religion was a danger that produced only three things: fanatics, war waged by fanatics, and the subsequent pain. Alec also had some personal knowledge of the Nastaturan military's opinions of the Grisamm themselves, having listened in to his father's and uncle's discussions on the subject.

But time was of the essence; Alec knew this, and therefore he couldn't be too picky. After having met Frances and some of his fellow monks and talking to them a week ago, he had signed them on, though not without trepidation. When they said they didn't want any pay beyond their basic expenses, Alec had become more confident about his choice. He had insisted that they would accept their pay, like everyone else, and if they didn't want their pay, then they could donate it to charity.

As it turned out, another reason it had been easy for Tota to hire the Grisamm for Alec's crazy plan was that he belonged to the same order. Alec was still shaking his head over that revelation—when he had the time. The moment they had signed on, they had taken the former slaves-come-pirates in hand and begun a rigorous training regimen involving hand-to-hand combat, computer hacking, high-tech battle gear, nano-armor, and anything else they could acquire that would give them an edge over the Wulsatures. The monks had even made them march and drill in formation—well, all except Myra, who was still in a local infirmary having new prosthetic legs fitted. She had been grateful to Alec for purchasing them—at first—and then had cursed him roundly when he refused to buy her a pair of cloned legs. He told her that if she was loyal to him, then he would consider buying her a pair, but due to their history she should be grateful for what she got. That was only partially true. She lacked any of the ancient gene-hacked Oman DNA, so it was very difficult to clone or stim new natural limbs for the big saurian woman; and it was certainly impossible at a frontier outpost like NF 16.

All in all, the former pirates had been very difficult to deal with at first. It had been a living hell for both Pier and Wolf to train them. However, in just two days, the Grisamm monks had turned everything around.

Now, Frances waved at the table, and a hologram of the space station emerged, perfect in every detail. Frances went over the strategy he had devised of getting aboard Lady Zoris' cruiser, so that they could locate and extract Alexa. Tota filled them in about the personnel he and his agents had bribed—people that they had to take with them and drop off at the nearest port, lest they be rendered desiccated space corpses or reeking piles of burnt protoplasm for betraying the Key Administrators.

During a lull in the conversation, Alec announced, "Mr. Tota and I have purchased a shuttle for them, and once they get to Mr. Tota's hotel, they can take off without knowing who we are."

Tota added, "You don't have to be concerned about them. Once they open the designated cargo door for you and your team, they will leave immediately for my safe haven."

"Good," said Frances, who continued, "As I was saying: you, Alec, with an escort of two attractive males or females—whichever you prefer—attend the ball the two Key Administrators invited you to, and..."

"Nina, what do you think will happen to us?" Tara asked quietly.

"No idea, but at least we're not in those slave blocks anymore. Those things were killing my wrists and ankles."

"You said it, girlfriend," Kirra agreed perkily.

"I'm just happy we're all together again," Zicci added as she scratched her left ear with her tail, "and not in some horrible prison."

"You might *wish* you were in a prison or harem before this is all over," Miska muttered.

"What are you saying?" Nina demanded.

"Let's see what develops, and decide what to do next."

"It's not like we can do much with these forsaken things attached to us," Kirra complained, tugging on her slave collar.

"Don't play with that!" someone shouted. Wolf walked up on the girls from behind. "Stand at attention, troops!"

Kirra quickly covered the slave collar with her tunic, and stood at attention with the other girls. They were all used to discipline, of course, but not this type. This discipline was stricter—but ironically, the punishments for breaking it were much less, and never lethal. But still, the drill instructors—especially the mad monks—were extremely picky, and they had no problems with punishing anyone who didn't obey.

The entire crew was lined up in formation in the main docking bay, each section isolated from the others. The first and second class officers stood together, as did the pilots and navigators, the Medical Officer and his staff, the Chief Engineer and his staff, the support crew, and the common soldiers. All in all, there were 412 individuals from over twenty different species (and admixtures thereof) represented in the hold. They were dressed in gray overalls and gray combat boots, with flashing in specific colors and patterns along either side of their uniforms. First class officers sported one wide white line, second class officers had two thinner white lines, the medical team had a yellow line and a large red crescent on their backs, the mechanics had a green line, the support crew a blue line, and the soldiers had a black line. The exception was the Grisamm monks, of course; they insisted on wearing their rope-belted robes, leaving only their boots and hands exposed.

Behl and Captain Zlo glanced apprehensively at each other as they waited for Alec to appear. When he did stride into the bay, he was dressed identically to Behl and Captain Zlo, in a first class offer's uniform. He walked up in front of his little army and made a perfect, 90-degree military turn to face them, then saluted them crisply.

"Welcome aboard the *Predator*," he announced.

There was a collective intake of breath among the crew. The name Alec had chosen for the former *K-13* was something no one had ever dared to name a ship. Any true pirate hunter loved their nickname of "Predator," a sobriquet that the pirates had given them, and they had long since claimed it as their own.

Someone applaused vigorously, breaking the silence. Alec looked around, finally noticing the one civilian among them. He stood on a landing leg of one of the runabouts, jumping up and down while clapping his hands. Mr. Tota, of course.

Alec rolled his eyes, and decided to ignore the laughter of the crew. He continued, "Now. I'll let you all in on a little secret I wanted to spring on you once we'd gotten everything shipshape. There will be a substantial bonus for anyone who completes his or her contract alive: one million credits for each of you."

His last words were met with cheers and applause from the entire crew, even Myra. Alec gestured with his arm for silence and stated grimly. "There is a catch. To receive the bonus, I expect your absolute loyalty and obedience in all things. If you can't give me that, leave right now."

Nobody so much as twitched.

Alec turned towards Captain Zlo and said sharply, "Prepare them for our departure." He saluted his crew and walked away.

Behl and Zlo looked at each other, shrugging, and then Captain Zlo started shouting out orders and instructions to his officers. They already knew what they needed to do, so his presence wasn't really needed; therefore, after a few moments of watching, he and Behl headed toward the bridge to take care of some administrative details. As the Grisamm split up to join their assigned crew groups, their leader, Frances, hurried after Behl and Zlo with a very confident expression. Alec watched them from his vantage point in a shadowy corner of the hold, as Tota joined him. Unsurprisingly, his were pants all wet. "Mr. Tota, have you started spreading rumors about our expedition?" Alec inquired softly as they ambled toward the nearest hatch.

"You need not worry, young master," the little fellow piped. "By now thousands, perhaps millions, of people in this outpost know about your treasure hunt...so you should have no problems running into your old friends."

"Let's hope you're right."

Tota nodded. "I have also spread the rumor that you are transporting a very large fortune to a secret destination, and I have thrown in a little evidence to support the story."

Alec stopped and peered at Tota with a puzzled expression. "And what evidence is that?"

"Oh, don't be concerned about it. Rest assured, my friend, you *will* find pirates waiting once you and your crew take off into space." Tota gave Alec a mischievous smile.

The rest of the crew returned to their respective training and work stations. Nina and her comrades had ended up in a fighter bay, where 20 swift and deadly little ships were fastened to docking positions on the deck and walls. The deck chief was scurrying around officiously, directing them on where to put the seemingly never-ending supply of munitions and stores that kept arriving from merchants all over the station. Any space available—and it was rapidly dwindling—was used for storage.

"They're beautiful," Tara breathed, cocking her head at a hovering fighter being driven into the bay by Pier, who had the cockpit open and was cursing loudly about the lack of room.

"You think they'll let us fly them?" Kirra asked brightly.

"We can only hope," Zicci called out. She was picking up one heavy box and putting it on top of another, her muscles bulging attractively.

"I like this," Nina told them.

That stopped them in their tracks. "What do you mean?" Tara asked.

"Becoming a civilian and working like this. Having a regular job and a chance for something better. Maybe I can even purchase a real citizenship on one of the colony worlds."

"Yeah, and grow fat and pregnant, too," Zicci laughed, and the others joined her. But Nina didn't hear. The dreamy expression in her eyes caught their attention, and for a long moment they fell silent, considering the possibilities for their own futures.

"That would be nice, maybe," Tara finally muttered, "but I'm not so sure about kids."

"I wouldn't worry about it if I were you. You ugly, you are," said Kirra, grinning.

The girls began laughing—all of them this time—and ignored Pier's shouts for them to move a crate.

They stopped laughing abruptly when one of the Grisamm, a robe-clad woman with ancient eyes, walked up to them and said quietly, "Keep laughing, sisters. It is good to spread positive karma into this dark universe."

Refusing to meet her eyes, their expressions upset, the former pirates returned to their work, much to Pier's satisfaction. The monk looked at them with sad eyes for a moment, then said loudly, "I want all six of you to meet me in Debriefing Room Two when you are done here."

The girls stopped what they were doing, and glanced at each other. Nina stammered, "Um, ah, w-we're supposed to report to Sergeant Wolf for training."

"We haven't done anything wrong...I think," Kirra protested.

"I'll take care of Wolf, and I'll see you in two hours. Or do you need more time with your chores?" the Grisamm woman asked in friendly tones.

"We should be able to finish up in an hour," Tara informed her, "and may I ask what you want from us?"

The woman inclined her head in a gentle nod. "My name is Nadia, and I will educate you."

"Educate us in what?" Nina demanded.

"I will educate you on freedom—how to be free, and how to live a life of joy and harmony."

"Planning to brainwash us to join your cult, are you?" Zicci shouted bravely.

The other woman stopped and turned back to look at them, her face serene. "No, nothing like that. I'm going to teach all of you how to deal with your freedom."

"I'll be there," Nina whispered, and soon all the others followed her example.

Nadia gave them a friendly smile, then turned and walked away gracefully.

TWENTY-SEVEN

"COMMANDER Korron Ezim reporting as commanded, sir!" The young man stood sharply at attention and snapped off a perfect salute to Admiral Cook. After Cook returned the salute, just as precisely, Ezim began his report. "Admiral, we count over three hundred Florencian ships in sector Green Four. They are stationed very near Admiral Busch's column. The ships bear the markings of the 9th Galactic Fleet of Handover, and our Intelligence Section believes they are commanded either by Admiral Jonas Nass, a citizen of Handover, or by someone by the name of Rimez."

"And does IS have any idea why the Florencians showed up when they did?" Cook asked. When the commander seemed reluctant to reply, he growled, "Speak up, man, I don't shoot messengers."

"Aye aye, sir. IS attaches no particular significance to this, but they did note that last evening, Admiral Busch left his column after having been invited to New Frontier Station 16 by the Key Administrators there; it was shortly thereafter that the Florencian Fleet arrived. Our sensors indicate that a corvette-class vessel of the same type that picked up Admiral Busch also picked up someone from the 9th."

Cook nodded. "Standard procedure when they want to talk. They don't want either our 11th or the Fish Fuckers' 9th too close to their beloved money factory. Go on."

Obviously trying not to smile at the Admiral's use of the derogatory term for the Florencian Federation, Ezim continued, "Sir, we've also detected two rather large columns of ships approaching NF16. Each is several hundred kilometers long, and consists of between two and three hundred ships each. They appear to be civilian cargo convoys, and are expected to reach the station within 36 standard hours. Neither our sensors nor our scouts have picked up anything else, except of course for the dozens of private ships coming and going from all directions."

Cook fell silent while thinking of his next move. *It appears that the 9th hasn't picked us up yet, which will give us an advantage in case this escalates into something more than a rescue-and-recovery mission,* Cook mused, then noted that the commander was still shifting from foot to foot, looking ill at ease. "Something wrong, son?"

"May I speak freely, Admiral?"

"You may."

"Isn't it unusual to see this much traffic this far from any major system?"

"Yes and no. Were we to draw attention to ourselves or the Florencian 9th, that would discourage traffic, certainly. If you're referring to the convoys, that could be anything from supplies to ships in need of dry dock, in case they're about to make a long trip elsewhere, say out to the Fringe Worlds. Maybe they just want to trade with the New Frontier stations. There are many different possibilities—we'll just need to keep on our toes, and make sure we follow all traffic closely and find out as much as possible. Got that?"

"Aye aye, sir!"

"Now inform the captain that we will remain here on standby, in case Admiral Busch needs us. As I'm sure he will." As soon as he uttered them, he realized that those last few words should have remained unsaid.

Ezim looked puzzled. "What was that, Admiral...?"

"Nothing important, Commander. Return to your station." They saluted, and Ezim went on his way.

Scowling, Cook spun his command chair to face several monitors, on which were presented bright, colorful representations of the local space traffic. The colors of the various dots indicated their ship classifications, and cryptic alphanumeric codes provided, to the practiced eye, each ship's name and planet of registration. Local astronomical bodies, mostly bleak, airless rocks belonging to the brown dwarf around which New Frontier orbited, were rendered and labeled in dull gray. He stared at the screen, his mind far away as he thought, until he realized that his eyes had registered something anomalous. Squinting, he zoomed in on a large asteroid cluster in the far distance, and had the computer clean up the screen. There were several more blips there representing ships, but they weren't color-coded or labeled. He pursed his lips in thought and then shook his head, his thoughts returning to Busch's meeting with the Key Administrators.

He smiled faintly, thinking of his old friend's past. Busch's qualifications as a diplomat were precisely zero— or less than that, if possible. That had slowed down his career somewhat, needless to say. By rights, he should have been commanding his own Galactic fleet by now, except for an incident that had occurred during his last civilian mission, just before he received his fleet commission. He had been appointed as a deputy ambassador on one of the new colony worlds that Nastasturus, which was hurting for resources, hoped to bring into their empire. During his third week at his new post, a war broke out.

By the end of the three-year long conflict, the Reltuban system was under the military control of the Nastasturus Federation, at the cost of fifteen million Nastasturan and three hundred million Reltuban casualties. A joint report by the Nastasturan Intelligence Department and the Intergalactic Police Organization indicated that the war had been triggered by something that the then-Plenipotentiary Busch had said to the planet's leader at a dinner function. That wasn't enough to cause a global conflict, of course, but the subsequent bungling of the Diplomatic Corps and the Nastasturan military had escalated that minor diplomatic breach into a bloodbath. The Nastasturan officials and officers whose malfeasance had caused the conflict to spiral out of control were tried for war crimes and executed.

Busch's error had been an innocent one, so he was spared; but the event had sealed Busch's fate as a fleet commander, and ever since then, or so he claimed, he had developed an exceptional dislike for any or all civilians. Admiral Cook, however, was aware that this was not true. Busch had always disliked civilians; Cook liked to joke that he'd probably cursed his mother for putting him in civilian diapers instead of camouflage ones.

Busch's only hope of advancement was to find civilian investors willing to help him expand his fleet, since the military certainly wasn't going to do it. But for the past fifteen years, investors had been impossible to come by. Busch was a close family friend, so the Hornets had come to his rescue and taken him under their collective wing. That wasn't enough, however, to scrub the stain entirely from his escutcheon, so to this day Busch's advance was limited. At the moment, his entire fleet consisted of the twenty-five cruisers that were acting point for Cook's main battle group. If Cook hadn't signed him up for the 11th, he would most likely be unemployed.

While Busch was ordinarily the last person Cook would ever send out as an emissary, he did make one exception to his rule: whenever they had to deal with Merchants or Traders. Both groups were unforgivably corrupt, and they deserved Busch's bluntness and scorn. And there was always the chance that, corrupt though they were, Busch could squeeze an investment out of the bastards so he could expand the fleet.

Nearly a thousand people representing hundreds of species had gathered inside the enormous grand ballroom. Alec peered around the vast chamber. It reminded him of the ballroom on the *Bright Star*: the décor was simple, but ostentatiously expensive. The conservative look, accented in pale pearl and gold—real pearl and real gold—left a lasting impression; the tall snow-white walls gave way to scores of crystalline ports, which offered an outstanding view of the universe beyond. The ballroom was poised at the very top of the station, and the ceiling was a huge glass dome that sparkled slightly; possibly it was nothing more than an electromagnetic shield. For anyone who entered here, the ballroom said one thing, and it said it very well: *Power.*

Alec hooked a finger under his tight collar and tugged. He was outfitted in his new dress uniform, which matched his eyes in color; the trousers folded into his new boots. His boots were made of an odd black leather, most unusually ornamented: there was a thin strip running up the outer side of each boot that appeared to be decorated with coarse, braided black fur. Around his waist was a black belt with similar decoration. The belt buckle was silver, bearing a sigil he had designed himself: a large triangle with an eye in the center. The eye was made of a blue pearl he had purchased for several million credits. To the left of the eye were two black lines, and to the right a single black line.

He wondered what people would think if they knew the design was similar to the mark he had burnt into Alexa's left buttock—with the exception that, then, it had been two lines next to a circle, rather than an eye or triangle, and there was one more line on the right side. He had seen his new design many times in a dream that had begun to disturb his sleep in recent weeks. He didn't understand the dream. It was as if someone else had controlled his hand when he had programmed the design into the pirate woman's brander.

One of the monks was a skilled blacksmith, and had made the belt buckle for him in the ship's smithy. The monk had liked the design, informing Alec that it reminded him of something—but he couldn't quite put his finger on what. And of course Behl and Captain Zlo had asked about the sign when he had it painted on the *Predator*'s hull, but Alec had difficulty explaining it. Frances, on the other hand, had simply nodded, while Tota stared at it with a concerned look, silent for once. One thing Alec hadn't done was put the ensign on the uniforms of any of the crew, including the officers' uniforms and his own; and when asked why, he had simply said, "You...*we* have to earn it."

Alec was flanked by former pirates Nina and Tara, to his right and left, respectively. Nina had clamped onto Alec's arm like a parasitic plant. The brunette wore a stunning dress made entirely of pale, shimmering pearls, which whispered faintly whenever she moved. The long gown shopped short of the floor to reveal her black boots, which any fashion designer would have said killed the outfit. She'd made herself up with cosmetics that matched the tattoo on her right side of her forehead, and carried a large sun feather that she idly fanned herself with. Tara wore an outfit much like Nina's, but hers was made out of golden pearls that matched the current color of her hair—and of course she hated the color, which Alec had selected. She wore little make-up, and making her wear that much had almost caused a minor mutiny until Wolf had threatened to get Myra involved; Tara felt it was humiliating to have her face painted, unless it was for combat or perhaps some wild dance. But finally she had consented to allow Nina to apply a little eye shadow. Later, when Nadia had shown up and nodded for Alec and Wolf to leave, things had become easier. Nadia and one of her Grisamm colleagues, Mikka, had completely given the girls a makeover, transforming them into two beautiful ladies. The biggest challenge, according to Nadia, was when they had to educate the two girls in table manners.

Alec had noticed the respect all the female crew had for Nadia and her friend Mikka. In fact, Kirra, Zicci, Mohamma and Miska, the other members of the little clique that included Nina and Tara, had complained bitterly when told they wouldn't be allowed to join their friends as Alec's escorts. Alec, feeling rather helpless, had informed them that he really only wanted to bring one girl, but had been advised to bring at least two. He told them that he'd randomly picked the two girls' names out of a hat, so to speak, but that had been a bald-faced lie, and the other girls called him on it, especially Kirra and Zicci. But when Nadia showed up and whispered something to them, their faces brightened and they hurried away. Nadia had bowed her head towards Alec, and left him shaking his own head.

Two of the Grisamm followed closely behind Alec and his girls, dressed in their standard robes, except that these were black and sharply pressed. Normally no servants were allowed to attend events like these, but because of Alec's high position and enormous wealth, an exception had been made for him. The same was true of about a dozen others, all of whom were allowed to bring an entourage.

The function was about to begin, and people were entering through the two main entrances in droves. The majority were arriving by limousines; a few were brought in by private shuttles in space, and could be seen through large crystalline ports in the far wall as they docked alongside. However they arrived, they all wore the latest fashions, with the exception of Alec, the monks, and the various representatives of the Commercial Traders and the Federated Merchants, who wore more conservative garb.

Outside the banquet rooms was a large park with a lake in the middle; birds and tiny feathered dinosaurs flew through the air and sang under a blue sky scattered with fluffy white clouds, the kind of sky that legend claimed arced over the ancient Oman homeworld. It was all artificial, of course, with the apparent exception of the avians; the sky was nothing more than mimetic paint. Soft background music issued from hidden speakers as the guests lined up to greet the host. Hundreds of servants stood along the walls like statues dressed in black, all willing to assist any of the guests in any whim. They had to, on pain of death; they were, to a being, slaves.

The two Key Administrators and their spouses welcomed each of the guests, and next to them stood several VIPs from different corners of the universe: politicians, celebrities, military officers from various polities, Traders and Merchants, and others less recognizable. Behind them loomed several large rooms, stuffed to the rafters with art of all types.

Alec glanced at his wristcomp.

"Stop that," Nina said, as she rapped his arm lightly with her sun-feather. "It doesn't look normal." She smiled toward a couple that was looking in their direction suspiciously, and her eyes silently advised them to go about their business.

Alec frowned as he noticed Nina slipping something glittery into a hidden pocket. "Speaking of looking normal," he muttered, "If you ever do something that stupid again, you'll wind up back with that frog friend of yours. Got me?" Nina smiled and nodded, but Alec could see the thinly-veiled terror in her eyes. He held out his hand, and Nina dropped an adamantine brooch into his hand, muttering something about a small fortune under her breath.

Alec turned to the woman who had just passed them and said, "Excuse me, my lady. Apparently you dropped this." Alec held up the brooch, and the old lady smiled and thanked him. Alec shot Nina a disappointed expression, and he just shook his head in reply.

They passed through the enormous ballroom room into a banquet hall, where four long tables seating perhaps two hundred and fifty people each had been arranged in a large square. In the center of the square were several gourmet chefs preparing, with the help of their assistants, a wide variety of dishes from dozens of worlds.

Alec had bypassed the line of guests being greeted by their hosts, and let out a long breath when he realized he'd managed to avoid their notice. Gesturing one of the many servants over to him, he asked her to escort them to their places at the dinner table, while another servant with several cocktail drinks on a silver tray hovering next to him offered refreshments. Smiling, Alec nodded thanks, then handed Nina and Tara a glass each while taking one for himself. It amused him to watch the girls as the two former pirates looked at the gilt-edged tumblers suspiciously before taking tiny sips of the brew. Both grinned widely, then emptied the contents in one big gulp each. They looked at him, disappointed that their glasses were empty, and he nodded toward the tray. They immediately swapped out their empty tumblers for full ones.

From behind them came a familiar voice; Alec closed his eyes and cursed when recognized it as that of Tobbis, the Key Administrator of the Federated Merchants contingent. Tobbis all but shouted, "Ah, Mr. Horn, there you are! We have been looking all over for you!"

Alec spun around with a broad smile on his face, showing all of his perfect white teeth. He greeted Tobbis and was introduced to the man's wife. She was a beautiful woman of the Asipa species, with long red hair that extended down her back in a carmine mane. She smiled shyly at Alec, who kissed her hand, making her blush.

"I hope your stay with us has been as pleasant for you as it has for me and my colleagues?"

"Why of course, Mr. Tobbis, but soon I must depart."

"Well, that *is* sad news. We were hoping that we might persuade you to purchase citizenship on our new colony world. A person of such esteem as yourself could easily find a very high ranking position in our government."

"Thank you for your offer, sir, but politics has never been my strong suit."

Tobbis smiled, but it didn't reach his eyes. "So, do you intend to liquidate your accounts with us?"

Alec looked politely baffled. "I had the impression that I could leave my money in my accounts here, and that I would be able to access them anywhere in known space. Or perhaps I was wrong?"

"Of course not," Tobbis said quickly, "you are absolutely right about being able to access your accounts anywhere. That's what makes our system so great."

"I bet," said Alec dryly.

"Oh, before I go and welcome some more of my friends, there is someone I would like for you to meet. As a matter of fact, he also is a citizen of the Nastasturus Federation." Tobbis turned halfway aside, while swinging his arm out in a grand gesture towards the back of a short, stocky uniformed man. He wore a light blue tunic with white trousers and dark boots, the basic uniform of the Nastasturan space navy. "He has a very nice business proposition that might interest you, considering you are in the market of hiring pilots and astronauts to explore the universe," Tobbis explained while the person he was referring to turned around with a drink in his hand, revealing a row of medals and other ornaments arranged on the left side of his chest. "Mr. Horn, allow me to introduce to you a Galactic Fleet Admiral from your own Federation...Lieutenant Admiral Alistair Busch."

Their eyes met—and their glasses of champagne fell to the floor in a twin tinkle of breaking glass. Tobbis looked surprised at both of them, but before he had time to make a comment, Alec grabbed Admiral Busch's hand fast while pumping it like mad. "My, my...I'm most honored to meet one of the famous Galactic Fleet Admirals. My name is Alec Horn, sir, and I can't wait to tell my entire family that I have had such an honor..."

"I'll bet you can't," muttered Admiral Busch, "you little bas..."

Alec cut him off hurriedly. "I hear you're in the market for a fleet investor? Or so my beloved friend Mr. Tobbis said."

"Why, you little..."

"I must say, the Admiral looks most pleasant in his uniform," Alec babbled. "Will you forgive us, Mr. Tobbis, while I get to know one of my Federation´s heroes better?"

"Why of course," Tobbis said graciously. "Later, then, Master Horn."

Alec, who was a head taller than Admiral Busch, grabbed the officer under his arm and walked him over to a quieter area. When they were out of earshot, Busch hissed,

"You little weasel, are you aware that your father's has sent *an entire fleet* looking for you? He and your mother are worried sick about you, and here you are running around like a lost asteroid pretending to be a wealthy little shit from the underground. I ought to lay you over my lap and let you have it with my belt, you no-good cadet from hell!"

"Let me know when you're finished," Alec said dryly.

"*Finished*! Stand at attention, you young whelp, before I tear your arm off and beat you with it! I..." Busch hesitated as two rather large men in black, monkish robes stepped up to them, and stared down at the diminutive admiral with the experienced eyes of hardened warriors. Nina and Tara hovered behind them, looking nervous.

"Are you done, sir?" Alec asked brightly. "Oh, good. I do have an explanation, you know, and I was going to send my parents a coded message as soon as I left this place."

"You need to send one *now*, and so do I. Your Uncle Hadrian is here with his entire fleet group, and he too is worried sick."

"Uncle Alistair..." Alec stopped himself when the older man gave him a chilling glare. "Your pardon, sir. Admiral Busch, please listen to me for just a moment, so I can let you know what's going on. See it as one upper-echelon officer reporting to another, if you will."

"You're not a damned general yet! You have to be sworn in, commissioned, and go back to school for several years, not to mention acquire another ten or twenty years of hardcore experience in the field, before you can use that rank," Admiral Busch growled.

"Except in the case of hostile action or an act of war perpetrated against the Nastasturus Federation or any of its citizens, property or allies. Then my brevet rank would be confirmed, correct?"

Admiral Busch gazed with suspicion at the boy in front of him. He corrected himself: Alec was a man now. Busch knew that Alec's question was a trap. Normally he would have knocked out the person who dared ask him a question like that—questioning his intellect, by Gull—but now he only scowled, eager to hear more. After all, at heart Busch was a simple soldier who, like any other simple soldier, longed for some action, though the young whippersnapper in front of him didn't know that.

Admiral Busch grabbed a new glass of champagne from a tray hovering nearby, and moved slowly toward a wide expanse of viewport. Alec followed, gesturing for Nina, Tara and his guards to remain behind.

"What are you up to?" Busch demanded.

"When the *Bright Star* was captured by pirates, I was taken prisoner along with thousands of others—including my entire cadet squad. I escaped, as I was taught to. I'm going back to rescue my friends, Admiral." There was a brief silence, and then Alec continued. "I must do this, sir. We're taught never to leave anyone behind..."

"Spare me, Alec, I know all too well that bullshit they teach you at the Academy—and I also know that most of its just propaganda. Most of you kids are from wealthy Elite families, and will never see any real action."

"We've seen it now, sir." Alec struggled to keep horrible memories locked in the back of his mind; especially the memory of Jack's fate. He realized very well what madness his little expedition actually represented; but something told him that he had to go on. Something deep inside of him had been awakened; he didn't know or understand what it was, but every time he thought of it, it filled him like a heady elixir. He craved for something to exhilarate his soul, it seemed; and perhaps, in some perverse way, it represented some type of satisfaction. He didn't know what it was he felt that he was missing; he just knew he had to do what he was doing.

Admiral Busch noticed the look in Alec's eyes, and his expression changed to one of concern. "Alec, your way of thinking and your actions honor you and your family, but they will not give you any credit in life. I understand what you're going through, and..."

"You understand shit," Alec hissed at Busch, catching the Admiral off guard. "They *ate* Jack. The monsters *ate him* while keeping him alive as long as possible, so they could prolong his agony. I killed him before I managed to escape, you hear me? He asked me to...or what was left of him did." He was panting, controlling himself with great difficult. "Uncle Alistair, I, we were the prisoners of monstrous pirates, all but slaves, and if you only knew what they did to us...and what I have been through since..."

His eyes flicked toward Nina and Tara, who looked like they wanted to vanish into their own boots.

Busch swallowed hard. "Alec, gather yourself. After all, you are an officer in the Nastasturan milit..." He broke off as Alec ripped open his jacket and shirt.

"They branded me! *Look* at it!"

Admiral Busch looked at Alec's scarred chest, which displayed the branded image of a circle with a triangle fitted inside, with the letter A inside that. His expression cycled from extreme sadness to cold, hard hate in an instant, and he whispered, "They branded you...?"

"Yes sir, they did." Alec buttoned his uniform tunic over his ruined shirt and stood tall, crisply saluting his superior officer. "Brevet General Alec Hornet of the Nastasturus Federation Army reporting, sir. Lieutenant Admiral Busch, it is my duty to inform you that an act of piracy and an act of conspiracy entered into and condoned by representatives of the Federated Merchants and the Commercial Traders has been perpetrated against the Nastasturus Federation and nearly ten thousand of its citizens. It is also my duty to inform you that under the Nastasturan laws against piracy, I am automatically commissioned to hunt down these perpetrators and obtain evidence to support such claim for a period of one year."

Alec fell silent, staring straight forward.

"At ease," Admiral Busch muttered, "we don't want to make a scene."

Alec relaxed and focused his eyes on Admiral Busch, who looked at him speculatively and said, "A declaration of war status by a high-ranking military officer does not apply in any neutral territory, even if an act of piracy occurs. It can apply only within our own territory, or that of our allies."

"It applies, sir, if the either the Merchants or Traders are implicated," Alec countered. "Military Code 36 CFR 60.4, Section 106, paragraph b."

Busch nodded. "You're right. What is your evidence?"

"Here's my primary evidence, gathered over the past 28 years by someone I trust. For various reasons, the individual has been too afraid to step forward until now." Alec popped a coin-sized disk from his wristcomp and handed it to the Admiral, who slipped it into one of his breast pockets. "Besides that," Alec continued, "when I escaped from the pirates, I happened to come across several other lines of evidence implicating the Traders and Merchants. I've hidden my documentation of that evidence in a secured location. And," he lowered his voice to a whisper, "I was also able to get my hands on some of their treasure."

Admiral Busch turned to the viewport, and gazed out into the Big Dark. "I take it that this treasure of yours is worth quite a sum?"

"More than you can dream of."

"I see." Busch turned back toward Alec. "I can't wait to hear your story—or to see your uncle's face, when I report having found you."

Alec nodded, thoughtful. "But sir, will you get in any trouble, if you let me act on my claim?"

Busch snorted. "That's a loaded question. On one hand, I'm required to allow you to chase your claim, assuming you're right about our law, and I suspect you are. On the other hand, your uncle will be pissed. Unless I can convince him otherwise, he'll come for you himself."

"I was afraid of that. Is his fleet far away?"

"No, the fleet is quite nearby, but... let me think."

Most of the guests had seated themselves by now, and a servant approached, advising Alec and Busch to take their own seats. Busch gave the servant a short but firm suggestion about where she could go, and she decided to turn her attention to more appreciative guests.

Admiral Busch turned to Alec with a serious expression. "Tell me your plan, son. If I like it I'll support it, and I'll do what I can to stall your uncle until he keelhauls me." Then he strode off toward the banquet tables as Alec followed.

There was a minor scuffle regarding the seating when Admiral Busch demanded to sit next to Alec, but it was quickly sorted out. On each side of them sat Tara and Nina, each apparently having the time of her life. Their young beauty attracted many hungry eyes—male and female—that they completely ignored, being far too busy inhaling all the glamour around them. An old Major from a distant minor federation and his wife sat next to Nina. After an exchange of pleasantries, the Major asked, "My, my, what a lovely young woman you are. Tell me, dear, what sort of trade is your dinner escort involved in?"

"Don't know," Nina answered with her mouth full of food.

"Oh, perhaps you're just his temporary escort?" the old man sniffed.

"No, not really."

Nina fiddled with one of the tools in front of her, trying to understand how to use it on the hard-shelled crustacean on her plate. The Major, meanwhile, became frustrated, and he leaned toward her, his face red. His wife grabbed his arm as he shook loose and continued, "You don't seem to know much, now do you? Do you know what trade *you* are in?"

Nina answered, with her tongue between her teeth as she struggled with the idiotic shell, "Well, not really. Not anymore." Just then, the shell decided to revolt, and slipped away at high speed toward the central island, where the chefs were busily creating the next course.

It struck one of the chefs between his eyes, sending him crashing to the floor, dragging several of his assistants with him.

Nina looked puzzled, then turned to the Major and said loudly into the sudden silence, "Well, I used to be a pirate." The Major and his wife stared at Nina in disbelief as she said to the chef in front of her, "Hey, you, that shell's mine. Can you toss it back to me?"

The Major smiled and was about to continue the conversation with what he thought was a prostitute—and a liar with no manners—when he was faced with a pair of dark blue eyes that silently informed him to mind his own business. When the old man looked hurriedly away, Alec transferred his own shelled delicacy to Nina's plate. Then, with a surgeon's skill, and to her childlike delight, he flipped the shell open with the tool provided.

By the third course, Tara and Nina had gotten over most of their shyness and were enjoying the dinner tremendously. Alec and Busch, however, were involved in a deep, quiet conversation and neither paid much attention to any of the fifteen dishes they were served. Alec made gestures with his hands several times during the conversation, while Busch played with his fork and listened intently without displaying any emotion.

When Alec made a brief pause to sip some water, Busch stiffened and dropped his fork on his plate, leaning toward Alec and scowling as if to say, "Now? Right *now*?" Alec nodded as he kept drinking.

WOLF and Frances, accompanied by ten of the Grisamm monks, drifted like shadows through the private cruiser's corridors. At the first junction, they split up in three groups and, in two-by-two formation, preceded towards their respective objectives.

They had confirmed, only hours before, that the eccentric art dealer Zoris Af Sun had in fact purchased a slave fitting Alexa's description. The trader who had served as their contact had also provided valuable information on the layout of Zoris' ship, which matched up precisely with what Tota had already provided. Since Zoris was attending the same event that Alec was, there could be no better time to reclaim the young woman. Thus emboldened, they moved forward with the operation.

No one questioned Alec's motives in risking the entire enterprise with this action, though they all suspected that said motives were more personal than professional. He had given them the excuse that this Alexa would be able to find Zuzack, or at least serve as bait to attract him. The fact that they had almost two hundred other former pirates in their custody who might be able to find Zuzack was something often thought about, but never mentioned in Alec's presence. Besides, most of the people involved considered this a minor operation that offered a chance for a little fun after a long, boring stretch of training.

Alexa lay on her stomach, enjoying a warm oil massage from one of the male servants. She still thought this must be hell. She was so aroused she was shaking, but none of the boys wanted to have sex with her.

"If you only know what I would do to you, Clen," she teased. She started in on very detailed story on how and what she could do to him with her mouth and tongue, but it was to no avail. *Bastard must be a eunuch,* she thought, *or maybe he only likes men.* She closed her eyes.

The hands stopped massaging her a moment later, and Alexa made a little sound of protest. Then the hands were back, and she stretched herself while yawning, "No, not there, Clen, lower..."

"Is that her?" a stern voice demanded.

"Check her. Hurry," said another voice.

That's when Alexa realized that the hands on her back had changed their size and texture. They were larger and rougher, and instead of soft skin touching hers, these hands wore gloves. Before she could process that, the towel around her waist was yanked off her while another hand touched the brand on her left buttock that her knight had left her with. Another voice said, "It's her. Take her."

Alexa reacted instantly, prepared to fight for her life—but someone had the audacity to shove a needle or something into her right buttock before she'd moved more than a few centimeters. She felt a hard sting, and then her body refused to obey her; and a second later, everything turned black.

The monk looked at Wolf as he rolled the girl into a thick blanket, and they smiled at each other. Alexa had almost ruined her own rescue. Wolf hefted the girl over his shoulder, and the two hurried down the cruiser's corridors, passing the pool room, where several servants and slaves were sleeping an unnatural sleep. Several more monks meet up with them at a bend in the corridor, and they all hurried together to a round opening in the bulkhead. Moving quickly, they carried Alexa into the tiny rounded chamber beyond, and were joined by four of the monks. It was a tight fit, but they wouldn't have to be in each other's pockets for long. After securing the hatch, the remaining monks watched as the escape pod blasted free of the cruiser and accelerated away into space. Seconds later, the pod was intercepted by a small shuttle, which caught it in a tractor beam and brought it aboard before accelerating at full throttle toward the inner system.

"Our turn. Let's move," Frances ordered as he ran lightly down the corridor, followed by his colleagues. They met up two other monks on the way, and all of them found their way into a second escape pod. As the hatch sealed, the Grisamm soldiers braced themselves for acceleration—but nothing happened.

"They must have locked the pods down after the first one launched," one of the monks said quietly, stating the obvious.

"Can you override it?" Frances asked calmly, glancing at the man as he popped a panel off the bulkhead and started peering into its guts.

"Nossir, not from in here. I'd need access to the ship's mainframe."

"Plan B," Frances said, as he pressed a button on his wristcomp. "Gaius, activate the beacon."

"Yes sir." The youngest monk pulled a slender rod from his sleeve and bent it in his hands. Both ends of the beacon immediately began to flash a brilliant white.

A millisecond later, an explosion inside the cruiser vibrated through the hull, causing several escape pods, including the one Francis and his men were on, to launch automatically. Immediately, their pod was intercepted by a second shuttle, that drew them in and then launched itself on a circuitous and confusing course through the various orbits of the space stations that made up the outpost. Once they were convinced they had shaken off any possible pursuit—not that there had been any that they could discern—they rendezvoused with the other shuttle behind a small asteroid further in-system.

After a tense few hours, the two shuttles made their cautious way back to the Star-Dice, Tota's private hotel and casino, where the *Predator* was now docked. With perfect precision, the two shuttles entered the vast ship's main docking bay, and settled down gently onto the deck.

Tota peered through the crystal wall of his office. He could see the bridge of the *Predator*, and he waved at the people he recognized on the bridge. He grinned widely as Captain Behl gave him the thumbs up. A moment later, *Predator* glided slowly away towards New Frontier 16.

Tota turned to a tall, attenuated omanoid. "Inform the Grand Master that I think we have found someone suitable for our purpose." He looked back into space, and noticed a large convoy approaching in the far distance. He smiled and said brightly, "Oh, good! More customers!"

COMING SOON

NASTRAGULL

—— BOOK TWO ——

HUNTED

ERIK MARTIN WILLÉN

ABOUT THE AUTHOR

ERIK Martin Willén has been creating science fiction worlds since the time he was a young boy, even working with a friend on a short-lived comic book version of Nastragull. Erik loves creating worlds of epic proportion and exploring those worlds in the stories he creates.

Erik currently lives in a small village in south Sweden and when he isn't writing, works as a lumberjack with nature conservation. *Pirates* is his first novel with the second installment, *Hunted* due to release in summer 2015.

Made in the USA
Charleston, SC
01 February 2016